Also by Kristin Cast from Bloom Books

TOWERFALL

The Empress

SWORDS TAROT TOWERFALL

(novellas co-written with Gina L. Maxwell)

King

Two

THE LOVERS

A Towerfall Novel

KRISTIN CAST

Bloom books

Published by Bloom Books, an imprint of Sourcebooks
1935 Brookdale RD, Naperville, IL 60563-2773
(630) 961-3900
sourcebooks.com

Cataloging-in-Publication data is on file with the Library of Congress.

Printed and bound in the United States of America.
LSC 10 9 8 7 6 5 4 3 2 1

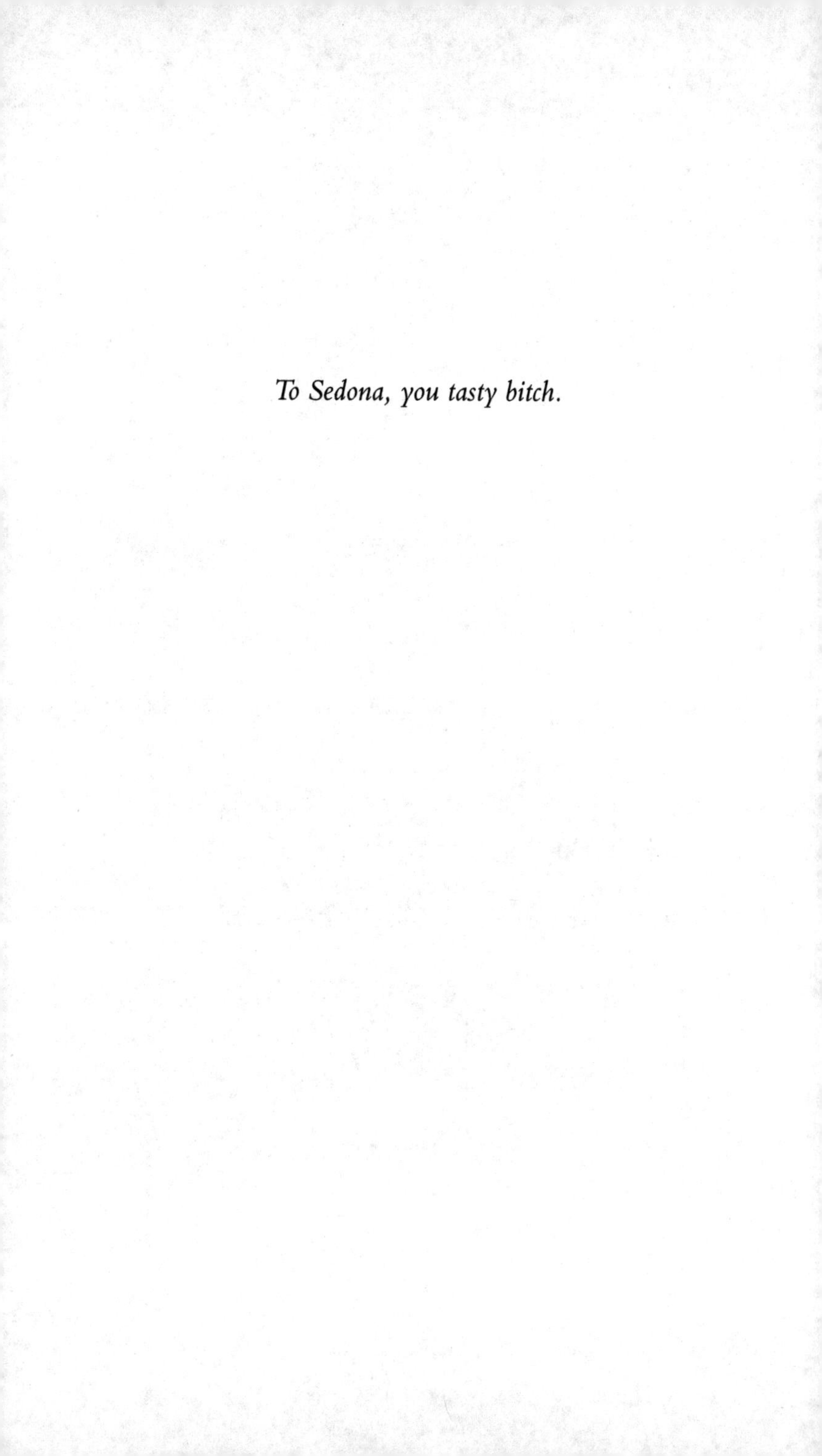

To Sedona, you tasty bitch.

3 2

5 1 4

6 7

8

TOWERFALL TAROT

The Heart Spread

REVEAL THE SHAPE OF YOUR LOVE STORY.

Love is never just one thing. It is a wound, a mirror, temptation, sanctuary. It's the choices we make again and again—to open, to stay, to leave, to begin. This eight card tarot spread is designed to trace the contours of your romantic path. What's shaping it? What's haunting it? What might it become if you choose yourself fully? Inspired by the card at the center of this novel, The Lovers, this spread forms the shape of a heart and offers a window into the truth behind your own love story.

USE THIS SPREAD WHEN:

Use this spread when you're at a romantic crossroads. When you're healing from heartbreak and need clarity to move forward. When you've met someone who stirs something delicious within you, and you want to know if it's fate or fantasy. Use it when you're ready not just to be loved, but to understand how you love. This spread will help you see the patterns, the possibilities, and the power that lives in your heart, and guide you toward the kind of love that was meant for you all along.

TIPS AND TRICKS:

Begin with The Foundation and notice how it impacts every card that follows. Pay close attention to the tension between The Dream and The Fear. What you want most may be tangled up in what you're most afraid of.

The Mirror can feel confrontational. It shows not only who you've loved, but who you've been within your own love story.

Let The Lesson anchor you before you reach The Choice where your path begins to shift.

And when you arrive at The Heart, don't rush. This is the truth you've been circling all along. It's the core of how you love, and the kind of love that's waiting if you're brave enough to claim it.

Keep a journal nearby. Breathe between cards. Let yourself fall.

THE CARDS:

CARD 1:

The Foundation—Your early beliefs or wounds around love. The origin of your love story.

CARD 2:

The Dream—The ideal love you crave, consciously or unconsciously.

CARD 3:

The Fear—What holds you back. A subconscious fear or block sabotaging intimacy or trust.

CARD 4:

The Mirror—Who you've loved and what they reflect about you.

CARD 5:

The Lesson—What love has taught you.

CARD 6:

The Choice—The crossroads you face on your current journey and what you must decide.

CARD 7

The Invitation—A person, experience, or realization asking to enter your heart now.

CARD 8

The Heart—Your love story. The core truth of how you love and what kind of love is fated for you, if you dare to choose it.

Content Warning

Hello friend,

Before you're thrown through a magickal portal back into the realm of Towerfall, I want to offer a content warning for themes that may be difficult or triggering for some.

This story includes depictions of emotional manipulation, gaslighting, and power imbalances in romantic relationships. It also explores themes of religious trauma, including the use of shame, control, and sacrifice within a faith-based system that closely parallels Christianity.

I grew up in the church and have experienced religious trauma firsthand. I've also been in a romantic relationship that was emotionally, verbally, and physically abusive. Writing this book meant navigating the deep emotional fallout of both of those traumas and the ways in which they intertwine, reinforce shame and fear, and complicate the process of healing.

Gemma's story isn't a mirror of mine, but it's rooted

in my truth and my lived experiences. Her resistance, her fire, and her refusal to be reshaped by a world that tries to make her small are reflections of my survival and healing. Throughout *The Lovers*, Gemma reclaims her voice, autonomy, and the right to redefine what love, power, and belief look like on her terms. And it completely changes her life.

If you've been through anything similar, please know that I see you. It's my wish that *The Lovers* offers both healing and hope. That said, please take care of yourself as you read. Your well-being always comes first.

With love + gratitude,

Kristin Cast

ONE

The Jaguar rental was a mistake.

Not because I can't drive it—oh, I can drive the hell out of this car. But because it looks like I belong in it.

And that's the problem.

Everyone here thinks I'm the hometown girl who made it big and never looked back. The girl who flew to the big city and lives in a loft and takes important meetings over brunch. They think I'm rich, successful, and have it all together. And I want them to keep believing that.

But the truth? I have about three weeks of savings left before I'll have to move back here to South Carolina and crash in my childhood bedroom like the cautionary tale of every failed entrepreneur.

The thought makes my stomach twist as I kill the engine in front of Wilder Ever After, a Gothic fairy tale of a bridal boutique nestled between an antique shop and a bakery.

Before I can continue second-guessing everything about my life choices, my phone buzzes against the leather console.

Mackenzie.

I sigh and answer. "If you're calling to make sure I actually showed up, the answer is yes."

"Good," she says, a little breathless. "I had a feeling you'd try to escape."

I roll my eyes, even though she's not wrong.

"I'm not escaping," I mutter, adjusting the thin strap of my dress that's already sticking to my skin in the South Carolina humidity. "I'm sitting in a very nice rental car outside the bridal boutique, trying to remember why I agreed with you that having your wedding in the South at the beginning of summer was a good idea."

Mackenzie snorts. "Because you love me, obviously. And because, if I had it in fall like my mama wanted, we both know she'd turn it into some sort of shabby chic barnyard-themed nightmare."

That earns a laugh. "Ah, yes. Now I remember."

"Stop stalling and get inside," she says. "I'll see you at the rehearsal dinner."

I hang up and exhale slowly, staring through the windshield.

The boutique is beautiful. Ivy-covered brick, arched windows draped in silk, sunlight catching on crystals that send rainbow prisms through the store.

I should be excited to be here. I should be thrilled to see Mackenzie, to celebrate, to pretend for one weekend that my life hasn't completely gone to shit. Instead, all I can think about is how quickly a month can disappear.

The bell chimes as I step inside, and cool,

lavender-scented air washes over me. The place is pure witchy romance. Bridal gowns hang like ghosts along the walls, shimmering with lace and satin. Vintage furniture is cluttered with crystals, tarot decks, and floral arrangements designed to manifest true love.

It's very Mackenzie.

I drag my fingers across a nearby velvet-covered chair, but my mind is already cataloging the space like I'm in a client meeting.

The lighting's too harsh for an intimate setting. The floral arrangements are too symmetrical. And those pink…vagina sculptures? Bold choice.

"This is a vacation," I mutter to myself, picking up a brochure about crafting your own magickal bouquet.

The irony isn't lost on me that I'm supposed to be here as a bridesmaid, supporting my best friend since diapers, but all I can think about is work even though I don't technically have a job anymore.

A burst of movement catches my eye as a girl rushes out from behind a display of tulle and crystal dildos—yes, dildos, because why not? Her wild red curls frame a round face dusted with freckles, her button nose scrunched in concentration. She looks both adorable and like she's on the verge of a breakdown, her wide brown eyes darting around the shop as if something is about to explode.

"Oh! Hi! Welcome to Wilder Ever After!" The girl—Elsie, according to her name tag—practically vibrates. "Are you here for a consultation? Or maybe a fitting? Oh, I bet you're here for the sample sale—we've got *the* most amazing deals today."

She's a whirlwind of energy, her red hair bouncing

as she springs toward me like she's been shot out of a confetti cannon.

"No, I, uh—" I start, but before I can finish, she's talking a mile a minute.

"Like, *seriously* amazing. And, oh, all our statues are 20 percent off! Well, that's just the fertility statues, though. The gods and goddesses—Aphrodite, Demeter, Priapus, Ostara, Dionysus—they're all still full price. But you know, if you're looking to manifest something…"

I blink. "Fertility statues?"

"Some say they work, some say they don't! But I always tell people: what's the harm in a little magick?" she trills, her grin wide and infectious as she shoves an iPad into my hands.

"You just need to fill out a few details," she chirps. "Nothing too intense—just your name, wedding date, style preferences, favorite colors, mood board links, venue details, guest count, all of your fiancé's info, and"—she winks—"a promise to give us your firstborn."

I bark out a laugh.

"Kidding." She grins. "Mostly."

I glance down at the screen like it's suddenly sprouted fangs. The questions glare at me, demanding answers I don't have. So, I fill in the only one I do.

NAME: GEMMA SUMMERS

It takes less than a second to bring back zero results. "It doesn't look like I'm in your system. Maybe the appointment's under—"

"Oh, you don't need to do that if you've already got an appointment!" she says, cutting me off. "Shoot darn,

I was supposed to ask that first." Her laugh is breathy and nervous as she bobs on her toes and holds up two fingers. "It's my second week." She beams at me like that'll explain everything. "And it's almost June. You know what they say about a June bride…"

I don't, but I nod along like I do. "It's close to your busy season?"

"*So* busy!" She practically bounces out of her skin. "And we just got a new shipment of gowns, and my manager's in the back dealing with that, so it's a bit chaotic—"

"I can wait," I offer.

"No, no, no!" Elsie insists, waving her hands. "It's a *special* day!" She motions for me to follow her toward an antique desk tucked along the side of the sales floor where a computer sits nestled among crystals and lace swatches. "*Your* special day."

"Oh, it's not my—" I start to tell her I'm the bridesmaid and not the bride, but she bumps into a toddler-sized clear crystal penis, and I have to catch it before it falls to the ground and shatters into a thousand pieces.

"Oh my goddess. Oh, wow," she says, staring wide-eyed at my hands wrapped around the gleaming shaft. She looks at me, panicked now. "Sorry. I mean, thank you. I swear I've had some training. Enough training. Totally enough training." She sits down shakily, fingers fluttering over the keyboard, and looks up at me. "So, what name is your dress listed under?"

I'm sure my smile is strained as I release the giant phallus and resist the urge to run.

"Roberts. Mackenzie Roberts," I say, suddenly a 1960s action star. "I'm here to try on and pick up my dress," I say, shifting my bag on my shoulder. "I submitted my measurements online, but this is my first time being able to make the trip back home."

Elsie nods enthusiastically, tapping away at the keyboard. "Ooh, exciting! Big trip home, huh?"

I hesitate. "Something like that."

"Charleston is *the* perfect place for a destination wedding." Elsie squints at the screen, her pale white skin blooming splotchy pink around her collar.

"It's not really a destination wedding—"

"Aha! Found it!" She presses her palm to her flushed chest. "I was worried there for a minute that I'd accidentally deleted your file." She straightens and clears her throat as if suddenly aware she's oversharing. "What I mean is, come with me to the Spirit and Silk Suite. We'll get you all set up, and I'll bring in your dress." She offers a nervous smile and gestures for me to follow.

The suite isn't much bigger than a closet, but it's trying very hard to be luxurious. Satin-lined walls gleam under the flickering glow of dozens of lit tea lights, and a puff of sandalwood-scented mist curls up from a corner diffuser.

My stomach twists. The dress that's waiting for me isn't free. Neither was the flight, or the rental car, or the gift I bought for Mackenzie, or the hotel I booked for appearances even though I should be staying at my parents' house.

I shove the thought away as Elsie flutters around like an excitable fairy.

"Would you like tea, coffee, water, or maybe a mimosa?" She claps her hands, not waiting for my response. "Grapefruit mimosa, perfect for the occasion!"

Before I can protest that day drinking in my thirties only leaves me puffy and tired, she disappears through a velvet curtain in a blur of red curls.

A moment later, she's back, thrusting a crystal flute filled with pale pink liquid into my hand. "Here you go!"

And just as quickly, she's gone again to fetch the dress.

"What the hell? Maybe this will be the thing that fixes me." I swirl the liquid and take a sip.

My phone buzzes. Amanda.

I don't answer. Instead, I take another drink, forcing the bubbles past the knot in my throat.

Amanda is the only one who knows the truth—that I'm drowning. That I got laid off from my job right after I'd spent my savings to leave South Carolina and move up to Manhattan for a promotion that was supposed to catapult my career. That the Jaguar rental and the bougie hotel are a lie. That in less than a month, I won't be drinking mimosas and pretending everything is okay. I'll be back in my parents' house, in the room I grew up in, trying to figure out where it all went wrong.

The phone vibrates again. I silence it and take another sip.

This is fine. Everything is fine. I have three weeks to figure it out. Three weeks to fake it till I make it.

The velvet curtain flutters open, and Elsie bursts in, holding a dress in front of her like it's a sacred offering. "Um, it looks like there's been a, uh, slight mix up with the sizing," she stammers, clutching the fabric tighter. "It might fit a little differently than expected."

I blink. "I sent in my measurements..."

"I know!" she says quickly, nodding too hard. "Totally my fault, probably. The system's been glitchy and—" She bites her lip, hesitating. "Or it could be the dress. Sometimes they run…unforgiving."

She doesn't say it outright, but I hear the undercurrent: Maybe you've changed. Maybe you've gotten bigger.

And yeah—it stings a little.

Elsie's chest once again flushes blotchy pink. "I didn't mean—I just— Ugh, I'm so sorry. I can help you into it, I swear. I should have handled this better."

I let out a slow breath, softening my expression. "It's okay." I take the dress from her, steady. "Seriously. Not a big deal."

Her eyes dart to my waist, then back to my face. "Are you sure? I—I didn't mean to offend—"

"You didn't," I say, more firmly this time. "Bodies change. Sizes change. That's not something you need to tiptoe around like it's contagious."

She looks like she might cry, so I offer her a small smile. "I've got it from here."

Biting her lip, she hangs the dress on a hook before scurrying out with a mumbled apology.

I take a breath, letting the air cool the flush creeping up my neck. I'm not ashamed of my body. But that doesn't mean moments like this don't still chip away at me, little by little.

I set down my drink and glance at the garment. Powder blue. An alarm bell goes off in the back of my mind. Wasn't Mackenzie's custom wedding gown also this color? I should remember, but getting fired after spending ten years working for the same company and thinking that there was a chance my life was finally turning into something I wanted has really fucked with my brain power.

My phone vibrates again, and I know before picking it up that it's Amanda and that I can't keep ignoring her video calls. "You didn't text when you landed, Gemma. I had to check your astrocartography map and pull three cards just to make sure your plane wasn't going to crash. Do you know how unstable your Mars line is over the Southeast right now? It's like cosmic turbulence."

"I don't even know what that means."

"It means—" She shoves another bite of noodles into her mouth, talking around it. "I was this close to calling the airport and demanding your flight number so I could channel a bubble of protective energy around your whole plane to keep you safe. Instead, I settled for burning mugwort and drawing a protective rune in vegan eyeliner on my bathroom mirror. You're welcome."

"You are completely unhinged." I try to laugh it off, but guilt prickles over my skin. I should have texted. I normally would have. Before I started floating in this panicked, directionless limbo. Before I started avoiding Amanda because she actually sees me.

I bit the tip of my nail, watching the candle flames dance. "I was going to. I just—"

"You didn't want to talk to me."

"That's not true."

She tilts her chin.

"Okay. It's kind of true." I exhale, rubbing my forehead. "I just...didn't know what to say."

"Gemma..." It's not an accusation. It's not even pity. It's just...knowing. And that makes my stomach hurt.

My vision blurs. My chest tightens. I'm not crying. I refuse to cry. Wiping at my eyes, I turn away from the phone and reach for the dress, needing something physical to focus on.

Amanda, mercifully, lets it go.

"So," she says, too casual. "Have you seen him yet?"

I freeze, dress half-unzipped.

"Who?" I ask like I don't already know.

Amanda scoffs. "Come on. There's only one man in that entire state you're avoiding."

She's right. But I wish she wasn't.

I force a shrug, still avoiding the phone screen. "Nope. Can't say I've had the pleasure."

"Good," she says. "Because you don't need that temptation in your life."

I snort. "Temptation?"

"That's what he is, isn't he? Not just the ex you can't shake. He's the promise of something bigger, something better. He makes you feel like you could have more. Be more."

I hate that she's right. Again. Because that's the problem.

Alder isn't just an old flame. He's success personified. He's what I lost, what I need, what I can't afford to chase but don't know how to stop wanting. And if I see him again? If he so much as looks at me the way he used to—like I'm the only thing in the room that matters? I don't know if I'll be able to walk away.

Amanda watches me. "Gem, you do get that you're a complete badass without him?"

"Of course." I try to smile. "And I told you—I'm done with him."

"You sure? Because you don't seem to understand how much you absolutely do not need him." Amanda arches a brow. "I worry about you, Gem. I've been on the other end of the phone when you and Alder go from together to not. I've listened to you cry and promise yourself that you're not going to get pulled back in by all his promises or let him make you doubt yourself or feel like you're not good enough. And yet"—she gestures at me, waving her fork like a magician's wand—"you're renting a car you can't afford, staying in a hotel you don't need, and avoiding my calls like I'm the IRS."

I groan. "You are so dramatic."

Amanda narrows her eyes. "Is it dramatic if I'm right?"

I don't answer. We both know the truth.

Coming back here means facing him. And no matter how much I tell myself I'm past this, past him, past what he represents…

There's still a tiny, desperate part of me that wants to see him. That wants to believe I could still have that life. That wants to stop struggling and finally take a break.

"Let's get through this fitting, and then we can figure out the rest of my life."

Amanda sighs but lets me shift the conversation.

I set the phone down, angling it so she can give a full commentary as I slip out of my outfit and into the baby blue bridesmaid dress.

The fabric shimmers under the candlelight, catching the flames like water. The lace-up corset back is pretty, or at least, it was before I had to wrestle myself into it like I was wrangling a wild animal into church clothes. I'm billowing out of the top.

"This dress is a problem," I mutter.

I twist, trying to reach the zipper and the laces, but the material refuses to cooperate. The pressure builds. From the corset. From my failures. From the weight of pretending I still have it all together.

I tug again, but the more I fight it, the worse it gets.

I can't breathe.

The air thickens. The candles flicker. The room closes in.

And suddenly, it's not just about the dress. It's about this town. This wedding. The fact that everyone here thinks I'm a success when in less than a month, I'll have nothing.

I yank on the fabric, but it won't budge.

The flames jump. The air presses in. The walls tilt.

Amanda's voice filters in from the phone, tinny and concerned. "Gem, babe, you okay? You look like you're about to faint."

"It's just the candles." I wipe the sweat from my forehead. "It's a fucking furnace in here."

The flames jump again. The shadows twist. My pulse hammers against my ribs.

I back away from the mirror, the hairs rising on the nape of my neck. There's something in this room. Watching. Waiting.

Goose bumps rise along my arms as my gaze swings around. The fire grows higher, taller, casting long, dancing shadows on the walls, and for a moment, I swear the room darkens except for those blazing flames.

My breath quickens, and Amanda's voice crackles through the phone, a distant, hollow sound I barely register. I sway on my feet, dizzy, disoriented as the flames reach toward me, higher, hotter, pulling me in—

"*Gemma!*" Amanda's shriek yanks me out of the trance.

I blink, my senses snapping back into place, and that's when I feel it.

Heat.

My hair. *My hair is on fire.*

Panic surges through me. I scream, slapping at the flames as they lick up the end of my ponytail.

I scramble out of the dressing room and finally manage to smother the flames when I crash straight into *him*.

TWO

I collide with a wall of solid muscle, my balance tilting dangerously as I grasp at fabric—expensive, tailored fabric. And then a scent washes over me. Crisp, clean, familiar, tinged with apples and linen.

My stomach drops.

I know that scent. I know exactly who I've just crashed into.

And of course. *Of course* he's here.

Alder.

He reaches out and grips my elbow to keep me upright. My pulse rattles through my veins as he braces me against his chest. His touch is steady, commanding, insistent—so sure it feels inevitable, like the sunrise or my own breath.

Alder Hawke always finds me when I'm at my weakest.

"Gemma." My name rolls off his tongue like he owns it, like he always has.

His blue eyes lock on mine, burning through every shield, exposing my raw nerves and hidden doubts.

I suck in panicked gulps of air, the dress squeezing me from every direction. I'm barely standing. Barely breathing. I must look like hell—flushed and flustered, corset strangling the life out of me while my boobs stage a prison break.

Embarrassment scorches my cheeks, and I know I'm tomato red, sweatin' like a sinner in church, smelling like burnt hair.

And all the while, he's just standing there, calm, composed, taking in every inch of the disaster that is currently me.

Elsie's voice pierces the air like a siren. "Oh my goddess! Your hair!"

Her wild red curls bounce with every step as she darts over, round face flushed with panic, brown eyes scanning me and the singed ends of my ponytail.

I barely register her approach, my brain still catching up to the fact that Alder is here. Alder is touching me.

"Are you okay?!" She stops a few feet short, wringing her hands in front of her chest. "How did that even happen?" she asks, her voice pitching higher. "Not that it's your fault! Obviously."

"I'm fine," I mumble and try not to collapse under the weight of his stare.

"The dress!" Elsie gasps, her attention shifting to the dress like it's the victim here. Her hands flutter like frantic little birds, patting every wrinkled inch of fabric. "Oh, thank goddess." She presses her freckled hands to her chest. "I mean, burning hair is one thing, but a *dress*? That'd be a whole other level of disaster."

Her eyes widen, and her cheeks brighten with a blush. "Not that your hair's a disaster! You look great! Really. Like...I've seen worse. *Way* worse."

I stare at her, trying to focus, but all I can feel is the heat radiating from Alder. He doesn't speak, doesn't move. He watches me like a wolf eyeing prey. It's a look that says he could pull me apart without lifting a finger, and I'd probably let him.

Elsie glances nervously over her shoulder at him before leaning in closer to me, her voice dropping to a whisper. "It was the candles, wasn't it? I've been telling the manager we need fewer candles. But does anyone listen to the new girl? *Nooooo.*"

I blink, still processing, but she's already moved on.

"I'm just glad you weren't standing near the crystal display," she continues, rushing to fill the silence. "Those things are practically weapons. Imagine impaling yourself right before the wedding."

She gives a nervous laugh before sucking in a breath.

"Oh! The wedding!" She smooths the dress again even though, after a good steam, it'll be perfectly fine. "I—I am so *so* sorry. This isn't your dress."

My mind buzzes, but I can't help the ghost of a smile that pulls at my lips. "That's a relief."

"My manager is looking for *your* dress—the bridesmaid's dress. That's why this one is a bit..." She waves her hands toward my chest, where my boobs are currently waging war against this corset.

Alder's gaze doesn't waver. His lips part slightly like he's about to say something—something I'm not ready for. But when he speaks, it's not a taunt.

"It's good to see you, Gemma." His voice is low and

smooth and rolls down my spine like melted wax. Just like it used to.

And then, there it is. That smirk. Like he's already forgotten every wrong thing he ever did.

But I haven't.

I brace myself for the cutting remark, the passive aggressive dig. Something that will remind me why I left.

"You look—" He pauses, head tilting slightly, like he's searching for the right word. His blue eyes catch on the tight corset, the mess of fabric, the fact that I am very clearly struggling.

I tense, waiting for the humiliation, the tease.

"Beautiful."

The word lands in the pit of my stomach. "I—"

His gaze trails from my face, over the wrinkled, too-tight dress, the flushed skin of my collarbone, the singed ends of my ponytail.

With that same effortless confidence, he murmurs, "I think this might be my favorite look on you."

It's not sarcastic, not mocking. It's soft, almost admiring.

But that's the trap, isn't it? Because Alder never just says things. Every word is placed like a chess move, every look is meant to pull me in, to make me second-guess myself, to make me feel like I was wrong for leaving.

My throat tightens.

He smiles. "Tell me, Gemma, did you set yourself on fire just for me?"

There's the teasing edge. Just enough to disarm me, to make it feel like he's being playful. Like this is normal and we aren't standing in the middle of a bridal store six months after I swore I'd never be with him again.

I swallow, my brain screaming at me to speak. But all I can hear is the way he said *beautiful*. Like he meant it. Like he's never meant anything else more.

A door along the back wall swings open with a creak, and the energy shifts.

A woman glides in. She's tall, draped in flowing black fabric speckled with silver moons, her long dark hair cascading over her shoulders in loose waves, a few white strands glinting in the light. The scent of sage and something metallic, almost electric, trails behind her.

She stops in front of me, her kohl-lined eyes locking onto mine in a way that makes my stomach clench.

"I found it," she says, her voice low and smooth.

She lifts the baby-chick yellow gown with reverence. Silver rings adorn nearly every finger and clink together like chimes as she touches the airy fabric.

"The powder blue is for the bride. *This*"—she raises the yellow gown a little higher—"is yours."

I try to thank her, but my mouth is dry.

The way she's watching me feels…off. It's like she's not simply seeing me. She's reading me. Every thought. Every secret.

A chill tickles my back, and I wrap my arms around my middle.

Her gaze flicks to Alder, then back to me. A knowing smile curves her lips.

"Such strange energy in the air today," she muses, almost to herself, her eyes narrowing slightly as she traces a pattern in the air with her fingers. "I felt it the moment you walked in." She steps closer, her voice dropping to a near-whisper. "You're standing at a crossroads, dear. Be careful which way you turn."

Her eyes hold mine, and it feels like she's waiting for me to say a thought she already sees swirling inside my head.

"Thank you?"

I take the dress and nod numbly, retreating into the dressing room with the new outfit and the singed ends of my ponytail. My fingers tremble as I pull off the too-tight wedding dress, the fabric sticking to my skin like a Band-Aid.

"Two things!" Amanda's voice buzzes through the phone, sharp and urgent. "One, I am so happy you didn't go up in flames. I'm way too old to find a new best friend. Two..." She leans closer to the screen, eyes wide. "Did I just hear *Alder Fucking Hawke*?"

I groan. "Yeah, yeah you did."

Amanda's brows shoot up so high they practically disappear beneath her bangs.

I hang Mackenzie's dress on the hook, my heart still hammering. "What the hell is he even doing here? This is a bridal boutique not a...a—"

"Corporate boardroom? Offshore tax haven? Or, I don't know, a fucking villain's lair?"

My laugh comes out shaky. "Exactly."

Amanda's eyes narrow. "Hand him the phone."

She crosses her arms over her chest, chin tilted at an angle that means she's ready to throw hands. And this wouldn't be the first time she's torn into him via FaceTime. Amanda's been my best friend since our first soul-crushing corporate retreat in our early twenties, back when we were both fresh-faced assistants at the publishing house. She may live in New York, but she's had front-row seats to every adult version of me—including the Alder years.

Shaking my head, I pick up the phone. I can't let her do that again. Not when my own emotions are violently rattling around inside me, already unraveling everything I've tried so hard to hold together.

"I have to go."

"Gem—"

"I'll call you later."

Before she can protest further, I hang up.

I press my back against the satin-covered wall and squeeze my eyes shut, trying to breathe through the storm raging in my chest. But it's useless.

The icy weight of his gaze. The way my name drips from his lips like a prayer. The smirk that told me he already knew I'd be back.

Six months ago I walked away from Alder Hawke. Now I am back in South Carolina standing dead center in a past I never fully let go of.

I clear my throat, flexing my fingers, willing them to stop shaking as I fumble with the zipper of the correct dress.

My hands are too unsteady, my body too hot, my mind too full of *him*.

There's a soft knock on the doorframe.

"Gemma." Alder's voice threads through the curtain like smoke, curling into places I swore I'd sealed shut. "We should talk."

A suggestion wrapped around a command. Silk over steel. He's always done this, made me believe I had a choice, when the reality is, I never do.

My pulse hammers, stubbornly unwilling to obey. “There’s nothing to talk about.”

But even I don’t believe it.

The velvet curtain flutters, and I catch the shine of his polished shoes just beneath the hem. Alder knows exactly what he’s doing. Standing close enough that I can feel him, even though we’re separated by a sliver of fabric.

My throat tightens, a hot, painful lump forming as I slip the silky dress down over my flushed skin and zip it up. It’s actually a pretty dress—surprisingly flattering for a bridesmaid gown—but I’m too overwhelmed to care.

“I heard about your job,” he says after a beat.

Of course he did. He’s not just a fixer. He’s *the* fixer. The one people call when the stakes are too high, the mess too dirty, the fallout too dangerous. He doesn’t just clean things up—he rewrites the narrative. He trades in secrets, spins lies into legends, and buries the truth so deep it forgets how to breathe. If there’s a scandal brewing, he’s already neutralized it. If someone thinks they can hide from him, they’ve already been seen.

Keeping tabs on me is easy.

I don’t answer. What the hell am I supposed to say that he doesn’t already know? That I spent ten years building something only to get pushed out? That I’ve burned through my savings trying to pretend like everything’s fine? That in three weeks, I’ll have nothing?

That I need help?

That I need *him*?

No. I won’t give him that.

My hands tremble as I tug on the zipper—I need to get out of this dress and out of this store—but it’s stuck.

He sighs, the sound low, knowing.

"Gemma," he says, voice smooth as honey, "you don't have to do this alone."

My stomach tightens.

That's the worst part. The way he says it—so gentle, so understanding—like I made some kind of mistake by leaving and that I should have stayed so he could take care of me.

I force my voice steady. "I'm handling it."

"You're *surviving* it," Alder corrects, a shadow of amusement in his tone. "That's not the same thing."

I grit my teeth, yanking the zipper again, but it won't budge.

Damn it.

"I'm Jason's best man," he continues. "We're going to run into each other again."

Frustrated, I shove the curtain aside and step out, chin high even though my confidence is slipping through my fingers.

"Alder, just—" I exhale sharply. "Just get whatever you came here for and go. I'm sure we can manage to avoid each other for a day."

I tug at the zipper again, harder this time.

Nothing.

His eyes flick to the struggle, laughter tugging at his lips. "Need help?"

"No."

It's a full sentence. A hard stop. But Alder never listens.

He closes the gap between us, moving with that quiet confidence that once hooked me and might still. His hands brush mine like I was never in control to begin with.

My body goes still. The air between us turns thick, heat coiling between my skin and his fingertips. Alder finds the zipper and slides it down in one slow, measured movement, his fingers grazing my spine just enough to set off sparks.

"You don't have to do everything the hard way, you know."

I hate that he makes it sound so simple.

His hands fall away, but his presence stays, heavy in the air, filling up every space I don't want him to.

"You're free," he murmurs.

I don't thank him.

He didn't do this to be kind. He did this to remind me how easy things could be if I just let him back in.

I retreat into the dressing room. The curtain falls between us, but it's not enough. I can still feel him.

I get back into my clothes and take one final look at the singed golden-brown ends of my ponytail before grabbing my purse and the dress and stepping out of the room.

Alder is still there, watching, waiting, and I hope he'll stay rooted in place in his polished shoes and his suit so perfectly pressed it hurts. I try to slip past, but he moves at the last second. Before I can react, his hand is on my arm. His grip is firm but careful, his thumb pressing against my wrist in a touch that feels like possession disguised as restraint.

"Gemma." My name is a warning, a promise, an order he knows I'll obey.

Heat ripples through me, slow and unwanted.

I pull away from his grasp because if I don't, I'll stay. "I'm only here for the wedding," I say, but the words taste like a lie.

I push forward, and I'm almost at the door when the shop manager's voice cuts through the quiet.

"Don't miss the cake pull!"

I freeze. Slowly, I glance back at her. "Cake pull?"

"Oh, yes." She nods, her dark gaze piercing from beneath spidery lashes. "It's a wedding tradition. Each ribbon in the cake leads to a charm...and a future." Her attention flicks to Alder, then back to me while her fingers brush the silver pendant at her neck. "Be sure not to miss it. The charm is magickal and always guides you to what's meant to be."

I want to scoff, to say something dismissive and sarcastic. I don't believe in fate, in magick, in charms and party tricks that claim to know my future.

But her words settle into my bones like a spell.

Even though I don't believe in magick, I do believe in Alder's hold over me, in the way he stands there, undeterred, knowing absolutely everything. Knowing I'm a breath away from giving in.

And I hate that, somehow, it does feels like fate.

The shop is suddenly too small, too white and pastel and full of magickal dreams I want no part of.

I catch Alder's eye again, and he shifts, moving like he's going to come after me, going to push, going to say whatever it is he thinks will break me down.

And I know, if he speaks—if I let him speak—I won't be strong enough to resist.

So I do the only thing I can. The same thing I did six months ago.

I run.

THREE

The wedding reception is in full swing. The tent, pitched near a sparkling lake on the perfectly manicured lawns of the Charleston Island Country Club, glows with golden lantern light. Tables are draped in soft ivory linens, centerpieces burst with blooms, and the air is fragrant with roses, gardenias, and sweet buttercream.

Southern weddings have a particular kind of charm—one part fairy tale, two parts local gossip—and this one is no exception.

I linger near the bar, nursing a drink that isn't nearly strong enough while I fidget with a monogrammed cocktail napkin. The event is a "phone free space" which means the wedding planner forced every single guest to drop their devices into a wicker basket before the ceremony, which means I have no way to distract myself from my thoughts.

"I am *so sorry* about Kendall and Alex." Beside me, Mackenzie's petite frame sways as she clutches her champagne flute. Her wedding dress, pristine despite its earlier suffering and the fact that she spent the entire cocktail hour twirling barefoot through the grass, shimmers under the lights.

I shrug. "They're fine." Or, at least they will be after I've had enough to drink.

She hiccups, swaying closer, and makes a pitiful groaning sound before dropping her forehead against my shoulder.

"My mom is in Bunco with their moms," she mutters. "I had to make them bridesmaids, or I'd never hear the end of it. Like—*never*." She leans back, eyes bleary. "I'd have died an old woman, and they'd still be saying, *remember how Mackenzie didn't make Kendall and Alex bridesmaids? What a selfish little bitch*."

I laugh into my glass. "We have to avoid that at all costs."

"Yep," she agrees, popping the p before taking a very unladylike gulp of champagne.

Her gaze sweeps the room, her grin going lazy. She hiccups again and turns back to me.

"God," she mutters under her breath. "Alder looks *so good*."

I go very, very still.

She gasps suddenly, hand flying to her mouth, the triangle of freckles beneath her left eye crinkling with a wince. "Wait! Am I still allowed to say that? I mean, I'm a married woman now." She extends her left hand and closes one eye to focus on the massive diamond. "*Is this illegal?*" she slurs.

"I think you're safe."

Mackenzie nods, satisfied. Her gaze sweeps the

reception tent again, catching on Alder once more. She exhales, her champagne flute tipping precariously in her hand.

"Not gonna lie," she says, voice just loose enough with alcohol to be brutally honest, "He is such an asshole. Not husband material. Not even boyfriend material. If he hadn't grown up literally next door to Jason, there's no way they'd be best friends. *Buuuut* I get why you keep going back." She waves her hand in his direction. "He's rich as sin and looks, well…like that."

I follow her gaze, even though I shouldn't. I know exactly what I'll see.

Alder, standing just beyond the crowd, effortlessly tall, perfectly composed, his presence suffocating even from across the tent.

I look away fast.

"I mean, Gem, let's be real." She leans in, voice low and conspiratorial, the kind of tone that precedes bad decisions and questionable life choices. "You're doing your *Sex and the City* thing in New York, and that's great. But Alder… He could buy you a penthouse up there tomorrow, no problem."

She's not wrong. And the thought makes me want to puke. "I don't want him to buy me a penthouse."

Mackenzie presses her lips together and blows. "Not saying you should do it, but you wouldn't be the first woman to sell her soul and that punani for money. Easy peasy, lemon"—she hiccups, giggling—"squeezy."

My throat burns as I down the rest of my drink and motion to the bartender for another.

Mackenzie has no idea how much easier it would be. How much I've already considered it. If I gave in,

I wouldn't be weeks away from running out of money and packing my bags to move back in with my parents. I wouldn't have to drown in shame when everyone realizes I didn't make it.

It would be so damn simple to let Alder take care of it. To let him fix everything. To let him buy me security, stability. An escape from the reality I don't want to face.

And I might even enjoy it.

I know without a doubt I'd enjoy the sex. That part of our relationship was never a problem.

I take a sip of my fresh gin and tonic, blessedly stronger this time, and glance over my shoulder at Alder.

Maybe my soul isn't such a high price to pay. Maybe it's not mine to bargain with at all. Maybe he already owns a piece of it.

"Mackenzie!" The wedding planner rushes up, clipboard in one hand, earpiece securely in place, moving with the focused urgency of a woman who has seen some shit. "It's time for the cake pull."

Mackenzie squeals in delight, clutching my arm. "Oh my God, Gemma, *the cake pull*!"

I try to protest, but she's already yanking me forward.

The cake sits at the center of the reception hall, a towering masterpiece of sugar and gold leaf. At its base, ribbons thread through the layers, each tied to a hidden charm. A fortune. A glimpse at what's to come.

"Go on." Mackenzie nudges me toward the cake and the other bridesmaids. "You have to. It's tradition."

I groan and playfully bump her hip with mine.

"Love *youuuuu*!" She shouts as the wedding planner whisks her to the front of the gathering crowd of guests.

Alex clears her throat and glances at Mackenzie, her

voice loud enough for everyone to hear, "Remember last fall at Sophie's wedding? I got a money charm. And then, boom! Three new clients."

"Yeah, well, I hope this pull actually works." Kendall, Thing 2 to Alex's Thing 1, snorts, her fingers twirling around her ribbon. "I could use some serious love luck right now."

Love.

The word burns through my thoughts along with visions of Alder. I shoot back the rest of my gin and tonic, wincing as it goes down rough.

Mackenzie drunkenly raises her arms like a race starter about to set us off. "On the count of three, you'll pull together!"

I grab a ribbon. The moment I do, a shock zips through me. It's static electricity but with a strange undertone—a tingling sensation that travels up my arm and settles in my chest.

"What the hell?" I mutter, shaking off the buzzing sting and flexing my fingers. The other bridesmaids don't seem to notice, too caught up in their own excitement, playfully elbowing each other, ready to see what their futures hold.

"Three, two, one—*pull*!"

A chorus of cheers rings out from the gathered crowd as we tug on our ribbons. The others glide out of the cake effortlessly, glinting at the end of their satin strings. Bridesmaids squeal and joyous gasps pop from the gathered attendees as their attention shifts to Mackenzie, her dark curls bouncing as she wiggles in the middle of a group hug.

But my ribbon stays stuck.

I pull again, harder this time. The satin catches, hung up somewhere deep inside the cake. I tug again. Nothing. Finally, I use both hands and yank on the string like my life depends on it.

The ribbon jerks free, and I stumble backward. A blob of frosting flies through the air, and something heavier than a charm lands with a wet slap directly onto my overflowing cleavage.

I glance down, my pulse whooshing in my ears, embarrassment rushing hot through my veins.

It's not a charm.

It's a card.

The frosting-covered card clings to my skin, smearing a sticky splotch of buttercream across the pale-yellow satin of my dress.

The din around me swells, laughter and giddy shrieks as the other bridesmaids compare their charms—tiny sparkling beacons of hope for their future. A tiny baby carriage for motherhood. A ring for an upcoming proposal. A four-leaf clover for good fortune.

I peel the card from my chest, my fingers tacky with buttercream.

This is wrong.

I catch Mackenzie's gaze across the cake table. She claps her hands, eyes still bright with alcohol and post-pull euphoria. As I step toward her and she sees the mess on my dress, her expression shifts. Her nose wrinkles.

"What's that?" she asks, tilting her head.

At the same time, I blurt, "What's this?"

Her eyes flick to the card in my hand. I hold it up, swallowing hard.

"It was in the cake," I say. "It's my charm."

Mackenzie blinks, trying to focus through the fog of champagne. She grabs my wrist and leans in to inspect the card.

"Gem..." she murmurs, shaking her head. "I—I've never seen this before."

Ice slides down my spine.

"What do you mean?"

She frowns and throws up her hands.

"All the charms..." She gestures vaguely toward the others. "We got them from Pandora. They don't sell cards. Well, gift cards..."

I stare down at the card, my pulse hammering.

Mackenzie sticks her finger in the frosting on my boobs and puts it in her mouth. "Is this vanilla?"

She's saying something about cake tasting and the bakery screwing up, but I don't hear her anymore.

Over her shoulder, past the glittering centerpieces and flickering lanterns, Alder cuts through the crowd, moving toward me like a shark.

I clutch the paper tighter, my fingers smearing buttercream across the edges.

I need to get out of here before he reaches me.

I snag a flute of champagne from a server as I slip away, weaving between the tables and guests without so much as a backward glance. The tent flaps rustle as I push my way outside and rush to the clubhouse where I duck into the bathroom.

It's blessedly cool as the door closes behind me, and the noise of the reception is long gone, leaving me alone with the quiet hum of the air conditioning and the soft whisper of my ballet flats against the polished marble floor. I take a sip of champagne and set the card on the edge of the sink before glancing at my reflection.

The frosting smear across my chest is more noticeable in this harsh lighting, a pale blue stain streaked with white buttercream that sticks to the satin like some kind of bridal scarlet letter. I press my fingers against the fabric, wiping at it uselessly before tearing a handful of paper towels from the dispenser. But it's not the wreckage on my dress that I'm drawn to cleaning up.

It's the card.

I brush away the frosting with the ball of wadded up paper towels. The air around me grows thick and humid, and a tingle washes down my back, electricity pulsing just beneath my skin. The world around me seems to slow, the edges of my vision growing hazy. My breathing stills as the last bits of frosting melt away under my touch and reveal the card's shimmering surface.

It looks like a tarot card.

No...it *is* a tarot card.

I swallow and peer closer. I can't explain the dread pooling in my stomach as I trace the shimmering figures on the surface. The card seems to vibrate, hum with an energy that pours lava hot through my veins.

Two figures are locked in a tender embrace, bodies pressed together like two halves of the same whole beneath towering, golden-leafed trees. A twisting green serpent curls up one of the tree trunks—temptation lurking in the shadows. The man and woman at the center look familiar. Too familiar to ignore, even as my mind insists it's impossible.

I touch my hair as I stare down at hers. Even with the singed ends I had to cut off in my hotel room with sewing scissors, my blond waves still drape across my shoulders and down my back—just like hers. She wears a deep blue gown, and a satin mask obscures her eyes, but I know that round chin, those cheekbones, that smile.

And him. I'd recognize him anywhere.

"Alder."

His golden hair, his chiseled features, those piercing blue eyes… They're locked on the version of me printed on the card while his hand cradles her neck. I can almost feel those hands, the way his fingers used to trace my skin with equal parts possession and command, like he couldn't decide if he wanted to protect me or mark me as his.

I clench my jaw, forcing away the memory, but the figures are unmistakable.

She looks like me. He looks like Alder. They look like us.

I grip the card tighter, trying to convince myself it's just a trick of my mind, just another silly wedding game.

A flicker of movement catches my eye, and my pulse quickens. The serpent, coiled around the base of the tree shimmers for a moment, its green scales catching the light like it's alive.

"You are on your way to being drunk, Gemma. Get your shit together." I shake my head. "And don't do this to yourself. Don't perform these mental gymnastics. Not over Alder. Don't give him the satisfaction."

I reach for more paper towels from the dispenser to clean up my dress, but it's empty. Of course it is. Leaving the champagne flute on the counter, I grab the tarot card and make a beeline for the nearest stall. I'll finish cleaning up with toilet paper.

The stall door closes behind me just as the bathroom door swings open, heels clicking across the tiled floor.

"Doesn't Mackenzie look *so* beautiful?" Kendall gushes, her unmistakable vocal fry on overdrive from too much alcohol. "Everything is just *so* perfect."

"Oh, I know. *Absolutely* perfect," Alex replies, her southern drawl coated in sugar. "Though, if I'm being honest, the lighting during the ceremony could've been a touch softer. Mackenzie looked a little washed out."

"*Mmm*," Kendall hums in agreement. "And those boutonnieres? I would have made *such* a different choice, but…"

Their passive-aggressive critique carries on, *bless her heart* and *it's just a shame* stabbing through their conversation like thorns among roses. I roll my eyes and tear off more toilet paper to wipe the last bit of frosting from the pale-yellow satin.

I just need to get cleaned up and get out of here. Seems like I'm going to spend this whole night running away from people.

Kendall's tone shifts. "Can you believe Gemma actually showed up?"

My fingers freeze. Here we go.

"*Oh my God*." Alex feigns surprise. "I wasn't going to say anything, but since you brought it up—the absolute audacity. She didn't come to any of the pre-wedding events. Not the bridal shower, not the bachelorette. Too busy playing *girl boss* in the Big Apple."

Kendall snickers. "Right? And then she flames out and comes crawling back like nothing happened."

"Seriously." Alex's voice drips with faux concern. "I

heard she lost her job, her apartment, and like—everything. Now she's acting like it's totally fine that she's back here, drinking champagne and acting like she's not seconds away from couch surfing."

Kendall clicks her tongue. "I mean, bless her heart. Mackenzie should've cut her from the bridal party. Would've made more sense to let someone who actually showed up to things hold a bouquet."

"And can we talk about how hard she pulled on that cake ribbon?" Alex huffs. "Like, this charm isn't going to save you, honey."

Kendall laughs. "You know she was hoping for a money charm."

Alex snorts. "Honestly, if I'd tanked that hard, I wouldn't be showing my face at all."

They cackle, oblivious to the fact that I'm standing mere feet away.

"I will never get what Alder saw in her." Alex pauses her cutting blows to rustle through her clutch, the sounds of makeup caps popping off. "He could have anyone, but he always went back to her. She's never been in his league."

"I know," Kendall scoffs. "We've been single this whole time, and he hasn't texted either of us once."

Alex cuts in. "It's fucking mindboggling."

My heart thumps harder, and my fingers press against the card as if it can reach the answer to something I can't quite grasp. I've let them go on for long enough.

I ball up the sticky wad of toilet paper and toss it into the bowl. It flushes with a satisfying *whoosh*. I throw open the stall door like I'm an old west sheriff and their luck has just run out.

Their laughter dies as I meet their shocked, wide-eyed gazes in the mirror. Alex's hand hovers midair, her blush brush poised over her cheek, and Kendall's lips move in a silent *oh shit*.

I step up to the sink beside them, slow and unbothered. I rinse my hands. Pat them dry. Then I smile, sharp and sweet.

What's a couple of mean girls compared to the rest of my life burning to the ground?

"Sorry to hear it's been so hard for y'all to get your lives together," I say, voice soaked in sugar. "Do you think it has anything to do with the fact that you're both clinging to the same hometown drama you peaked with at seventeen?"

Their horrified gazes lock on mine.

"Here's a tip," I continue, reaching for my champagne flute and raising it in a mock toast. "You don't need a money charm—you need therapy and a personality."

Alex's cheeks flame pink. Kendall sputters.

"But hey," I say, tilting my head, "I'm rooting for you. Genuinely. It must be exhausting being that bitter all the time."

I take a slow, luxurious sip of champagne, letting the bubbles fizz and pop against my tongue, savoring the moment before I swallow. Then, without another word, I turn on my heel and stride out of the bathroom.

The door swings shut behind me with a satisfying thud, cutting off their sputtered outrage.

For the first time since coming back home, I feel like I won.

FOUR

I find a secluded spot at the edge of the reception on the dock overlooking the lake, where the glow of lanterns gives way to shadows. At the edge of the water, the humid air presses against my skin, thick with the croak of toads and the rhythmic hum of crickets.

I lift the champagne flute, downing what's left in one long sip. The bubbles fizz through my bloodstream, numbing the edges of my thoughts.

Now that I'm alone—no Mackenzie, no Amanda, no wedding drama or job-hunt stress—it hits me.

I am fucking exhausted.

I am so tired of clawing my way toward a future that keeps getting yanked out from under me. Of almost making it. Of falling short. Of failing. Of knowing that, in less than a month, I will have nothing left.

No apartment. No money. No plan.

And why? Because I believed in myself? Because after ten years of working my ass off—of grinding through eighty-hour weeks, of sacrificing sleep and sanity, of building a career out of nothing but sheer fucking determination—I thought I had earned my place.

A bitter laugh catches in my throat.

I was supposed to be safe.

I was supposed to have finally made it.

Being the Director of Marketing for the biggest publishing house in New York wasn't just a job. It was everything.

I had connections, I had momentum, I had a future.

I wasn't just coordinating launch parties for debut authors—I was rubbing elbows with editors, with CEOs and CFOs, with the very people who could have launched me into the next stage of my career.

And then one day, out of fucking nowhere, they called me into HR and told me it was clear I wasn't ready for the promotion. That they'd already filled my old position. That they had no choice but to let me go.

I had to sit there, smiling through a meeting to keep from sobbing, while they danced around the real reason they were letting me go.

I wasn't good enough.

I thought I was. I thought I was ready for that promotion five years ago, but clearly, I was wrong.

My boss looked me in the eye and told me I *wasn't* ready for the next step in my career.

Maybe I never will be.

Maybe the future I built my whole life around is just a story I tell myself—one more thing I want so badly that I can't see the truth staring me in the face.

And now?

Now, I have three weeks left on my lease and an overdrafted checking account.

Now, I have LinkedIn rejection emails clogging my inbox and exactly zero prospects on the horizon.

Now, I'm staring down a future I never planned for, a future where I crawl back to my parents' house, humiliated, broke, and a failure.

And the worst part? The ugliest, most shameful part?

There's one person who could fix all of it.

One person who has the power to put me back on my feet with a single phone call.

And I'm so tired of fighting that I don't know if I have it in me to say no to him again.

I let my fingers brush over the tarot card in my palm. The serpent glints in the moonlight, twisting, watching. I don't need a reading to understand the warning.

"Drinking alone?"

I turn, and there he is. Like an answer to my prayers. Like I summoned him with a thought, a need, a weakness.

Alder stands confidently in that quiet, composed way that always makes my stomach twist.

My hand tightens around the tarot card, its edges biting into my palm, the only thing keeping me steady against the pull of everything he has to offer. The only thing reminding me that this isn't fate—this is a choice.

Alder tilts his head, eyes shining like ice in the moonlight. "You came back."

"I'm not here for you," I say.

His lips curve. "We both know you don't believe that."

He lifts a hand, brushing my hair back with deliberate softness. Then he twists a strand around his fingers, his touch light but so, so unbreakable.

His lips dip to my ear, his breath warm, coaxing, indulgent.

"You're struggling," he murmurs, his fingers skimming down my arm. It's not a question. It's a fact. A truth he knows too well. "Wouldn't it be easier if you let me help you?"

"I don't want your help," I lie, but even I hear the vulnerability in it.

His lips graze the corner of my mouth in the softest tease.

I sway forward, body betraying me before I can stop it.

He plucks the champagne flute from my hand and, without looking, tosses it onto the bank. The crystal thuds softly against the grass.

Alder's hands find my waist, and he pulls me closer, closer, closer, until I feel him everywhere.

"You saw what's out there, Gemma," he breathes, his lips skimming my jaw. "You left. You tried it your way. And you taught yourself a lesson."

His teeth graze my pulse, and I can't help the shudder that rolls through me.

"Now..." He drags his mouth up to my ear. "It's time to come back to me."

"Why me?" The words fall from my lips before I can stop them. "Why not find someone else? Someone more on your level."

He smiles against my skin, his fingers trailing lower, his touch so hot it burns through the fabric. "I blame it on growing up in a small town." His hands wander, sliding down, gripping my hips, guiding me exactly where he wants me. "You got your hooks into me early."

"So it's my fault?"

He hums, low and indulgent, like I should be flattered. Like I should be grateful that a man like him wants me. "And you soften my image, the company's."

His hand slides down my back, slow, possessive. He pulls me flush against him, and I feel him. All of him. The thick, undeniable swell of him through his slacks, pressing hard against my stomach.

Heat floods my veins, my pulse jumping, thighs clenching around the want, the need, how familiar and how right it feels.

"See?" he murmurs, his mouth so close to mine it's torment. "You still fit against me perfectly."

I bite back a whimper, nails digging into his chest.

I hate him.

I want him.

God help me, I can't tell the difference anymore.

"Even when I went off to Stanford," he murmurs, his lips dragging down my throat. "Even when I'm traveling the world. When I could have anyone." His teeth graze my collarbone. "I only want you."

His hands slip under the thin straps of my dress. His fingers brush my bare skin, and I swear I can feel his smirk against my throat when I shiver.

"You keep me grounded, Gemma," he murmurs.

His lips find the hollow of my collarbone, his tongue skimming slow, deliberate.

"I could remind you of home too," he whispers, voice so soft, so lethal.

His hands lower the straps, his mouth tracing the newly exposed skin.

"Hell," he breathes, dragging his lips lower. "I could build you a home, Gemma. A castle, if you want."

A promise.

A trap.

I exhale sharply. "So you can lock me away in a tower?"

His lips curve against my skin. "So I can save you."

I should walk away. I should tell him to fuck off, to take his money, his power, his promises and go straight to hell.

But the thing is—he's right. About all of it.

If I let him, he could fix everything.

He could save me.

He could buy me security, stability. A life without struggle.

Would it be so bad to trade my pride for peace?

Alder's fingers tilt my chin up, forcing my eyes to his. He waits. Just long enough for me to catch my breath. Just long enough for me to pretend I have a choice.

Then, he crashes his mouth into mine. His lips part, and his tongue sweeps in, claiming every inch of my mouth as a groan escapes from my throat. I can't stop the whimper that follows, my hands fisting in his shirt.

"Let me save you, Gemma."

My body answers for me. And I let it.

Because tonight, I don't want to fight. Tonight, I want to be taken care of. Tonight, I want to be his.

Alder's hands are everywhere, mapping me, memorizing me like he hasn't already spent years doing it. His fingers slide lower, finding the hem of my dress, pushing it higher, inch by agonizing inch.

Cool night air skims over my heated skin, and I shiver. Not from the cold—from him. From the way he's looking at me like I belong to him. Like I always have.

His strong hands grip my thighs, lifting me against him. He squats, lowering us both until my butt hits the dock. Then he eases me back, guiding me down with those strong hands until I'm lying flat and breathless beneath him. And fuck, there it is. The thickness of his cock pressing right where I need him.

I whimper, instinctively rolling my hips, chasing the friction.

Alder chuckles—low, rough, and entirely too satisfied. "There she is."

His fingers skim higher, teasing the edge of my panties.

I shift against him, hips tilting in silent demand.

He cups me through the fabric, his palm pressing just enough to make my legs weaken around him.

Heat floods me, pooling low and deep, an ache that only he can satisfy.

His lips drag up to mine. "Tell me something, sweetheart," he murmurs. "This." His palm presses harder, moving in slow, agonizing circles. "This doesn't feel like a casual, just-catching-up kind of situation."

I bite my lip, nails digging into his shoulders. "Shut up," I pant, but it sounds more like a moan than an actual objection.

Alder laughs, the sound so low, so wicked, I feel it in my body.

"Oh, that independent streak is cute." His fingers slip beneath my panties, skin against skin, finding the wetness that's already waiting for him.

He strokes once, slow and devastating, his other hand gripping my thigh, keeping me right where he wants me.

My head falls back against the dock, a sharp gasp breaking free.

"This doesn't mean we're back together," I manage, my voice wrecked, breathless.

"No?" Alder makes a thoughtful hum, his fingers still stroking, unhurried, cruel. "You mean to tell me"—another stroke, firmer this time, like he's testing me, taunting me, coaxing me closer to the edge—"you let me get you like this, let me touch you like this, but we're just…what? Two exes catching up?"

He strokes again, and my hips jerk into his hand.

"Alder," I gasp, nails scraping down his back, desperate.

"I love this little act you're putting on, sweetheart," he murmurs. His fingers move faster, working me open, owning me. "Like you don't already know how this is gonna end."

I choke on a moan, my thighs shaking, my hands pulling him closer, but it's not enough. I need more. I need all of him.

The ache is excruciating, unbearable. I press closer, hips tilting, chasing him—chasing what I know only he can give me.

"Please," I cry.

I don't care if it's desperate. I *am* desperate. In so many ways.

The corner of his mouth lifts. "I won't give you what you want, Gemma."

His fingers slow. Then he pulls back, removing his hand completely, leaving me aching, empty, furious.

A broken, frustrated noise escapes me, but he just leans in, brushing his lips against my ear, his voice so dark and thick with promise, I swear I can taste it.

"Not until you give me what I want."

I shudder, my nails digging into his shoulders, because I already know what he wants.

It's not just my body. It's everything. My admission. My surrender.

He wants me to come back. To say it. To beg.

"You need me, Gemma," he murmurs, his thumb skimming my bottom lip. "I see it. I feel it." His hand trails down my throat, lower, lower, stopping just above my breasts. "You're shaking for me. So wet for me."

I suck in a breath, my legs quivering from how badly I need him inside me.

He leans in, his mouth just barely grazing mine. "Say it."

I shouldn't say it. I shouldn't mean it. But, God, I do.

"I need you, Alder." My voice is wrecked, raw, ruined, my body shaking. "Save me. Please."

His growl is pure sin, and with a sudden, sharp tug, he yanks my panties to the side. The fabric rips, the sound loud in the quiet night, as he makes damn sure there's nothing left between us.

Alder hooks his arms under my knees, yanking me closer and spreading me wide with a strength that's both thrilling and utterly terrifying.

As he moves me, my gaze catches on the swaying grass, and the tarot card I don't remember letting go of. It pulses with an otherworldly glow, the faint light drawing my attention as the figures on its surface shimmer and shift. Their limbs entwine, melding into one another, hungry for each other, pulsing and changing and very much alive.

That's impossible. I blink, my vision swimming, unsure if it's real or a trick of my alcohol-soaked mind. I've had too much to drink. Too much Alder.

"Look at me, Gemma." His deep, impossible-to-ignore voice snaps me back to exactly where I belong.

I can't fight him. I don't want to.

"You don't look away." He brushes his thumb over my jaw, his fingers down the column of my neck. "You keep those pretty fucking eyes on me. Understand?"

"Yes," I whisper, my voice trembling.

"Good." The clink of his belt buckle echoes in the stillness followed by the slow, torturous slide of his zipper. "Now let me remind you what it means to belong to me."

I whimper, anticipation coiling tight, making every nerve in my body scream for him.

He spreads me wider, his cock replacing the ruined lace, the thick, swollen head brushing against my entrance, teasing, taunting.

"Fuck," he groans, his jaw clenching as he watches me struggle to stay still.

The slow, unbearable drag as he pushes into me makes me cry out, the mix of pleasure and pressure stealing my breath. He fills me completely, stretching me, spoiling me.

I arch into him, legs tightening around his waist.

"You don't ever have to worry again, sweetheart." He thrusts, slow and teasing. "You need a house? Done."

Another thrust, deeper this time, punishing.

"You need a new car? Consider it yours."

I moan, my body tightening around him, every syllable dragging me closer to the edge.

His pace quickens, rougher, more demanding, driving into me like he knows exactly what I need before I do.

"You'll never have to check your bank account again." His words are hot and sharp, each one punctuated with a stroke that steals my breath.

"You'll never have to struggle, never have to wonder if you're gonna make it."

He thrusts again, his cock hitting that spot that makes my vision blur.

"I'll put a black Amex in your name and deposit six figures in your account just to see you smile."

I whimper. Nothing has ever sounded so fucking good.

"I'll buy you whatever the fuck you want." His mouth is everywhere, kissing, biting, licking. "You want diamonds? Pick 'em out."

Another thrust, another shock of pleasure that has me clawing at his shoulders.

"You want your own driver? I'll have one waiting in the morning."

The promise drags me under, the idea of never worrying again, of being wrapped in this life, in him, safe, secure, and fucked-out.

My hips tilt, body desperate for more, for everything.

"Say it," he growls against my throat, his tongue flicking out to taste me. "Say you want it."

I do. I want all of it. The money. The security. The life. Him.

I want to never have to fight again, to never have to wonder if I'm going to make it.

"I want it," I whisper.

He groans, deep and satisfied, his hips snapping forward.

"You fucking have it."

His thumb slides between us, pressing against that aching bundle of nerves, stroking in perfect, practiced circles.

I shatter around him, pleasure crashing through me, his cock still driving deep as I come hard, gripping him like I'll never let go.

Alder groans, thrusting faster, chasing his own pleasure. "You're mine now, Gemma."

My vision flickers, and black spots dance around the edges. The world tilts, and a strange dizziness twists in my chest as the stars above swirl and spiral. The moon dims for a heartbeat, its light faltering, sputtering, then blazes again.

I blink hard, trying to ground myself in Alder—in his hands gripping me, his body moving against mine, anchoring me in his promises. But the world around us continues to spin, and I am untethered, out of sync, floating between pleasure and something I can't quite name.

My gaze falls to the tarot card, its faint glow pulsing in time with the punishing rhythm of Alder's thrusts. The lovers depicted on the card shift, their forms blurring, melting into one another, becoming something whole, something eternal. A shimmering energy radiates from them, hypnotic and alive, and I can feel it breaking open within me.

My skin tingles, static crawling beneath the surface, and I dig my fingers deeper into his back, desperate for something solid, something real. But the dock beneath us seems to tilt, dissolving into the same surreal haze that's creeping into my mind.

Alder's rhythm stutters, his grip tightening, and

with a low, guttural groan, he spills into me, his body shuddering against mine.

For a moment, everything halts.

The only sounds are the ragged echoes of our breaths and the gentle lap of water against the shore.

My body hums, my limbs heavy, every nerve throbbing from the aftershocks of him.

Alder's forehead presses against mine, his breath warm and uneven, and when he finally pulls back, his hands are still on me, smoothing down my thighs, gripping my waist, like he's reluctant to let go.

"You won't run from me again." His voice is quieter now, but it's no less commanding. "Not tonight. Not ever."

Acceptance twists deep in my chest.

For the first time, I don't want to run.

I don't want to face the reality waiting for me beyond this dock—the bank account that's running dry, the career I have to rebuild, the months ahead filled with uncertainty and exhaustion—the cold, sharp edges of a life that doesn't want me back.

With Alder, there's none of that.

There's certainty. There's security. There's money.

And right now, those are worth more than any promise of love ever could be.

I swallow hard, adjusting my dress as he fastens his belt, the lingering warmth of him still inside me, still on my skin.

Alder stretches out on the dock beside me. His chest rises and falls, his eyes half-lidded as he looks at me.

"Lie with me," he murmurs. "Just for a minute."

I settle beside him, and the moment I do, his arm drapes around me, pulling me in like I never left.

"We'll only stay for a minute," he says again, but his voice is thick, lazy, satisfied.

And I know we'll stay as long as he wants us to.

I breathe out slowly, sinking against him, my cheek pressed to his chest.

"Only a minute," I whisper, like I'm still pretending I have control. Like I haven't just made the choice I swore I never would. Like I haven't already given in.

I let out a long breath, my gaze drifting to the stars. They're brighter now, scattered like diamonds across the dark expanse of sky. The moon catches my eye, a crescent sharp and thin as a sliver of glass. My brow furrows. I could've sworn it was full earlier. I blink, my eyelids growing heavy, vision blurring with the pull of sleep.

The night feels…different. The sounds of the lake are faster, rushing, sweeping, as though we're no longer where we were before. But that's absurd. That's impossible. That's the champagne talking.

The steady beat of Alder's heart, his promise of security, his unshakable certainty lulls me into that space between awake and asleep. I close my eyes, letting the warmth of his body pull me deeper.

And for the first time in a long time, I let myself go.

I let myself rest.

I let myself be taken care of.

FIVE

Icy cold water slaps my face, yanking me from the edge of a dream.

I gasp, bolting upright, my fingers clawing at my soaked dress. For a bleary-eyed second, I'm sure it's spilled champagne, but the chill seeps through the fabric and covers far too much of me. I blink hard, wiping water from my eyes, squinting at the rising sun—a runny yolk smeared across puffy white clouds.

"Wake up, lovebirds!" a rough voice snaps through the morning quiet, slicing through my disorientation.

Alder stirs beside me, groaning as he sits up, golden hair plastered to his forehead in wet strands. Slowly, he drags a hand down his face, blinking against the brightness.

I turn toward the voice, and my surprise lodges in my throat.

A man stands on the dock holding an empty wooden bucket, water dripping from its rim. He looks like an actor who stepped straight out of the Enchanted Renaissance book event I coordinated last spring, only dirtier, rougher, more authentic—like he belongs in the past instead of playacting in the present. His mud-stained tunic clings to his wiry frame, his boots caked with clay. His weathered face twists into a scowl as he glares down at us.

The venue must be putting on some kind of medieval faire. Maybe a cleanup crew in costume, working the early shift.

"You two better clear out." He leans down, his voice rougher than the wooden planks beneath me. "Can't have the likes of you sleeping here. You'll drive away the fishes."

Beside me, Alder tenses, water dripping from his chin. "What the hell?"

I force my stiff, aching limbs to move, scrambling to get to my feet as my mind tries to catch up. The wedding. The drinks. The dock. My head throbs, last night's events returning in jagged fragments.

"I understand, we overstayed," I say in a rush, brushing at the damp fabric of my dress as I struggle to shake the feeling that something isn't right. "We're with the wedding party, and we'll get out of your way. But was the bucket really necessary?"

The fisherman's eyes narrow. "Wedding? Ain't no wedding 'round here, missy."

My stomach plummets.

No wedding?

That's not possible.

Did we sleep so long they've already cleared the whole venue? We couldn't have. It's barely sunrise…

I glance around, expecting to see the tent and remnants of last night's celebration, but—nothing. No chairs. No flower arrangements. No distant clatter of a cleanup crew. Just an endless stretch of wild grass and a dense tree line, framing a river I don't recognize.

Wait. A river?

I blink, trying to clear the fog in my brain.

This wasn't a river last night. It was a lake. A calm, glassy lake on Charleston Island Country Club's perfectly manicured grounds.

My heart stutters, and my legs wobble as a flare of panic goes off in my chest.

Alder exhales sharply. He's taking it in too, but his face is unreadable, his jaw ticking as his sharp gaze sweeps the horizon.

"What the fuck," he murmurs.

The fisherman snorts. "You lot done gawkin' yet?" His scowl deepens, his gaze fixed on us like we've trespassed on sacred ground.

I stumble back a step. My mind reels, trying to root itself in logic.

"I—I need to get back," I stammer, more to myself than anyone else. "Is there a shuttle? Or…or a car service?"

The man barks out a humorless laugh. "*Car service?* What in the devil's name are you goin' on about?"

The words hit like another splash of cold water.

I look to Alder, expecting a plan, a response, anything, but he's still watching the horizon, lips pressed into a firm line.

"Young people've all gone barmy, haven't they?" The fisherman mutters the words under his breath and scratches his bearded chin. I catch a glimpse of his calloused fingers, the dirt caked under his nails, the deep, dry cracks around his knuckles—this isn't costume makeup or part of some quaint getaway experience. This is real.

He turns back to the river and dips his bucket back into the rushing water, pulling it up with a grunt.

Alder grabs my arm. "We're leaving."

The unease that's been clawing at me only sharpens its talons as we turn away from the water and head toward the incline. But my feet drag, my body hesitating. Something is pulling me back toward the river.

My fingers twitch and my skin tingles, an electric hum buzzing at my side. My gaze shifts to the dock, drawn by a force I can't explain.

The tarot card.

It lies on the damp wood, still and ordinary, its edges dulled in the early morning light. It's not glowing. The figures aren't moving. The strange energy that seemed to hum from it last night is gone. It's just a card. Just ink and paper.

Except…it isn't.

Is it?

I scoop it up, hesitating when my thumb brushes over the smooth surface, searching for the spark I felt before, the faint glow, the shimmer of movement. Nothing. It's just a card. Just a silly, meaningless card.

At least, that's what I'm telling myself.

I shove it into the pocket of my dress, but I don't let go. My fingers curl around it, grip tightening, because somehow, letting go doesn't feel like an option.

Alder's hand clamps back around my arm. His patience is gone.

"Move, Gemma." The command is quiet but absolute. His grip tightens around my wrist, his palm warm, steady—unchallenged. He doesn't hesitate. Doesn't question. Because to him, this isn't a debate.

Alder steers me toward the incline, his pace brisk, purposeful, like the world will rearrange itself the moment he decides it should.

"We'll find the clubhouse," he says smoothly, as if nothing about this situation is wildly unhinged. "I'll call us a car, get us back to my condo." His voice dips into familiar, honeyed persuasion, all the while leading me exactly where he wants. "I'll even order the eggs Benedict you like from that café—you know the one."

"Wait." I plant my feet, yanking free. "Hold on. This is…"

"Sweetheart…" His voice is low, even, but there's a razor-thin edge beneath it. "There's no running away to New York this time."

I stiffen. "I'm not running—"

His grip finds my wrist again. It's not tight, not rough. Just firm. As sure and certain as he is.

"What happened to last night, Gemma?" It's a question that isn't really a question at all. "What happened to you finally admitting you were done fighting? What happened to me taking care of you, saving you, giving you everything?"

Alder leans in, his heat pressing against me, crowding out the chill, the doubt, the tiny voice still telling me to run.

"I don't say things like that lightly." His grip hardens, but his voice turns coaxing. "I meant it—every word."

My throat tightens, my pulse pounding beneath

his fingers where they brush my jaw, where they trail down the curve of my neck. Barely there—but I feel it everywhere.

"Your life isn't in Manhattan." His fingers skim the hollow at the base of my throat. "Your life is here."

His thumb traces my collarbone, sending a ripple of something deep and unshakable straight through me.

"With me." He lets the words hang between us, sinking into the space where I should fight back, where I should say he's wrong.

But I don't want to keep fighting. And he knows it.

His lips quirk, just slightly, because he sees it—the cracks forming, the exhaustion pooling, the continued fall into something I was never strong enough to resist. He sees the moment I truly give in.

Then Alder turns and strides through the dewy grass like he owns the whole damn world.

And I follow.

***

The early morning chill bites at my skin as we push through waist-high grasses.

Alder's tone was so certain, his resolve so firm, I almost expect to hear the bustle of workers dismantling the wedding tent, the murmur of voices, the clatter of metal. Even though I know something is very wrong, I keep going. Because when Alder speaks with that much conviction, it's hard not to believe him.

But as we crest the top of the hill, an eerie silence presses in. It's too quiet. Unnaturally quiet. The silence is so loud, my ears ring and the hairs on the back of my neck lift.

There's no tent. No tables. No stray decorations littering the ground. Not even the smallest scrap of confetti or pastel place card. Just grass stretching and rolling toward a dense forest of trees so thick the shadows seem to swallow the sunlight.

Alder stops beside me. His body goes rigid, his narrowed gaze sweeping across the empty field.

"This isn't right." His voice doesn't waver, but the confidence in it falters for the briefest second.

Unease sinks its claws deeper into my chest, and my breaths come faster, shallower.

This is where the reception tent should be. Where Mackenzie's wedding should be.

But there's nothing.

I swallow, reaching for him before I even realize what I'm doing, my fingers clutching the sleeve of his suit.

"Alder..." My voice barely makes it past my lips. "Where's the tent?"

His frown deepens. He glances at me, then back at the empty expanse of grass. A flicker of doubt creases between his brows, but then his expression smooths. "They must've cleared it out early. Packed it up while we were asleep."

I stare at him, my disbelief bubbling to the surface. "When? The sun's been up for, what, an hour? There's no way they cleaned it all up that fast." My voice cracks, rising with something that's not panic—because I am *not* panicking—but something dangerously close. "Where are the trucks? The crew? A frickin' napkin!"

Alder's jaw tightens, his mask slipping. For a brief moment, the arrogance and assuredness that define him flicker, replaced by an expression unsettlingly close to fear.

Then, just as quickly, it's gone.

"Maybe we should head back," Alder says, rolling his shoulders. "Figure out what's going on."

Back where?

I wrap my arms around myself, hugging against the sudden chill.

"I don't see Charleston Island Country Club, do you?" I demand, my voice sharper now, the edge of my fear hardening into something I can actually hold. "None of this looks familiar, and I know for a fact Mackenzie didn't have her wedding reception in grass that's damn near up to my tits!"

I gesture wildly at the empty stretch of land.

"And that man—who was pretty much in medieval cosplay—kicked us off the dock at the lake. Except, no, now it's suddenly a river?! And he said the words *car service* like we were speaking German. So, you tell me, Alder, where are we supposed to *go back* to?"

He doesn't flinch under my outburst. He stands there, still and sure, his piercing blue eyes scanning the horizon once more.

The weight of his silence is infuriating.

"Are you seriously just going to stand there?" My voice cracks, and I press a trembling hand to my forehead. "You haven't changed a bit. Always so sure you're right. I should have listened to Amanda. I should never have—"

I stop, choking on the words.

"I swore to myself I wouldn't let you—"

"Gemma." The single word is a command. "Listen to me."

I do, because there's no ignoring him when he speaks like that. No fighting the pull.

"I know this doesn't look right." His voice is even, measured, like he's already figured it out and there's nothing here that can't be fixed. Like I'm the only variable he can't predict. "I get it. But spiraling won't solve anything."

"I'm not spiraling." My voice trembles, my mouth goes dry. My chest rises and falls too quickly, and I hate that he sees it. Sees everything.

His frown deepens, but then his jaw sets, and his eyes harden. "If everything really did vanish, if we're somehow...somewhere else, then standing here falling apart won't get us back."

His voice is so damn steady, it almost grounds me. Almost.

"We need to stay clearheaded."

"And do what?" I shrug. "Wish really hard? *Thoughts and prayers* our way back to reality?"

"We act." His voice is final. Certain. "We move forward. We don't waste time standing here pointing out everything that doesn't make sense."

A shadow streaks across the ground, and my gaze flicks up. A hawk wheels overhead, its wings cutting through the pale morning light. My racing thoughts cling to the idea that it's a sign. A cosmic reassurance that if I just let Alder lead, we'll find a way through this mess.

His last name is Hawke, after all.

The thought is absurd, and the rational part of my brain rejects it immediately. I've never believed in omens or signs, never put my faith in charms or superstition. But, right now, I'd gladly sacrifice a whole herd of farm animals if it would undo whatever disaster I unleashed last night.

I drag my gaze back to him, but he's staring past me.

"What is it?" I ask as I turn to follow his line of sight.

At first, I don't see it. Just the endless stretch of the river, the way it glimmers under the sun's first rays. But then my breath whooshes from my lungs, and my heart stutters. The clouds shift, and something dark and massive cuts through the rising light.

I blink, my throat tightening as I take in the impossible silhouette stamped against the dawn. The details sharpen as the sun creeps higher, each ray carving the shape into something undeniable. My mind stutters and struggles to process what I'm seeing even as the truth of it turns to stone before me.

A castle.

It's in the distance, massive and towering, its walls stretching impossibly high. Turrets twist upward and gleaming spires pierce the sky like silver lances. It's impossible—a fantastical mirage from a fantasy novel. The kind of place that belongs in the pages of the books I read before planning a marketing campaign.

To the right of it, a copse of trees looms—taller than the castle itself, their thick, jagged outlines stabbing at the sky. They rise like sentries and cast long shadows over the surrounding land.

My stomach churns as I realize both the castle and the trees sit on their own islands, surrounded by water that stretches endlessly into the horizon, shimmering like molten silver under the rising sun.

Untouchable. Inexplicable. And yet...undeniably there.

The tarot card hums in my pocket, a low vibration that seeps through the fabric of my dress. A steady pulse of heat radiates from it, matching the rhythm of my galloping heartbeat and intensifying the wrongness of this place. I press my palm to my pocket, and the edges of the card tickle my skin with a strange energy.

The card is reacting.

Reacting to the castle. To the islands. To whatever it is that brought us here.

"Alder…" My voice is a broken whisper. "There's nothing like that in South Carolina."

Cool air whips around my still-damp dress, and I hug my arms to my body. I am cold and wet and surrounded by more unblemished nature than I've ever seen.

He exhales slowly, his gaze unflinching as he takes it all in. "Sweetheart, I don't think we're in South Carolina anymore."

SIX

The forest is dense and endless. Towering trees loom overhead, their thick branches knitting together to block out the sky. Sunlight slips through in shards, casting sharp beams over the moss-covered ground. The river snakes alongside us, our only real marker in this unfamiliar world.

"This is it, Gemma." Alder's voice breaks through the hush as he moves ahead of me effortlessly, his long strides cutting through the undergrowth like he's been here before. "The impossible. The unexplainable. Do you understand what this means?"

I tighten my grip on a low-hanging branch as I duck beneath it, my ballet flats squelching against the soft earth.

"We're walking into something no one's prepared for," he continues. "This is multiverse theory. This is the kind of shit that governments bury and billionaires weaponize."

That sends a chill through me. Alder doesn't speak in maybes. He doesn't speculate. He *knows*. This is what he does. He finds the cracks and exploits them before anyone else even knows they're there. He spins chaos into opportunity, disaster into power. He's built his empire by getting to the truth first. And now, he's looking at this world like it's the next story he'll control.

I should be more frightened than I am. Should be planning, analyzing, trying to figure out our next move. But my mind is sluggish, trapped under the weight of exhaustion and the overwhelming reality that we are nowhere.

No phones. No roads. No signs of life.

But Alder is so sure. And he's the only thing I recognize in this place. And, if anyone can get us back, it's him.

"We are exactly where we're supposed to be."

I glance around the endless stretch of trees, my stomach tightening. "We are lost."

Alder stops, turns. "Lost implies we don't have options." His lips curve slightly, the ghost of a smirk. "I always have options."

He walks to me and places his hand on my lower back, steering me forward.

"Alder." I exhale, forcing my feet to keep moving. "I'm trusting you to get us home."

He looks down at me, gaze unreadable. Then, slowly, his smirk deepens. "You made the right choice."

I don't respond. I just keep walking. There's nowhere else to go.

We trek in silence for a while, the sound of the river our only company. My thoughts swirl and tangle, forming a tight knot in my chest. This is too much. Too big. Too unknown. And I made the decision to trust Alder Hawke completely, no matter the price.

What would Amanda say? And Mackenzie, if she knew… Well, she would probably say that it's worth it, but she's not here. Nobody is. No one except Alder.

And I'm already losing myself in him. Already slipping back into the pattern of letting him call all the shots.

I slow my steps and inhale deep breaths. "I need a minute."

Alder's head tilts slightly. But then he nods once, decisive. "Don't go far."

I walk farther into the trees. Thick branches tangle around me, blocking out this world and the reality I can't process. I push deeper, past gnarled roots and ferns, until the shadows swallow me whole.

Finally, I stop and press my back against the cool bark of a moss-covered tree. My chest rises and falls in shallow, uneven pulls. I can't get enough air. I'm drowning.

I woke up somewhere different than I fell asleep. Not just another bed, another bad decision, but a whole new world.

And worse—so much worse—I let myself fall back into him. I gave in. Stopped fighting.

"This wasn't supposed to happen."

I worked my ass off, made the smart choices, built something from nothing. And still, the ground caved beneath me.

Back in South Carolina, I chose to let Alder save me from the world, from myself. Yes, it was a moment of weakness that felt...*unbelievably good*, but I might not have stuck to it if I'd woken up and the worst thing I had to do was the walk of shame to find my phone.

Now is a different story. I've run out of plans, out of pride, out of every damn thing except him. Plus, I want out of whatever this is. I want to get back home. So why shouldn't I let him save me? That's what he does. He finds answers no one else can. Gets what he wants, no matter the cost.

And if I let him, he'll get me out of this.

I squeeze my eyes shut, forcing air into my lungs.

Focus. Don't spiral. Just breathe.

The scent of damp earth fills my chest, the rustling trees overhead shifting in rhythm with the too-fast thump of my pulse.

It's fine. He's got this.

He's got me.

My pocket vibrates, and my breath catches.

I yank the card free. It pulses against my palm, a warm and steady heartbeat as the image shimmers like a mirage.

The card gets hotter—too hot.

"Shit!" I yelp, dropping it as fire licks through my fingers. It lands on a dew-covered fern with a hiss, tendrils of smoke curling into the air.

The edges glow like embers. The image shifts, flickers in and out of focus.

I shake out my hand, rubbing my fingertips together, still feeling the heat.

What the hell is happening?

My teeth clench against the scream building in my throat.

“What do you want from me?” The question bursts out, ragged and loud.

I don’t know what I expect from this impossible, inexplicable thing. To explain itself? Of course it doesn’t. I’m only met with the soft whisper of wind and the distant rush of the river.

I swallow hard, shaking my head. “This is ridiculous. I am being ridiculous.”

But the card pulses again, brighter this time, like it’s breathing with me. Like it’s waiting.

Snap!

The sound is loud and close. The sharp crack of a branch underfoot followed by the whisper of movement through the trees.

My body goes rigid, every nerve lighting up with the need to flee. The hairs on the back of my neck prickle, and a warning crawls up my spine.

I whip around toward the sound, gripping the nearest fallen branch like it’s a weapon. My pulse pounds through my limbs, muscles coiled, ready.

The forest is suddenly too dense, the shadows between the trees darker. I don’t know where I am or where to run.

Something moves.

I tighten my grip on the branch, swinging with everything I have as the figure steps into view. But before the wood makes contact, a hand snaps up, catching it midair with almost lazy ease.

My fingers loosen on the branch, and I suck in a breath.

Alder’s naked—completely, unapologetically naked.

Sunlight breaks through the trees, dappled patterns

sliding over his bare skin. Broad shoulders, sharp lines of muscle, every inch of him honed and gleaming. My gaze catches on the ridges of his chest, the sharp cut of his abdomen, and then—

A scar.

Jagged and long, slashing across his stomach.

For a second, I swear it glows gold in the fractured light. I blink, convinced I'm imagining things, but the breeze shifts, throwing shadows across his body before I can be sure.

Alder tilts his head, watching me with mild amusement. His grip is still firm around the branch, but it looks like he's barely exerting effort.

"Is this how I am to be greeted?" His voice is too casual for someone who just got attacked with a stick. His blue eyes gleam, familiar and yet…not. "With a branch to the head? Or were you aiming somewhere else?"

Heat floods my face, and I yank the stick back with a scowl. I retreat a step, trying to ignore the way my pulse spikes and my gaze stubbornly refuses to stay above his shoulders—but something is off.

I can't put my finger on it.

I know Alder. I've spent years knowing Alder—every smirk, every look, every ridge of that body like a Greek god come to life.

And yet, something about him feels…different.

"You can't just—" I sputter, waving a hand at him. "For heaven's sake, why are you naked?"

His grin widens, disarming and boyish, and not quite right. "I'd apologize, but I feel like this says more about your aim than my wardrobe."

I scowl harder. "That's not an answer, Alder."

There's a second—barely long enough to notice—but his expression shifts. His brows knit together for the briefest moment, a flicker of confusion in his gaze. But then it's gone.

His smile returns, effortless. "Right. Of course."

The knot in my stomach tightens.

"As for the, uh, lack of clothing..." He gestures vaguely to himself. "I went for a swim to rinse off. The current swept me down the river a bit, and now I'm a little...lost."

"A swim?" My voice cracks, and I grip the stick tighter. "You decided now, of all times, was the perfect moment for *a swim*?"

He shrugs, wet strands of golden hair falling into his eyes as a sheepish smile tugs at his lips. "Well, it seemed like a good idea at the time." Embarrassment colors his cheeks, and he clears his throat and takes a deliberate step back, disappearing behind a massive fern.

Something inside me twists. I don't know why. I should just let it go. But my gut—it's screaming at me.

"So, let me get this straight." I force my voice to steady, desperate to ground myself. "You wandered off for a swim, and I'm just supposed to...what? Pretend that's normal?"

His brows knit together again. There it is—that flicker of hesitation. Barely there. Gone before I can fully process it.

"I wasn't—"

"Doesn't matter," I say quickly, needing this conversation to be over. Needing space from him, from this place, from the twisting wrongness curling inside me.

I shake my head, stepping back. "Just…go find some pants."

He laughs, a low, easy chuckle, and rubs a hand over his jaw like I've just said something ridiculous, like we're sharing some inside joke. Then he flashes me that lopsided grin that makes my stomach flip.

And for the first time since stepping into this forest, I feel real fear.

Not because of where we are. Not because of what's happened. But because I don't fully recognize the man in front of me.

His laugh is too easy. Too natural. Too much like Alder…but at the same time, not.

I inhale sharply, forcing logic to override instinct. Of course he's acting differently—we woke up in some unknown place. He's rattled. I am too. Who wouldn't be? And what, I'm suddenly suspicious because he smiled at me and decided to go for a swim to clean his body after a night of drinking and sex?

I need to get a grip.

I turn away before I can talk myself in circles. "I'm taking another minute."

"Wait!" he calls after me, but I don't stop.

I don't want to think about this. I don't want to consider the fact that something inside me is screaming to run.

"You forgot—"

"I don't care!" I throw the words over my shoulder, quick, breathless as I duck into the shadows of the forest. I just need space. A minute to clear my head, to breathe, to stop feeling like my world keeps falling out from under me.

I don't know how long I walk before I realize I've gone too far, that the sound of the river has faded and my surroundings look even less familiar.

I retrace my steps. Or at least, I try to. But the forest twists and folds in on itself, the shadows growing heavier. My breath quickens. I'm never finding my way back.

Then I hear it—the faint, distant rush of water. Relief floods me, and I pick up my pace, weaving through the trees toward the sound. The forest opens and sunshine greets me as the river and the path along its edge come back into view.

I stumble out of the trees and stop dead in my tracks.

Alder stands by a boulder, his back to me, tugging a pair of fitted breeches up over his hips. The leather fits his frame like it was made for him, though it's far from the tailored slacks he was wearing earlier.

My pulse stutters. Wait…what?

I blink, my gaze tracking the rest of the outfit laid out on the rocks—a deep burgundy coat, intricate gold embroidery forming a five-pointed star enclosed in a circle. A matching vest, an elegant, high-collared white shirt, the kind you'd see in a museum exhibit, not on Alder Hawke.

This…this isn't his.

A chill slides down my spine, but I push it away. There has to be an explanation.

"What are you doing?"

Alder turns at the sound of my voice, one brow arched, as if I'm the one acting strange. "There are no roads, no power lines, no sign of anything from the twenty-first century." Alder's voice is even, unshaken. Like nothing about this situation unnerves him. Like he isn't even considering the possibility of being afraid. Because Alder doesn't do fear. He does control.

"And the fisherman back on the dock?" he continues, pulling my focus back to him. "He looked like he walked straight out of the Dark Ages. These"—he gestures to the clothing draped over the boulder—"might help me blend in when we finally come across someone else."

I can't stop staring.

The pants look too perfect on him. Like they weren't abandoned but made for him.

A nagging voice in the back of my mind whispers that something isn't right—but I shove it down, bury it under the comfort of Alder's confidence.

"What about the man they belong to?" The man who's out here naked in the woods. But…that was Alder. It had to be. Any other explanation will prove that I've lost my mind and this whole situation is a hallucination, and that is something I cannot handle right now. "What happens when he comes back?"

"I haven't seen anyone." He holds my gaze as he slides his arms into the white shirt, the fabric settling over his shoulders, clinging to every sharp line of muscle like it was tailored for him. "Have you?"

A small knot tightens in my stomach, but I swallow it down and shake my head. He's the only person I've seen out here…right?

"We'll be long gone by the time whoever owns these clothes comes back."

I open my mouth to argue, but then he picks up the coat and slides it on. The way the deep maroon fabric falls over his shoulders like he was born into royalty, the way the embroidered sigil gleams in the shifting light—he looks right.

Not just like he belongs in them. Like they belong to him.

His lips curve into a slow, knowing half-smile, his blue eyes sparking. "Like what you see?"

I narrow my eyes at him to hide the way my pulse spikes. "This isn't a game, Alder."

His smirk fades as he steps closer. "You think I'm not taking this seriously?"

I swallow hard, my throat tightening, but I don't look away. "You're certainly not acting like it."

Alder leans in, so close I feel the warmth of his breath when he speaks. "Gemma, I am doing exactly what needs to be done to ensure you're taken care of and that you're where you belong—with me."

The air between us crackles, and my heart pounds in my chest as I search his ocean-blue eyes. Before I can respond, heavy footsteps crash through the underbrush behind us. My heart leaps into my throat, and I spin around.

A group of armored guards bursts through the trees, their polished breastplates glinting in the sunlight. Their heavy boots churn up the forest floor, swords swinging at their hips. The leader—a broad-shouldered man with a close-cropped beard and sharp eyes—scans the pathway before his gaze locks onto Alder.

"There you are, Lord Lockhart!" His voice booms with relief as he strides forward. He stops a few paces away before dipping into a deep, practiced bow. The others follow suit, their heads dipping in perfect synchronization.

Lord Lockhart?

I glance up at Alder.

He doesn't react right away. Just a slight tension in his jaw before he smooths it away, his expression settling into something unreadable. Then, like flipping a switch, his gaze sweeps over the guards, assessing, calculating. "Yes, you've found me. What seems to be the problem?"

I gape at him. *What seems to be the problem?*

The lead guard's gaze flicks to me, and he flashes Alder a gap-toothed grin. "My lord, you could find a lady to sweep off her feet in the middle of a cyclone."

Alder's lips quirk into the faintest smirk. "You know me well."

What the actual fuck is going on?

The guard gestures farther up the path. "We must resume our travels, my lord, if we're to reach the Kingdom of Cups before nightfall."

The Kingdom of *what*? My mouth opens, ready to protest, to tell them they've got the wrong guy. Alder is not a lord, and this isn't some medieval fairy tale. But before I get the words out, Alder's fingers press against my shoulder.

It's not a warning—not exactly. It's the action of a man who expects to be listened to. And it's enough to make my words stick in my throat.

"Very well." Alder inclines his head without hesitation. "Lead the way."

My heart pounds as the guard nods and starts back up the path.

The others follow—but then, one hesitates. His gaze shifts to me, then back to Alder. "And the lady?"

"She is mine." It's a statement of fact. A simple truth.

"And as her knight in shining armor, I am duty-bound to protect her." Alder casts a glance down at me, his mouth just barely curving at the edges. "A noble cause, wouldn't you agree?"

The guards chuckle. "A noble cause, indeed, my lord."

On the surface, the words are sweet, charming. But I hear the weight in them. It's a statement of ownership, of certainty.

I stare up at him. I've made my choice, and there's no turning back now.

Slowly, my hand finds his arm, slipping into place right where he expects it to be.

The guards march ahead, their armor clinking with every step, their boots crunching against the forest floor.

Alder leads, and I try to keep pace, but my mind is spinning, my pulse hammering in my throat.

"What is going on?" I whisper under my breath.

One of the guards glances back, his bushy red brows knitting together.

Alder's hand tightens where it rests on mine. The silent message is unmistakable. *Not now.*

We follow the guards down an offshoot of the narrow path, the dense forest gradually thinning until the trees break and we emerge onto a wide, beaten dirt road lined with wildflowers and scattered boulders.

My steps falter as my gaze lands on the carriage waiting ahead. Its dark wooden frame is carved with swirling patterns of golden pentacles that glitter in the sunlight. Ruby embellishments are embedded at each corner and gleam like hot coals.

The horses hitched to the carriage are just as

dreamlike. Their glossy black coats gleam like polished onyx, and their braided manes shimmer with threads of gold. They paw at the ground, powerful hooves kicking up dust as they snort and toss their heads impatiently.

This can't be real.

My heart pounds as I take it all in, my mind struggling to make sense of what feels like a scene from a book.

A guard opens the carriage door and gestures for us to climb inside, but my feet stay planted. I don't move. I can't. My legs refuse.

I glance back to the forest, toward the path we took to get here.

I'm having a psychotic break. That's what this is.

But then there's the ache in my legs. The raw blister on my heel. The dirt under my fingernails. The sharp scent of horses. The solid weight of Alder's grip on my arm.

This isn't a hallucination. This is real.

And I am so, so far from home.

Alder's palm presses against my lower back. A silent command wrapped in the illusion of guidance. "After you."

Now is not the time to question. Alder isn't, and I won't either. And then, before I think too hard about it, before I let the rising panic overtake me—

I step inside.

SEVEN

The moment my butt hits the bench, the plush velvet cushions envelop me. The fabric is deep red and impossibly soft. The rest of the interior is just as opulent. Golden filigree spirals along the walls, tracing intricate patterns that catch the light filtering through small windows etched with designs of pentacles and twisting vines. The ceiling is lined with embroidered silk, its pattern mirroring the patterns on the glass, while the floor is covered in a thick, luxurious rug that makes me want to rip off my dirty flats and spread my toes.

Too bad I don't have time to revel in the fantasy.

Alder steps in behind me, and as soon as the door shuts with a heavy click, I whirl on him. "What the fuck are we doing? I'm trying, Alder, *really* trying, to let you lead here, but this is getting out of hand. Armed guards are taking us to an undisclosed location. That's literally the start of a true crime documentary."

"They're taking us to the *Kingdom of Cups*," he corrects smoothly, settling onto the seat across from me.

"Oh, well, that clears everything right up," I snap, crossing my arms. "A kingdom. My bad. That's so much better."

He props his ankle on his knee, unbothered. "You're spiraling."

"No shit! You do see the suits of armor escorting us, right? The horses? The carriage? We've stepped into an alternate dimension where Amazon Prime hasn't even been invented yet. Not that that would be a particularly bad thing."

He leans forward, resting his forearms on his thighs, his voice maddeningly calm. "You told me last night you wanted me to handle it, and that's exactly what I'm doing."

I press my fingers to my temples, inhaling deeply through my nose. "Alder, handling it means calling a car service, booking a flight home—not being kidnapped by men who sound like they've stepped out of a Ren Faire."

"Gemma. Sweetheart." His voice is all honey and steel, sliding down my spine and settling low in my stomach. "I don't need to call for a car. I am the car service." He gestures around us, the movement lazy, arrogant. "This is what it looks like when I take care of things."

I gape at him. "You're insane."

"I'm the only one with a plan."

My jaw clenches. "And what exactly is the plan? Because I must have missed the part where we discussed you waltzing into a fairy tale and becoming the main character."

With a chuckle, he leans back and stretches his long arms along seat. "We're going to Cups. We're going to play along. And then we're going to get home. You don't have to worry about the details." His eyes flick over me, slow, deliberate. "You just have to sit there and look pretty."

My mouth falls open. "Excuse me?"

"Relax," he drawls. "You're always working. Always fighting. You made the right decision, letting me take over." His voice dips lower, coaxing, persuasive. "You deserve this, Gemma. You deserve not to have to worry."

I shake my head, trying to clear it. "Alder, I don't—"

"I know, I know you don't want to admit you need help. But you do. And that's why I'm here."

I swallow hard, my fingers curling into the plush velvet seat. "And what exactly do you get out of this arrangement?"

His smirk sharpens. "You."

A war rages in my chest. Every single thing he's saying is everything I've ever wanted, everything I've agreed to. Safety. Security. The end of the constant fight to survive.

It's so easy to let him take over.

And that's the problem.

I force a scoff. "You don't own me now, you know."

His blue eyes darken, amusement flickering into something more dangerous. "Sweetheart, I owned you the second you decided I was your best option."

I open my mouth, but nothing comes out. Because he's right.

As Mackenzie would say, I sold my soul and punani for comfort. For money. For *him*.

Maybe he could fight back against the guards, maybe he'd even win. But me? I'm at their mercy—and his.

Alder watches me, head tilted, like he's waiting for me to catch up to something obvious. Then he sighs, low and indulgent, like I'm a child throwing a tantrum over a scraped knee. "Come here."

Before I can react, he grips my wrists, shifts his weight, and pulls me firmly enough that my body follows, sliding across the plush carriage seat with zero resistance. The soft cushions absorb my stumble, and then I'm right beside him, my thigh skimming against his as the scent of him—apples and linen and something darker, warmer—fills my lungs.

His hand comes up, fingers threading into my hair with a touch so gentle it unravels something inside me, something I should keep locked up tight. He strokes down the length of it, slow, like he has all the time in the world, and then he bends, brushing a kiss to the top of my head.

"There she is." His lips move against my scalp, sending a slow, unwelcome shiver down my spine. "I told you. I've got this." His hand shifts, his palm smoothing over my shoulder, his breath warm against my temple. "Everything is going to be okay."

I keep my back straight at first, my shoulders tense and stiff beneath the weight of his arm. My gaze locks onto the passing blur of green fields and distant trees beyond the carriage window, but I can't focus. The questions spinning in my mind are loud, but Alder's voice is louder, stronger, curling in the spaces between my ribs, coiling into a steadiness that almost feels safe.

The tension bleeds from my body in slow increments.

My shoulder softens first, leaning ever so slightly into his chest. The steady rise and fall of his breathing pulls me closer, and it's comforting. So, so comforting.

My head tips until it finds the curve of his chest.

He strokes his fingers through my hair again, and I let myself relax.

I don't trust him. But right now, I need him.

Outside, the guards ride alongside the carriage on horseback, their polished armor catching the light and glinting like mirrors. Beyond them, endless fields stretch out, the tall grasses bending in the breeze. Their pale tips shimmer like liquid gold under the relentless sun, a living, breathing sea of light and movement. It's beautiful, almost hypnotic, but my attention is quickly pulled to the horizon.

I sit up and shove the curtain aside, pressing closer to the glass as my gaze sweeps over the landscape. Massive structures dot the field, their hulking forms grotesquely beautiful. One strides on long, insect-like legs, its spindly joints clicking and whirring as it moves. Steam hisses from pipes that jut out at odd angles, shrouding the giant contraption in shuddering mist.

Another machine—a huge, gleaming sphere—spins lazily in place. Its exposed inner workings are a maze of burnished steel that pumps and pulses with the fire of pistons and faint puffs of steam. Gears line its outer shell, spinning in perfect harmony, their silver teeth glinting.

The air seeping into the carriage is thick, heavy with a metallic tang that coats my tongue. It's sharp and salty and laced with the acrid bite of oil and tinged with electricity, like a storm waiting to break.

I press a hand against the glass. "What are those things?"

Alder leans forward beside me, peering out like we're simply admiring the view. His fingers rest casually on the edge of the window, as if we're not lumbering toward something unnatural and inexplicable.

"Impressive," he murmurs, brows lifting in appreciation.

"*Impressive?*" The word sticks in my throat like a splinter. "You cannot be serious."

He glances at me, the corner of his mouth lifting. "Come on, sweetheart, don't tell me you're not at least a little awestruck."

"Awe isn't the word I'd use," I mutter. My skin prickles as the low hum of the machines vibrates through my chest and the carriage lurches forward. "Those things could crush us. What if they're weapons? What if they're—"

"They're not weapons." His tone is maddeningly casual, as if we're discussing weather and not towering metal nightmares that could stomp us into the dirt. "Look at how they're moving. They're working. See the pipes on that one?" He nods toward the massive sphere. "They're likely venting heat. It's regulating itself."

"And nothing says safety like machines the size of buildings needing to regulate their own heat."

Alder chuckles and drapes an arm over the back of the carriage seat, fingers idly playing with the loose strands of my hair. "You worry too much."

I whirl back to face him. "No, you worry too little! We"—I gesture between us wildly—"don't know where we are. We don't know how we got here. And we don't know what those things are! But you"—I jab a finger into his chest—"you're leaning back like we're on a damn honeymoon carriage ride through the English countryside."

His smirk deepens, his blue eyes sparking, and I realize, too late, that I played right into his hands. "Sweetheart, if this was our honeymoon, you'd be in my lap screaming for an entirely different reason."

My stomach flips. "You're impossible."

"And you're adorable when you're spiraling."

I press my lips together, exhale sharply through my nose, and sink back into the plush velvet.

The carriage crests a small hill, and the town sprawls out around us. Our pace slows as we descend over cobbled streets and into the village. Buildings rise on either side of us, their stone facades weathered with age and interwoven with gleaming metal. Silver pipes twist along the walls like veins, carrying plumes of steam to and from towering machines that hum and click from where they're mounted on top of thatched rooftops.

Vendors line the streets, their carts overflowing with shimmering trinkets and polished gears that catch the light like jewels. Children dart between the carts, laughing as they chase the shadow of a massive clockwork bird perched on top of a spire. The bird's metallic wings twitch and steam hisses from its joints as it lets out a mechanical cry that echoes across the square.

Noise grows in the distance, faint at first but unmistakable.

"Are people…cheering?" It's not long before my question is answered and the celebration swells, vibrating through the carriage as it slows to a crawl, and we roll into the heart of the bustling village. Townsfolk pour into the streets. People lean out of windows, climb onto rooftops, and wave blue and silver banners. The fabric ripples in the breeze, and I catch the emblem embroidered on every flag—a chalice surrounded by swirling waves.

The carriage creaks to a halt in the center of the square, and the noise swells again.

Alder takes a deep breath and claps his hands against his thighs. "Guess we're about to find out why."

The door swings open, and Alder moves first. He steps out, and renewed cheers ripple through the crowd. He turns and extends a hand to me.

As he helps me down, the world explodes into bursts of soft, fragrant color. Petals rain down from every direction, a kaleidoscope of flowers cascading through the air like perfumed confetti. The crowd surges forward, tossing blooms with wild abandon. Daisies, violets, and an unfamiliar pale blue flower cling to my skin, catch in my hair, and scatter across the cobblestones, painting the ground in a rainbow of blossoms.

"Three cheers for Lord Lockhart!" someone shouts, and the cry is echoed again and again until the sky feels like it might crack open with the force of it.

I glance up at Alder, expecting to see some sign of confusion, some acknowledgment that this is as baffling for him as it is for me. But no. Of course not.

He's thriving.

He stands tall, his broad shoulders squared, his head held high like he was born to bask in this kind of praise. His dazzling smile radiates confidence, his blue eyes scanning the crowd with an ease that makes my stomach twist. He soaks it all in, not just unfazed but energized.

And why wouldn't he be? After all, that's the luxury of being Alder Hawke—a gorgeous, tall, white alpha male.

Meanwhile, I'm left standing in the center of this storm of petals and applause, the cobblestones unsteady beneath my feet, and the suffocating realization that whatever is happening here, Alder isn't just playing along. He's already claiming it.

Just like he's claimed me.

A trumpet blares, and I whirl around, craning my neck to see around the carriage. My heart slams against my ribs as my gaze lands on the castle, looming impossibly large and imposing in the late-afternoon sun. Its spires and domes shimmer in shades of blue and silver, fracturing the light into glittering shards.

My gaze drifts past the walls of the castle to a dark copse of trees that rises just beyond them. Their jagged peaks spear the sky, stark and menacing against the shimmering blue and silver. I saw them both from a distance before, but up close, it feels like they're watching me back.

Unease churns in my stomach—but, no, that's not quite right. I don't feel *uneasy*. It's deeper than that. I feel…pulled…trapped…summoned? It's as if those trees are calling to my heart and etching hidden messages in my bones.

My chest tightens. I force myself to look away, but the sensation lingers—an itch I can't quite reach, a whisper of something just out of earshot. It hums low in my veins, tugging at the edges of my thoughts like a half-remembered dream.

Boots crunch over gravel as one of the guards steps around the carriage and bows sharply.

"My lord." He gestures to the other side of the carriage, where my view is blocked. "The ferry awaits. We must be on our way if we're to keep schedule."

I blink, trying to shake off the fog of whatever just gripped me, and nod almost absently. "The ferry?"

The driver snaps his whip, and the horses jerk forward, pulling the carriage toward the edge of the path. Their hooves clatter against stone as the sound of rushing water grows louder, more insistent. And then I see it.

The castle's outer walls are alive with pipes and steam and waterfalls that cascade down in silken torrents and catch the light like molten silver. The streams twist and tumble through carved channels, their paths feeding into a vast, shimmering lake of dark, silvery waves that encircle the castle and ripple like liquid mercury.

Beyond the moat, the ocean stretches into the horizon, a frothing expanse of white-tipped waves crashing endlessly into one another. It's overwhelming—so much movement, so much sound, so much power—and my pulse sputters as I take it all in.

Alder is already walking, following the guards, but I barely notice until his hand clamps firmly around my elbow.

"Try to keep up, Gemma." His grip is unyielding, but there's a spark of mirth in his gaze that makes my teeth clench. "I can't keep an eye on you if you're always lagging behind."

I yank my arm free with a glare, but despite my irritation, I follow him. My steps falter as we near the platform, and the sound of rushing water grows louder.

One of the waterfalls splits like a curtain. It doesn't slow or lessen in force, it simply...parts.

The water cascades to either side with a hiss that reverberates through the air and shakes the ground beneath my feet. Mist sprays outward in delicate arcs, catching the sunlight and scattering it into colored light that shimmers against the burbling moat below.

Behind the parted veil, the ferry emerges, its dark, polished wood glinting as if freshly lacquered. The sharp prow cuts through the waves as the vessel glides forward.

The ferry's hull is massive, sleek, and carved with deep serpent-like grooves that funnel the water away, keeping it gleaming and mostly dry despite the churning spray. The railings are lined with ornate silver filigree patterns that twist and curl like the flow of the water around it, their edges catching the light and throwing it back in dizzying swirls.

As the ferry nears the platform, steam hisses from hidden vents along its sides, curling upward in ghostly tendrils that mingle with the mist.

The figure at the helm steps forward, their silhouette sharpening. They're cloaked in deep midnight blue, and their face is obscured by a smooth metallic mask gleaming cold in the sunlight. The mask is expressionless, featureless except for the faint ridges where eyes, a nose, and a mouth should be.

A chill skates between my shoulders. "Are we crossing the Styx?" I mutter under my breath, my voice trembling slightly despite my attempt at sarcasm.

Alder hears me. His lips twitch. "Sweetheart, if this is the afterlife, you're stuck with me for eternity."

I shoot him a look. "Then I'd rather take my chances with the underworld."

He tsks, shaking his head. "That's no way to talk to the man who's saving you."

"The man who thinks he owns me," I correct, folding my arms.

"Tomato, tomahto," he drawls. "Either way, you're mine."

The ferry halts with a smooth, almost imperceptible motion, bobbing gently in the rippling moat. The parted waterfall continues to hiss behind it, a shimmering veil just waiting to trap us inside.

The masked figure at the helm tilts their head in silent acknowledgment.

My stomach twists. Nope. Nope, nope, nope.

The guards march ahead, boots thumping against the wood as they file onto the ferry. Alder, of course, follows without hesitation, stepping onto the deck like this is a VIP yacht experience. I advance slowly, every cell in my body screaming not to, but I force my feet to step on board.

The ferry glides forward, the oars cutting through the silvery water in steady, rhythmic strokes. The metallic tang grows sharper as we move toward the castle, and I grip the edge of the ferry, my knuckles white against the polished wood.

It's salt. I tell myself, my gaze flicking to the cascading waterfalls and the churning moat. *It's just salt from the water. That's it.*

But the taste lingers on my tongue, metallic and wrong, coating the back of my throat like blood.

Alder leans against the rail beside me, his golden hair

catching the sunlight. "You look like you're about to throw up." His voice is far too amused for the current level of *holy shit* we're experiencing.

"I'm fine," I snap, even though I'm absolutely not fine.

"You sure?" He eyes me, and the corner of his mouth lifts. "You get this cute little wrinkle right here"—he taps his index finger between my brows—"when you're spiraling."

I swat his hand away. "I am not spiraling. Stop saying that."

"Really?" He leans in, voice dropping to a lazy murmur. "Because you're gripping that railing like it owes you money."

I glance down. My fingers are clenched so tight around the polished wood that they look about three seconds from snapping off.

Slowly, I peel them away and shake out my hands.

"Unclench," Alder advises, grinning like a bastard.

"Unclench?" I repeat, my voice pitching higher. "We're being ferried across a moat by a masked…Grim Reaper impersonator to a castle that looks like it was designed by Tim Burton, and you think *I'm* the problem?"

Alder sighs like I'm exhausting but adorable and steps behind me, wrapping himself around me, his warmth pressing against my back. His arms don't cage me in exactly—but they could. Easily.

"See, this is what happens when you spend too much time away from me." His lips brush the shell of my ear. "You get all wound up."

My mouth falls open. "I was only away from you for six months."

"And in those six months, you clearly worked

yourself into a state." His hands slide up my arms, then settle at my shoulders, kneading gently. "You need me to keep you occupied. Trust me, Gemma. I know what's best for you."

The waterfall towers above us now, its thunderous roar vibrating through the ferry, through me. The mist clings to my skin, and I feel so lost I could cry.

I exhale slowly, forcing my shoulders to stay tense beneath his hands. "I don't actually trust you."

"No?" Alder makes a low sound, something between a chuckle and a hum of disapproval. "That's cute."

I scowl. "It's not cute, it's a fact."

His thumbs press deeper into the knots at my shoulders, working the tension apart like he has the right to undo me.

"Oh, sweetheart." His tone is thoroughly unimpressed. "It always takes people a minute to reacclimate after they realize they've been outmaneuvered."

My stomach clenches. It's a throwaway comment, meant to needle me, to remind me that he's always three steps ahead. But the way he says it?

I stiffen, shrugging away from his touch. "I hate this…everything. Being stuck in some strange world with you." The lie tastes like chalk, dry and crumbling.

The waterfall closes behind us with a roar, the sound swallowing the air as the shimmering curtain seals us in. There's no turning back.

"You don't hate being here with me," Alder murmurs, his voice all whiskey and smoke, his fingers just shy of entwining with mine. He leans down, close enough that I can feel his smirk without even seeing it. "You just hate that, even in another world, I'm still always right."

My lips part—for what, I don't know. Because the truth, no matter how much I want to avoid it, is painfully, undeniably clear.

He's not wrong.

EIGHT

The castle's outer walls ripple with intricate designs of waves frozen mid-motion. Silver pipes twist and curve through the stonework, catching the light and reflecting the shimmering water below in a way that makes the entire castle seem to move, to breathe. It's beautiful in a haunted ghost story sort of way, and I am not big a fan of the horror genre.

The guards disembark first, their boots striking the stone dock with sharp thuds. They fall into formation and march ahead, leading us toward the towering entrance. But just before we reach the doors, they part—wordlessly, seamlessly—leaving us to continue alone.

My steps slow, the knot in my stomach tightening as my gaze lifts to the massive doors ahead. They loom over us, carved from the same dark, polished wood as the ferry and inlaid with silver gears and cogs. The instant we approach, a low groan vibrates through the metalwork. The gears engage, clicking and spinning, and the doors swing open to reveal a grand hallway that stretches deep into the castle.

Figures line the interior, draped in the same midnight blue cloaks as the one who guided the ferry, their smooth metallic masks glinting like moonlight on water.

Alder looks like he's arriving at a five-star resort, while I stand there, gaze darting between the endless corridor and the masked figures flanking the walls like a very niche horror movie ensemble.

"Ladies first." Alder gestures for me to go ahead.

I don't move. "What if it's booby-trapped and giant axes come swinging out of the walls? Or—" I point at one of the smooth, unlit sconces lining the entrance. "Or poisonous poo-covered darts fly out, and I end up looking like a toxic pin cushion?"

His lips twitch. "Poisonous, poo-covered darts?"

I fold my arms. "It's called self-preservation."

Alder tilts his head, considering. "How about this? You walk in first, and if you die, I'll have a wing added to the Library of Congress in your honor."

I pause. That actually sounds…incredible. A whole wing dedicated to me. Floor-to-ceiling books, a plaque, maybe even a reading room.

Damn him.

"If I die, I'm haunting you," I mutter, and a chill skates through me as I step over the threshold.

Alder follows close enough that I feel the heat of him at my back. "Sweetheart, you're already haunting me."

My skin prickles as the thud of Alder's stolen boots echoes in the silence.

Behind us, the doors groan shut, and a sharp click locks them in place.

I yelp involuntarily. Fear frosts my veins and curls cold around my ribs. I want to puke. I didn't like the guards, but at least I knew they were human. These cloaked figures? I don't know what's behind their masks.

One of them steps forward as though pulled by invisible strings. They motion for us to follow, and without hesitation, Alder starts walking. It takes me being left behind in the giant hall with these silent figures to decide to cling to his confidence rather than resent it. Holding a grudge won't get me out of here. And right now, I need his certainty more than I need my pride.

As we move deeper into the castle, the silent figures surge to life like a wave. One by one, they step forward, their cloaks billowing softly, silently guiding us like a living, breathing map.

Silks cascade along the walls in shades of blue, shimmering with silver accents that shift like ripples across still water. The walls are interrupted by tall, narrow windows pressed into the stone, their frames etched with cresting waves. Sunlight streams in, painting the hall in muted blues and greys.

Above us, chandeliers spiral downward from the soaring ceiling, their arms curling like frozen whirlpools. Each fixture cradles dark, unlit globes that glint faintly, waiting for a spark that doesn't come.

Pipes coil along the walls, their sleek, serpentine patterns gleaming in the sunlight. They twist and curve, utterly silent. There's no hiss of steam, no hum of machinery. Shouldn't they make some kind of noise like the machines outside the castle? Only the constant distorted murmur of the waterfalls beyond the walls and my shallow breathing break the silence.

The deeper we go, the more the air vibrates with an unspoken tension. I swear I'm the only one who feels it because neither Alder nor these…*people*…show even the slightest hint that anything is out of place. But the closer we get to the heart of the castle, the more I want to run away.

We're guided down another hallway, this one narrower, darker. The flicker of light from distant windows barely illuminates the space, leaving shadows to slither across the walls. My gaze is drawn to the unlit chandeliers, the empty, cold sconces lining the walls.

"This is basically a horror novel," I mutter. "And I know damn well we're walking straight into the climax."

Alder snorts, because of course he does. "Drama, sweetheart."

I glare up at him. "Why don't they turn on the lights?"

He shrugs, entirely unbothered. "Maybe they're environmentally conscious."

"Yeah, that's the first thing I thought when we took a ferry through a waterfall and ended up in *The Infernal Devices* meets Versailles castle. I'm sure conservation is their top priority."

"You should try a little optimism, Gemma."

"I'll try optimism when we stop walking directly toward our gruesome deaths."

"You always assume the worst," he muses, unaffected by my impending nervous breakdown.

I cross my arms, irritation simmering beneath my panic. "Tell me, Alder, do you always know what you're doing, or are you just really good at faking it?"

His lips curve, wicked and knowing. "Tell me, Gemma, what's the difference?"

"One of them means you'll get us killed, and the other means you'll *definitely* get us killed."

He chuckles. "Sweetheart, if we were going to die, it would've happened already."

We take another turn, and the hall widens abruptly, spilling us into a vast chamber with towering double doors at its end.

The figures in cloaks fan out, taking their places along the walls in synchronized silence, their metallic masks gleaming faintly in the dim light.

I swallow. Hard.

The doors ahead are massive, inlaid with silver gears and sigils. As soon as we stop, they begin to move—clicking, grinding, unlocking.

"This is it," I whisper, pulse thrumming in my ears. "This is where they murder us, sacrifice us to some eldritch god, or feed us to whatever fantastical nightmare they're hiding in the heart of the castle."

Alder scoffs. "You've read too many books."

"I don't think I've read enough books to prepare for this."

The gears embedded deep into the polished wood whirl and groan. The vibrations hum through the stone floor and up through my feet.

I'm pretty sure I'm hyperventilating.

Alder takes my hand, and his thumb sweeps over my knuckles.

The tension in my shoulders eases just a little. My pulse doesn't stop racing, but it shifts, no longer sharp-edged panic, but something else. Something warmer.

I exhale, and the massive doors groan open.

The air inside hits me like a wave—warm, heady, and thick with the mingling scents of spiced wine, salt, and musk. It clings to my skin, sinking into my senses before I even step forward.

Quiet bubbles of laughter and the clinking of glasses mingle with music that pulses like a heartbeat, too slow to dance to but too seductive to resist.

My gaze locks onto the massive machine dominating the center of the grand hall, a monolith of gleaming silver and steel. A steampunk style Trojan horse. It looms silent and imposing, its intricate gears frozen in place. The hiss of steam and the clatter of metal we heard from the devices outside are absent. It's silent. Dormant. Everything that thrummed with life before—the humming contraptions, the pulsing energy—has been smothered by the castle.

I take a deep breath and let it out slowly. What has to happen to awaken it? And what happens when it does?

The thoughts linger, floating like steam in my mind, but I tear my eyes away, drawn instead to the tide of movement that flows through the room. Dozens of bodies sway and mingle. Sheer skirts ripple like water, teasing glimpses of sculpted thighs and bare skin as the women move. Shimmering silver corsets wrap around waists, the boning inlaid with glittering blue gemstones that catch the flickering glow of countless candles.

The honey-colored tapers have been lit and replaced so many times their melted wax forms stalagmites throughout the room and thick, frozen waterfalls across the buffet tables lining the walls.

The men are equally decked out, their waistcoats

embroidered with threads of silver and midnight blue, their collars open and shirts unbuttoned to reveal chiseled chests and the hint of muscled torsos beneath.

Female attendants glide through the crowd, their naked bodies painted entirely in gleaming silver. Their faces are hidden behind smooth metal masks that reflect the flickering candlelight like living mirrors.

One attendant holds a tray with deep garnet-colored wine. Another displays delicate crystal goblets filled with a golden, fizzy liquid that sends trails of vapor curling into the air. There are flutes of blue cocktails, the rim of each glass dusted with silver sugar that shines like stardust.

Tiny pastries shaped like cresting waves are filled with glistening creams in shades of navy and aqua, their petals dusted with edible glitter. Miniature towers of glazed fruit rise in stacks and are covered with threads of spun sugar as delicate as spider silk.

An attendant walks past, her silver-painted skin gleaming like polished metal. She stops beside a man dressed in an unbuttoned blue waistcoat embroidered with delicate silver chalices. The fabric clings to his broad shoulders, and the cut of his jaw is softened only by the devilish grin curling his lips.

Without a word, she extends the tray toward him. Its surface is covered in tiny orbs, like liquid sunsets trapped in glass. He inclines his head, and she plucks one from the tray with slender, silver-painted fingers. Slowly, she lifts it. His smile widens as he opens his mouth, and she places the orb on his tongue. As it dissolves, his eyelids flutter shut, and he tilts his head back. A low, contented sigh escapes him, and the tension in his shoulders ebbs like the ocean receding with the tide.

Alder steps closer, his voice a soft tickle against my ear. "Told you no one's getting sacrificed. Looks like we've been invited to a party."

I watch as another woman throws her head back, moans spilling from her lips as two men practically devour her with their hands, their mouths, their touch. My stomach twists.

"A party..." I shake my head. "This doesn't feel like a party. It feels like a trap."

Alder laces his fingers through mine, anchoring me in place. He doesn't argue. Doesn't tease. Just squeezes, firm and steady. *I've got you.*

His attention drifts to the far corner of the room where a tangle of bodies lounges on a nest of deep blue velvet cushions all pressed against the dormant machine's cold, gleaming surface.

A woman cranes her neck, exposing the long, elegant column of her throat. The man behind her traces his mouth along her jawline, his hand disappearing beneath the shimmering fabric of her skirt. Another woman sprawled across the cushions sighs as two men press in closer, their mouths teasing against her bare shoulders. Bodies shift, lips meet, hands roam. It's a tide of movement, a slow, rolling wave of pleasure.

I feel Alder tense beside me, and I've known him long enough to know what he's thinking.

"Oh no," I mutter, cutting him a look. "Absolutely not."

"But, Gemma..." He pulls me closer, his lips sliding into a smirk as he licks them, already savoring the idea. "It looks like fun."

"It looks like way too many balls."

As if on cue, there's a sloppy, slapping sound and one of the women lets out a moan, her head falling back against the shoulder of the man supporting her.

Alder chuckles, dragging his knuckles down my arm, a featherlight touch that makes my breath catch. "Lucky for you, sweetheart, I'm the only one allowed to touch this."

The words hit like a spark against kindling. My body betrays me, heating instantly, and my stomach tightens at the sheer finality in his tone.

I should hate that. Hate how easily he stakes his claim. But instead, a treacherous little ember of satisfaction burns in my chest.

Along with a feeling a helluva lot worse—jealousy.

Not of the tangled limbs and whispered sighs and gasping mouths. But because I don't want to share him.

Shit.

I cannot actually let myself fall for him again. Selling my soul for security is one thing. Getting swept up in his...*Alder-ness* is another.

He leans in, his breath teasing against the shell of my ear, his fingers stroking over the pulse at my wrist. "Doesn't watching them turn you on? That's all you'd have to do...just watch."

I clench my jaw, heat rushing to my face. "This is not the time for whatever fantasy you're working up in that morally questionable mind of yours."

Alder hums thoughtfully. "Morally questionable, huh? I'll remind you of that next time you're begging me to—"

I slap a hand over his mouth. "Finish that sentence, and I will personally sacrifice you to that pile of sex goblins. No mythical god or magickal beast needed."

His laugh rumbles beneath my palm. And then, God help me, he presses a slow, lingering kiss against the inside of my wrist.

The spot burns.

His eyes glint as he pulls my hand away from his mouth. "We should at least be considerate guests and sample the cocktails."

Alder starts to walk into the room, and I snatch his arm, halting him mid-step.

"They think you're someone else," I hiss, my fingers tightening around his sleeve. "What happens when they realize you're not? What happens when—"

He tilts my chin so my gaze lifts to his. "Sweetheart, all these fears you have, they'll come true if we don't play along. Now, breathe."

I inhale, dragging in a breath against the anxiety squeezing my chest.

His hand slides down my arm, finding my fingers, threading them through his own.

"I'll take care of everything." His voice wraps around me as he lifts my hand to his mouth, feathering a kiss across my knuckles. "Ready to admit that you trust me?" he asks against my skin.

"No."

His smirk deepens. "There she is," he purrs, leading me forward.

NINE

Hushed whispers trail in our wake, heads turning, eyes tracking our every move. Or rather, *his* every move. I won't waste time kidding myself—they're not looking at me. They're looking at Alder.

A group of scantily clad guests gather near the far wall, bare skin gleaming with a faint sheen of silver glitter. Their laughter is soft, coy, and their gestures entirely too suggestive as they watch him with unguarded hunger.

"We're in over our heads, Alder," I whisper, barely audible over the sensual hum of music, conversation, and wet ball slapping.

"Good thing I'm such a strong swimmer," he drawls and plucks two crystal goblets from a tray offered by a silver-painted attendant. He hands one to me without looking, swirling his own as though we're at a fundraising gala instead of in the middle of a sex cult.

My fingers tighten around the glass, the delicate stem pressing into my palm.

Alder drapes his arm across my shoulders and leans down. "You're thinking too hard again, sweetheart."

I exhale, my shoulders relaxing before I can stop them. I swallow down the instinct to regather my defenses, to argue, to resist. Instead, I let myself sink into his warmth.

If he's not afraid, I don't have to be either.

Plus, he's right. Again.

Every fear clawing at me, every horrible possibility racing through my mind, is more likely to come true if I don't play along.

The crowd parts as a man in a dark waistcoat strides forward, his polished shoes clicking against the stone. His presence commands attention, and the entire room shifts, quieting to a hush as he nears.

"Lord Lockhart," he begins, his voice smooth and rich. His piercing gray eyes flick to me briefly before they fully settle on Alder. "I am Victor Rothmore. Welcome to my kingdom." His dark, wavy hair brushes his tanned forehead as he inclines his head.

I stiffen and lean into Alder. "Should we kneel?"

"I kiss no man's ring." He winks down at me, and my stomach flips.

"Your Majesty," Alder replies, nodding slightly. "You know how to make a guest feel…welcome."

Victor's black brow arches and the corner of his bearded mouth quirks upward in a faint smile, but before he can respond, another voice cuts in.

"Yes, I do." The words slither over my skin, wrap tight, and squeeze.

I turn, my hackles instantly rising as a woman steps out from behind us.

I know her.

Petite and poised, her dress clings to her slight curves like liquid silver. Black curls frame high cheekbones, and three freckles form a triangle beneath her left eye.

Mackenzie?!

Wine red lips smooth into a grin, and there's an edge to her gaze that lands like ice in my veins.

No. Not Mackenzie. Not *my* Mackenzie. It can't be. Can it?

My heart stumbles, my brain locking up as it tries to reconcile the impossible resemblance. Same face. Same body. Identical down to the last freckle, yet utterly different. Where my Mackenzie is warm and open, this woman is cold, every inch of her a weapon.

I'm so distracted that I barely process the shift in Alder—the tightening of his grip, the way his breath slows just slightly.

He has to see it too. Has to recognize her. This is his best friend's wife.

But if he does recognize her, he stops short of showing it.

"Queen Delphara Rothmore." Her name slides off her tongue like venom, her smile all teeth.

She stops beside her husband and tilts her head as she studies Alder. "My scout watched you and your men enter the boundary of our kingdom this morning. And you, Lord Lockhart, made quite the entrance."

Alder doesn't miss a beat. "I'm usually the one doing the watching."

A flash of amusement flickers in Delphara's dark eyes. "I had to ensure the same fate did not befall you as befell our Lord and Lady Ashwood when they journeyed to Pentacles."

Alder's smirk doesn't falter, but I swear I feel the air around him shift.

They're two predators circling, testing, sizing each other up. A game is being played, and I have no idea what the rules are.

"Although," she adds, her gaze finding mine, "the scout neglected to inform us you were…accompanied." Her lips curve just slightly, like I'm a bug she'll delight in crushing under her heel.

I recoil, my shoulders drawing in, my grip tightening on Alder's hand.

Nope. This is not my Mackenzie. This is Wrong-Mackenzie. Evil-Mackenzie. Possibly-Murderous-Mackenzie. But somehow, she's here.

Oh fuck. Alder's *multiverse theory* bullshit is true.

"Perhaps," the king interjects as he raises a glass to his lips, "if you had used Wolrick as I suggested instead of one of Droskyn's men—"

"I trusted Droskyn," Ice-Queen-Mackenzie snaps, her composure cracking for the briefest moment.

"Bedding someone isn't the same as trusting them," Victor replies coolly, not bothering to hide his disdain.

My hand gets sweaty in Alder's, and my cheeks flush with the effort to keep my expression neutral. I know exactly what he means.

"You're one to talk, aren't you, husband?"

Okay. Wow.

I clear my throat, desperate to break the tension before this turns into a *Game of Thrones* spin-off. "We appreciate the warm welcome, but—"

"As I was saying," Rude-Bitch-Mackenzie continues, not bothering to even look at me as she tramples all over my sentence, "you made quite the entrance."

She gestures around the room, her attention lingering on the dark, unlit chandeliers and the massive dormant machine at the center of it all.

"The devices activated the moment you crossed the border into our kingdom."

Alder raises an eyebrow, taking it all in stride, but I feel like I'm sinking deeper into quicksand.

"Everything *came to life*. The bulbs illuminated, the machines thrummed, the air itself felt…restored. I am disappointed that, since your carriage arrived in town, it has all gone dormant again." With a shrug, she twirls her fingers through the air. "But that is of little consequence. It only reaffirms what I've known all along—a partnership between Cups and Pentacles is destined for greatness."

Alder takes a deep breath, and his broad shoulders seem to get even broader. "Usually, after I wake something up, it stays awake."

Oh, for fuck's sake.

I'm not a huge fan of wine, but that line makes me down a giant gulp as I will myself not to roll my eyes so hard I see into the past.

"They make a pill for that, you know?" I mutter.

Delphara's gaze cuts to me. "Do *you* have something to add?"

The emphasis on "you" sends a jolt of anger through me. "I was literally speaking, so—"

"*Excellent*." Wicked-Witch-Mackenzie returns her attention to Alder. "I do so look forward to discussing the details of our…*alliance*." Her voice drips with suggestion, and I don't miss the way she trails a single, teasing fingertip along the inside of Alder's arm as she says it. She has all the subtlety of a loaded gun.

I down the rest of my wine in one long pull.

Whatever's written on my face must be clear enough to see from space, because King Victor clears his throat, his glossy gray eyes flicking toward Veiled-Innuendo-Mackenzie. "My wife forgets herself."

Oh, I do like him.

"And, it seems, she has also forgotten your recent losses. Your father's passing was so sudden. And what with your advisor's machinations and beginnings of what I could only call a coup—"

Delphara waves a manicured hand. "We all agree Four got what he deserved."

Victor's nostrils flare. "The man was killed, Delphara."

"And we've all since moved on." She silences him with another dismissive flick of her wrist, her sapphire rings catching the light. "Enough of the maudlin, Victor."

She pivots before I can blink and hooks her arm through Alder's. "Come, Lord Lockhart. While I show you the pleasures Cups has to offer you must tell me what life has been like since abdicating your throne. I do hope the sentiment isn't catching."

Alder's thumb grazes the back of my hand once, twice, before he releases it and lets her pull him into her orbit.

"No, you go on ahead. I'll stay right here," I mutter to absolutely no one.

And, like I'm back at my Mackenzie's wedding reception, I exchange my empty glass for a full one as another silver server drifts past.

A hand brushes my shoulder, and I turn to find King Victor watching me with an expression I can only describe as sympathetic.

"Don't take it personally," he says dryly, offering me his arm. "My wife has a…singular talent for alienating even the most patient of us."

I hesitate a beat, but hunger, exhaustion, and the sting of being so easily discarded win out.

"I did notice that," I say, my gaze zeroing in on the queen, who's leaning so far into Alder's towering frame she might as well start taking notes on his molars. "I assume you've been dealing with that talent for a while, then?"

"Long enough to know when to stop fighting it and just let her tire herself out."

I take a long sip of wine, purely for survival. "Like a toddler having a tantrum."

"Except with more jewelry and sharper claws."

I snort laugh before I can stop myself.

"It's refreshing to speak with someone who isn't afraid to say what they're thinking."

That sobers me slightly. As much as I want to laugh this all off, to let myself get swept up by this decadent setting, by a literal king, the truth settles like lead in my stomach. Alder isn't the only one who needs to tread lightly.

I force a placid smile and lift my glass in a mock toast. "I'll take that as a compliment."

"It was meant as one," Victor replies, leading me toward a gilded table draped in midnight blue silk and arranged with platters of food so decadent it would make a Michelin chef weep. "No one should endure Delphara's company on an empty stomach."

I eyefuck the table, then side-eye him. "You say that like she gets worse."

He plucks a grape from a bunch and pops it into his mouth. "She hasn't even gotten started."

The double doors groan open, and a cloaked, masked figure barrels inside, their robes flowing behind them like dark water with the force of their strides. The hush spreads like a ripple, the party's soft laughter and music strangled by the steady clink of their metal-tipped boots against polished stone.

They move with purpose toward Victor, and I don't realize I'm holding my breath until the masked guard whispers a hushed message to the king.

The energy shifts the moment they speak.

Victor stiffens. His grip tightens around his glass, knuckles white. His jaw locks so hard I swear I hear the grind of his teeth before he finally speaks. "How did he get past the water?"

Awareness prickles against my skin.

The cloaked figure gestures sharply, their gloved hands slicing through the air with quick, clipped movements. Whatever they're saying, it's not good.

Victor exhales through his nose, his fingers flexing against the goblet before he sets it down. His gray eyes cut across the room, scanning, hunting.

I don't know what he's looking for. Or who. But I do know what it feels like when the air shifts before a storm.

The floor vibrates, a low, ominous hum that slithers up my legs and coils tight around my chest. One by one, the chandeliers flicker to life, spilling golden light across the room. The pipes lining the walls hiss in unison, releasing spirals of steam that twist toward the ceiling.

Partygoers gasp and squeal, but the sound is brittle and too sharp around the edges to be anything close to delight.

"What fresh hell is this?" I suck in a breath, my gaze automatically searching for Alder across the room. His broad frame is rigid, his expression composed, but even from here, I catch the slight shift—the faint crack in his mask as his eyes dart from me to the massive machine at the center of the room.

With a grinding screech, the contraption lurches forward. Gears turn, metal grinding against metal in a shriek that sets my teeth on edge. Its once dormant mechanics roar to life, sending energy pulsing through the castle walls, shaking the very foundation beneath us.

Near its base, the lovers untangle in a frantic blur of limbs and silk. A woman stumbles backward. The silver chains draped around her bare waist and cascading down her legs like a decorative gown catch in the machine's grinding gears with a sickening snap.

She freezes. Her wide, terrified eyes dart to the chains as if disbelief alone could stop what's coming.

The machine jerks. The chains pull taut.

A scream tears from her throat as she's yanked off her feet. She flails, grasping desperately at the hands that reach for her. They grip her arms, her legs, straining against the machine's relentless pull. But the gears devour the chains inch by inch, dragging her higher, tangling tighter.

Another jerk. Another cry.

And then her final, desperate wail is cut short, swallowed by the wet crunch of bone snapping beneath the relentless grind of metal. The machine roars, a guttural, mechanical growl as it pulls her under.

Blood sprays in a wide arc, warm and slick. It splatters across the polished floor, streaks the pristine walls, beads along the silver pipes. The copper tang fills my throat, clogs my nostrils.

The machine moves again. It lumbers forward, seeking its next kill.

The room explodes with panicked cries, the screech of grinding metal, the pounding of frantic footsteps as bodies shove and stumble, each person fighting for escape.

I whirl, searching. *Where is Alder?*

He promised to save me. And here, in this kingdom, the value of a knight in shining armor outweighs any deposit into my bank account. Right now, survival isn't about power or money—it's about protection. His protection.

The hum beneath my feet intensifies, climbing up my legs, spreading through my body like a fever.

Run, the thought screams in my head. *Run now!*

And for the first time since this nightmare began, I listen.

I run.

TEN

My ballet flats slip against the crimson-slick floor, blood smearing beneath my frantic steps as I weave through the throng of screaming, panicked bodies. The metallic tang clings to the back of my throat, and every breath rasps like sandpaper in my chest. Elbows jab my ribs, shoulders slam into mine, and silver painted nails rake down my arms, but I grit my teeth and keep going. Keep running. Keep moving. Keep trying to get away.

Until someone barrels into me from the side.

I stumble, slip, and go down hard—my shoulder slams into the floor first, but it's the sharp crack of my head against stone that steals the breath from my lungs.

Stars burst behind my eyes. The world tilts. Sound warps, everything dull and echoing as if I'm submerged underwater.

I blink hard. Once. Twice. My eyelids feel heavy.

The chaos around me slows, softens, and the sharp edges blur like a watercolor painting left in the rain.

Someone screams. I try to push myself up, but my limbs aren't cooperating. They're numb and fuzzy, like they belong to someone else. My head throbs. I can't tell if I'm bleeding or just dizzy. Maybe both.

I think I hear my name.

And then I'm being lifted, moved, gripped by hands I'd know anywhere.

Alder. His gaze locks on mine. His eyes burn with something I haven't seen before—something fierce, unshakable.

Fear.

For me.

"You're safe, Gemma. I'll make damn sure of it."

It's not a reassurance. It's not even a promise. It's a vow.

Then we're moving.

He shifts me against his chest like I weigh nothing, and barrels through the chaos without hesitation. Bodies slam into us, but he doesn't stop. Doesn't flinch. The crowd bends around him, parts for him.

My head lolls against his shoulder. The pain pulses in and out, afraid to commit. Everything feels floaty. I feel floaty. Like I'm watching from above—like I'm dreaming someone else's dream.

But I still cling to him. Even when the world spins. Even when I'm not sure if I'm standing or being carried. He's the only solid thing I have.

Someone slams into us, but Alder doesn't go down. His arms are steel around me.

"I've got you," he murmurs into my hair.

For a moment, I forget the carnage. Forget the blood and the panic and the monstrous machine tearing through the room. I only feel him. His breath against my temple, the steady rise and fall of his chest.

The roar of the machine and the shrieks of the panicked crowd fade into the background as we race down a dimly lit corridor. Shadows stretch along the walls, fractured by the flicker of fading sunlight streaming in through narrow windows.

At last, he shoulders open a heavy wooden door. The hinges cry out in protest. He charges across the threshold and kicks the door shut behind us, the bolt sliding into place with a brutal clang. The silence that follows is broken only by the harsh, uneven sounds of our breathing.

He sets me down carefully, and I try to stand but my legs fold. The wall catches me, cold and unforgiving. I slide down to the floor, my back pressed to the stone, my head pounding like a war drum.

Everything's spinning again.

My hands are sticky with blood. Her scream won't stop echoing in my skull.

I choke back a sob and press my shaking, blood splattered hands to my cheeks, the tears spilling over before I can stop them.

Alder is suddenly there, crouching in front of me, his warm hands on my shoulders. "Gemma, look at me."

I try. God, I try.

"Gemma." He says my name like a tether, like something meant to bring me back.

I blink blearily up at him. "You're here. You saved me. You said you would and then you did."

He's…gorgeous. Ridiculously so.

And those eyes.

They're not just blue. They're the ocean. The kind that swallows ships and drowns sailors but also cradles them, carries them, brings them home.

I must have hit my head harder than I thought.

More tears. I hate it. Hate that I'm crying. Hate that I need him. But he's all I have.

"You're right, I'm here," he says, and his hands tighten on my shoulders. "And you are safe."

For the first time since this nightmare started, I start to believe it.

He stands and his assessing gaze scans the room before landing on a door on the far side.

"Wait here." It's not a command—it's something gentler.

Panic flares again, and my hand shoots out, wrapping around his wrist. "Don't."

It's not just fear. It's a raw, vulnerable, terrifying feeling I don't want to name.

His eyes soften. He kneels, fingers sliding between mine, his thumb brushing over my knuckles so tenderly I could break. "I'm not leaving I'll be right back. I promise."

I nod. Or at least, I think I do.

The moment he disappears through the side door, I sag against the wall. The world tilts sideways. My vision warps at the edges.

The room is…nice. Luxurious. Silk panels. Silver accents. Like something from a magazine. I'd appreciate it more if the floor would stop pitching.

A muffled curse makes my ears prick. Then a crash, the hiss of steam, another curse.

"For the love of all that is sacred!"

A weak laugh escapes my lips. That's new.

He returns, holding a steaming towel and drops to his knees in front of me.

"This should help."

He drags the towel gently over my cheeks, my forehead, my nose, catching the smudges of blood and grime clinging to my skin. The warmth is heavenly, chasing away the cold like sunlight on frost. I let my eyes drift shut.

Six months ago, even when he said I'd never leave him, I did.

No promises, no penthouses, no Library of Congress additions could make me stay. Because I always knew I was his property, not his partner.

And that's not love.

Maybe leaving proved my point.

My eyelids flutter open, and his gaze meets mine. He watches me as he works, his thumb grazing my jawline, his fingers brushing my temple like I'm fragile… precious.

It makes my stomach flip.

It makes my heart ache.

What would it feel like to trust him to hold the jagged pieces of me and not be afraid he'll use them as weapons?

The thought is so sweet, so terrifying, that it tightens my throat and leaves me shaking. I press my lips together to keep the emotion from spilling over, but I'm unable to keep it in. I let out a shuddering breath and fresh tears spill over.

He lowers the towel and cups my face with both hands. His thumbs brush against my cheeks, catching the tears as they fall.

"You're okay." His whisper is rough around the edges. "You'll be okay."

The way he's looking at me… It's everything.

"Forgive me," he murmurs, voice like velvet against my skin. "I've wanted to do this for far too long."

My heart skips a breathless beat as his face tilts closer. His lips barely brush mine. A question, not a demand.

Gone is his crispness of apples and linen. I'm surrounded by woodsmoke and dark chocolate—a scent that makes me want to curl up and stay.

The kiss deepens, slow and teasing, like he's savoring the taste of me, committing it to memory.

It's not like him. It's better.

I melt into it, into him, letting the heat burn away the fear, the doubt, the distance between who we were and who we might be.

When he pulls back, he's breathless. So am I.

"You taste like sugar," he murmurs, tongue flicking across his bottom lip. "Sweet…addictive. Like dessert."

My pulse hammers. My skin is on fire.

His smirk returns, but it's softer this time. More dangerous.

"And, Gemma?" He strokes my jaw, touch featherlight. "I spent years cursed, the flavors of life stolen from me." He leans in, breath warm against my cheek. "I could no longer indulge in my favorites. No more chocolates, no more berries, no more honey. It all turned to ash on my tongue. You're the first woman I've tasted since I've been free. My first dessert." His lips brush my ear. "I've always had a weakness for dessert."

It's too much. It's all too much.

His nearness, his words. What is he even saying? He

was cursed… Curses aren't real.

The room sways. My vision tilts.

So consuming. So dizzying. So…warm.

Who knew a kiss could do this?

Who knew love could do this?

No. Not love. Never love. I won't love Alder Hawke again. No matter how many times he kisses me like that.

Although…I wouldn't mind him trying.

God, he's hot.

I lean forward—just a little—because I want more. But the world lurches.

I blink.

Suddenly, I'm on my back.

How did that happen?

He's saying my name. Repeating it. But he sounds far away. Like a voice echoing down a long tunnel. A train tunnel. Are we on a train? Is he a bandit?

Laughter bubbles up my throat.

He's a bandit on a train, stealing off into the night. Stealing away with my heart.

Another hiccup of laughter, then everything goes dark.

ELEVEN

The sound of drapes being pulled open drags me back. Fabric rustles. Sunlight explodes into the room. I blink against the gold spilling across the walls.

Ow. My head.

I wince, pressing my fingers to the back of my skull. There's a bump the size of a goose egg pulsing there like a neon sign: *You fell. Hard.*

The room around me is aggressively gorgeous. Sunlight filters through dew dappled windowpanes and pours across the intricate waves carved into the bedframe and inlaid with mother-of-pearl. A canopy hangs above, gauzy and sheer as a cloud.

Through the open balcony doors, jagged cliffs bite into the sea. Waves crash violently against them, and across the moody waters, I spot an island—mist-shrouded, wild, connected only by a crumbling stone bridge that screams death trap but in an Instagram-worthy kind of way.

Two maids bustle around the room, completely unaware that I'm conscious. One lights a fire in the hearth, coaxing kindling into a crackling flame. The other flits past a line of delicate glass decanters with her feather duster, their contents glowing in strange shades of green and cobalt blue.

I shift, the silk blankets tangling at my feet as I take in the room.

A chaise lounge sits in the corner, its velvet upholstery dyed the color of midnight seas, the fabric plush enough to drown in. The faint scent of the ocean and pine needles wafts in, mingling with the floral sweetness that lingers in the air and something else—something warm and mouthwatering.

My gaze shifts, and my stomach growls at the decadent tray perched on a silver pedestal. Delicate pastries, their golden crusts glistening with sugar crystals, are arranged alongside slices of fresh fruit. Crispy bacon curls beside a bowl of yogurt crowned with flower petals and nuts, and a steaming pot of tea sits beside a crystal carafe of wine.

My fingers graze the edge of the silk sheets before finding the rough crustiness of my dress. It's still on me. Stiff with dried blood. Crumpled. Filthy.

I slept in this? The thought alone makes my stomach twist.

And then another thought—a hotter, more intrusive one—flares to life. *Alder should have undressed me.*

Actually, no. I want to be awake for that.

My cheeks flush as memories crowd in. The way Alder looked at me, how his voice softened when he spoke my name, the way his touch steadied me, soothed me, made me feel like I was worth holding together.

The kiss—God, that kiss. And then…fade to black. Literally.

Where is he, anyway?

I kick off the blankets and slide to the edge of the bed. My bare feet hit the cold floor, and I rise with a grimace, still tender all over. I need a shower. And caffeine. And maybe a different life.

"Excuse me," I begin, voice sleep roughened.

The two maids spin around like I just pulled a knife. Their eyes widen as they take me in—bare feet, blood-streaked dress, tangled hair.

"Oh," the taller one says, halting mid-swipe of the mantel. Her dark hair is pulled into a severe bun that tightens her already severe features. Something about her feels familiar, though I can't quite place where I've seen her before. "We weren't expecting his lordship to have… *company*."

She says the last word like a curse, like I should be embarrassed.

Beside her, the shorter maid flushes, her round cheeks coloring as she averts her gaze to the floor. She shifts awkwardly and clears her throat. "We should, um…" Her voice is soft, almost timid. "Perhaps we should have waited—"

Her gaze flits up to mine briefly before darting away again, and I freeze. She looks just like Elsie from Wilder Ever After. It's uncanny—the same red hair twisted into a simple braid, the same round eyes, freckled cheeks, and delicate features.

Another doppelgänger, clone, multiverse look-alike.

"Sorry." She winces. "No one told us Lord Lockhart wasn't…sleeping alone."

"It wouldn't be the first time a visiting lord enjoyed a bit of *entertainment*," Pinched Face adds, the edge of her smirk deepening as she glances pointedly at the bed and then back to me. The insinuation hangs heavy in the air, unspoken but crystal clear.

The redhead elbows her. "Clara, stop."

Clara waves her off. "She knows I'm right."

My jaw twitches. "What's that supposed to mean?"

"I think it's fairly clear, don't you?"

Heat scorches my cheeks. I'm too stunned to clap back. Too thrown by the not-Elsie clone and the fact that this entire morning already feels like an outtake from a Regency-era sex scandal.

"*Clara*," the redhead whispers.

Again, Clara waves her off with a flick of her wrist, her sneer widening as she crosses her arms. "No trunks. No other belongings. Just a mysterious woman asleep in his lordship's bed? A mysterious *paid woman*."

I clench my teeth, but I force the words out evenly. "You've got the wrong idea."

But honestly, who the hell cares if I were a sex worker? And, side note: If I were, I'd be charging a hell of a lot more than whatever she would guess.

"For heaven's sake." I square my shoulders and draw in a steady breath, meeting her gaze head-on. "I don't know what story you've built in your head, but I am not the villain."

The room falls into a strained silence, the weight of my words pressing against the tension like a hand against a bruise.

Clara's mouth puckers, and for a fleeting moment, something flickers across her face—regret, maybe, or recognition. Whatever it is, I take it as a win.

Beside her, Not-Elsie nods, her round face flushing as she offers a hesitant smile.

I glance down at my dress and grimace. "Any way you can help me figure out how to look like less like a horror show and more like a human being?"

The door flies open.

Alder barrels in, shirt partially unbuttoned, coat flung over one arm, his hair a perfect mess. He sees me standing and stops. Blue eyes rake over me, wide and sharp and furious with worry.

"Gemma, God." His voice cracks down the middle as he crosses the room in three long strides. He tosses his velvet coat over the bed and cups my face with both hands like he's checking for damage. "You scared the shit out of me."

His thumbs brush my cheeks, his eyes scanning every inch of me as though cataloging what's left. "You look like hell." He swallows hard, his jaw tightening. "I can't have you depreciating now. Not after everything I've done to get you back."

My brows shoot up. "Did you just refer to me as an investment?"

"The castle physician is across the kingdom delivering some noble's baby," he continues, ignoring me. "And unfortunately, I left my on-call concierge and team of specialists in a different fucking world."

"My lord," Clara says, executing a stiff curtsy. "We've come to prepare you for your session with the council. I assumed you'd want to send your…*guest* on her way."

"She was injured. She's not going anywhere." Alder's head snaps toward her. "I won't have her walking off, blacking out, and forgetting where she belongs."

My stomach squeezes. My pride snarls. I hate how both reactions hit me at once.

Clara's eyes narrow, but before she can muster another cutting remark, Alder raises a hand to silence her. "Your concern is noted."

His gaze cuts to me. "You shouldn't be on your feet. You need a bath, clean clothes, and then a day in bed drinking tea or doing whatever women here do with their time."

I blink. "Excuse me? I like tea just fine. It's great, in fact. What I don't like is being told what kind of woman I'm allowed to be."

He smirks. "Believe me, sweetheart, no one could ever tell you what kind of woman to be. But maybe someone should tell you not to charge into danger while still bleeding."

My lips thin, and I cross my arms over my chest.

"Sweetheart, I found you bleeding, half-conscious, and barely able to stand."

"I'm fine now."

"You hit your head so hard, you wandered off and passed out."

"I don't need a babysitter."

"No," he says smoothly, stepping closer, "you need a bodyguard and a GPS tracker."

"If you think I'm staying in this room all day like some delicate little flower, you're out of your mind."

Alder's voice drops to that maddening murmur that gets under my skin in all the worst—and best—ways. "And if you think I'm letting you wander around this castle after yesterday, you are sorely mistaken. You belong in bed."

I arch a brow. "And what exactly do you think I'll be doing in bed all day?"

He leans closer, lips brushing my ear. "With me around? Let's just say rest won't be the priority."

My breath catches. My toes curl into the plush rug, my body betraying me with a rush of heat that spreads from my cheeks to places I'd rather not admit.

Clara and not-Elsie gasp in tandem.

"You," Alder says sweetly, "be a doll and draw Gemma a bath."

"*Me?*" Clara squeaks.

"You seem eager to help."

Her mouth opens and closes like a fish out of water, before she dips into a curtsy. "Of course, my lord. It's just that…a woman of her station—"

"I'll help you, miss. If it's all right." Not-Elsie jumps in.

Clara grabs her and hisses something I don't catch. Alder's already moved on—grabbing a slice of toast like this is just another day.

I stalk toward the breakfast tray and grab a piece of fruit, the sugar-dusted edge crunching between my fingers. "We need to get back to our world."

"I'm working on it." He chews, unbothered. "I want you resting today, back to yourself. If we were home, I'd give you my card and tell the driver to take you to The Shops, lunch, and then a massage."

"We're not home, Alder. And this is not a spa."

He shrugs and plucks a pear slice from the tray like we're standing in his penthouse kitchen instead of a castle that's literally mistaken him for some medieval lord. "I've already spoken to Victor and Delphara. The man I'm impersonating is here to negotiate trade. I'll play along, get the intel we need, and find a way back."

"You don't negotiate royal trade deals," I say flatly, watching him eat like this is all so casual, so normal. Like he hasn't fully grasped the fact that people are literally dying in this place.

"A negotiation is a negotiation," he says, licking juice off his thumb. "And you know better than anyone how good I am at getting what I want."

My stomach twists, and I chew slowly, letting the tart flavor distract me. But the truth is there, pulsing at the back of my mind. I let him take over back home because it was easier than fighting the world alone.

"I need more than that," I say. "Who are these people? Why do they think you're someone you're not? Why aren't they suspicious?"

He pours himself a glass of wine—of course it's wine at this hour, because Alder Hawke has never been ruled by a clock—and raises it lazily. "Sweetheart, the less you know, the safer you'll be."

"Spoken like every man who's ever lied to my face."

He smiles like I've complimented him, like my outrage is a cute little display he can fold neatly into his morning. "You're getting room service in a castle. Doesn't that count as a win?"

"No. A win would be not being confused for medieval escort Barbie."

His smirk grows, infuriating and smug. "Admit you're enjoying this."

"I don't have a choice," I shoot back, my grip tightening on the fruit in my hand.

Clara clears her throat. "My lord, the council awaits."

Alder sighs as if playing lord in a fairy tale is taxing. He rakes a hand through his golden hair and turns to me with that lazy half-grin that always means he's about to do something wildly annoying. "We'll talk later. Try not to get into any more trouble while I'm gone."

He follows Clara into the attached room. The door clicks shut behind him, and I'm left standing there, clutching a piece of fruit and absolutely drowning in the knowledge that nothing—absolutely nothing—is what it seems.

TWELVE

Apparently, taking a bath in a castle is a lot like being at a spa—if that spa was designed by a Gothic architect with a flair for drama and a questionable relationship with candles.

The tub is enormous, claw-footed and made of something that glints like moonstone. Steam curls through the air like a lover's sigh, and the oils poured into the water smell like citrus and spice. For a few blissful moments, I soak in silence, letting the heat lull the ache from my muscles and blur the edges of the chaos still echoing in my mind.

I dress quickly afterward, tugging on the simple cotton dress Not-Elsie left folded over a nearby screen. It's soft and freshly laundered, and although it's a maid's uniform, it feels…safe. I snag a croissant from the breakfast tray and duck into the hallway before Alder can come back and order me to stay where he can see me.

It's not lost on me that I'm actively sneaking away

from my boyfriend like a teen from their parents, but I would rather wait to have an honest conversation with myself about that when I'm back in the land of electricity and indoor plumbing.

The castle halls are an eerie blend of grand and grim. All labyrinthine corridors, haunting echoes, and foreboding shadows. It's exactly the kind of place where the heroine would get swept off her feet by a darkly brooding hero with a secret—and, despite my best efforts, I know exactly which brooding hero my thoughts keep drifting back to.

"For heaven's sake," I scold myself and take a bite of croissant. "Being thought of as an investment property and an image softener isn't sexy."

But, being rescued, literally carried away from danger, and then kissed like the ending of a rom-com…

"Get it together, Gemma."

I follow the scent of something warm and roasted through the maze of corridors and eventually find a spiral staircase, its stone steps worn from centuries of use. I descend, the temperature rising and the delicious smells intensifying with each step. At the bottom, I'm met with light.

The kitchen is unexpectedly cheerful, sunlight streaming through a row of wide windows that look out onto the castle grounds and endless ocean. It's beautiful, almost surreal, like it doesn't belong in the same world as the cold, oppressive halls I just left behind.

For a moment, I allow myself to sink into it, the warmth of the space wrapping around me like a soft blanket. This, right here, is part of a world I don't mind falling into.

Copper pots hang from iron hooks, their surfaces catching the glow of a massive hearth at the center of the room. Steam drifts from various pots and kettles, the air filled with the rich scents of fresh bread, roasted meat, and something sweet that makes my mouth water.

Silver gears and steam-powered contraptions line the walls, their polished surfaces gleaming despite being frozen in place, as if waiting for some unseen signal to start again.

I pop the last bite of croissant into my mouth, savoring the buttery flakiness and wishing I'd grabbed at least one more. As I brush the crumbs from my borrowed dress, a plump woman with wild blond curls and a smudged apron barrels past me with a pot balanced on her hip, shouting an order before I can so much as blink.

"Fetch that sack of onions from the corner and get peeling!"

"Oh, no, I don't—" I stammer, shaking my head. "I don't work here. I'm—"

"Too good to work in the kitchens, are you? Think peeling onions is beneath you?" She slams the pot down on the counter, snatches a knife, and starts chopping carrots.

"No, that's not what I—" I try again, but the sharp *thwack* of the blade hitting the wooden board punctuates her conversation.

"Some of the finest women I know started out scrubbing pots and peeling onions. You think that work is beneath you? Find another castle. This one'll chew you up and spit you out."

"I don't think I'm too good for anything," I say quickly, holding up my hands in surrender. "I know I'm dressed like it, but I'm not here to work in the kitchens. I'm with…Lord Lockhart."

Her eyes widen, and her tone shifts so fast it gives me whiplash. "Oh, my stars, you must forgive me."

"Please, don't apologize," I say. "I completely understand. One of the attendants gave me this to wear while my dress is being washed. I—I don't have any trunks, but I'm not—"

"No need for explanations. A woman's work is a woman's work, no matter how she finds it." There's a fierce protectiveness in her tone. "And don't you let anyone tell you otherwise."

It takes me a second to register her meaning, and when I do, my cheeks flush. Before I can correct her assumption, my stomach growls loudly enough to echo off the stone walls.

The cook lifts an eyebrow. "Hungry?"

"Starving."

She chuckles, already turning back to the counter. "Well, lucky for you, I've got plenty. Sit yourself down. You look like you could use a good meal."

She gestures toward a small scrubbed wooden table near the hearth, and I take a seat on one of the worn stools. A moment later, she places a loaf of crusty bread and a jar of golden honey in front of me.

"Eat," she says, planting her hands on her hips. "And no complaining if I do end up putting you to work. These are my kitchens, and I can be a bit bossy. Might as well warn you now."

Before I can respond, Not-Elsie appears at the bottom of the stairs, an empty breakfast tray in hand. "A bit bossy?" she snickers. "That's putting it kindly."

The cook rolls her eyes but doesn't argue. I tear off a piece of bread and dip it into the honey. The first bite is like a revelation—warm, golden and floral. The sweetness blooms across my tongue, so pure it makes my eyes flutter shut.

"I must apologize for earlier. For Clara." Not-Elsie dabs her brow with a linen cloth embroidered with faded red flowers. "I'm Sylvie, by the way. This is Bernice."

I brush crumbs from my fingers and offer a small wave. "Gemma. Nice to meet you."

"Don't mind Clara," Sylvie adds with a shrug. "She's nice enough—deep down."

Bernice snorts and resumes chopping carrots. "Keep making excuses for Clara, and you'll find yourself sent back across the water. That girl's not worth the effort."

"She's harmless," Sylvie says, plucking a slice of carrot from the cutting board.

Bernice inhales sharply, clearly ready to argue, but Sylvie leans in and kisses her cheek. "You know I'm right," she teases, sliding into the chair across from me before the cook can swat her.

Bernice grumbles, shaking her head as she turns back to her work.

"Glad to see you survived the party yesterday." Sylvie takes a bite off her stolen carrot slice. "Your dress is a bit… Well, let's just say Althea is doing her best. But it might be a lost cause."

"Yeah, thanks." I set the bread down. "Last night was…a lot."

"That's putting it mildly." Bernice drops a handful of chopped carrots into the pot with a splash. "Lights going on and off, then coming back on again like they'd forgotten why they were made. Not to mention all the gears and pipes firing up then going dead just as fast. I feared I would faint dead away," she says, pressing her palm to her chest. "None of this has worked since my grandmother's grandmother was a cook here in this very kitchen. Then it all comes alive at once? Well." She stirs the broth harder than necessary. "Suppose it's none of my business."

Sylvie leans forward slightly, lowering her voice as though the castle itself might be listening. "Cups used to be the most advanced kingdom in the realm. Steam powered machines, running water, light—it was the envy of everyone. Although, before yesterday, I'd never actually met anyone who was alive to see it all come on at once like that."

Bernice's wooden spoon clatters against the pot. "*Sylvie*," she warns.

Sylvie doesn't flinch. "Gemma was here. She saw it. She watched the machines turn on. She watched that woman—" Her voice falters. "We all know this kingdom isn't running right."

Bernice clears her throat, but her jaw tightens. "Doesn't mean we go filling her head with stories. Some things are better left unsaid."

"They're not stories. And, Bernice, she's from Pentacles," Sylvie presses, leaning toward the cook as if to drive the point home. "It's only a matter of time before magick is no longer outlawed in their kingdom. I've heard their new king himself wields it."

"Sure he does." Bernice crosses her arms. "And I'm a dragon."

"You hoard enough copper pots to convince me," Sylvie fires back, grinning.

Their laughter and banter fade into the background as my mind spirals. Magick outlawed? A king wielding it? It sounds like something out of *Lord of the Rings*, but it scratches at the edge of a truth too real to ignore.

I take another bite of bread, but the honey turns bitter as my thoughts jump to Wilder Ever After. To the moment I pulled that card from the cake, its gilded edges catching the light like it knew I'd find it. The delicate chain of events leading me here begins to snap into place, each link tightening in my chest.

Each ribbon in the cake leads to a charm…and a future.

The tarot card. The Lovers.

I stop chewing, the bread lodging in my throat as a chill crawls along my neck.

Maybe it was magick.

Absurd. Ridiculous. Impossible. But the thought digs its claws into me and refuses to let go. Haven't I been surrounded by the impossible ever since?

The charm is magickal and always guides you to what's meant to be.

I swallow hard, the piece of bread scraping its way down.

Holy shit.

That card *was* magick.

My pulse quickens, panic creeping in. I haven't seen it since…since I was in the woods with…naked Alder.

Where is it?

I shoot to my feet and brush my hands over my borrowed dress like it holds the answers.

That card matters more than I let myself believe.

Damn it. Why did I let Alder distract me?

The wall sconces flicker and flare. One bulb explodes

with a sharp pop, sending a spray of glass skittering across floor. Steam hisses from the polished silver pipes along the walls. The floor trembles, dishes rattling and clattering in the cupboards.

Bernice rushes to brace a stack of pots. Sylvie lunges for a basket of eggs but is too late. Shells crack against the stone, runny yolks trembling on the quaking floor. I rush forward just in time to catch a crystal bowl before it shatters.

The clanging and clicking grows louder as a mechanical whisk on the counter sputters to life. It whirs violently, its gears screeching as it plunges into the soup pot, sending a geyser of broth splattering across the counter, the floor, and Bernice's apron.

"See?" Sylvie shouts, wrestling the rogue whisk from the pot. "There's something more going on! You can't keep pretending there isn't."

A silver mixing contraption explodes. Dishes rattle. Steam blasts from the walls. And just when it looks like something is going to catch fire, the door slams open with a dramatic crack.

All three of us yelp in surprise, our heads snapping toward the noise. Alder stands there, tousled and grinning like he didn't leave me hanging an hour ago. Sometime while I was wandering the halls, he went back to our room and changed into a loose white tunic tucked into dark breeches that fit just right. He's rumpled and radiant, and his eyes are sparking like I'm the answer to a question he didn't realize he'd been asking.

"Well," he says, cocking his head, "looks like I arrived at exactly the right time."

THIRTEEN

My heart stutters.

It's embarrassing, really, how my body betrays me before my brain can catch up. One look at him and I'm warm all over, like someone flipped a switch labeled *disastrous attraction to men who've emotionally ruined you.*

My breath quickens. Heat blooms in my cheeks.

Damn him.

Why does he always show up like the misunderstood hero—the kind of brooding asshole with a six-pack and a smirk that could undo a decade of therapy?

I grab Alder's arm and yank him toward the back corner of the kitchen, away from Bernice and Sylvie. "Aren't you supposed to be at the council meeting?" I hiss. "You know, figuring out how the hell we get home?"

His eyes crinkle at the corners. "I had a better offer."

"What, food?"

"No." His gaze drops to my mouth. "You."

Just one word. One ridiculously effective word. And it slices through my defenses like a hot knife through butter.

His hands close over mine, and before I can yank them back, he raises them and presses the lightest kiss to my knuckles. The gesture is maddeningly smooth—Alder at his most infuriating. And yet, there's a softness in it too. Something familiar and foreign all at once. It makes me want to slap him and maybe straddle him, which is deeply unhelpful.

"You didn't get enough to eat in the room?" I ask, more clipped than I mean to be, trying to shore up the cracks he always seems to find.

I'm not falling for this again. I'm not falling for him. No matter how pretty the packaging or how well he plays the role of hero, I'm not the girl who gets fooled over and over…and over and over again by the same asshole.

His grin turns wicked, the kind that used to spell trouble for my clothes. "I always need a full meal before I enjoy dessert."

My knees go wobbly. I want to throw a spoon at his face.

Instead, I scoff. "Disgusting."

He shrugs like he's proud of it. "Delicious."

And just like that, I'm twenty-one again, hiding a blush and pretending his teasing doesn't make me feel like I'm standing at the edge of something dangerously enjoyable. I hate how easily he does this. I hate how much I don't hate it.

"You look…" he starts, and there's a shift in his tone that pulls all the air from the room. "Lovely." His gaze lingers. "Good enough to eat."

"Don't think you can distract me with sexy flattery."

He leans in, thumb brushing the corner of my mouth. When he pulls it away, it glistens with a smear of honey. Without breaking eye contact, he lifts it to his lips and licks it clean with the kind of deliberate, slow drag that belongs in a wet dream.

"Sweet," he murmurs. "Just like I thought."

My brain short-circuits. Images of last night crash through me—his hands, his kiss, the impossible softness in it and the promise I thought I felt tucked into its warmth. That stupid heat blooms again, curling low in my stomach, desperately wanting to set up permanent residence.

His scent hits me all at once, a heady mix of woodsmoke and dark chocolate. Before I can stop it, I let out a sigh. A real sigh. Like a swoony Victorian heroine fainting over a discarded cravat. I want to fight him. Or maybe kiss him until he forgets whatever he's hiding from me. Or maybe I want him to kiss me until I forget too.

I open my mouth to say something—maybe to challenge him, maybe to lie and tell him that he's gross and I feel nothing—but Bernice saves me from myself.

"If you two are quite finished," she says, voice flat as a cast-iron skillet, "there's a task that needs doing." She thrusts a wicker basket between us. "Couldn't save the eggs, and a new batch won't gather themselves."

I grab it, grateful for the excuse. For the distance. For the chance to get away from the magnetic pull of this man who is both my ruin and reason.

The lights in the kitchen still burn too bright, and the steam-powered contraptions still hiss and sputter, but

Bernice and Sylvie have managed to settle the worst of it by the time Alder and I step into the misty courtyard.

The cool air kisses my skin and is tinged with the scent of damp stone mingled with the sweetness of nearby blooming flowers.

Without hesitating, Alder sets off down the narrow stone path, basket swinging easily from one hand. I fall into step beside him, grateful to not have to think about where we're going.

As we round the corner, the roar of water crescendos, and one of the great waterfalls cascading down the castle's exterior comes into view. Its torrents crash against jagged rocks far below, shattering into glittering spray that hangs in the air like fairy dust.

I glance at him as we walk. "How did you learn your way around this place so quickly?"

He shrugs, his grin softening into something almost wistful. "Some places unfold themselves to you," he says. "People too. Those you're meant to know… You find them, and suddenly, the map appears."

My breath catches. For a moment, everything slows. The spray, the sunlight, the low thrum of the castle behind us. All of it fades beneath the weight of his gaze.

This doesn't feel like the Alder I know.

This feels like someone seeing me—not as an accessory to his success, not as some carefully curated image of stability and charm, but as I am. The woman who walked away. The woman who had nothing left but her pride and a few bruised pieces of her heart she couldn't bear to hand over again. The woman who's scared, if she's being honest. Scared of what happens if she keeps standing still. Scared of what happens if she moves forward.

I swallow and quickly look away, tugging at the scoop neck on my borrowed dress like it's suddenly suffocating. "Well," I say, too brightly, "lucky you. A magickal map and all the answers fall into your lap. Meanwhile, the rest of us are hoping we don't get flattened by a rogue mechanical whisk or eaten by a weird machine."

He laughs under his breath, but it fades as he reaches out and brushes a hand against my elbow. "Watch your step."

The narrow path is slick, the stones glistening like they've been polished with moonlight. His touch is steady, casual, protective, and it sends a shiver through me that has nothing to do with the cool air.

We follow the trail as it curves into a garden that looks stolen from a fairy tale. The roar of the waterfall quiets behind us, replaced by the soft rustle of leaves and the sigh of a breeze that smells of sea salt and summer flowers.

"It's beautiful," I whisper, reaching out to trail my fingers along the velvety petals of a white rose the size of my palm. The bloom is soft and cool, and for a second, everything else slips away.

"What's it like? Where you're living?"

He's watching me. I can feel it before I look up. "You probably know better than I do. You've spent more time flying up there for work than I ever spent living there."

His lips twitch. "Still. I want to hear it from you."

I hesitate, but only for a beat. "It never felt like home. Not really."

I glance over at him, expecting him to say something smug or teasing, but he just waits.

"I get why you don't want to leave South Carolina,"

I say softly. "I was itching to get out. I thought if I just got far enough away—got somewhere shiny, somewhere impressive—then I'd…become someone else. Someone more."

I exhale through my nose, eyes fixed on a cluster of pale blue blossoms at my feet.

"I was supposed to love the city. Everyone does, right? I got out of the sticks and landed somewhere with rooftop views and twenty-four-hour everything and noise that never lets up. It's what people dream about." My voice hitches, a little laugh slipping out. "But I never stopped feeling like a visitor. Like I was just borrowing someone else's life for a while."

I don't look at him when I add, "And you know how that turned out."

The silence stretches. Not heavy, exactly. But full.

"Honestly, if we'd been…different, I might not have left."

The words hang there, raw and too honest. My chest tightens. I didn't plan to say that part. But it's the truth.

And it's the first time I've said it out loud.

A long, aching beat passes. His eyes are locked on mine, and the weight of it feels like standing on a precipice.

I've never spoken to him like this. Never been vulnerable without expecting him to twist it, spin it, use it for a pitch or a photo op or a campaign about how relatable we are. But this Alder, he listens.

And that's the most dangerous thing of all.

"Mackenzie's convinced that if I asked, you'd buy some ridiculous high-rise in Manhattan and I'd never have to leave."

He's still silent, still listening.

The vulnerability makes my pulse stutter, so I take a right turn, desperate to pull myself back into safer waters.

"Being dropped into a place like this has to feel at least a little familiar. You're used to walking into a mess and taking control."

He hesitates. His eyes flick to the ground, and for a second, the grin falters. "It…is."

There's more he wants to say. I can feel it in the way his lips purse, in the pause that stretches too long. Like he's weighing something, wondering if he should let me see past the surface.

Finally, he clears his throat, and when he speaks again, his voice is lower, careful. "I think I've been waiting," he says. "Waiting for something—or someone—to show me where to go next."

He reaches for a nearby flower—deep blue with petals like satin and snow—and gently tucks it behind my ear. His fingers brush my temple. The touch is light, fleeting, but it's enough to make my breath hitch.

"There," he says, voice like dusk. "Perfect."

My cheeks heat, and I quickly turn away, pretending to admire another flower. Anything that isn't his face, his hand, his words.

But I can't lie to myself.

This moment feels like the start of something. Something I didn't ask for. Something I don't know if I'm strong enough to stop.

I can't give him my heart again. He's proven what he'll do with it.

This man walking beside me isn't the Alder I knew six months ago. He's still dangerous, still devastating in that tailored-suit kind of way—but there's a new edge to him now. An ache beneath the armor that makes me wonder if maybe, just maybe…the storybook ending I swore I didn't believe in is walking right beside me.

And that's what terrifies me most of all.

When we finally reach the coop, I'm almost grateful for the distraction. The soft clucking of hens drifts on the breeze, mingling with the earthy scent of hay and feathers.

Alder strides ahead and opens the narrow wooden door with a flourish before bowing dramatically. "Ladies first."

I roll my eyes. "Chivalry isn't dead, it just smells like chickens." I duck inside, brushing past the weather worn frame and into a surprisingly elegant space.

The floor crunches beneath my feet, straw layered thick over flagstones. Sunlight streams through leaded glass windows, scattering jeweled light across the carved mahogany beams overhead. Nesting boxes, crafted from dark wood and decorated with silver inlays, line the walls in neat rows.

It's the fanciest henhouse I've ever seen.

Even the hens look expensive. Their feathers shine like polished copper and gold, and one of them hops onto a stool with the same energy as a disapproving headmistress. She eyes me like I've broken the dress code and lets out a sharp cluck before pecking the hem of my borrowed dress in protest.

But I'm not thinking about chickens. Not really. I'm still back in the gardens, his voice echoing through me.

I think I was waiting for something—or someone—to show me where to go next.

Was he talking about me?

The Alder I knew didn't wait for anyone. He didn't follow maps—he bought the damn compass company and charted his own course. But today, he wasn't leading. He was listening. And maybe that's what unsettles me more than anything.

I'm so deep in my own thoughts about him, about us, about everything that I don't notice the bold hen at my feet until it's too late. My foot lands squarely on her claw.

The hen lets out an ear-piercing squawk, her wings flapping wildly against my legs like she's trying to take flight.

"Ah! I'm sorry—" I stumble back, arms flailing as I try to regain my balance. My slipper catches the edge of a small stool, and it topples over with a loud clatter, sending a basket of corn kernels and chicken feed flying.

Cue full-blown poultry pandemonium.

Feathers fill the air. Hens shriek like they've just heard the sky is falling. Beady little eyes glare at me as they scramble for the scattered feed.

"Gemma!" Alder calls, his voice rich with laughter.

"I didn't mean to!" I shout back, trying to sidestep the hens that are now darting around my feet, pecking at the ground with alarming determination.

He chuckles as he moves closer, his hands up like he's approaching a spooked animal. "Hold still!"

"Hold still?" I squeal, flinching as one particularly aggressive hen flaps past my shoulder, nearly hitting me in the face. "They're everywhere!"

"They're chickens," he says, still laughing. "They're not going to hurt you."

"Easy for you to say!" I snap, hopping on one foot as another hen pecks near my ankle. "You're not being attacked!"

One pecks my ankle. I squeal and spin, tripping again, and before I know it, my feet tangle together. With a startled yelp, I go down, landing flat on my butt in the middle of the henhouse.

Alder's laughter is full-bodied now, the kind that doubles him over. He crouches beside me, grinning like the absolute menace he is. "Are you okay, Your Majesty of the Coop?"

I blow at the feathers floating in front of my face, huffing when one stubbornly sticks to my cheek. "Oh, you're hilarious," I grumble, brushing at my straw and feather tangled hair. "I swear, if you call me the Mother of Hens, I'm throwing feed at your face."

"You've become their queen." He leans forward and plucks a feather from my shoulder. "It's majestic."

I lunge for a handful of the scattered kernels, but he catches my wrist with a warm, gentle grip—and just like that, the world slows. The flurry of feathers fades. The ridiculousness of it all slips out of focus.

He's close, his hand holding mine, his fingers brushing a feather from my cheek. "You've got something…"

His thumb lingers next to my mouth, and the warmth of his touch makes my lungs squeeze. Our eyes lock. My heart forgets how to function properly.

This shouldn't feel like a moment. Not here. Not covered in feathers and straw. But it does. It's just him. Just me. Just us. The way his blue eyes soften. The way his grin melts into something quieter, something that makes my chest ache.

I inhale, slow and shaky, and the scent of hay and sunlight fills my lungs, grounding me in a space that feels too surreal to be anything but. His thumb brushes my jaw ever so slightly before he leans in. My lips part, my breathing shallow.

But then a hen flutters up behind us, squawking indignantly as it lands on the tipped-over stool.

The spell breaks.

Alder pulls his hand away, the absence of his touch making the air between us cold. I jerk back and scramble to my feet.

"I'm fine," I mutter, cheeks flaming.

He rises too, extending his hand to me with a playful tilt of his head. I pointedly ignore it, brushing off my skirt instead, bits of straw and feathers floating to the ground.

"I don't need your help."

"You sure?" he teases. "Although, you do wear chicken feathers well."

"Get back to your egg collecting duties, *Lord Lockhart*."

I glance at him as he moves past me. The light streaming through the windows catches in his golden hair and softens his angles until they're almost tender. My heart gives a small, unexpected flutter.

The hens, now happily pecking at the scattered feed, pay us no mind as we gather the eggs we came for. We work in silence for a while—well, mostly silence. He hums. Loudly. Off-key. I try not to smile. And fail.

With the basket full, I squeeze through the narrow doorway, glad for the cool breeze on my flushed face. Behind me, Alder turns to the hens with a sweeping, exaggerated bow.

"Ladies," he says solemnly. "Your service has not gone unnoticed"

I roll my eyes but can't stop the smile tugging at my lips. "You're ridiculous."

"I'm charming," he corrects.

I tilt my head. "Completely unrealistic."

He ducks under the doorframe. Well, he tries to. His broad shoulders catch with a solid *thunk*.

There's a beat of silence.

"Little help?" he grunts.

I stop in my tracks, staring at him before the realization sinks in. "Wait…are you actually stuck?"

"No," he says, immediately followed by a resigned, "Yes."

I slap a hand over my mouth, laughter bubbling out anyway. "Oh my God, this is…this is the best thing that's ever happened to me."

"It's not funny."

"It's *deeply* funny. Like, tears-streaming-down-my-face funny."

He shifts, trying to twist himself free, but the movement only wedges him in tighter. The side of his shirt rides up, flashing a sliver of tan skin, and I have to bite my lip to keep from making a comment I'll regret.

He groans theatrically. "This might be it for me, Gemma. I've lived a good life. Tell my story. Tell them I died heroically."

"In a henhouse?"

"With honor," he insists.

"I'll be sure to have a plaque made and hung on this very coop, and we'll host an annual memorial egg hunt."

He grunts again, shifting his weight. "Careful. Mocking a helpless man is bad luck."

I scoff. "Says the one percenter who spies on people for a living and is now stuck in a doorway."

"Alright, new plan. You pull, I push."

"Perfect." I set the basket down and grab his outstretched hand.

We tug. We twist. We accomplish absolutely nothing.

"I think the hens are judging you," I say between laughs.

"They've turned," he deadpans. "I can feel it. Any minute now, they're going to start pecking for blood."

I yank harder. "Stop talking and wiggle!"

"I am wiggling!" he shouts, but he's laughing now too—really laughing. The sound of it does something to me. Loosens a screw that's been wound tight since the moment I landed back in South Carolina.

Finally, with a grunt and one last tug, he pops free, stumbling into the sunlight with a dramatic gasp for air like he just escaped the underworld.

He brushes himself off with wounded pride. "That was graceful."

"Graceful in the way a baby giraffe is graceful, sure."

He places a hand over his heart and bows deeply. "Thank you, Lady Gemma. You've saved me from a poultry-related demise. I am, henceforth, your humble servant."

"You're lucky I didn't film that for the village TikTok."

His grins softens, warmer, less performative. His eyes find mine. The air between us changes, tightening with a new kind of awareness. He steps closer and reaches out, plucking a feather from my shoulder like it's a thread of silk.

"You're shedding."

And just like that, my laughter stumbles. My chest tightens. Because it's not just a feather. It's the way he's looking at me. The way his touch lingers. The way my pulse trips and my knees soften.

My chuckle is thinner now. Tense at the edges. "If I start clucking, take me out back and put me down."

"I don't do mercy killings." His lips twitch. "But I'd absolutely build you a luxury coop."

"Oh good," I mutter. "A girl can never have too much real estate."

I pick up the basket again, but he takes it from me and hooks it over his forearm.

We head back toward the castle in silence, the waterfall's roar rising to greet us. I sneak a glance at him. Mist clings to the golden strands of his hair, making him look like he belongs in a painting or on the cover of one of the very smutty books piled on my nightstand.

He's quiet now, thoughtful.

Which is almost worse than the flirting.

When he's not performing, not teasing or smirking or turning everything into a punchline…when he's just walking beside me like this—warm and solid and not being a total ass—it's easy to forget all the reasons I've kept my walls up.

As we round the last bend, the castle's towering silhouette slices into the sky. A flicker of movement in one of the high windows catches my eye—just a shift of shadow, maybe, but enough to make me pause. I pause and glance over to see if Alder noticed.

He has. His stride falters, sharp blue eyes narrowing as they lock on the same window. He stops suddenly, tense and calculating. With an exhale, he turns to me and thrusts the egg basket into my arms.

"What—?"

Before I can finish, he takes my free hand, lifts it to his lips, and presses a kiss to my palm. The gesture is light, but it sparks like static down my spine.

"I should return to those very important council meetings you're so fond of bringing up," he says, his voice low, his breath warm against my skin. "If anyone asks, tell them I was detained by chickens and a woman who looks far too good in a borrowed dress."

I open my mouth—no idea what I planned to say—but the moment disappears as his fingers brush against mine one last time.

And then he walks away. His long strides carry him toward another part of the castle. He doesn't look back.

I hate how much I want him to.

I stand there like a lovesick girl holding a basket of eggs, watching his broad frame disappear through an archway, the dim light swallowing him whole.

Even then, I don't move.

Because I want more.

More of that smile. More of the way he slips into my space like he's always belonged there. More of the man who kisses my hand like it's sacred and looks at me like I'm something he's not ready to let go of.

I want more of Alder Hawke in every way that's ever mattered.

And for the first time in all the years I've known him, I think he might actually be ready to give it to me.

FOURTEEN

I'm lost.

After returning the basket of eggs and joining Bernice and some of the other attendants for lunch, I tried to retrace my steps back to the room I share with Alder—all while secretly hoping his covert, intelligence-gathering meeting was over and he'd be there waiting for me. Preferably shirtless, chest gleaming, and ready to report back on our chances of returning home. But only after we defile every surface we can find. And I have multiple orgasms. And he has an emotional catharsis that finally cracks his I'm-such-a-moody-asshole exterior.

You know…casual weekday stuff.

Instead, I'm somewhere between tapestry thirty-two and tapestry fifty, maybe, wandering the castle's stone hallways like I'm stuck in a really elaborate, dimly lit IKEA.

Every corridor looks the same—endless stretches of gray stone and brooding images featuring long-dead royals and overcompensating heroes, all slowly being devoured by time and moths. The torches lining the walls cast flickering shadows that shift and stretch like they're waiting for the right moment to pounce.

My borrowed slippers, half a size too big and aggressively unsupportive, whisper against rugs as I walk. The runners are obnoxiously plush. The kind I envision in a villain's lair or the home of someone who enjoys twirling their mustache and hoarding cursed objects.

I run my hand along the cold, uneven wall and turn another corner only to find an identical stretch of hallway.

Nope. Still not my room.

A familiar buzz of panic starts in my chest, fluttering just beneath my ribs. I slow my steps, half hoping that someone will pop out and rescue me, preferably with a tray of pastries and a helpful little map that says: YOU ARE HERE and ROOM WITH HOT MAN IS HERE.

But no one comes.

And it's quiet. Too quiet.

Not just castle quiet, which I've learned is a mix of library plus cathedral plus abandoned museum at midnight quiet, but eerie quiet.

My stomach twists, and my thoughts sharpen in the worst way.

What if I never get home?

It slides into my brain like a slow-moving tide, seeping into the cracks of my composure. What if I really am stuck here? What if this is it? No more morning coffee runs, no more talking to Mackenzie using TikToks and memes, no more drunken late-night truth-bomb bonding sessions with Amanda. No more real world.

Just stone walls. Crowned queens with bad attitudes. And Alder.

Alder, who I am definitely not emotionally dependent on in any way. Obviously.

I shake the thought off—violently, like a dog shaking off water—and refocus.

Find my room. Find Alder. Don't panic.

I square my shoulders, take a breath, and turn down the next hallway.

That's when I feel it.

A breeze.

It's faint but unmistakable—cool, unexpected, and tickling the inside of my forearm. I stop in my tracks. There's no window here, no reason for wind in this part of the castle. But it's there, whispering against my skin like it has secrets to share.

My heart beats a little faster. It's irrational, but something about the crisp, shifting air feels…purposeful.

I follow it.

The breeze grows stronger, carrying a scent that's different from the castle's mustiness—cleaner, wetter, like rain on stone. It dead-ends at a massive painting. The canvas stretches nearly floor to ceiling, depicting a regal woman draped in blue. Her pale face serene but her unnervingly sharp eyes are not. They seem to follow me, tracking me like she knows something I don't.

The frame is ringed in silver serpents, coiling and gleaming in the torchlight.

The draft tugs again, and my fingers follow it to the seam where the frame meets the wall. And there, just under a snake's forked tongue, is a small, almost invisible button.

Because of course there's a secret button in the creepy snake frame.

I press it before my brain can think better of it.

Click.

With a shudder, the floor shifts. My stomach lurches as a hidden panel beneath my feet pivots, and swings inward. I yelp, a tiny, panicked noise, when the castle spins around me, and I tumble into the darkness.

The painting slams shut behind me.

And I'm alone.

In the pitch black.

Awesome.

My hands find the wall, rough stone cool beneath my fingers. I press my palm flat against it, as if I can absorb some kind of guidance through sheer contact. Of course I can't, but it gives me something to do while I wait for my eyes to adjust and my heart to slow down.

"This is how people die in fantasy worlds," I mutter. "Secret tunnels. Paintings with weird buttons. I know this trope. I've read this book."

Up ahead I see a faint golden glow seeping through the worn weave of another canvas.

I creep closer, my fingers skimming along the wall as I shuffle forward and try not to think about spiders or ghosts or the fact that I left behind both safety and my home.

My hands skim the back of the painting, and the rough fabric prickles my skin. I lean in, pressing one eye to the small gap in the weave. It's a peephole, not much but enough. And through it, I have a perfect view of the bathing chamber beyond.

The room glows, lit only by flickering candlelight

and the watery shimmer of the cloudy gray sky pouring in through a pair of open French doors. Steam curls around everything, softening edges, but not hiding what's about to unfold. A silver tub—ornate, massive, gleaming, carved with images of waves and writhing serpents—sits at the center.

A glittering, endless stream of water spills from the gaping mouth of a silver serpent mounted high on the wall. The tub overflows, water cascading over the edges and spilling down stone steps and across the floor in a rushing current. The stream flows across the room in a path that slips straight through the open doors and vanishes into the black abyss beyond the cliffs.

Four masked guards take their places on either side of a man already standing near the tub, their robes the color of a moonless sky. Their faces are hidden behind smooth silver masks, identical in every way, hollow-eyed and expressionless.

The man is tall, still, with a robe as pale as bleached bone and as luminescent as moonlight. His mask is similar to the guards', but the top is adorned with two curved points that jut out like viper fangs above his eyes. He cradles a book in both hands, thick and old and bound in tarnished silver, its cover etched with waves and sigils that shimmer when the candlelight catches them.

When he opens it, the air shifts. Cold slithers in, licking at the edges of the room. The guards raise their hands, palms up, and the man begins to chant.

His voice is not…right.

The mask distorts it, making it hollow and disembodied, like it's echoing from a cave somewhere far beneath the earth. The sounds are low and strange and rich with unfamiliar syllables that curl through the air like smoke. The guards join in, their voices weaving together in a dissonant, hollow harmony that bounces off the stone and reverberates in my bones.

A door opens, and two women enter.

Queen Delphara Rothmore glides into the room like a specter made flesh. Her ceremonial cloak ripples around her ankles like water. The fabric is impossibly fine—midnight blue kissed with silver—the color of a lake lit only by stars. On her head rests a delicate crown of entwined silver serpents, pale blue gems glinting in their eyes. Apple blossoms are woven around the polished coils, fresh and white, like they bloomed just for her. Her dark curls fall down her back in loose ringlets beaded with moisture as if she's been walking through mist.

Clara follows her—barefoot, pale, her own cloak a softer echo of the Queen's in color and style but there's no crown, no embellishments. Only her hands, clenched into fists, and the kind of stillness that comes right before someone breaks.

Together, they descend the stone steps into the steaming tub, the water seeming to rise to greet them. Their cloaks float on the surface like petals.

Delphara straightens, tall and motionless in the center of the tub, water curling around her hips. Clara bows her head, her shoulders hunched like she's bracing for pain.

The chanting grows louder. The masked man's voice rises, but it's Delphara's that reaches my ears—clear, resonant, and undeniable. It rings out like a bell struck underwater, threaded with a power that doesn't simply join the ritual but commands it. Her voice bends the air. It pulls the steam into spirals. The candle flames bow toward her. Even the masked guards hesitate for a breath, their chants faltering as if something ancient has stirred. The magick doesn't come solely from the book or the masked man. She sets it free.

And the room answers.

The candle flames flicker violently. The temperature drops. The shadows twitch. The current in the tub picks up speed as the water takes on an iridescent sheen. The surface glows from beneath, suddenly lit from below. Threads of color shimmer under the water—blue, violet, silver—twisting like fish just out of reach.

Wind rushes in through the French doors, sudden and forceful. Every apple blossom in Delphara's crown lifts, suspended in the air. The silver on her robes catches the light and flares like a mirror to the moon.

She dips her hands into the tub, water streaming down her arms like liquid glass as she lifts them.

Then, she touches Clara's forehead.

Two fingers. That's all. But the moment they make contact, the magick manifests.

A line glows neon blue where Delphara's fingers trail—fluid, ancient, like it's been pulled from the depths of the sea itself. It's a sigil that loops and arcs with unnatural grace as it hovers, gleaming against Clara's skin like bioluminescence in the dark.

The sigil pulses once. Twice. Then it begins to shift.

The blue deepens into silver, burning brighter for one long heartbeat—and then it sinks into Clara's skin like ink into paper, leaving nothing behind.

The chanting hums through the floor. The air tastes electric.

This is magick.

Not metaphorical magick. Not the kind I read in books or whisper over birthday candles. Not fairy tales or wishful thinking or childhood fantasies about Santa and the Tooth Fairy.

Real magick.

My thoughts flash to the card from the cake. The Lovers. The way it shimmered. The way it felt warm in my hand. The way it pulled me toward Alder and this castle and—

It wasn't coincidence. It wasn't chance.

The pull always reveals what's meant to be.

Magick is real.

And it's terrifying.

Clara's breath hitches.

She lifts her head—eyes wide, mouth slack—and for a moment, it looks like awe. Wonder.

Then her whole body jerks.

Her hands claw at the water. Her limbs thrash. She convulses once. Again.

Delphara doesn't move.

The masked man chants louder, his voice rising above the others like a thread pulled taut.

Clara's eyes roll back. Blood leaks from her nose, the corners of her eyes, from her mouth. Crimson foam bubbles down her chin as her lips part in a silent scream.

My hand flies to my mouth.

A final ragged, wet gurgle, and Clara sinks. Her body slips beneath the surface. The water froths. Blood weaves like silk ribbons through the waves and coils around Delphara's pale skin.

The air shivers. A faint hum pulses through the chamber—like a chord struck on an instrument that doesn't exist in this world, in any world. The surface of the water glows faintly, then brighter, a shimmering white light that radiates outward from where Clara vanished. It casts dancing reflections on the walls, the ceiling, Delphara's face.

And then Clara rises.

Not floating, not bobbing—but lifted, slowly and deliberately, as if the water itself is obeying a silent command. Her body breaks the surface like an offering. Limbs weightless. Hair fanned around her like a crown of kelp. Eyes closed.

Delphara touches Clara gently, reverently, as though this isn't a murder but a farewell. She presses her forehead to Clara's, their brows touching in a quiet, brutal blessing.

Then Delphara steps back.

Clara's body tips over the edge of the tub, limbs loose and limp, a doll discarded, her blood-slicked skin glistening in the candlelight.

With a sickening splash, the current grips her. Drags her. And I watch, numb and frozen, as she's carried across the stone floor, out the open doors, and over the cliff into the abyss beyond.

Gone.

Like she was never here at all.

The chanting stops.

Silence slams into the room like a fist.

The masked man closes his book with a soft final thud.

Delphara brushes two fingers through the blood-slick water, then raises them to her lips. She kisses them, eyes fluttering closed.

A ritual sealed. A promise kept.

And, for the second time in as many days, I run.

FIFTEEN

I can't breathe.

The air is thick and wet and wrong, the taste of blood still sharp on my tongue. My legs move before my brain catches up, sprinting down the stone corridor as if I can outpace the image of Clara's lifeless body slipping into the dark.

My shoulder slams into the hidden panel. I'm frantic and shaking, and my fingers scrape over the cold stone. I find the button—press it hard.

Click.

The floor shifts beneath me again and I'm thrown back into the hallway, staggering away from the painting like I've been spit out by the castle itself. I slam into the opposite wall and suck in a breath like it's the first I've ever taken.

Run.

My slippers skid across the rugs. I round corners too fast. My breath punches out in short, shallow bursts. I don't know where I'm going—I just need distance.

Distance from that room, from that tub, from that sigil that shimmered and changed and sunk into Clara's skin like a key into a lock.

They killed her. They killed her like it was nothing. Like it was sacred.

I reach another intersection of hallways, my pace faltering as I clutch my aching chest and swallow ragged gulps of air. My legs burn, exhaustion catching up with the terror surging through my veins.

A tapestry ripples beside me from the force of my movement, and I force myself to slow down and duck into the shadows. I cannot get caught looking like this—wild-eyed, trembling, covered in sweat.

Think. Breathe. Do not get found out and dragged in front of Queen Magickal Human Sacrifice.

Inhale. Exhale. Again.

I smooth my trembling hands down the front of my skirts, force my spine to straighten. Act normal. Just a normal woman in a normal castle on her way to…tea drinking? A modiste fitting? Letter writing?

I push off the wall, walking fast but controlled. Head down. Eyes on the ground.

I'm fine. This is totally fine.

And I'm also ignoring the fact that my brain is playing the trauma reel on a loop behind my eyelids.

I turn a corner—and slam straight into a wall of solid muscle and tailored velvet.

A sharp gasp escapes me as I stumble back, hands catching soft fabric.

Strong hands catch my elbows, steadying me before I can fall. "Whoa there," a familiar voice says, stretching the words with a lazy drawl. "Where's the fire?"

Alder.

Relief crashes through me so hard my knees almost give out, and I lean into him.

He grins down at me, golden hair tousled, blue eyes gleaming. "God, you're warm," he murmurs, pulling me against his chest. "Where have you been?"

"Alder, I—" My voice catches, cracked and raw. I don't know where to begin. I don't know how to make the words come out. "Something happened."

But he's not listening. His arm slips around my waist, the other brushing a loose strand of hair behind my ear as his mouth finds the curve of my neck. "I thought I told you to stay in bed."

I plant a hand on his chest, firm but not enough to push him away. "Seriously. Something is wrong."

"Mmm. Of course something's wrong," he murmurs against my jaw, like this is all a game. "Something always is when you're involved."

"I watched a girl die," I blurt. "Clara, the maid from this morning. In some kind of bathing chamber. With the Queen. And a masked man who—I don't even know what he was chanting—and it was magick, Alder. Real magick."

He goes rigid for half a second and then exhales a soft laugh. "You must have hit your head harder than I thought."

"I'm serious!" I snap. "There was chanting, there were guards, the Queen painted a glowing sigil on Clara's head—and then Clara started bleeding from her eyes and nose and mouth. And then she—she just—she died. Her body went over a cliff. I saw it."

He pulls back slightly, his eyes narrowing in

something that looks like concern, but feels patronizing. "Gemma, sweetheart, you need to lie down."

"No, I need you to listen," I say, words tumbling out in a rush. "There's something happening here. Something bigger than us getting swept up into this world. Magick is real. I felt it. I saw it. And Sylvie—she mentioned the Kingdom of Pentacles. She said they have magick there. That's what she said. That their new king uses it. This whole state or country or—"

"Realm," he corrects. "This whole realm is called Towerfall."

"Yes," I say, my voice pitching up. "They have magick here. *Real magick.* And I think—" My breath hitches. "I think there's so much going on that you and I cannot even begin to understand."

He exhales through his nose and drags a hand through his hair. "Gemma…"

It's not just his tone. It's his whole body—tense, jaw tight, muscle in his temple ticking like he's barely keeping his irritation in check. Like I'm the problem.

"You said you'd find a way home," I push. "Have you? Have you actually found out anything that will help us?"

He doesn't answer right away. Instead, he shifts, stepping toward our door like he's heard all he's willing to hear. "You need to get into bed," he says finally.

I blink. "What?"

"You're rambling. You're exhausted. This entire ordeal has clearly brought on some sort of episode, and you running around the castle unsupervised isn't helping. What you need is to lie down and let me handle things."

He opens the door to our shared room and places a

hand at the small of my back, nudging me forward like I'm some fragile thing he needs to tuck in and medicate.

I step into the room but stop just past the threshold.

He's different now—colder, sharper, like the man from the chicken coop never existed. And I understand. Pretending to be someone else during high-pressure trade negotiations in front of literal royalty would rattle anyone, even him. But it doesn't explain why the Alder who joked with me about being the ruler of hens and made me feel like being vulnerable was a strength is now treating me like I'm made of glass.

"Don't make this sound like I'm having some sort of issue," I snap, spinning to face him. "This is real, Alder. We have to get out of here."

He steps in behind me, closes the door, and turns the lock with a soft click. "You're hysterical."

My gazc darts to his. "Don't you dare."

But he's already moving closer, his hands skimming my sides, brushing the edge of my dress, his voice low and coaxing. "You're exhausted. You've been through too much. You need to let me take care of you."

"I don't need to be taken care of. I need to be believed."

He dips his head, pressing a kiss just beneath my ear. "Don't I always know what you need?"

I jerk away. "Do you?"

His smile doesn't reach his eyes. "Of course I do."

"I'm not making this up. I'm not hysterical. I'm not suffering from some head injury. *This is happening*. And the sooner we stop pretending like it isn't, the better chance we have of getting out before we end up..." Words clog my throat as the image of Clara's body sliding beneath the water flashes behind my eyes. "Before something worse happens."

His jaw tightens. "You didn't used to question me like this."

"Yeah, well, it's amazing what six months away from a toxic relationship will do to a woman."

That gets his attention. His eyes narrow. "What the hell is that supposed to mean?"

I cross my arms, nails digging into my sleeves just to keep from shaking.

It's dizzying, how fast he's changed—how the man who smiled at me by the waterfall feels like a fever dream compared to the one standing here now. But anger's easier to hold onto than confusion.

"It means I've had time to think. Time to breathe. Time to remember who I am when I'm not constantly trying to be whatever version of me you've decided you want that week."

His mouth twists, but before he can find a comeback, I add, "And if you think I'm going to stand here while you try to dismiss everything I just saw—everything I felt—like it's some kind of stress-induced hallucination, then you really don't know me at all."

"You're spiraling," he says, too quickly, like he's been waiting to use that word. "You've always done this—blown things out of proportion when they're out of your control."

"You think this is me spiraling?" I ask, incredulous. "I watched a woman die. I saw blood and chanting and a glowing sigil disappear into her skin, Alder. You want to try and tell me that was my attempt to regain control?"

He doesn't answer. He just looks at me like I'm being ridiculous. Like I'm embarrassing him.

"You've always had a flair for drama," he says with a sharp little laugh that grates across my skin. "You used to love making things bigger than they were. It's probably why the publisher thought you weren't ready for a promotion."

I freeze.

The air shifts.

Alder doesn't notice. He's moving toward me to distract me with another touch, another charm offensive.

But I'm stuck.

The publisher thought I wasn't ready for a promotion.

That phrase—those exact words—came from a meeting with HR the day I was fired. Those words gutted me.

I never told him that. And he just said them like he'd heard them before.

I can't unravel that thread right this second. Not now. Not after everything that's just happened.

So I tuck it away. Mentally file it somewhere behind the images of Clara's blood, the chanting, the queen and that man, and the overwhelming truth that magick is real and people here die for it...because of it.

"But none of that is important right now," Alder says. "You're here. With me. Isn't that all that matters?"

I shake my head. "No. It's not."

His jaw ticks. "Why are you being like this?"

"Why am *I* being like this?" I shake my head. "I shouldn't have to justify having an emotional reaction to the fact that I just witnessed a ritual sacrifice."

"Gemma, stop." His expression shifts. "You're exaggerating."

"Am I?" I scoff. "Or is it easier for you if I'm the

one being dramatic? That way you don't have to actually see me."

"I've always seen you."

"No," I say, my voice quiet but cutting. "You've always seen the version of me that needed you. The one who'd fold when you said fold. The one who didn't push too hard or ask too many questions."

He laughs bitterly. "That's rich. Considering you've never stopped running long enough to let anything between us actually stick."

"Oh, don't turn this around on me," I say. "You want to talk about the last ten years? Let's talk about how every time I needed you, you turned it into a test. Every time I came back, it was just another game of control. You pull me in, push me away. You dangle what I want just far enough away to keep me reaching."

"I've always been there," he growls. "You think I stuck around because I liked the power trip? No, Gemma. I stayed because you were mine. Because no matter how far you ran, you always came back."

"Maybe that's the problem," I whisper.

A silence stretches between us, jagged and raw. We're both breathing hard, both flushed with more than just anger.

He takes a step forward like he might try again. But then he stops. His hands ball into fists at his sides, his expression twisting into something bitter and mean.

"Forget it," he barks, voice rough. "I'm not doing this with you." He spins on his heel and stalks toward the door. The echo of his footsteps is thunderous, every step vibrating like a slammed drawer in my chest.

"Right," I say coolly, arms crossed tightly around

myself. "Let's not actually be honest. Let's not deal with anything."

He freezes, just for a second. His knuckles go white around the brass doorknob, but he doesn't turn back. Doesn't say a word.

The door swings open.

And then he's gone.

The door slams shut behind him, leaving me alone with the mess he always makes but never bothers to clean up.

SIXTEEN

Alder didn't come back last night.

I don't know why I expected him to. I fell asleep facing the door like a tragic, languishing Victorian heroine abandoned by her lover—except I'm not in a corset and this isn't a novel.

My dinner tray remains untouched by the fireplace, the once-warm bread now stale and hard, the butter congealed like a sad metaphor.

I don't regret what I said. Not one word. We've been circling each other for a decade—hot, cold, together, apart—and I've been complicit in every messy, muddled part of it. But yesterday morning…that was different. The henhouse. The laughter. The flower he tucked behind my ear. That felt like something real. Something whole. And now here I am—alone in a cold castle room that smells like soot and rejection.

The door creaks open.

"Good morning!" Sylvie sings, balancing a new tray with practiced grace. "I brought—oh."

Her smile falters the moment she sees the dinner tray. Her gaze flicks to me, sitting upright on the edge of the bed, hair a mess, eyes gritty, dress wrinkled, then back to the tray.

"I guess you weren't hungry," she says gently, setting the breakfast tray down beside the untouched one.

"I lost my appetite somewhere around sunset," I mutter and pull the blanket tight around my shoulders.

Sylvie doesn't press. She moves around the room, fluffing pillows, lighting the hearth. She doesn't hover, but she doesn't rush either. She's quiet in the way only someone who truly understands heartbreak can be.

I clear my throat. "Thanks for breakfast."

She glances at me over her shoulder. "Be sure to add honey to the porridge. Bernice says it helps sweeten a sour mood."

"I think I might need the whole hive."

Sylvie chuckles and brings the tray over. "Here. Eat. Even misery needs energy."

I manage a small smile and accept the bowl, stirring the porridge absentmindedly. "You're good at this," I say.

"At what?"

"This." I gesture vaguely. "The whole…knowing-what-to-say-and-when-to-bring-honey thing."

She shrugs, settling onto the windowsill. "Castle life teaches you quickly. You either learn how to read people, or you get eaten alive—sometimes literally, depending on what room you wander into." She laughs, but the words hit a little too close to home.

I force a smile, pretending my stomach isn't turning itself inside out over everything I'm trying not to think about. Namely, a certain golden boy who managed to ruin a perfectly good fantasy in record time.

Focus on something other than your spectacularly bad taste in men.

"Speaking of wandering…" I glance up, watching Sylvie in the soft morning light. "I was touring the castle last night, and I didn't see Clara. Is she…okay?"

Sylvie's smile flickers. She fiddles with a frayed thread at the hem of her apron, the picture of someone trying very hard not to lie. "Clara is…complicated."

Complicated. That's certainly one way to describe a woman who was just sacrificed in a bathtub by Queen-Serpent-Crown.

I set my spoon down carefully, keeping my tone light. "Complicated how?"

Sylvie shrugs, her hands smoothing over her apron like she can iron out her own tension. "She…tended to ask questions. Go places she wasn't supposed to."

"She sounds a lot like me," I say, smiling a little too sweetly.

Sylvie's gaze sharpens for just a second before she drops it back to her lap. "Castle life doesn't suit everyone," she murmurs. "Some people get…into things they shouldn't."

I pick up my spoon again, swirling it idly through the porridge. "Is that what happened to Clara?" I glance up, watching her carefully. "Did she get into something she shouldn't?"

A beat. Sylvie doesn't move. Doesn't breathe.

When she finally speaks again, she says, "There are a lot of rules here. Most of them aren't written down. But everyone knows who enforces them."

"Delphara?" I ask.

She stiffens slightly. "Maybe it's better if you don't worry about Clara."

Maybe it's better if I didn't know there's a secret bathroom/death chamber hidden in this place, either, but here we are.

Sylvie huffs a small, humorless laugh. "Worrying isn't exactly encouraged around here. Not unless you want to end up on the Queen's list, which, trust me, is a lot easier to get on than off."

I let her pivot. Let her shove the conversation back onto safer ground even though every instinct in me wants to keep digging, keep clawing for the truth.

I stir my porridge again, the honey dissolving into cloudy swirls. "Yeah," I say lightly. "I'm pretty sure I made the Queen's list the second I breathed near her."

Sylvie huffs a laugh. "That's about as warm as she gets, honestly."

I flash her a crooked smile, leaning into the easy rhythm. "Good to know I'm not the only one she's got it out for."

Sylvie shifts, relaxing a fraction against the window frame. "No. Definitely not." She hesitates, then adds, "Queen Rothmore has a very...specific view of women. Mostly that we're soft, and delicate, and inherently lesser."

I blink. "Wait, what?"

"Every attendant within the castle is a woman. Every masked guard? Man. The message is pretty clear. Although it's a lot harder to keep the palace running than it is to stand around in a mask and look vaguely menacing," Sylvie says, rolling her eyes. "But in the queen's mind, power looks like masculinity. Women are for cleaning, fetching, and bed sport."

"That's...deeply depressing." My spoon clinks against the side of the bowl. "And confusing. I mean, when women think so little of other women, what does that say about how they see themselves?"

Sylvie lifts her shoulders in a slow, tired shrug. "I feel bad for her, really. The only value Queen Rothmore has ever had has been tied up in the man who chose to marry her. It's no wonder she wears a crown and still feels like she's not enough."

Sylvie props her elbow against the window frame, gaze drifting toward the water. For a second, she almost looks sorry for Delphara. Almost.

"You didn't hear that from me," she adds quickly, her voice lower now. "And don't repeat it. Not unless you want to earn a higher position on that list."

A chill slides down my spine. I lean in slightly, dropping my voice to match hers. "Cone of silence. Whatever we say here stays in the vault."

Sylvie's eyes brighten, and she shifts closer, until we're like two girls sneaking secrets at a sleepover. She tucks a loose strand of hair behind her ear, voice dropping conspiratorially. "You'll think me foolish," she murmurs, "but there was a time I believed I might be chosen as a lady's maid. I thought if I worked hard enough, learned enough, perhaps the Queen would take notice."

"Did she?"

"Oh, yes." Sylvie's smile turns brittle. "Her Majesty said I was too outspoken to be trusted in any position of importance. That a woman's job is not to think, but to serve."

My mouth falls open. "She actually said that?"

Sylvie nods, her nose wrinkling in a look of pure disgust. "And right after, she sent me to muck the stables for a full month." She pulls a face like she's just tasted something rotten. "And I don't know what they feed the royal horses, but whatever it is, it doesn't sit well with them, I can tell you that much."

We both let out a laugh, but it fades fast.

"Gemma?" she asks gently, looking down at the untouched tray from last night still sitting near the hearth. Her gaze flicks back to me. "You didn't eat your dinner, and I know I'm being forward, and it's not my place, but…you look so sad. Did something happen?"

I open my mouth. Close it. What do I say? I saw her friend die in a ritual bath? That magick is real and bloody and terrifying? That I'm letting the man I promised never to love again mess with my heart?

She fidgets with the hem of her apron again, nervous. "I too know what it's like to arrive in a place and feel completely alone."

My throat tightens. "Thank you," I manage, voice small. "I'm…I'm okay. I just need time to think."

She nods. "Often enough, that's all that's left to us."

Sylvie crosses the room and sits beside me on the edge of the bed, smoothing her skirts as she settles. I set the porridge aside, suddenly too full to eat, and before I can think too hard about it, Sylvie reaches over and takes my hand.

Her palm is calloused, her fingers warm. Solid. Steady.

For a moment, neither of us speaks. We just sit there, two women who don't quite fit, caught in a place that chews up the soft and spits them out.

"I was never meant for a place like this," Sylvie says quietly. "Too curious. Too stubborn." She squeezes my hand gently. "You either learn to bend into something they'll keep—or break with the attempt."

A lump rises in my throat. I blink hard, trying to will it away.

I want to tell her everything. About what I saw. About the secrets clawing at the edges of my mind. About how alone I feel, trapped in a castle of lies and blood, trying to hold on to a version of myself that's slipping through my fingers.

I want to trust her. I want to trust someone.

But I've already trusted the wrong man. And I don't know if I can even trust my own heart anymore.

The words tear free before I can stop them.

"I need to get home," I say suddenly. "I need to find my way back home and…figure things out."

Sylvie watches me with an unreadable expression. "And Lord Lockhart? Is he part of that home you're trying to get back to?" she asks softly, tilting her head. "He was seen sleeping in one of the libraries last night."

My heart lurches like a startled bird. I press my free hand to my chest, willing it to slow. "That's part of what I need to figure out."

Even though I've told myself—over and over—that money and security matter more than messy things like love and vulnerability, I'm starting to feel the crack in that logic. I can't build a future on something that empties me out. Not when I've glimpsed what it could feel like to be truly seen. To laugh and tease and flirt and feel something that was a hell of a lot like joy. What we shared yesterday morning—it mattered. And I'm not sure I can go back to pretending it didn't.

A knock rattles the door, and Sylvie jumps up,

brushing her hands on her apron as she rushes to open it. I catch a flash of another attendant in the hall before Sylvie returns, holding a sealed envelope.

"It's for you," she says, "from Lord Lockhart."

My heart stumbles.

She hands it to me, and I stare at the wax seal. I break it with a flick of my thumb but hesitate, the note trembling between my fingers.

This is so much worse than a text I can preview and pretend I didn't see. There's no swiping this away. No three dots bouncing at the bottom of the screen to warn me something's coming.

"I can't," I mutter. "You read it. Wait—no. Don't read it. Not if it's bad. Don't tell me what it says if it's bad."

Sylvie blinks. "*Oookay…*"

"Wait—no, do tell me," I say, collapsing back on the bed and yanking a pillow over my face. "Okay." My voice is muffled now. "I'm ready. What does it say?"

I feel her weight settle at the edge of the mattress. She clears her throat and reads aloud, "'Meet me at the west dock after breakfast. Come alone.—A.'"

"Romantic," I mumble into the fluffy down. "If you're into cryptic letters from billionaire spies with mood swings."

"What was that?" She looks deeply confused now, her brow furrowed.

"Nothing," I say, tossing the pillow against the headboard.

Sylvie folds the note then tucks it into my palm. "Whatever this is between you two…you don't have to decide everything right now. But if it matters, and it very much seems to, don't leave the table just because the first course didn't go down easy."

I blink at her. "Did you just compare my relationship to a meal?"

She shrugs. "I've been working in kitchens too long."

I laugh, rustily but real.

"Thanks, Sylvie."

She stands, hands on her hips, her chin lifted. "Now then, let's get your hair sorted and find you something decent to wear, so you don't look as though you've spent the entire night pining."

I groan. "Oh, for heaven's sake. Is it that obvious?"

She lifts both brows. "You look two blinks away from fainting into the nearest chaise."

I sit up straighter, dragging a hand through my tangled hair. "Well, that's exactly the look I was going for. Fainting, but fashionable."

"Well, my lady, you have succeeded," she says, already moving toward the vanity. "Although I'm not entirely sure we should be excited about it."

It only takes a few minutes—some clever pinning, a borrowed ribbon, and a fresh dress Sylvie must have sent for, one that falls against my curves in all the right ways—before I feel like I've been at least partially reassembled.

I smooth the fabric over my hips and glance in the mirror. I still look tired, and a little too pale, but there's a bit more of me there now. Enough to move forward.

"Wish me luck," I say as I pause at the door.

"Oh no, you do not," Sylvie replies, folding her arms with mock severity. "You cannot answer a mysterious summons from a handsome lord and not swear to tell me all when next you are able."

I smile despite myself. "Is that your way of admitting you're invested?"

She lifts her chin. "I have a sharp eye for trouble, and a soft heart for tales that end well. Of course I'm invested."

Impulsively, I step forward and wrap her in a quick, grateful hug. "Thanks again, Sylvie."

She hugs me back tightly. "You are most welcome. Now off you go. And remember, I shall be waiting for every detail."

As I open the door and step into the hall, a nervous flutter builds low in my stomach. Because I'm not just heading to the dock. I'm heading toward answers.

And maybe—because magick *is* real—a chance at the kind of love I've spent far too long pretending I don't care about.

SEVENTEEN

I step onto the dock, the salty sea air curling around me, brushing cool against my cheeks. The water, the sway, the soft creak of wood beneath my feet—it all feels too familiar.

It was only three days ago. *Three days.*

Alder and I were tangled in each other's arms, breathless, making promises, the night air brushing our skin as we fell asleep on a dock so much like this one. That dock was supposed to be a pause, a weekend escape. Instead, it became a portal. A threshold. The end of one life and the beginning of something I still can't name.

So much has happened since then. Too much.

It feels like I've lived an entire lifetime in the span of a few sunrises. Like I've shed one version of myself and stepped into another—raw, aching, unsure of the terrain but still somehow stronger than before.

And the Gemma who stood on that dock with Alder just a few nights ago? She would've said yes to anything he asked. Let him possess her, parade her around like an accessory to his perfect all-American image. All smiles and angles and glossy PR-approved photos. She would've swallowed her doubts with champagne and let the press call it love.

And I really thought I was okay with that.

But I'm not. Not anymore.

I'd rather move back in with my parents, red-faced and broke, than sell my soul for a lifetime of money and sex and nothing more. I'd rather start from nothing—be humiliated, be lost—than lose myself.

Because now I've seen something else. I've seen him. Not just the curated version, the one built for boardrooms and magazine covers, but the one who has depth and is all kindness and fun and who looked at me like I mattered.

I want that man.

And I want him to see me—all of me. Not just the polished, poised version he used to show off at fundraisers. Not the woman who stayed quiet, smoothed the edges, and did whatever it took to stay in his orbit. I want him to see the woman I'm becoming—the one who's scared and brave, who stumbles and still keeps going. The one who deserves more than admiration or control. Who wants partnership. Who wants to be *chosen* not because she's easy to parade around, but because she's real and messy and still worthy of being loved.

Who saw magick with her own eyes.

Who watched someone die and still has no idea what to do with that knowledge.

I hope he's ready to talk. Really talk. And I hope he's ready to listen—the way he did yesterday morning in the gardens, when for a moment, it felt like we'd finally stopped pretending.

Because I'm not just here to say yes. I'm here to be heard.

And if he can't give me that…I'm walking away.

A small, beautiful sailboat moored in a slip catches my eye as I pass it on my way to the end of the dock. It rocks gently on the water. The hull gleams in the midmorning sun, the sleek, polished wood curving elegantly. The navy sail is neatly furled, secured with knotted ropes worn soft with use.

Sunbeams scatter across the great moat that surrounds the castle isle, shattering into flashes of gold and silver. But beyond it—past the glimmering waters and the gently bobbing sailboat—shadows stretch long and dark through the towering pines. The bridge that connects this island to the next is crumbling, ivy strangling the stone, its arch broken and sagging like a spine that can't hold the weight anymore. One good storm, and it'll collapse.

Maybe I will too.

The breeze picks up, sharp and cool as it rolls off the water. It lifts the ribbon from my hair, and I let it go. Let it flutter away like the white flag I'm no longer willing to raise.

I brace my hands on the dock railing, fingers curling around the weathered wood. I breathe in the scent of salt and pine, let it sting my lungs, let it keep me from unraveling.

Maybe he won't come.

Maybe he'll make it heartbreakingly easy to walk away.

The seconds stretch. A gull cries somewhere overhead, its call sharp and lonely. I shift my weight from one foot to the other, the wood creaking beneath me, and pretend I don't keep glancing over my shoulder to scan the path behind me every few heartbeats. The wind picks up again, tugging at my sleeves, like even it's trying to pull me back.

Behind me, boots thud softly against the dock's planks. Then his voice—familiar enough to hurt.

"I'm glad you came."

There's warmth in his tone, teasing and light, as if this is just another morning, just another conversation. Like we haven't been dancing around each other in this endless push and pull that's left me aching and raw.

I don't turn around.

My eyes stay locked on the water, on the fractured reflection of the castle shimmering in its depths. The wind slips around me, and the distant crash of the sea feels louder than it should—like the ocean's trying to drown out everything I don't want to say but have to.

My fists clench at my sides. Every emotion I've swallowed down for the past decade is stacked, one on top of the other, until they're too heavy to carry.

"What was the point?" My voice comes out quiet, but sharp enough to cut. "Sleeping in the library. Not coming back to the room last night. What message were you trying to send, exactly?"

I turn to face him, bracing for his smirk, for the deflection, for another round of whatever passive-aggressive game he thinks we're still playing.

But he's just...standing there.

A picnic basket hangs from one hand, a rolled blanket

tucked under his arm. The breeze ruffles his golden hair, and his eyes—his blue, wide, confusingly soft eyes—look almost startled. Like I've caught him off guard. Like he doesn't know how to play this particular game because he never agreed to it.

"I—" He blinks, and his smile tilts, uncertain. "That wasn't meant to be a message. I didn't want to wake you."

His voice is too gentle. His words too careful. There's no sharpness, no familiar edge of condescension or control.

I falter. Just for a second. Because this isn't how Alder fights. He throws jabs, backhanded comments, guilt-laced apologies meant to keep me tethered. But this version—the one standing here holding a picnic and a blanket—he's not playing defense. He's not playing at all.

"I just thought…maybe we could spend the day together." He lifts the basket slightly in an awkward peace offering.

And suddenly I don't know what to do with all the fire I brought with me. I crossed this dock ready to rage. Ready to demand apologies, answers, accountability. But instead of a storm, I've run headfirst into sunlight.

I cross my arms. "Why, Alder? So you can play the part of the charming, brooding lord with a picture-perfect brunch spread and sweeping gestures and hope I forget everything that's happened?"

My voice rises, sharp and cracking around the edges. "What, were you planning to distract me with champagne and ocean views and just…reset us? Pretend last night didn't happen? Pretend the last ten years didn't happen?"

He opens his mouth, but I steamroll over him.

"I can't do that anymore. I won't go on like nothing's changed."

"Gemma—" His voice is soft, caught between caution and concern.

"No," I snap, shaking my head. "Don't *Gemma* me. Last night I was trying to tell you something real. And you—" My voice cracks, and I hate it, but I keep going. "You brushed it off like I was being dramatic. Like I was imagining things."

His brows knit together, but I'm already on a roll, fury and heartbreak burning through me.

"I gave you honesty. You gave me avoidance and hands that wouldn't stop touching me even when I was begging you to listen."

"I didn't mean—" he starts.

"You never mean to!" I explode, throwing my arms up. "That's the problem, Alder. You never mean to hurt me. You just do. You say something shitty, or you don't say anything at all, and then I'm left making excuses to convince myself that I'm not naïve or dense for still hanging around."

He flinches at that, and I almost feel bad—but not enough to stop.

"You always do this," I say, voice lower now, biting. "You show up with your charming smile and your credit card, and you expect that to be enough."

He runs a hand through his hair. "I didn't come here to fight with you."

"Well, too bad," I snap.

I step closer, my heart thudding, every nerve in my body electric with hurt and want and a decade of unspoken things.

"I need more than this. More than mood swings and breadcrumbs and sweet moments that vanish the second it's inconvenient for you to care."

His jaw tightens. "I *do* care."

"Then why didn't you come back to the room last night?" I fire back. And I know I'm talking in circles, but there's something he's not saying, and I want the truth. "Why did you leave me alone after what I told you?"

He hesitates. Just long enough to say everything without saying a word.

"I needed you." The wind off the water whips my hair into my face, and I shove it back with shaking fingers. "For more than your money or security, I actually needed *you*—the man who looked at me like I was more than something he could just…win."

His expression shifts and the color drains from his cheeks. He doesn't flinch, doesn't look away, but something in him staggers. Like a blow landed. Like he didn't expect it to hurt.

"I'm sorry," he says softly.

No excuse. No sidestep. A real, honest apology.

It knocks the breath out of me.

I blink, stunned, because this isn't the man who once turned a fundraiser into a PR stunt and called it romance. This isn't the man who missed birthdays and canceled dates and always made me feel like I was the one asking for too much.

"Oh," I breathe. It's all I can manage. Just that one tiny word, because my chest is too full, and my throat is too tight, and I don't trust myself not to cry.

"I should never have left you," he says. His voice is

still low, but steadier now. "I should have stayed. I should have listened."

He takes a step toward me, slow and careful, like he knows just how close he came to breaking whatever's left between us.

"I'm still the same man I was gathering eggs with you yesterday morning," he adds, eyes locked on mine. "Let me prove it."

I look down at the basket in his hand, at the blanket tucked under his arm, then up at him again, wary. "This your idea of proving it?"

He lets out a quiet breath. "It's a start. Just…come with me. Please."

"I don't need a romantic field trip," I say, but the bite in my voice is already fading. My edges are duller now, the anger bleeding out of me, leaving behind nothing but tired muscles and too many feelings.

The corner of his mouth lifts in a half-smile. "Don't think of it that way. Think of it as breakfast."

I stare at him. At the wind-tousled hair. At the soft lines around his eyes, at the quiet way he's standing there. Not forcing, not charming, not telling me I'm spiraling. Just waiting.

"Where?" I ask, arms still stubbornly crossed.

He gestures toward the sleek little sailboat bobbing gently next to the dock. "There. Other side of the island. Just a little while."

"I'm not done yelling at you."

That half-smile tugs at his lips again. "I'd be disappointed if you were."

I stare at him for a long beat. My pulse thuds hard in my throat, tangled with too many feelings—anger, confusion, something terrifyingly close to hope. I don't want to give in. I don't want to make this easy. But I also don't want to stay stuck in the version of us that's always *almost* worked.

"Fine," I say. "I'll go. But you're on *extremely* thin ice."

"Wouldn't expect anything less."

I step past him, jaw set, my flats thudding softly against the dock as I head for the boat. My heart kicks with every step, still thrumming with leftover frustration and a feeling I don't want to name.

He doesn't reach for me. Doesn't guide me with a hand on the small of my back like he always used to. He lets me move ahead. Lets me make the first move. He gives me space.

And maybe that, more than the apology, more than the picnic, is what begins to thaw the part of me that still has hope.

He follows behind, and for the first time, it feels like we're not falling back into old patterns. It feels like we're choosing something new.

EIGHTEEN

The sailboat wobbles beneath me as I clamber aboard, and immediately, I regret every life choice that's brought me to this point. My balance vanishes and I flail, arms windmilling like I'm starring in a slapstick comedy I didn't audition for.

The boat rocks harder, and I lurch sideways, seconds from tumbling overboard in what would surely be the least dignified splash of my life, when a warm, calloused hand wraps around mine.

"Careful," Alder says, steadying me like it's nothing. "Dramatic exits are usually more effective after the date, not before."

My eyebrows shoot up. "This isn't a date. We're just...changing the location of our conversation."

"Of course. Yes. Simply a conversation," he says with a mock-serious nod. "I mean, what else would it be called when two people are alone on a sailboat with a picnic and unspeakable tension. Very casual."

I open my mouth to fire back, but the boat sways again—harder this time—and I stumble straight into him.

His arms catch me without hesitation, strong and warm and way too solid for my emotional safety. My hands land on his chest, and unfortunately, it's still as annoyingly perfect as I remember—broad, steady, stupidly well-built beneath his linen shirt.

"Think of it like riding a horse," he murmurs, still holding me a little too close.

"A horse?" I ask, trying to sound unimpressed even though my pulse is tap-dancing behind my ribs.

"Well," he says with a lazy shrug as he gently guides me toward the center of the boat, "a horse made of wood. With no saddle. Or reins. And floating."

"Oh, perfect," I mutter, catching my balance again. "So basically a death trap with a nautical flair."

"I prefer to think of it as charmingly adventurous. Besides, it's only a death trap if you fall overboard."

"Comforting," I say, eyeing the shifting water.

He flashes a crooked smile. "You're the one who agreed to come."

"Yes, well, I also once agreed to get bangs, so clearly my judgment is flawed."

His laugh slides right under my skin. It feels good to make him laugh.

"Sit," he says, motioning toward the bench. "I promise to keep all death-defying heroics to a minimum."

I slide onto the bench and grip it for dear life, stomach fluttering in that traitorous, giddy way that only happens when you're in mortal danger or about to fall in love. I'm not sure which one this is yet. Possibly both.

If only Amanda could see me now.

The thought makes me snort.

"Something funny?"

I open my mouth to respond, but laughter tumbles out instead—uncontrollable, impossible to stop. The sound bubbles up, bigger than me, breaking free of the knot that's been sitting heavy in my chest for the past three days. It spills out until I'm doubled over, gasping, tears gathering in the corners of my eyes.

Alder watches me with the same reverence most men reserve for a home-cooked meal or football. Then, slowly, he closes his eyes, inhales, and tilts his face toward the sun like he's soaking up the sound.

"I can't—" I try to catch my breath. "It's just...this."

I gesture wildly at everything—the boat, the ocean, the towering pines, the castle behind us like a Gothic fever dream.

"We're in another realm, Alder. A literal, actual different world. I was supposed to be crying into my boxed wine while I packed up my life this week. Instead, here I am. On a boat in a magickal kingdom with a man who may or may not have spent the past decade emotionally wrecking me."

He chuckles. "When you put it that way, I suppose it does sound a bit unconventional."

I burst out laughing again. "You think?"

Alder's tall frame is silhouetted against the sparkling waves as he moves to the mast. The wind teases his hair, brushing it across his forehead. In a few deft movements, he hoists the sail, and the fabric catches the wind with a satisfying snap. The boat jerks forward, the sudden motion pulling a startled yelp from my throat. My hands fly to the edge of the bench, gripping tight as the hull wobbles beneath me.

But then the wind catches the sail just right, and we're gliding. The lurching steadies, the rocking evens out, and the world around us melts into the hush of water against wood.

I exhale a pent-up breath, and the tension in my shoulders loosens. The breeze tangles my hair, salty and crisp against my skin, and for the first time since this whole bizarre storybook saga started, my brain stops buzzing with questions and contingencies. Just this moment, this feeling.

A thought blooms within me, slow and unexpected. It takes root, deep and certain, warming me from the inside out.

I'm proud of myself.

For standing up for myself. For not backing down when it would've been easier to let him charm his way out of the truth. I didn't cave. I didn't chase. I didn't shrink to fit the space he offered.

I release a slow breath, my fingers loosening their grip on the edge of the boat. How many times have I mistaken control for safety? How often have I convinced myself that being wanted was the same as being chosen? How many versions of myself did I minimize to keep the peace—to keep him?

And now, with the wind on my skin, the vastness of the water, the horizon wide and unexplored, every fear, every second-guessing thought feels so unimportant.

I glance at Alder, and his gaze is already on me. A slow smile tugs at his lips. "Gold coin for your thoughts."

"I was just thinking..." I inhale. The crisp air fills my lungs, scrubbing away the weight of everything I've carried for too long. "That for the first time in a long time, I feel like I finally belong to myself."

I expect the words to feel fragile, like they might shatter the moment they're spoken aloud—but they don't. They're solid, real. True.

The ocean stretches out before us, an endless expanse of shimmering blue that melts into the sky. The wind rushes by, and the sunlight warms my skin as I let the feeling sink into my bones, let it expand and take up space inside me, claiming every part of me that once felt worthless and afraid.

The breeze picks up, the sail snapping taut, and the boat surges forward. We skim across the water, cutting through the waves like we were always meant to, and a flicker of exhilaration sparks to life in my chest. It builds, burning like wildfire, consuming hesitation, doubt, and every reason I've ever given myself to play small.

I tip my head back, laughing as the wind rushes past, lifting me higher, setting something free inside me that I didn't even know was caged.

And then, without warning, the wind turns.

A sharp gust slams into the sail, yanking it sideways. The boat lurches violently, one side lifting out of the water, and my laughter shatters into a startled scream. My stomach plummets. The once-soothing rhythm of the waves transforms into a crashing roar beneath me.

"Shit." Alder's grin vanishes as he scrambles to steady the rudder.

My fingers dig into the edge of the boat, my breath ragged as panic seizes my chest. "Shit?" I echo, my voice pitching higher. "What do you mean, *shit*?"

"We're off course," he says tightly, wrestling with the

tiller. The boat groans in protest, the sail flapping wildly overhead. His calm demeanor is gone, replaced with tightly wound urgency. "The wind's too strong. If we don't get it under control, we're going for a swim."

My stomach somersaults as the boat tilts again, the hull groaning against the surge of the waves splashing dangerously close to the edge. "Swim? As in *the ocean*?"

"Unless that island is closer than it looks to be," he shouts back, his voice strained as he fights the wind. "Gemma, I need you to help me."

"How?" My heart hammers so hard I feel it in my throat. "I don't know boats! I'm not a sailor!"

"You don't have to be," he hollers, tossing me a coil of rope. "Just pull when I tell you. Got it?"

I hesitate, my fight or flight response settling on securely on freeze.

The sail flaps violently, the wind screeching through the rigging. The boat could capsize at any second.

My palms sweat against the rope heavy in my hands. "No, I definitely *don't* got it."

"You do! You've got it!" His blue eyes meet mine, clear and steady despite the storm of movement around us. There's fear there, sure—but also belief. In me. "You can do this."

I nod, swallowing hard.

"On my count—one, two, three, pull!"

I yank the rope with everything I have. It burns my palms, and my muscles scream as the wind fights me at every turn. Alder is beside me, bracing the sail, his jaw clenched and his body taut with effort. The boat pitches wildly. Saltwater sprays my face. But I grit my teeth and pull harder.

"Almost there!" Alder shouts, his voice barely audible over the howling wind. He's a windswept mess, but he doesn't waver. "Pull, Gemma!"

I give one final, desperate tug, and the sail snaps back into place with a loud crack. The boat rights itself and steadies beneath us, slicing forward again in a clean, steady line.

I collapse onto the bench, chest heaving, hands trembling as I drop the rope, and the tension drains from my body all at once. "We were about two seconds away from a full *Titanic* moment."

The wind whips around Alder, his shirt clinging to his chest like he's starring in a nautical romance novel as he exhales a slow breath. "You didn't fall in. I didn't crash us into anything. And the sail is still attached. I think of this as a win."

"Is that your benchmark for success? Not sinking and not dying?"

He grins, shameless. "You say that like I didn't just take your breath away."

I groan, tipping my chin toward the sky. "Why do I talk to you?"

"Because I'm charming," he says, sitting beside me. "And alarmingly handsome. And you're secretly having a good time."

I glance at him from the corner of my eye. "You forgot modest."

"I left that one out intentionally."

We sit in silence for a moment, the boat swaying gently, the wind curling between us.

When he speaks again, his voice drops lower, velvet and vulnerable. "I never stop thinking about you, you know."

The words land with a quiet thud in the center of my chest, knocking the breath from my lungs. When I look at him, Alder's grin lingers, lazy and devastating. That look is the first sip of whiskey on a cold night, slow-burning and bracing, curling low in my stomach.

My heart stumbles.

I swallow. Sit a little straighter. Pretend like I'm not seconds from combusting.

Then he shifts closer.

His finger grazes my thigh, barely there, a whisper of contact that turns molten the second it lingers. Heat blooms beneath my skin, embarrassingly fast.

His gaze drops to my mouth.

"Do you like it?" His voice is so deep, I shiver. "The sailing, I mean."

I scoff, but it's weak, breathless, my pulse already in free fall. "It was great. If you're into mortal terror with a side of saltwater in your nose."

His thumb brushes higher on my thigh, slow and casual and anything but. "You're welcome…for the thrill."

"Thrill?" I manage, my voice tighter than I'd like.

He leans in, his mouth close enough that I can feel the heat of his breath. "We could also think of it as foreplay."

My breath hitches. Loud. Obvious.

His hand flexes against my leg, not moving higher, not moving away. Just…there. A promise wrapped in restraint. My skin tingles beneath his touch.

"You always get this handsy after a brush with death?" I ask, aiming for snark, landing somewhere between winded and wrecked.

"Only when the brush is with you."

Heat crashes through me, a slow, aching pulse that I can't ignore. My thighs clench like I can contain the sudden, sharp air-stealing want.

"Say the word, Gemma," he murmurs, his voice thick and slow and toe-curlingly confident, "and I'll drop anchor and have you on your back before your next breath."

My pulse stutters. My mouth goes dry. I bite my lip—hard.

"And if I want to stay upright?" I whisper, barely trusting myself to speak.

"Then I'll make you beg for it while you're sitting pretty."

A choked sound escapes me. It might be a laugh. Might be a moan. Who even knows anymore?

His thumb strokes the inside of my thigh again, and I swear, my bones melt. My body is seconds away from surrendering. From throwing me at him like some desperate groupie.

The island is right there, close now. Forest green and sun-dappled against the endless blue, a whole new mystery waiting. But I barely see it.

Right now, all I see is him. The wind in his hair, the salt on his skin, the fire in his eyes blown wide and dark with want.

And God help me, I want to burn.

Thud.

The boat jerks violently as it hits the rocky shallows, grinding over the shore with a teeth-rattling scrape. I shout and lurch sideways, catching myself on the edge of the bench just before I go sprawling. Sand grates the hull, halting our momentum like nature itself has called a time-out on our foreplay.

Alder curses, scrambling to grab the tiller as I push myself upright and try to regain my composure and what's left of my dignity.

He hops into the knee-deep water and drags the boat closer to shore with obnoxiously flexed arm muscles.

I climb out with as much grace as I can fake while my legs are still trembling and my libido is screaming, *What the hell just happened?*

As soon as my feet hit the sand, I blow out a breath and brush the hair from my face. The breeze off the water hits my skin like a slap, and I silently thank the universe for that crash because I was two seconds away from committing a very stupid, very public sex mistake.

But Alder is no easier to ignore now than he was in the boat.

The way his shirt clings to his chest, damp with sea spray and sweat, the fabric molding to every lean, sculpted line like it was tailor-made to ruin me. Those breeches—tight, sinful, displaying the kind of ass that should come with a warning label.

God, he's fucking sexy.

Heat washes down my spine as he kneels beside me in the sand with the picnic basket he retrieved from the boat. He unties the woven lid and unpacks its contents with deliberate care—an aged wheel of cheese, fresh baked bread still dusted with flour, glistening strawberries, a bottle of wine. And then, nestled among the linens, he lifts out a small jar of golden syrup, sprigs of lavender suspended within like tiny blossoms trapped in amber.

He uncorks the wine first, pouring deep red liquid into two delicate glasses. Without a word, he hands one to me, his fingers brushing over mine as I take it. I hesitate, studying the glass.

"I don't think we should drink," I say finally, my voice softer than I intend. "I want to be clearheaded. If we're going to talk—if we're going to make decisions about whatever this is—" I gesture vaguely between us. "I want to use my brain. Not my other...parts."

His eyes darken, showing his amusement. "Your other parts?"

"You know what I mean."

"I absolutely do." His voice drops, velvet-soft and dangerous. "And I'm not interested in clouding your judgment."

Then, without breaking eye contact, he tips his glass and pours the wine into the sand. The red liquid soaks into the earth like blood. He takes mine and does the same.

"I don't need wine to want you," he says. His voice is low, husky, threaded with a heat that makes my stomach do something unholy. "And I'd rather you remember every second."

The air between us thickens—charged, electric, impossibly heavy.

"Jesus," I breathe. "You are entirely too good at this."

"I'm good at a lot of things," he says, leaning closer, his eyes on my mouth. "You want a list?"

"I want a perimeter," I mumble, but my voice is shaking.

He grins. "Gemma, if you wanted distance, you shouldn't have gotten in my boat."

"Oh my God," I groan, trying to get my bearings. "This is exactly what I mean. I'm trying to be smart, and you're making it impossible."

"If you want to make decisions with your head, do so, but what about your heart?"

The question lands hard.

I glance away, trying to breathe past it. Trying to remember why I can't just fall into this man like I always do—headfirst, heart open, consequences be damned.

I reach for a strawberry, desperate to shift the focus. Anything to ground me, to pull the moment back from the edge of whatever it's becoming.

But before my fingers can close around it, his hand finds mine, fingers wrapping gently around my wrist.

"Let me."

My lips part on instinct. The air hums with possibility. Every nerve ending is screaming *danger.* The smart thing would be to pull away, to say something witty, something sharp and self-protective, something that builds a wall between us. But I don't move, don't speak.

Because the heat of his skin against mine is a tether. Because in this moment—on this beach, in this realm, with him—there's nowhere else I'd rather be.

He plucks a strawberry, red and gleaming and still kissed with dew, from the bowl, cradling it between his thumb and forefinger. Then, with a slow, deliberate movement, he dips it into the jar of honey. The thick amber clings to the fruit, dripping in lazy ribbons down his fingers.

His eyes lift to mine and hold.

"You'll tell me if it's too much?"

The sincerity in his voice. The gentleness. It scrapes

against every raw, aching place inside me, places I didn't know were still bleeding.

"I will," I whisper.

He drags the strawberry across my bottom lip, smearing the honey, letting it linger. The moment stretches, unbearably slow, unbearably tender.

The fruit touches my tongue, and I bite down.

Sweetness bursts against my lips, ripe and sun warmed, tangled with the floral depth of honey. The syrup coats my teeth, my tongue, melting through me like golden sunlight spilling over bare skin. It sinks deep and leaves me flushed, restless, hungry for more.

He watches every second.

Watches the way I lick a bead of juice from the corner of my mouth.

Watches the way my breath catches when his knuckles graze my cheek.

"You are the most dangerous thing I've ever wanted," he says, barely louder than the wind.

My heart squeezes.

I swallow, the flavor of strawberry thick on my tongue, but it's nothing compared to the taste of that sentence. Nothing compared to the way he's looking at me like I've already ruined him, and he wants me to do it again.

I reach for the stem still in his fingers, but he doesn't let go. Our hands stay tangled. Our eyes stay locked. And that ridiculous, terrifying hope starts to rise again.

Maybe this is more than lust and loathing.

Maybe this is something real.

Something that could finally be ours—if we don't ruin it first.

"I want to tell you a story," he says, his voice low, smoky.

I blink up at him.

"A story about a king who was cursed," he continues, "starved of every pleasure. Would you like to hear it?"

I nod, the movement small, my breath caught somewhere between my ribs.

There's this feeling I get—right before I open a book I know is going to ruin me—a kind of electric stillness, like the moment before a storm. That's what this feels like. Like I'm about to be undone, and I'm turning the page anyway.

"One day, the cursed king was saved." Alder drags the honey-drenched strawberry in a slow circle around the rim of the jar. "Washed clean in a golden light."

He lifts the fruit to my lips, his voice low, coaxing. "Open for me."

A soft, involuntary sound slips from my throat as I do.

"And when the king awoke from his curse"—he leans in, his breath warm on my cheek—"he was hungry."

The strawberry grazes my bottom lip—sticky, sweet, slow.

"Ravenous," he breathes, his voice a raw ache now, something that lives between want and worship. "Desperate for sugar and spice…for what he had been denied."

He brushes a stray drop of honey from the corner of my mouth with his thumb, the barest graze of his skin sending a pulse of heat straight through me.

His story is only half tale. It's a parable wrapped in something older, something deeper.

Or maybe it's not a story at all.

Maybe it's a confession.

He presses the fruit to my lips again, and I part them without hesitating, anticipation coiling tight inside me. The syrup spills, warm and decadent, trickling down my chin in a slow trail.

I don't have time to wipe it away before his fingers follow. The rough pad of his thumb traces the sticky path down my skin, collecting the honey with unbearable slowness.

My breath stutters as he brings that honey-slicked finger to my bottom lip, dragging it across the sensitive skin, smearing the syrup in teasing glides. The warmth of it—of him—seeps into me, and I press my thighs together, desperate for relief, for friction, for anything.

Then, before I can prepare, before I can even breathe, he pushes his finger into my mouth.

My lips part, and I close around him, the taste of honey and salt thick on my tongue. A slow, involuntary hum vibrates in my throat.

Alder inhales, and the sound that rumbles from his chest is deep, dark, possessive, and so raw it makes me ache. His pupils dilate, his lips parting like he's about to speak, but he doesn't.

He only continues watching.

Watching the way my lips close around his finger. The way I swallow. The way the honey disappears, leaving only the heat of him behind.

"Tell me, Gemma." His voice is low, barely more than a whisper, but it slides over me like silk, like temptation itself. "Do you think the king ever got his fill?"

I don't answer. I can't.

Because his finger is still resting heavy on my tongue. Because his body is so close, his warmth pouring into me, making my head spin, making my heart trip over itself.

Because I already know the answer.

No, the king never got his fill.

The king is still starving.

NINETEEN

Heat pulses through me, thick, relentless, curling low and dangerous. It begs me to close the distance, to give in. Because I want to. God, I want to. Every inch of me aches with it, a dull, hungry throb that says, *just one more time.*

No.

No, no, no.

This is how it always happens. This is how I lose myself in him.

This is how I ended up in a magickal kingdom, a whole dimension away from anything that makes sense, sitting on a beach with an unfairly gorgeous man who smells like salt and seduction and makes my brain go soft just by existing.

Alder watches me, waiting, his finger still resting against my lips, his breath uneven, his eyes dark with promise. I know that look. That look is a trap. That look is a spell I can't afford to fall under again.

I rip myself away, scrambling to my feet.

The loss is immediate. His heat vanishes, the touch disappears, but the ache he leaves behind, that hollow, open ache, burns hotter.

"I can't," I say, voice rough, splintering. "We can't."

His brows crease, lips still parted like he's about to say something. Like he's about to stop me.

But I don't give him the chance.

I turn and walk fast toward the tree line, away from the beach, away from him, away from every stupid, dangerous part of me that still wants him more than air.

My pulse pounds in my ears. My steps crunch hard against the sand. I need space. I need air. I need to remember I'm not that woman anymore—the one who used to melt under his touch, fold herself into the shape he needed.

But he looked at me like I was still her.

And the worst part?

A tiny part of me wants to be.

A groan tears from my throat, all frustration and ache. I rub my temples. "Emotional maturity is wildly overrated."

But dammit, I am proud of myself.

This isn't running away. This is clarity. This is growth. This is the seasoned, evolved Gemma Summers making a goddamn smart choice.

At least, that's what I tell myself as I keep walking.

There's a rustle of movement behind me, the soft drag of footfalls in the sand. He's not chasing me. Not yet. But he's following. Because of course he is.

He always follows.

I don't turn around. I don't need to. I can feel him

like gravity—like heat and memory and inevitability. His presence wraps around me like the tide, slow and sure, stealing all the space I thought I carved out.

The terrain shifts beneath my feet. The sand gives way to packed earth and beach grass. The world narrows to a cliff's edge, jagged and wild. The sea churns below, waves smashing against stone like they're trying to shake the island apart. Mist rises, clinging to my skin, cooling the fire simmering inside me.

I inhale, bracing myself. One breath. Then another.

"Gemma," he says, voice lower now, closer. "Don't run from this. Don't run from me."

I force a laugh, but it's brittle. "I'm allowed to want space." My arms cross, locking tight over my chest.

But he's there now—not as near as I want him but closer than he should be.

I whirl. "You don't get to—"

And then I see him.

He's flushed, lips parted, chest rising and falling like he just survived a battle. And maybe he did. Maybe we both did.

I try to hold onto my anger—it's easier, safer—but I can't.

His hands cup my face. His thumbs stroke along my cheeks, and it undoes me. This tenderness is more deadly than anything he's ever said.

"Is it me you're running from," he asks softly, "or is it what you feel when we're together?"

I want to tell him it's both. I want to tell him I'm terrified. That he still has the power to shatter me, and that's not a fair thing to give someone.

But I don't say any of that.

Instead, I look at his mouth.

It's reckless, stupid—but I can't help it. My gaze rises to his lips like they hold the answer to the question my body keeps asking. His breath brushes my cheek, and I don't step back. My hands twitch at my sides, desperate to reach for him. My lips part on an inhale I never finish.

He kisses me, warm and honey-sweet, and I forget everything but the taste of him.

The world tips beneath my feet, and a low hum rolls through the air, vibrating through my skin, through my very being. The ground pulses as if something beneath us is stirring, awakening.

My eyelids flutter open, and I catch a shadow moving beyond the trees. I gasp against Alder's mouth, breaking the kiss as my gaze lifts over his shoulder. The massive trees groan as they shift, pine needles rustling and branches swaying, their ancient trunks bending like weary giants parting to reveal a long-buried secret.

A stone tower rises from the earth, its craggy surface weathered. It's a relic half-swallowed by the trees as if the island itself has tried to erase it from memory. The twisted boughs of dead apple trees cling to its sides, brittle branches curling like skeletal fingers, strangling the stone in their lifeless grip. Deep cracks wind through the stone like old wounds long scarred but never truly healed.

The hum grows stronger, vibrating in my chest, rattling through my teeth.

Alder's narrowed eyes are fixed on the tower, brows furrowed and posture rigid.

I step back, my heart still racing from the kiss, from the energy pulsing in the air, from the way he looks at that tower like it's a piece of himself.

"You know what this is." My words barely rise above the hum.

His jaw tightens, his throat working as he swallows. "A doorway," he says finally, his voice rough. "A forgotten one."

His fingers drift to his stomach, brushing absently over the gold buttons of his shirt. His gaze flickers, distant for a moment, before he exhales and walks toward the structure.

"It's the tower," he murmurs, voice laced with something almost reverent. "The heart of the Kingdom of Cups."

While I've been busy trying to keep up, trying to find some footing in a world I don't belong to, Alder's been in meetings gathering knowledge. He's been putting the pieces together.

Dry, withered leaves float down as he pushes aside a low-hanging tree bough before trailing his fingers along the rough stone, slow and searching.

"There's one in each kingdom," he continues, his voice almost lost beneath the rhythmic whisper that seems to rise from the very earth. "They were once connected by magick—gateways that could transport the people of Towerfall from one end of the realm to the other."

I blink at him, at the tower, at the moss that clings to the crumbling stone like it's trying to keep it whole.

"So, this thing was like a…a wormhole?"

A couple days ago this would have sounded ridiculous, but I've seen too much to laugh at magick. I've watched a girl die in a chamber full of chanting and silver light. I've felt the air thrum when someone speaks the right words. I've tasted honey that made me forget my own name.

I've seen it. All of it. And somehow, this is just another piece.

I swallow, heart thudding in my chest. "But this can't be how we got here..." My gaze drifts to the tower, but my mind is already somewhere else—on Mackenzie's wedding. On that card. The Lovers. The pull. The dock on the lake.

There was no tower at Mackenzie's wedding.

Only the card.

And Alder.

The magick wasn't in the stone. So, was it in the card, or was it in us?

"This magick only exists within this realm." He presses his palm flat against the rock, his fingers splaying as if feeling for a heartbeat beneath the surface. "Or it did. Until it was outlawed. Until the ruling families severed the connections, and the towers and their magicks were left to wither and die.

"But now..." He turns to me, his blue eyes shadowed, their teasing glint dulled by something heavier, something that settles deep in my chest and refuses to let go. "They're waking up."

I step closer to the Tower, drawn by a pull I don't understand. Like a thread tightening in my ribs, tugging me forward, demanding I listen, I feel it. Ancient. Beckoning. Familiar in a way that makes my skin prickle.

"Like your story about the king." My voice is light, teasing, but the words taste of strawberries and honey, of his fingers brushing against my lips, of the warmth that curled through me as he fed me. My body still remembers, still purrs with the ache of something unfinished.

Alder tilts his head, watching me closely, like he hears what I'm not saying.

I swallow and drag my attention back to the tower. The moss-covered stone looms over us, its deep cracks rough and pitted as I press my palm against its cool surface. The moment my skin meets stone, something inside me shifts.

A pulse. Deep, reverberating.

It rolls through the air, through me, through every nerve in my body, sinking into my veins like a second heartbeat. The very stone beneath my hand groans, as if stirred from an impossibly long slumber, a beast shaking itself awake.

Bits of rock and moss tremble loose, drifting down like the tower is shedding old skin. Alder's arm locks around my waist, and he pulls me against him, all warmth and unwavering strength as he shields me.

A thunderous crack as stone grinds against stone. Another bone-rattling roar, and a jagged fracture tears the tower's surface. A dark void yawns open, exhaling a gust of air thick with the tang of iron and forgotten things.

I feel the pull of this place carve a path beneath my skin, around my heart, a whisper of what I've lost and desperately want to find. Like iron drawn to a lodestone, like breath to starving lungs, I am pulled forward, every part of my body responding to an unseen force, my feet moving before I can command them not to.

The hum rises, no longer a distant beat but a living force that vibrates beneath my skin, in my ribs, sinking deep, curling into something inside me that has always been there, waiting.

Alder stiffens, but he doesn't fight it either. There's a shift in his breathing, but his body moves just as mine does—as if neither of us has a choice.

My slippers scuff against the uneven threshold, and the sound ricochets through the space, the echo stretching long and thin before fading into silence.

The air chills the deeper we're pulled into the belly of the giant, the damp scent of stone wrapped in something richer, darker. It smells old, untouched, abandoned by time.

The fingers of sunlight that manage to stretch into the cavern flicker weakly against the walls that shimmer faintly, laced with veins of burnished silver, slick with condensation that drips in slow, measured rivulets against the stone.

As my eyes adjust to the dark, a faint, ghostly glow emerges from the center of the chamber, pale and cold as moonlight. A monstrosity of silver and steel rises from the center of the cavern in a tangle of gears and pipes that sprawl outward from its wide base, twisting and coiling like serpents poised to strike. Some plunge deep into the stone floor, disappearing into the earth. Others stretch skyward, reaching, straining toward a ceiling lost in darkness.

Rust streaks down its sides like ancient wounds. Cobwebs sag in thick sheets between the gears, and dust lies undisturbed, dulling the once-bright gleam of metal.

A faint, hollow groan emanates from deep within it, as if it's breathing in its sleep. As if something inside is still waiting to awaken.

A chill lances my spine. I swallow hard, my voice barely a whisper. "It's like those machines outside the city…a massive version of the one inside the castle."

The one that killed that woman.

"It doesn't look like it's worked in ages," I murmur, but the words feel thin, as if the cavern itself is swallowing them before they can take shape.

Alder steps closer, his fingers drifting across a nearby pipe. The faint, spectral gleam catches on his face, blurring his features, making him look otherworldly, unreadable. Like he belongs here in a way that I don't.

"It's magick," he says simply, and something in his voice prickles against my skin.

I move forward without thinking, drawn to the machine the way I had been drawn to the tower itself. The air thickens as I step closer, the cavern pressing in on all sides. Dust clings to my fingertips and spiderwebs catch on my sleeves, draping like ghostly threads across my arms as I brush the edges of the machine.

I exhale sharply, my pulse skipping. "I think…I think I walked right into a spell."

Alder tilts his head, a question etched between his brows. "What do you mean?"

I drag my fingers through my hair before letting them fall helplessly to my sides as I try to form the words around the impossible truth. "When we did the cake pull… When I pulled out my ribbon, I didn't get a charm." I glance at him, throat tight. "I got a tarot card."

He says nothing, so I keep going, even though the truth feels ridiculous, even though there's a small voice inside of me screaming that I'm in for another round of disappointment.

"The figures on it…they *moved*," I whisper. "The snake slithered, and the people…the people looked like us. They clung to each other. Their bodies moved together. Melted into each other."

I brace for the disbelief. For the brush-off. For the casual dismissal that always follows any hint of my intuition. But then I remember he said he wanted to prove to me that he was the kind of man I need him to be. So I meet his eyes, hold my breath, and give him a chance.

"It was magick," I continue. "I didn't know it then, but I do now. That tarot card—it did something. It forced us here."

Finally, softly, he says, "I believe you."

I nod slowly, unable to speak, emotion crowding my throat.

He studies me for a long moment. "What if it didn't force you anywhere? What if it simply revealed where you were always meant to go?"

The words hit me low and deep, blooming in the space behind my ribs like something inevitable. Maybe it didn't pull me off course. Maybe it pulled me into alignment. Not just with this world—but with myself. With the truth I've been running from, with the version of me I was too afraid to believe in.

My fingers brush the base of the machine, and a flicker of heat pulses beneath my skin. I lean closer, breath fogging against the cool stone, and blow away a layer of dust.

A carving emerges.

Two hearts, delicately entwined, their curves interlocking like the endless loops of an infinity symbol. It's a language I don't know but instinctively understand, and the longer I stare, the more the details emerge.

One heart is slightly larger, more dominant, its edges bold and smooth and deeply etched. The other, a breath softer, its lines more fluid, its form almost unfinished, as if it hasn't quite decided what shape to take.

The longer I look, the less it feels like a symbol and the more it feels like a mirror.

Like me.

Like him.

Like us.

The hearts aren't static. They're in motion, circling each other, pulling and pushing in an unending dance. Not symmetrical, but balanced in their own imperfect way.

A shiver rolls through me as I glance up at Alder, his profile lit by the faint glow from the mouth of the cavern. His hand rests on the machine, steady, as if he's grounding himself. Or maybe it's the other way around.

I reach out. It's not much. My fingertips brush the back of his wrist, barely there, barely anything at all. Just a question I don't know how to ask.

His eyes find mine. And everything else—the hum of the tower, the weight of this world, even the tension in my own limbs—fades.

We simply look at each other.

Not in that earth-shattering, I-can't-breathe kind of way. But in the way people do when they finally see each other without all the noise.

He doesn't move at first. Neither do I.

And then, I whisper, "The carving. It feels like us."

Alder's throat bobs, and he nods. "It does."

Another breath. Another beat.

"Why are you looking at me like that?" I ask, my voice quiet but steady.

He doesn't smile. Doesn't joke. Instead, he tilts his head, eyes full of something that could crack me open if I let it.

"I'm trying to memorize you."

I blink, startled.

He shrugs, like it's the simplest truth in the world. "In case I never get to see you like this again."

The moment stretches. The intimacy of it settles over us like dusk, gentle and certain.

A low, resonant hum rolls through the cavern, and the massive piston above us shudders faintly, releasing a curling wisp of steam. The vibrations beneath my feet intensify, their rhythm syncing to the frantic pounding of my heart.

Alder steps closer. His arms slide around my waist with the ease of someone who's done this a thousand times, and yet still holds me like the act is holy. His hands settle low on my hips, anchoring me to the present, to him, to this impossible moment where everything in me finally stops struggling.

The machine hisses, a sharp exhale that feels like the room itself is bracing for what comes next.

I reach up, thread my fingers through his hair, and pull him down.

The kiss isn't tentative. It's wildfire—hungry and immediate and merciless.

He kisses me like he's been starving for it, like I'm the first breath after drowning. Like he'll never get enough. His mouth claims mine, teeth catching on my bottom lip, tongue sweeping in to taste, to take, to give. I press against him, desperate and gasping, and he meets me with equal force.

I feel the hard lines of his body everywhere.

His fingers sink into my waist. His chest rises fast against mine as he moans softly into my mouth when I deepen the kiss.

The machine roars—a guttural, grinding sound that vibrates through the walls, through the floor, through me. Gears shriek. Steam hisses. The whole Tower shudders, as if it's been holding its breath for centuries and has finally decided to exhale.

It's not just noise.

It's response.

I flinch against Alder as metal clangs above us like a warning shot fired in the dark. My breath catches. We both freeze, still tangled in each other, eyes wide as the heat between us mixes with something ancient and awakening.

For one suspended second, I'm ripped back to where we are. To what this is. The Tower—this machine—is shifting, breathing, waking up.

"I thought it was broken," I whisper, terrified of what this means and of the fact that I don't want any of it to stop.

"So did I."

Silence follows. Then his hands find the curve of my waist, and the moment is over. The pause between heartbeats ends. My body responds like it was built for him.

He kisses lower—along my jaw, down my throat—and each brush of his mouth is a spark to dry kindling. I shudder, breathless, helpless against the way he devours every inch of me.

"You're delicious," he growls against my neck, voice rough and reverent, a scrape of need that sets every nerve in my body alight.

My knees nearly buckle, and I clutch his shoulders.

"I want to taste every inch of you."

The Tower moans again—stone grinding, metal clanking, steam rising like breath from the lungs of a sleeping god. The walls shiver. The air thickens, electric and charged and watching.

The machine isn't just waking.

It's bearing witness.

Still, I don't pull away. I don't ask questions. I don't run. Because deep down, somewhere beneath the rational voice screaming at me to get a grip, I know this connection, this hunger, this impossible, dangerous thing between us is what I've been waiting for.

The boundary between us dissolves, melting into the kind of hunger, the kind of *need*, that doesn't ask permission—it just takes.

And I let it.

For the first time since reuniting with Alder, I don't want to be saved.

And then—

A scream.

Sharp, piercing. It splinters through the cavern like a crack in glass. The sound is so sudden, so wrong, it doesn't register at first.

Another scream. Battered. Choked.

I jerk back.

The machine keens, a high, metallic whine that rakes down my spine like cold fingers.

There's a screech of pain and terror and everything that should not be as the world crashes back into focus.

Something is happening outside these walls. Something we were never meant to hear.

TWENTY

Alder is already moving, stepping in front of me like a shield. But I'm rooted, breath ragged, every hair on my body standing on end.

Another scream tears through the air, shrill and broken.

We bolt.

The tower's magick must've turned us around, because this isn't the side of the island we came from. We're at the far edge now, where the land narrows into a crumbling stone bridge draped in ivy and rot. It stretches across the churning moat like a broken bone.

And beyond the bridge, the castle rises. Its turrets pierce the storm-colored sky. From here, it looks like something carved from a nightmare. A gilded cage. A kingdom steeped in blood.

The wind howls against the cliffs, cutting and briny as it kicks up sea spray and grit that drag through my hair like restless fingers. Salt stings my lips, and the cold sinks into my skin. Below, the crashing waves feel like an echo of something inside me, relentless and breaking, breaking, breaking.

Alder goes stone-still beside me.

Down the slope, beyond the tangled wilds of beach grass and jagged rock, a young woman is running.

Or trying to.

She stumbles through the sand, limbs flailing and clumsy with exhaustion, frantic with fear. Every desperate kick of her legs, every panicked glance over her shoulder tells the same story—she knows she's not going to make it.

Behind her, the Masked guard advances like shadows slipping through water. Their silver masks glint as they move without urgency, without hesitation, without mercy. Their flowing navy cloaks trail behind them like spilled ink across the earth, swallowing the light.

They move like this hunt is routine. Like they've done this before.

The girl screams again—a high, desperate sound that slices through the cold salty air.

She stumbles. Her feet slip, her knees buckle, her fingers claw at nothing as she slams into the sand.

The guards don't break stride. They move with the patience of inevitability.

Alder tenses, his muscles coiling, flexing, his fingers twitching like he's seconds away from drawing a weapon he doesn't have.

The girl tries to crawl away, her body curling in on itself, hands digging furiously into the loose grains as if she can bury herself, as if she can stop what's coming.

But it's too late.

Two of the Masked guards descend upon her. They yank her up like she weighs nothing, gloved fingers locking around her arms in a grip that's unyielding and final.

She wails. A sound so raw, so broken, so full of knowing that something inside me breaks open too.

She twists, kicks, thrashes with everything she has left. The masked guards shift with the impact of her struggling, but they don't falter, don't waver.

Movement ripples from the mass of guards who've crossed the bridge and stand in the sand. It's the pull of the tide retreating to reveal what lurks beneath.

Something stirs within their ranks. And then, he emerges.

The man with the fanged silver mask. The man who chanted as Clara was murdered. He's draped in bone-white robes, the fabric billowing like steam around him. He moves with the unshakable confidence of a man who has never doubted his own power. The calm of a predator who has never once feared being prey.

The girl's screams claw at my ears, raw and desperate, each one slicing into me like a blade, cutting me open, exposing the memory, pulling it closer, closer—

I can't breathe. My knees tremble, and for a terrifying moment, I think I might collapse.

But then Alder shifts. His body coils with intent, his jaw tight, his hands flexing like he's about to do something.

Oh, God, no.

A bolt of panic rips through me.

I know what he's thinking. I know what he wants to do.

And I can't let him. I can't lose him.

Not here. Not like this. Not when I need him to live.

I move without thinking, grabbing his arm, anchoring myself to him as much as I'm trying to anchor him to me.

"No." The word is barely a whisper.

Alder whips his head toward me, eyes blazing. "She needs help."

"I know." My voice breaks, but I don't let go.

His body vibrates beneath my hands, a live wire barely restrained. He's seconds away from throwing himself into the fire, from charging headlong into death.

I suck in a breath, steadying myself, gripping him tighter. "But you can't."

His shoulders jerk, his breath stutters, eyes flicking to mine, searching.

The truth lodges in my heart like shrapnel—too small to kill me, but sharp enough to hurt with every breath.

I need him. Not just now. Always.

But right now, there's more at stake than just us.

The young woman wrenches free, her body twisting violently, a last, desperate bid for escape. Her head turns, her wide-eyed gaze swinging between the guards and the forest beyond—prey realizing too late that there's nowhere left to run.

The man in white doesn't hurry. He closes in on her with terrifying calmness.

She barely makes it a handful of steps before his hand lashes out, catching the back of her maid's uniform. He yanks hard. The force rips her off-balance, her body snapping back like a marionette.

She crashes to the ground. Her scream splinters through the air—not just a cry, not just terror. It is a plea, wrenched from the deepest part of her, from the part that still believes someone might come.

Alder moves, instinct driving him forward. Every muscle flexes, prepares.

I tighten my grip on his arm, digging my nails into his skin.

"She's not the only one." My voice is low but urgent, thick with the weight of everything we've seen, everything we can't ignore as I nod toward the girl. "There are others. Others like her."

Images slam into me like waves: the woman in the castle who was consumed by the machine, Clara in the bathing chamber… One death after another, all dismissed. All forgotten.

Alder's fists clench then unclench as he looks at me, his expression darkening.

I see the fight in him. The same persistence that made him chase me down this beach, that won't let me go, that makes him succeed at whatever he puts his mind to. But this focus is different. He's never been the type to risk himself for someone else.

"We save her, and what?" I continue, voice rising. "We get thrown out of the kingdom? Or worse—we die trying. And it won't stop anything. They'll just replace her.

"If we want to stop this, really stop it, we don't do it by charging down there and playing the hero. We do it by going after the ones responsible. The Queen. This man. The guards and whoever else knows and looks the other way."

His fingers twitch, and his chest rises and falls in one slow, measured breath as my words settle. Then he nods, just once, his only sign of surrender.

Down on the beach, the girl cries out.

The man in white rears back and slaps her. The crack of his knuckles against her cheek is brutal and merciless. Her body jerks with the impact, head snapping to the side, blood spraying from her mouth before she crumples.

The guards close in. They scoop her up like discarded cloth, her unconscious body dangling between them.

The man in white scrubs at the smear of blood his robe as if he's wiping away an inconvenience rather than the proof of his cruelty. Then he lifts a hand, gesturing for the team of guards to move.

The girl's body sways in their grip, arms slack, head lolling, dragged toward whatever fate awaits her as they disappear into the forest. The shadows stretch long, greedy fingers, swallowing the last flicker of movement, the last glimpse of her pale limbs vanishing between the towering trees. Only the faint rustling of pine needles and the metallic clink of steel-plated boots remain.

And then nothing.

"I think that's the same man from yesterday." My words are a whisper, brittle and trepidant, like saying them too loud might bring him back. "The man with the queen. The one who was chanting—he was wearing that mask."

Alder doesn't look at me. His gaze stays locked on the tree line.

"Droskyn Vayne," he murmurs. "A priest." A beat of silence. Then, lower, rougher, "He should be…" Alder exhales through his nose, jaw tight, throat working like the words are strangling him. "He should be dead."

I swallow hard, forcing myself to push through the fear, through the revulsion curling in my gut. "Now do you believe me? That it wasn't all some emotion-driven hallucination? That I really did watch him and Queen Rothmore kill Clara?"

"Why didn't you tell me this before?"

"Are you kidding?" A sharp laugh catches in my throat, and I shake my head. "I did. You wouldn't listen."

Neither of us speak.

The waves crash below. The wind batters the cliffs.

Alder exhales. A slow, heavy sound, like he's absorbing my words, like they landed somewhere deep. His jaw flexes. The silence between us stretches, taut and thin, straining under the weight of something unspoken.

My pulse stumbles. There's a shift in him, not big, not obvious, but enough. A flicker in his eyes, a tension in his shoulders. Like he knows something I don't. Like he's been waiting for me to figure it out.

I take a step closer. "What aren't you telling me?"

The bushes rustle behind us, and I whip my gaze over my shoulder. There's motion between the trees. There, then gone.

Alder tenses. His stance shifts, sharp and ready. His eyes scan the shadows, narrowing as another branch sways.

Then I see it.

A flash of red hair, vibrant and unmistakable, catching the light before vanishing into the green.

My breath hitches. "Sylvie?"

No. No, it can't be her. She wouldn't have followed us. She shouldn't even be out here.

But I know what I saw.

My mouth goes dry. I'm still buzzing from the maid's abduction, from the knowledge that danger is closer than anyone wants to believe. And now Sylvie's out here, alone?

"Sylvie?" I call again, louder now. "Are you—are you okay?"

No answer. Just wind and the whisper of leaves.

Another rustle. A shadow shifts deeper in the brush.

My pulse kicks. Something's wrong.

She wouldn't run from me. She wouldn't hide. Not unless she had a reason. Unless she saw something. Unless someone saw her.

Panic flares, sharp and sudden. If the guards even suspect she's spying on them, they won't hesitate. They'll give her to Delphara like they did Clara, like I'm sure they're going to do to this girl.

We can't save the maid I don't recognize, not with the Masked guard crawling over the beach like maggots on a fresh kill. But Sylvie? We still have time. We still have a chance.

"Sylvie, wait!"

Still no answer. Just the echo of her name swallowed by trees and wind.

But I'm already moving. My slippers slap the path, breath heaving as I break into a run. Instinct drives me forward, faster than I thought I could go.

Branches scrape at my arms as I tear through the trees, fear surging behind my ribs, Alder shouting my name as I disappear into the brush after a girl who should not be here—and maybe never should've been trusted at all.

She ducks between the trunks, weaving through the

forest like she knows every inch of it, slipping in and out of the fog-draped shadows like a ghost.

My breath saws through my lungs as I push harder, faster, the trees whipping past as I close the distance between us.

And then she's gone. Like she was never here at all.

My heart pounds as I spin, breath ragged, scanning the dense trees and shifting shadows.

Alder crashes through the underbrush and comes to a stop beside me, sharp-eyed and silent.

"Where did she—" I choke out, freezing when a branch to my left snaps.

A blur of movement explodes from the brush. Steel flashes, and I stumble back.

Alder is fast. His hand whips out, catching the attacker's wrist mid-strike. The blade glints an inch from my throat before it's wrenched away.

Sylvie struggles against his grip, twisting, kicking, wild-eyed, and feral, but he doesn't let go. Her chest heaves. Her hair's tangled, damp with sweat or mist or both. Her eyes dart between us, bright with panic and something sharper.

"I'll let you go," Alder says, voice even, "but I need to know you won't come at us with that blade again."

Her gaze flicks between us, calculating, cautious, weighing options we can't see. Her fingers tighten around the hilt of her dagger. Then, slowly, she nods.

Alder releases her, but his posture stays rigid, his eyes never leaving her.

Sylvie jerks her arm back and rubs her wrist where he held her. Then her attention snaps to him.

"You," she snarls, nostrils flaring, "*blistering asshole*!"

Alder's brows shoot up. "Asshole? You came at Gemma's throat with a knife." He gestures toward me, incredulous. "Forgive me if I thought that warranted a response."

Sylvie's jaw twitches. Her fingers squeeze around the dagger again, the leather-wrapped grip creaking under the force of her hold. Then, abruptly, she turns to me.

"What are you doing here?" she demands. "I thought the two of you had stolen away for a tryst. Yet here I find you, skulking about the woods on an island where you have no rightful business."

"I could ask you the same thing." I cross my arms and tilt my head. "You ran after I called your name. Twice."

Her expression doesn't soften. "And you chased me. Why?"

"Because I was worried. Because I thought—" With a shrug, I throw up my arms. "I don't know, you were doing something nefarious."

"Nefarious? *Me?*" Sylvie scoffs. "Hardly. More likely you feared I'd seen something you wished to keep hidden." Her eyes narrow. "You're the one sneaking around in the shadows."

Alder lets out a breathy chuckle. "That's rich coming from someone hiding in the forest with a dagger."

Sylvie's lips press into a thin line. "I came to find Clara."

The wind rips through the trees, bending the branches and carrying the scent of the forest and the sea.

I swallow, but the words still taste like iron. "Sylvie…" My voice cracks. I try again, softer this time, like gentling my tone might lessen the blow. "Clara's dead."

"I know."

Her words land like a stone. "You know?"

"I found out. I—" Pain cracks across her face, raw and sudden. Her hands tighten into fists at her sides. "I've been looking for her. For her body. I thought—" She cuts herself off, breathing hard. "She deserves a proper burial. Not to be left on this deserted island like she was nothing."

Alder shifts beside me, but before he can speak, Sylvie rounds on him.

"And don't pretend to be innocent in this." Her voice turns to venom. "I heard you speaking with Queen Rothmore."

A ripple of tension rolls through Alder, his entire body locking into place.

I blink, turning to him. "What is she talking about? I thought you were discussing trade deals and our way back home…"

"There are matters within the palace you cannot begin to understand, Gemma." Sylvie's voice drops, fierce and trembling. "If you have any sense, you'll leave. Return home and forget you ever set foot in Cups."

The wind howls through the trees as the sky presses lower, thick with a coming storm.

Sylvie steps closer, her gaze boring into mine. Something in it roots me to the ground, holds me captive. "And you'll run far away from *him*."

She doesn't raise her voice. She doesn't need to. Because in the way she says it—in the steel behind her softness, the fear she's trying to hide—I hear it for what it is.

Not a warning.

A death sentence.

I glance at Alder, expecting him to react, to snap back with a comment that will make everything Sylvie is saying make sense. But he doesn't.

Instead, his fingers flex at his sides. His jaw tightens. His breath is slow and measured. His gaze is distant, calculating, like he's rewriting something in his head—some timeline he thought he could control.

Goose bumps prickle across my arms. Something is wrong. Not just with Sylvie. With him. It thrums in the space between us like a silent alarm.

I glance at him. Then back at Sylvie.

The wrongness of it all coils around my ribs, tightening, waiting.

I could go. I could turn around, walk away, try to figure out my way back home, pretend none of this ever happened.

But I don't.

Because I can't.

Not just because this world makes no sense, not just because I don't know how to fight masked guards or survive in a forest or find my way home. But because as messed up as this is, as confusing, as dangerous, there's something between Alder and me that I can't walk away from.

The gravity of him, the force that holds us together, isn't just attraction. It isn't just survival. It's deeper, woven into my being, stitched into the spaces between my heartbeats.

With him, I don't feel like I'm drowning.

With him, I feel like me.

Sylvie looks my direction one last time, and there's

something in her gaze—grief, regret, resolve. And then she turns.

She runs.

And this time, I let her go.

TWENTY-ONE

The sailboat ride back to the castle's isle is cold and silent. A storm is coming, swallowing the last traces of sunlight in thick, iron-hued clouds. The wind claws through my damp hair, and the tang of salt is thick on my tongue.

Alder doesn't speak, and neither do I. The rhythmic slap of waves against the hull fills the void between us. The longer we drift in silence, the wider it gets.

By the time we reach the docks, the air is buzzing with electricity, the promise of rain hanging above. I leave Alder to deal with the boat, my feet moving before I've fully decided where I'm going.

I just know I need to think, and I can't do that next to him while pretending I don't hear Sylvie's warning circle in my mind, gnawing at the edges of every thought.

If you have any sense, you'll leave. Return home and forget you ever set foot in Cups.

And you'll run far away from him.

I know he's keeping something from me. I know it

with the same certainty that I know the tide will rise and fall. That storms will come whether I'm ready or not. There's something beneath the surface, something he's not saying.

And I'm going to find out what it is.

I won't let him control what I know, what I don't. I need answers. I deserve them.

If we have any chance of salvaging what's been building between us, any hope of a real relationship, he'll be honest. He'll tell me everything. He'll prove he's the man he swore he wants to be.

And if he doesn't? If he lies? Then at least I'll know for sure we're done.

I square my shoulders and exhale, shaking off the lingering chill as I make my way through the castle's winding halls. I push open the heavy wooden door to our room as thunder rumbles through the castle. Wind rattles the windows, rain lashes the glass in sideways sheets, and a flash of lightning paints the world white before it vanishes back into shadow.

I sag back against the door—and immediately regret it.

It swings open behind me, and I yelp as I tumble forward with a graceless thud and crash onto my hands and knees.

Boots appear in my periphery. Followed by a familiar voice, low and amused. "If you wanted to be on your knees, all you had to do was ask."

Alder stands in the doorway, rain-speckled and flushed from the storm. He's wearing a deep maroon velvet jacket he didn't have on the boat, and the effect is…infuriatingly distracting.

"Read the room, Alder." I push myself upright, wincing as my knees protest. "And if you laugh, I'll make sure you regret it."

"Wouldn't dream of it." His lips twitch as he steps into the room and holds out a hand. "We need to go."

I let him help me to my feet, my brow furrowing. "We just got back."

He doesn't hear me—or he doesn't care. His gaze flicks over my damp dress, the salt still clinging to my skin. "What you're wearing will work. Not like you have any other options."

My spine straightens. "Excuse me?"

Before I can object, his hand finds the small of my back, guiding—no, *pushing*—me out the room and into the hall.

"Look, Alder, we need to talk."

His exhale is long. "Fine, but not now. Right now, I need you to come with me."

I cross my arms and plant my feet. "Nice to see we're back to this again. Guess your good moods don't last long. Or is this because of what Sylvie said?"

His expression hardens. "I have more important things to do than try and figure out whatever game you're playing."

My mouth drops open. "Game? Are you serious?" I laugh, but there's no humor in it.

Alder curses under his breath, his patience threadbare. "I'm trying to show you something that will change your life forever, but you would rather throw a fit and act like a child."

Lightning streaks the sky, casting jagged shadows through the corridor as thunder crashes in the distance.

I step to him, toe-to-toe, and tilt my chin up to meet

his narrowed gaze. "I'm not acting like a child. I'm just done with your bullshit. You can't yank me around like I'm wearing one of those little leash backpacks."

"You don't need a leash, sweetheart. You've always followed me willingly."

My retort rises fast—something vicious and biting, something that would feel good in the moment. But I choke it down. This isn't about scoring points. This isn't about name-calling or shouting until one of us folds. The fight that's coming matters more than that.

"Unless this thing you're dragging me to can get me home, I don't care. I don't want to see it. I don't need my life to be forever changed. That's already happened. I need it to go back."

His breath hisses out between clenched teeth. "You don't know the things I've done. The things *I'm doing* to make sure this kingdom survives. To make sure—"

"*This kingdom?*" I shake my head, my voice rising over the wind that batters the castle and rattles the windows in their iron frames. "I get there are things here that need to be dealt with, but this isn't our home!"

Lightning flashes again, illuminating his face in a harsh silver glow. His jaw flexes. His fists clench.

"For fuck's sake, Gemma, you're still doing it," he snarls. "Still clinging to that naive little fantasy where everything works itself out. You think if you just run away from it, it'll fix itself."

My brow furrows. "What are you talking about?"

"This is your Manhattan move all over again. Running like that solved nothing. You thought leaving me was the answer, but it was the worst decision you could've made—and you know it."

Something cold settles in my chest. "You think I regret leaving you?"

"You should," he spits. "I had to fix it. I had to. Because you don't know what's best for you, Gemma. You never have."

My stomach drops.

"When do I get a break? When is it my turn to be done cleaning up your fucking messes?" He laughs, low and bitter. "This small-town, homegrown, sweet-Caroline romance bullshit is not worth it. No matter what my PR team says about making you come back being *the smart risk*."

The cold in my chest turns to ice.

I blink once, twice—and then it clicks. The missing piece. The thread I tugged but never followed.

"Oh my God." My voice is quiet. "You sabotaged my career."

He says nothing. But he doesn't need to.

The moment when he parroted the exact words the publisher used when they let me go—words I never repeated out loud, not to anyone, not even Amanda—I should've known immediately. I would've had I not been distracted by this…world. Wherever it is we are.

He knew. He's always known—because he orchestrated it. Because the moment I walked away from him for good, he made sure I had nowhere else to run.

"You left me," he growls. "What did you think was going to happen? That I'd just sit back while you made a mess of everything I built?"

Rage crashes through me. Hot and immediate. My chest caves around it, my heart a live wire sparking behind my ribs.

"You're unbelievable," I spit. "You lied to me. Manipulated me. And now you're standing here justifying it? Do you have any idea what my career meant to me?"

His jaw clenches.

"You ruined my life," I yell, the words ripping out of me. "You've been the villain in my story this whole time—and I didn't even know it."

And before I can take another breath, he grabs me.

His fingers clamp around my wrist. Heat sears through the fabric of my sleeve. His face is inches from mine, eyes wild and furious, mouth twisted.

"You are so fucking delusional," he hisses. "You think I did this because I have some evil agenda? I did what I had to. You were destroying everything and were too ignorant see it. And then I tried to save you. I tried to give you a soft landing. But you're too damn proud, or, I don't know, too fucking stupid to comprehend the reality of our situation."

"Let me go, Alder," I grind out, wrenching against his hold.

Wind howls down the corridor. Thunder shakes the windows. My heart thrums hard and fast, my breathing shallow as I strain to free myself.

"Stop fighting me," he growls, his other hand latching onto my arm.

"Then stop forcing me!" I shout, fury rising like a tidal wave.

Something cracks. Not in the storm. Not in the stone. In him.

Alder stills. He looks at me then, really looks at me, and whatever rage had consumed him drains in an instant. His grip loosens and his hands fall away.

I stumble back, chest heaving, my wrist throbbing from the pressure of his fingers.

He shakes his head, a hollow laugh breaking free. The storm howls outside, lightning flashing again, catching in his golden hair like a crown of fire.

"It's not just the fake romance PR stunt bullshit that isn't worth it." His voice drops, quiet and cruel. "It's you, Gemma. You're not worth it."

The words cut like glass.

I take a shaky breath and force myself to meet his eyes. My vision blurs, but I refuse to look away. Refuse to cry any more tears because of him.

"How can you say that?" My voice fractures. "After everything we've been through. Was it all an act?" My throat tightens, but I force the words out. "This version of you—you're breaking my heart." I shake my head, blinking hard. "What happened to you?"

He turns halfway, spine rigid, hands flexing at his sides. Then, through gritted teeth, he snarls, "*You* happened to me."

Alder walks away, boots echoing down the corridor like distant thunder. Before he disappears around the corner, he glances back over his shoulder.

"If you still want answers…" A pause. A muscle ticks in his jaw. "Come to the chapel."

He doesn't wait for a response. Doesn't look back again.

And just like that, the storm isn't only outside anymore.

TWENTY-TWO

Rain lashes the stained-glass windows. Thunder murmurs and wind wails, slipping its cold fingers through the cracks in the stone as I slide into the shadows behind a crumbling pillar. I'd followed Alder through the castle, hiding just far enough behind to stay unseen, my footsteps cloaked by the storm. I hadn't wanted him to know I was following—hadn't wanted to give him the satisfaction.

The chapel stands at the heart of the castle. A masterpiece of reverence and ruin, rising from an open courtyard where the storm has full reign. Cracks snake through the marble pillars, thin as veins, and the once-lustrous frescoes high above are peeling, their faded edges curling like shedding skin. The air inside is heavy, humid, thick with the cloying scent of incense, damp stone, and that ever-present metallic tang that clings to everything in this kingdom and rests against my tongue like rust.

Lightning flares, illuminating the stained-glass

murals—waves crashing against jagged cliffs, a hand rising from a dark lake, fingers clenched around a chalice, rain pouring down on bowed heads in a benediction…or a curse.

And there, at the far end of the chapel, carved across the back wall, a serpent.

The sight of it makes my skin crawl. Its stone scales gleam wet in the flickering candlelight, and from its gaping mouth pours a thin stream of water into a basin below. The trickle distorts the candlelight, and, for a moment, memory drowns me—stone, silver, sacrifice. The hidden chamber. Clara's death.

Is this chapel tied to that chamber? Is it the origin of whatever rot slithered into that room with its chanting and magick and blood?

My stomach churns.

Nobles file in, and I scoot tighter into the shadows of the crumbling stone. They're draped in rain-slicked silks and velvets in shades of slate, seafoam, and storm, heads bowed, voices hushed, hands clasped in obedient devotion.

But this isn't reverence. It isn't worship.

It's hungrier.

Fear and fascination braided together. A wide-eyed submission that slides over them, then over me, like oil, slow, insidious, choking.

I scan the crowd, heart starting to race. Velvet shoulders, bowed heads, rain-spattered cloaks. My pulse kicks harder, searching for the familiar line of his jaw, the unmistakable gold of his hair. But he's gone. Lost somewhere in the sea of nobles welling into the pews like a tide.

For a heartbeat, panic flickers. But I squash it just as fast.

It doesn't matter where he is. I don't need Alder to get the answers waiting here. I don't need Alder at all. I can find my own way home.

At the front of the chapel, on a raised dais, stands Queen Rothmore.

She still wears Mackenzie's face. Still has Mackenzie's willowy limbs, that graceful, ballerina-like poise—but the resemblance ends there. Everything that made Mackenzie my friend—warmth, kindness, honesty—is gone.

The queen's eyes gleam like the point of a dagger, sharp and cold. And the moment she opens her mouth, the congregation stills. The silence is instant. Breathless.

"The gods have sent us a sign," Queen Rothmore begins, the crowd hanging on her every word. "For decades, we have labored, prayed, sacrificed. And now, for the first time in generations, we are close—so close—to the return of our kingdom's heart."

Behind her, her empty throne looms, flanked by two others. In one, an elderly woman, spine stiff, lips pursed, gray hair swept up on top of her head and secured with sapphire pins. In the other, King Rothmore sits scowling, his shoulders as tense as mine.

But he isn't watching the queen. He isn't listening. His attention is elsewhere. Victor scans the room, his gaze flitting over corners, faces, shadows with a precision that makes the hairs on the back of my neck stand on end.

What is he looking for? *Who* is he looking for?

"We are not alone in this effort," Queen Rothmore

continues, her voice dropping to a hush that somehow fills the entire chapel. The congregation leans forward, heads tilting like flowers bending toward the sun.

The silence thickens. Something in me coils tighter.

"Our former priest was reclaimed by the gods some time ago and taken to his final reward," Queen Rothmore says smoothly. "We honor Droskyn Vayne. We cherish his memory. However, the Kingdom of Cups does not dwell in the past."

A ripple of agreement rolls through the crowd like a wave as thunder rumbles overhead.

I tense. Alder said the man we saw *was* Droskyn—that he should be dead. And if the Queen isn't lying about Droskyn now…if that *wasn't* him on the island hunting down that girl…

Then who the hell was it?

My question is answered before I can finish formulating it.

"The gods, in their infinite wisdom, have sent us a new herald. Their new messenger. Their angel of restoration."

The crowd shudders, a collective inhale sweeping through them like wind through brittle leaves as white robes emerge from the shadows behind the altar.

The new priest steps forward and into the water pouring from the serpent's mouth. It spills down his body, soaking his white robes until they cling to his tall frame, outlining every corded muscle. The fabric is nearly transparent now, a second skin slicked against him.

Streams slip down the silver mask that hides his face but not his presence. It radiates through the room like a current. The congregation breaks into applause, a wave of sound that fills the chapel and crashes against my ears.

Delphara moves toward him. Her fingers trail along the curve of his mask like she's blessing him. He catches her hands before she can pull away and presses them to his unmoving mask.

She murmurs something I can't hear over the swell of cheers. Her eyes shine as she clutches him like he's the answer to her prayers, to the kingdom's.

The crowd responds in kind. A sound of rapture. Of surrender.

"My steady flock..." The priest's voice warps, distorted by the silver mask that obscures his face. It ripples, wavy and choppy, as though his words are being dragged through deep water.

My blood runs cold.

That voice—

It sounds like the one I heard during the ritual. The one echoing through the chamber while Clara died.

I can't be certain. But my body knows before my mind can catch up.

It's him.

He stands at the altar now, anointed. Worshiped. And all I can do is watch as they devour every word.

"We are called to endure. To sacrifice. To restore. The gods demand it, and we answer."

The rhythm of his voice is hypnotic, his words rising and falling like waves, lulling the congregation into something just shy of trance.

A shiver crawls over my skin, and I tuck my arms against my middle.

I know this cadence. This kind of tone. This kind of

power. Not just from Cups. From home. From childhood. A too-small church in the south. The pungent scent of lilies, thick and sickly sweet. The sour tang of sweat. A preacher with a voice like this one—soft, steady, never needing to shout. His power wasn't in volume. It was in the whispers that slipped under locked doors, in the words that seeped in like dark water, warping thoughts before they fully formed.

This is how it starts. This is how control nests inside devotion.

"We stand at the edge of salvation. At the brink of restoration," the new priest continues, arms spread wide. The storm howls against the glass as if trying to drown him out, but he doesn't falter. His words twist and writhe, a tangle of lies and half-truths that wind their way into the crowd. And the congregation devours it all, their hunger endless.

"The gods have heard our cries! But the path is not easy. It is one paved with sacrifice. With the blood we give freely to the waters that sustain us."

I glance around, half-expecting someone to resist. To rise. To question. But they're all staring at him. Drinking in his words. Cries of *amen* slash the air like a whip, and I'm not in the Kingdom of Cups anymore.

I'm back in that small, creaking church in South Carolina, sitting stiffly next to my mother. The heat of the day pressing in through the windows despite the rattling box fans. The wooden pew beneath me sticking to the backs of my legs. The pastor preaching about the holiness of suffering, about how pain and endurance will bring us closer to God.

My eyes burned with guilt, with confusion and

humiliation. With the weight of sins already committed and those still lurking, unimagined. I didn't always understand what I'd done wrong, only that my body was dangerous simply because it existed. Because I was a girl. A future woman. A vessel of temptation. A burden of shame.

Eventually, I got older and stopped going altogether. My mother called it rebellion. I called it self-preservation.

But now I'm back in church, listening to that same tone, those same promises, dressed up in new words but still the same ol' poison. It drips out of the priest's mouth and swirls around the chapel, a riptide pulling them under. And they don't fight it. They drown.

I don't need to know exactly what gods he's referring to or the kingdom's past to grasp the weight of his sermon, the power he holds. This isn't just belief. It's control. It's a hand wrapped around a throat. Not with violence but possession. The kind that will teach Cups to whisper instead of scream.

The priest's voice rises, smooth as still water, unshaken by the storm raging beyond the chapel walls.

"For generations, our kingdom's heart has been silent. But the path to restoration is before us." His hands spread wide overhead, wet robes dragging against the damp floor.

A murmur moves through the pews. There's the rustle of silks, the shift of weight, quick, darting glances.

The priest tilts his masked face toward the high ceiling.

The congregation seems to hold its breath in collective anticipation, hanging on his every word, caught in the pull of his tide.

"The High Priest before me, Droskyn Vayne, spoke of our great contraptions of steel and iron. He said the machines withered because the apple blossoms faded. Because the royal line lost its power."

My chest tightens. Apple blossoms. The Tower. The dead trees.

"But I have found a way for the trees to bloom once more."

A breathless silence.

"The Rothmore bloodline is not lost," he says, his fingers splaying wide as if reaching for the heavens themselves. "And neither is its power. A great sacrifice is coming. A celebration. A ceremony!"

A gust blows through the chapel, and his damp robes billow like the wings of a carrion bird. The congregation leans in, a sea of eyes shining with devotion, desperation, hunger.

"And it, my loyal flock, will be the last sacrifice the Kingdom of Cups will ever need."

TWENTY-THREE

The rain is merciless. It comes down in sheets, soaking through my dress, plastering the fabric to my skin as I stumble into the courtyard. The chapel's weight still clings to me—its incense, its lies, its worship. My lungs feel too full. My ribs, too tight.

As soon as the final blessing fell from the priest's lips and the nobles surged forward like a river breaking free of its dam—pressing toward the dais, clamoring for closeness, for purpose, for proximity to power—I ran.

Because if I hadn't, I would've screamed.

I press my back to the stone wall beneath one of the crumbling archways and tilt my chin toward the sky, letting the rain wash over me.

Footsteps splash through the puddles behind me.

My hands are fists at my sides. My spine rigid. My heartbeat like a ticking bomb.

I don't turn around. I know it's him.

"So, what did you think?" Alder's voice is rough,

worn thin by the storm and everything that came before it.

I laugh. It's not soft. It's not kind. It's a hollow, bitter sound that scrapes out of my throat like it's been lodged there for years.

"What did I think?" I echo, still facing the rain, still refusing to give him the dignity of eye contact. "I think I just watched a kingdom bow to a murderer and call it salvation."

He doesn't respond. Not right away.

The silence stretches, sharp and tense, broken only by the slosh of his footsteps closing in.

Finally, I turn.

He's beautiful in the way villains always are—wet hair clinging to his forehead, storm light catching on his cheekbones, eyes dark with something that used to look like love and now looks like possession. His maroon velvet jacket is soaked through, black with water, molding to the cut of his shoulders, the lines of his arms.

"You told me you were trying to get us home," I say, my voice barely above the rain. "All those meetings, all that posturing... You made it sound like you had everything handled."

"I do."

"No, you don't, Alder." My voice breaks open, sharp and rising. "If you did, you wouldn't have wanted me to follow you to a sermon led by a murderer." I swipe rain from my face with the back of my hand, breath hitching. "I don't know what the point was, but it wasn't anything that would get us home."

"I wanted you to come so you'd understand what we're up against," he says. "You needed to see the power we're dealing with. The control they have. The kind of belief they're feeding. So you'd stop dreaming about escape like it's a door we can just walk through," he snaps. "So you'd see that surviving here doesn't come from wishing for home. It comes from learning how to play the game."

I take a step back, fury curling tight beneath my skin. "You think I don't understand? That I haven't seen enough to know there is dangerous shit going on here?"

"I am protecting you."

"Stop lying!" The words tear from my throat like lightning. "You're protecting yourself. You want me to believe you're the only thing standing between me and disaster. And I did. God help me, I did. I believed you. I thought you were the way out, but—"

"No, Gemma. You still don't get it. There was never going to be a way home."

The words hit like a slap. I blink, stunned, the rain blurring the edges of him as if the storm itself wants to erase him from my life.

"I told you what you needed to hear," he continues, stepping closer, the rain sliding down his face, slicking his hair to his temples. "Because you weren't ready to hear the truth. You still aren't."

"What truth?" I breathe.

"That this"—he gestures to the castle, the chapel behind us, the drenched stone courtyard glowing silver with lightning flashes—"is the plan. This kingdom, this power, this future. There is no South Carolina anymore."

I stagger backward, the ground seeming to tilt beneath my feet. "You said—"

"I said what you needed me to say so you'd let me

do what I had to," he bites out, no softness left. "Because if you knew I'd made this choice for us, you would have fought me. And I couldn't have you messing this up for me like you did back home."

I blink against the rain, against the sting of betrayal. My pulse thunders in my ears, drowning everything but the terrible, inevitable truth.

"Oh my God," I breathe. "How could I be so naïve?" I laugh, but it breaks apart halfway out of my mouth. "You were never trying to escape Towerfall. You were always going to stay."

His lips part, but I hold up a trembling hand.

"Don't."

His voice dips, gentle now, soft like his manipulation always is. "For us, Gemma."

"Fuck off, Alder!" My voice rises again, cracking at the edges. "Don't you dare make this about us. You're carving out a place for yourself here, building a life in this kingdom, playing politics while I've been running around trying to survive it."

"Sweetheart—"

"Were you ever going to tell me?" I demand. "Or were you going to keep stringing me along with half-truths and sweet little moments until I forgot what I wanted altogether?"

The rain continues to fall, pooling in the space between us.

"You know what's pathetic?" I whisper. "I let you lead. I let you steer our whole relationship because it was easier—because you always seemed like you knew what you were doing, like you had a plan." I shake my head, my breath ragged. "But it wasn't easier. Letting you lead landed me here. In a strange kingdom, in a soaking wet dress, standing in front of a man who lied to me and ruined my life."

He flinches, barely.

"Actually no," I say, voice steeling. "I'm not giving you that kind of power. I made those choices. And, I'm proud of them. Because they did bring me here. To the truth about you. About me."

I take a shaky breath. "Without that tarot card, without this place, I would've spent my whole life thinking I was weak. That I needed someone like you to shape me. But I don't. I never did."

The rain streaks down my cheeks, tears I refuse to cry.

"But tell me, Alder. Just one thing. *Why?* Why stay here? In a Renaissance kingdom with no electricity, no hospitals, no modern anything? Why abandon a life of power and money and control for this?"

For a second, he doesn't answer. Then he straightens.

"Because, if you saw it like I do, you would know this kingdom could be paradise. And that is exactly what I deserve."

He steps forward, his voice darkening, deepening. "After everything I've done—for politicians, for corporate royalty, for billionaires who couldn't wipe their own asses without a fixer—I earned this. I pulled the strings. Cleaned up the messes. Protected people who didn't deserve it. I built empires, and the second things got complicated, they turned their backs on me."

He looks at me then, his gaze wild. "*You* turned your back on me."

My mouth opens, but no sound comes.

"I needed you," he says, and it's the most honest thing he's ever admitted. "When you left, everything unraveled. The company. The board. The press. I was going to be indicted, Gemma. For fraud. For wiretapping. For things no one was ever supposed to tie to me."

"And what?" I whisper. "You thought if you brought home your sweet, small-town ex, it would all just...go away?"

"You made people believe in me," he says quietly. "Even when I didn't deserve it."

"Was I always just a PR move?" My voice cracks. "Have the past ten years meant anything to you?"

His silence is a confession.

"God," I whisper. "You are so much worse than I thought."

Lightning cracks overhead, and somewhere in the distance, the chapel doors creak open.

"Lord Lockhart!" The queen's voice cuts across the courtyard, sharp and clear through the storm.

He stiffens.

Her silhouette appears in the archway—framed by candlelight, shrouded in shadow, her silver cloak snapping in the wind.

"You should go," I say, nodding toward the chapel. "Your crown is calling."

He hesitates. Just for a breath. Then he turns and walks away. Back to her. Back to the kingdom he's chosen. Back to everything I now know he was never planning to leave.

TWENTY-FOUR

The storm fades, but it leaves behind ruin—emotional if not physical.

I stepped out of the courtyard, away from the stone halls that echo with power and betrayal. Now, the castle looms behind me, its dark towers jagged against a sky washed clean by rain and studded with cold, indifferent stars.

God, if I could leave this kingdom entirely, I would. I'd carve a door into the sky and walk through it without looking back.

The path softens as I descend, the harsh cliffs giving way to gentler curves where waves kiss the shoreline with quiet insistence. The air is different here—salt-tinged, threaded with the scent of wet pine and earth.

My body moves without thought, as if it knows where to go even when my mind doesn't. And when I look up to see the small dock nestled at the edge of the moat, something in me splinters.

There, tethered to the worn wood, is the sailboat.

It rocks gently in the water like it's been waiting for me. Like it remembers.

The sight of it punches through me—grief and memory crashing together in my chest. The wind in my hair. His laughter. Strawberries and honey. The moment I let myself believe I was seen. That my heart was safe.

I hesitate at the edge of the dock, breath clouding in the cool night air. I take a tentative step as if I can walk backward through time, and the wood creaks softly beneath my feet.

"You shouldn't be out in weather like this."

I turn, breath trapped in my throat.

Alder leans against the sailboat. He's perfectly dry. A soft white tunic clings to his chest, tucked into black breeches that look entirely untouched by the storm. Moonlight brushes the edges of his golden hair, and in his hand, a knife gleams as he slices a pear, slowly, methodically, eating piece by piece with devastating calm.

He's too perfect to be real, and he can't be.

Because I left Alder at the chapel.

For a moment, I wonder if I did step back in time. Back to earlier today, before we left for our picnic. Because this doesn't make sense.

Then again, nothing has for days. Not waking up on the dock. Not being in this world. Not the machine. Not the Tower.

So maybe this is just one more impossible thing in a long line of impossible things.

The silver water ripples behind him, the gentle lap of waves against the hull the only sound in the thick silence stretching between us.

I can't move. Can't speak. My mind lurches, scrambling to reconcile the impossible.

"You—" My voice fractures, thin and trembling, barely able to carry the weight of the question forming behind it.

His lips curve into a tired half smile. "Me."

I shuffle backward, my body acting on instinct, every nerve screaming at me to run. But I don't. I can't. Not yet.

First, I need answers.

My breath comes faster, uneven. "No." I shake my head. "No, you're not—you can't be— You're in the chapel with the queen, and the nobles, and the…the…" My voice pitches higher, the words tumbling too quick, desperate. "You can't be here. It's not possible."

But he doesn't deny it. He doesn't move. Just watches me, his face cast in shadows beneath the moon's watery glow.

I retreat another step.

"How are you down here?" My voice quivers, barely audible over the rush of the waves. "How did you—"

The answer crashes through my skull before I can even finish.

This isn't Alder.

Not the Alder I know.

Not the Alder I left back at the chapel.

The man before me exhales slowly, like he's giving me a moment.

And then, finally—softly—he says the words that steal every trace of warmth from my body.

"I'm not him. I'm not Alder."

A gasp scrapes the back of my throat. The air around me stills.

"No," I whisper, the denial automatic. I shake my head as if I can physically push the idea away. "No, that doesn't make sense. That's not— It's not possible."

He doesn't argue. He just holds my gaze like he's waiting for me to catch up.

I try to force the pieces apart, but they continue to slide together, clicking into place with horrifying clarity.

The way he was on the island—warm, kind, soft in a way Alder never has been. The way he steadied me on the boat, laughed with me, made the world feel soft and manageable for the first time in what felt like forever.

And then the Alder I've always known—calculating, cold, manipulative. The man who crushed my trust, who ruined my life like it was nothing.

Not two sides of the same coin.

Two different coins altogether.

My chest tightens. The world tilts. I grip the dock's wooden railing as the truth crashes over me.

This kingdom has been full of faces I recognize but don't truly know. Mackenzie's face worn by a queen who's nothing like her. Sylvie, her red hair and freckles identical to Elsie's. This world is a mirror, a parallel universe full of people I've seen before, echoes of lives from my world.

And now, standing in front of me, is the cruelest reflection of all.

I shake my head again, harder this time. My breath whooshes from my lungs like I've been hit, and my fingers ache from gripping the railing so tightly.

"Gemma..." he says softly.

"How?" I manage to say, my voice a dry rasp in my

throat. "How is this possible? How did I not see it? *How do you know my name?*"

He sets down the knife and the half-eaten pear and steps off the boat onto the dock.

I want to run. I want to scream. But my mind won't send the commands to my limbs. It's spinning too fast, unraveling everything I thought I knew.

"I've been watching you," he says gently. "Since the forest. Since the first morning you arrived and you went in my carriage, with my guards, with a man who looked exactly like me. I thought…I thought it would be easier to—"

"Easier?" I snap, voice trembling with fury and something rawer, something closer to grief. "It doesn't seem to matter how many versions of you there are. You're all liars."

Tears sting the corners of my eyes, but I blink them away. I won't cry. Not for any version of him.

His gaze doesn't falter, but it shifts—turns sorrowful, maybe. Or is maybe tinged with shame. I don't care.

The truth is here now, staring back at me. Two men. Two versions. Two pieces of a puzzle I didn't know I was trying to solve.

"You're the Lord Lockhart everyone keeps talking about. The Lord Lockhart everyone assumes Alder is."

He nods. "I am."

"Of course you are," I whisper.

"Lord *Alderic* Lockhart." His name is a falling star, burning through the dark. "Former ruler of the Kingdom of Pentacles. Invited to Cups to discuss trade alliances and…" He shakes his head, his gaze dropping to his feet. "None of that matters anymore."

"You're the one I saw in the forest. You were naked and—" I gasp. "The henhouse. And this boat. The island. The machine after that woman—after she—"

"You were hurt," he says quickly, stepping forward. "I couldn't leave you—"

"So you whisked me away?" I spit. "Kissed me? Tucked me into bed after I passed out like some twisted fairy tale?"

"No, I found—"

"Shut up." I drag my hands through my wet hair, every inch of my skin buzzing with betrayal. "I knew it. I knew it in the forest after I first woke up here. You were different. Warmer. Softer. Too good to be true."

I press the heels of my hands against my eyes, but it does nothing to quiet the tempest inside me.

"I ignored it. I told myself I was being paranoid. That it was just trauma, stress, displacement—whatever the fuck people like to call it when a woman's gut screams and she chooses not to listen."

My breath hitches. "So I did what I always do. I stuffed it down. I followed Alder. I tried to be reasonable."

I look up at him. Moonlight spills over his body, tracing every edge in soft silver. He looks like a fallen angel. And it makes me want to scream.

"All those moments I thought we were building something…" My voice fractures, fragile and splintering. "Do you have any idea how much that hurts? Did you even think about me at all?"

His head snaps up at that, his blue eyes locking onto mine.

"Gemma," he says, and my name on his lips is so full of emotion it makes my chest ache. "You've been the only thing I've thought about since the moment you came upon me in the woods." His voice deepens, and he takes a step closer, the dock shifting beneath his weight. "Everything I've done in this kingdom—*everything*—has been because of you."

I clench my jaw, anger rising like a shield. "Don't. Don't try to make this about me."

"But it is. It's always been about you." His voice is raw, earnest, desperate. "I should be in the castle. In meetings. Fulfilling the duties I was summoned to perform. But I'm not. I'm here. Living on this boat. Waiting for a moment like this. For a moment with you."

My lungs squeeze, and tears press hot against my eyes. "You lied to me."

"I know," he says, not flinching. "And I won't stop you from being angry. I deserve that. But I won't lie to you again."

He presses a hand to his chest, like he's trying to hold himself together. "I've been adrift for so long, Gemma. My whole life I've been a tool for other people's gain. A pawn, a purse, a weapon. But the moment I saw you—" Alderic's voice breaks slightly, and that rough edge slices through me. "Something in me shifted. I wasn't just surviving or serving or existing. I *wanted* something for myself. I *felt* something real. For the first time in my life, I was just…me."

The words linger between us, warm and devastating. He's standing there, baring his soul, and I can feel the pull between us, as undeniable and scorching as fire itself. It's a thread of heat that winds through the air, connecting us in a way that feels ancient, fated, like our souls were forged from the same flame and are only complete when they're together. The way he looks at me, like I'm something sacred, like I'm the answer to every question he's ever asked—the weight of it nearly brings me to my knees.

But fire isn't just warmth and light. It consumes. It devours.

I take another step back, the distance between us both a relief and an ache. No matter how far I move, the pull doesn't lessen. It's still there, burning between us, tethering me to him with an intensity that feels like it will either save me or destroy me.

But the pain of betrayal pulses just as fiercely. It's a wound too fresh, too deep, to ignore. His words may ignite something inside me, but they can't erase the truth of what he's done.

Alderic reaches into his pocket and pulls something out.

The tarot card.

The one from the cake pull. The one I lost in the woods on the day he and I met.

My heart trips.

He holds it up between us, the intricate artwork catching the moonlight. The Lovers. Their entwined bodies shimmer faintly, magick still clinging to the edges like dew. Their connection is obvious, undeniable, fated.

"This is us," he says softly, his voice gentle now, careful. "This card brought you here. It wasn't chance, Gemma. It was meant to find you. To find us."

I shake my head, breath catching. "No. Don't do that."

"It's the truth."

"No," I whisper. "It's just a card."

"It's everything," he says, stepping forward.

"You know it. You've felt it. You believe in magick now—how could you not? You've seen it. And you know this wasn't random. You dropping it where we met, that wasn't coincidence. That was the Tower drawing us together."

I cross my arms over my damp dress. "You're twisting this. You're trying to make it into some grand love story, but it's not."

His jaw tightens. "It is a love story. You just don't want to admit it."

"No," I snap. "It's betrayal. It's manipulation. It's lies stacked on lies stacked on even more lies. You and Alder—you both made me feel something real only to rip it out from under me."

He flinches, but I don't stop.

"You don't get to stand here and rewrite everything as some fated-mates romance just because it makes you feel better."

"I'm not rewriting it," he says, voice rising. "I'm telling you what is. This card—The Lovers—is not only about love. It's about duality. Choice. A union that alters the path of everything around it. That's what this is, Gemma. Us. I've seen this before. Back in Pentacles with The Empress and The Hermit. Only after they succeeded in healing the kingdom did the Tower release them. They told me more would come to heal the realm. I didn't think it would be us. You. Me. This card found you because you're the key."

His voice grows more urgent, more insistent, tumbling over itself with conviction.

"The Tower. The island. The machine we found. The gears turning, everything starting up again, it all began when you and I arrived. Delphara thinks it's Alder, that it's some prophecy fulfilled, a sign from the gods. But she is wrong. It's not him. It's you. *It's us*."

My thoughts churn, trying to make sense of it. The magick. The machine. The way the Tower revealed itself to us. How it all came alive around us.

And still, I shake my head. Because none of it excuses the lies.

"The Kingdom of Cups is dying, Gemma. Towerfall itself is dying, and if we don't—"

"Stop."

He blinks, startled, his urgency faltering, caught off guard by the edge in my voice.

"If what you're saying is true…" He opens his mouth to respond, but I don't let him. "And I'm not saying it's not. But I wasn't brought here to fall in love." The words scrape out past the lump in my throat.

He stills.

A gust of wind rolls off the water, sharp with salt and the ghost of rain. And in the space between us, the card flutters in his hand like a dying flame.

"Gemma—" My name is a prayer, a plea, a broken thing falling from his lips.

And I'm breaking too.

Because yes—I believe in magick. I believe that card brought me here. I believe there's something bigger happening, something ancient and wild that's been weaving itself into my life without permission.

But this is not our love story.

"There's a lot here that needs to be fixed," I say, my voice steadier now, stronger for the pain beneath it. "And I will do what I have to do to get back home. To make it right. But whatever this is"—I motion between us, a trembling hand slicing the air—"it's not the answer."

I turn and walk away.

The dock creaks beneath my steps. The breeze bites at my skin. The tears come hot and unrelenting, blurring the world as they streak down my cheeks.

I don't wipe them away, and I don't look back.

TWENTY-FIVE

The castle kitchens are separate from the gilded lies of the palace above. Down here, the air feels heavier but somehow cleaner—like the truth is allowed to live in the cracks between the stone. It's the only place that feels remotely safe to me now. Maybe it's the warmth that lingers in the hearth's low-burning embers. Or maybe it's the people who work here, the ones who truly keep the kingdom running, who don't have the luxury of deception. There's no room for secrets when hands are stiff from kneading dough, when bodies ache from hours over a fire.

Unlike the nobles, they don't waste time pretending.

I wish I could say the same for myself.

I came here instead of returning to my room. Now that I know every bit of the truth, I can't look at Alder. He was always the man I feared he was, ruin wrapped in a beautiful smile. And Alderic, his counterpart on the boat, the man I let in, I'm not sure he's any better. Not really.

The kitchens are quiet at this hour, the usual clatter of pots and barked orders replaced by an expectant stillness. The dwindling fire casts ribbons of orange light across the stone floor. The scents of flour and rosemary still linger, mingling with the faint spice of clove. The air is heavy with the ghost of heat and the quiet hum of something waiting.

My gaze drifts over the empty counters and the neat stacks of wooden bowls left to dry by the basin. So much has unraveled, but the threads are still tangled, looping back on themselves in ways I don't yet understand.

But this is what I do know.

I turn chaos into clarity. I've managed national campaigns with a thousand moving parts, juggled bestselling authors with last-minute demands, sold books I hadn't even read off a two-line pitch. I've wrangled book tours, pre-order giveaways, launch strategies, influencer roundups, TikTok reveals. I've taken disasters and turned them into five-figure launch weeks. I've made magick out of mess.

And I can do it again.

"Okay, Gemma, think." I exhale and tuck my damp hair behind my ears. "What do you actually know?"

I square my shoulders and start mentally storyboarding the path forward, the way I would in a pitch meeting for a book with an unclear audience.

Step One: What do I know?

I know the Tower is connected to whatever's going on—and to me. I know Clara's dead. I know another girl has been taken. I know the queen and her new priest are killing women. And I know, with the final sacrifice the priest mentioned in his sermon, that I'm running out of time.

Step Two: Identify potential.

Delphara: Villain. Power-hungry. Dangerous.

Priest: Delphara's weapon. Identity unknown. Definitely a monster.

Alder: Manipulative liar.

Alderic: Complicated. Not off the hook. But… maybe not the enemy.

Sylvie: Cautious, capable. She knows more than she lets on. I can work with her.

The other women working in the castle: They've been surviving this place longer than I've been breathing its air. They'll help me. If I can convince them to trust me.

Step Three: Weigh the risks.

If I can't stop this, more women will die. The kingdom will collapse—or worse, become something even darker than it already is. And I'll never get back home.

Step Four: Craft the strategy. Execute the plan. Fix everything.

"Shit."

A muffled shout cuts through my brainstorming session, shattering the quiet like a dropped glass.

I go still, breath caught, heart slamming against my ribs.

The sound doesn't come again, but I know what I heard.

And I'm done pretending things away. Done rationalizing the strange or brushing aside what I feel in my gut. I've ignored too many instincts since stepping into this world. Looked away from too many truths.

Not this time.

My eyes sweep the room. I move to the hearth,

fingers grazing the worn mantel until they close around a thick pillar candle nestled in a silver holder. It's heavy in my hands, the metal cool against my skin as I crouch beside the embers and coax the dying flames toward the wick. It catches on the second try.

Faint, flickering light pushes back against the dark. Shadows slither across the stone walls, darting through the gaps between counters and cupboards like things with teeth.

Another shout—louder this time. A single word too muffled to understand. But I know what fear sounds like.

My pulse spikes. I tighten my grip around the candleholder, and the flame wavers as I move toward the pantry.

The larder is cavernous, carved deep into the bones of the castle. Shelves stretch to the ceiling, heavy with jars of amber and ruby colored preserves that catch the candlelight like jewels in a dragon's hoard. Burlap sacks of grain are stacked in neat rows, their rough edges softened by dustings of flour. Bundles of drying herbs are strung from the rafters, their earthy scents mixing with the brine of cured meats hanging on iron hooks.

The air is colder here. My breath fogs in the low light as I press deeper into the room, the candle's flame trembling with each step.

The shouting has stopped, but the silence it leaves behind is worse.

I move carefully toward the back of the pantry, where my candle throws just enough light to illuminate bare stone walls. And a seam in the stone.

I move closer, holding my breath. A golden glint slices vertically down the stone, thin as a blade. I press my palm against it and feel it—a groove, almost imperceptible, like the hidden switch in the frame of the painting. A crack in the castle that leads to something secret.

The wall shifts beneath my hand, and the panel moves with a soft grind, stone scraping against stone, revealing a narrow passage.

A rush of cold air spills out. Beyond, a spiral staircase winds into the dark. Oil lamps hang from the low ceiling at irregular intervals, their pale flames throwing long, nervous shadows.

I glance back. The kitchen remains silent. No one is coming to save me. I have to do that myself.

I blow out the candle and set it on a shelf. Then I suck in a breath, brace my shoulders, and squeeze through the narrow gap.

The panel slides shut behind me with a quiet click, sealing me in with the cold and the dank.

The voices are clearer now. Low. Urgent.

I hesitate, my fingers tightening into fists at my side, but I can't lurk in the shadows or wait for answers to fall into my lap. That's what I've been doing, and it's not working out. Instead, I descend the stairs with a steady breath and a clear purpose.

The cold intensifies with each step, curling around my sodden slippers and biting through my damp gown. The flickering lanterns overhead do little to banish the dark, but my eyes have adjusted and I no longer need the flames to see clearly.

The stairway opens into a wide, low-ceilinged chamber. The air is sharp with salt and smoke. The temperature drops further here, the cold clinging to the walls, seeping into the wooden beams overhead. To the left, a row of shelves gives way to heavy barrels and stacks of sealed crates. A collection of dusty wine bottles line one wall, their corks sealed with thick, dark wax. A single lantern flickers on a hook, illuminating a rack of cured meats hanging near the back wall.

But it's the women gathered around a central table, its surface strewn with maps, ledgers, and loose pages, that draw my focus.

Sylvie. Bernice. Castle maids. Noblewomen with their daughters who I recognize from the chapel, dutifully seated beside their husbands. The lines that divide these women above don't exist down here.

The women startle when they notice me—hands flying to chests, chairs scraping, whispers sharpening into alarm. One of the noblewomen steps in front of her daughter like a shield, while another grips a rusted meat hook from the wall.

"How did you find this place?" Bernice demands, eyes narrowing. "Who sent you?"

Sylvie doesn't wait for an answer. "Lord Lockhart sent you, didn't he, on behalf of Queen Rothmore—"

"Or her filthy priest." Another cuts in.

Sylvie resumes, "You found this place for them."

"No," I say quickly, hands raised, palms out. "I wasn't sent here. I didn't even know this room existed until I heard shouting."

The oldest woman rises slowly, her presence commanding even in silence. She looks familiar. She sat next to the Queen's empty seat during the sermon. A trusted ally. Or so I had thought. "You expect us to believe that you, an outsider, a stranger, simply happened upon our only sanctuary?"

Panic ripples through the chamber. A few of the younger women back toward the far wall. One of the older noblewomen whispers, "We need to move. If they know we're here, that we've been traitors to the throne, we shall be next."

Bernice slams her hand down on the table. "We are not traitors! Loyalty to the throne is not loyalty to a person, no matter how powerful. It's allegiance to the people. To this kingdom. Delphara Rothmore is the traitor."

"I'm not here to harm you or spy on you," I add, holding their wary stares. "I'm here because the Tower brought me."

Sylvie folds her arms tightly across her chest. "How have you seen it?" she demands, suspicion curling in her voice. "The tower vanished. Faded from the land, from records, long ago."

I swallow, my voice low. "When I was on the island it...appeared. Covered with moss and dead branches, just waiting to be seen again. Inside, there's a machine. It's huge and motionless, but not dead. It's dormant—like it's holding its breath."

I don't mention the Lovers card. I don't mention Alderic. I'm not sure what they mean. Not the card, not him, not the way I felt when the Tower opened its door like it had always known I was coming or the way being with Alderic made me feel like I was finally finding myself.

But there's no more waiting for men with secrets and power to save me, or lead me, or tell me what to do. I'm done with that.

"Bernice, I know you don't want to believe in magick, but it's out there. It's in this kingdom."

Bernice's expression turns to ice. "Magick is outlawed. Magick is dead."

I square my shoulders. "Magick brought me here. The Tower brought me here."

The tension doesn't dissolve, but it hesitates, shifts, curiosity prickling beneath suspicion.

"During the priest's sermon, he spoke about a great sacrifice," I continue, stepping closer to the table. "And I don't know how to explain exactly why I feel this way, but I think it's connected to the Tower. To the machine. To whatever's waking up in this kingdom."

The words taste like certainty. Like truth.

"And if I'm right, then we're running out of time."

The old woman exhales slowly and sinks back into her chair. Candlelight flickers across the deep lines of her face, etching shadows beneath her sharp, knowing eyes.

"When I was a girl," she says, "the machines ran on their own. We never questioned why. The royal family flourished. The kingdom prospered. Life was gilded, effortless."

"Until it stopped," another woman finishes. She's younger, but her voice is just as tight. "One day, without warning, the machines went quiet."

The old woman nods grimly. "And when our king and queen passed, their son Victor took the throne. He was young, foolish. He sulked and drank and wished for his father's grandeur. He was too busy pitying himself to notice that his new wife had taken hold of the kingdom."

"She turned to prayer to heal Cups," the woman still clutching the meat hook adds.

The old woman scoffs. "Delphara's answer was Droskyn. Her only tie to the land she left behind."

A shudder moves through the gathered women. The daughters inch closer to their mothers, drawn toward the warmth of something protective, something that still stands between them and whatever is coming.

"She claimed her priest had communed with the gods. That they were angry. That the machines' silence was a divine punishment. That they demanded renewed faith and allegiance—not just to them, but to her, to Droskyn, to Cups."

A bitter sting of recognition lances through me. I know these words. I've heard them before, in a different place, in a different kind of sermon. But the message is the same: power belongs to those who take it, and suffering is the price everyone else must pay.

"He claimed that the gods demanded proof of our loyalty," says a sharp-faced noblewoman near the wine racks.

"And when the first girl vanished, the machines roared back to life." The older noblewoman's voice turns flat, matter of fact, as if dulling the edges of a horror too unbearable to hold.

"Let me guess," I say, my heart pounding so violently I can feel it in my teeth. "Delphara and Droskyn claimed it was a miracle. Proof of divine favor."

The old woman lifts her chin. "But the machines did not require blood before. And what kind of gods reward the slaying of innocents?"

"More women went missing before we could stop him," another noblewoman says tightly as she reaches out and grips the older woman's hand. "But we did stop him."

"We poisoned Droskyn Vayne." The eldest woman's

words land with the weight of a gravestone. "We thought it was over. Without Droskyn, the Queen lost her grip on the magick he funneled into her. The machines fell silent again."

"And we believed we had done enough," the other noblewoman continues. "But we were wrong."

"She suddenly found someone new," Sylvie murmurs. "Not only loyal—powerful."

The old woman nods, slowly. "And worse. More strategic, more careful. Even less concerned with who we are as people."

A chill scrapes across my skin.

But even through the fear, something sharp and certain clicks into place.

"With your help," I say slowly, "I think I can finish what you started."

Bernice arches a brow. "And how do you propose to do that?"

"Delphara believes blood is the price of power," I say. "That sacrifice fuels the machine. But she's wrong. I've seen it. I've touched it. It doesn't need blood to work."

Sylvie crosses her arms. "Then what does it need?"

The answer rises unbidden, heavy, icy. I don't want it to be true, but every instinct screams that it is.

I swallow hard. "It needs the Lovers."

TWENTY-SIX

The next morning, I find Alderic where I always seem to—brooding on the deck of his sailboat like some exiled prince in a tragic love story. He's staring out over the water, shirt slightly rumpled, hair still damp from a rinse in the sea. It's obnoxiously poetic.

He looks up when he hears my footsteps, and that ruinously handsome face softens when he sees me, like I'm the very thing he's been waiting for.

Something inside me tightens. I hate that look. Or I want to climb into it—maybe both. The sunlight gilds his damp hair, his half-unbuttoned shirt clinging in just the right places, and I have to force myself not to stare at the sharp V of exposed skin.

Don't do it, Gemma. Don't remember how his mouth felt. How his hands felt. You are here for a reason, and how good he looks has nothing to do with it.

"I have a plan," I announce, climbing aboard without waiting for an invitation.

Alderic's brows lift. "Hello to you too."

"Don't get excited," I say, brushing past him and ignoring the way his presence makes my nerve endings buzz. "You're still on my shit list."

He leans against the mast, arms crossed, looking far too handsome for someone I'm absolutely still furious with. "Are you sure you don't mean the *Men I'd Throttle If They Weren't So Devastatingly Attractive* list?"

"You wish," I mutter.

"I do. In fact, I've been imagining the throttling."

His eyes rake over me when he says it. Not crude. Not even cocky. Just a low, smoldering promise that pools heat low in my stomach.

And God help me, my body answers. A flush creeps up my throat, hot and traitorous.

He crosses the space between us, and before I can stop him, his fingers brush a strand of hair behind my ear in a touch that feels like it knows every version of me—the furious one, the afraid one, the one who still remembers how he tasted.

I do everything in my power not to lean into him.

The moment stretches, tight and trembling, his face so close, the warmth of his breath blowing against my cheek. My lips part before I realize they have, my whole body tilted toward him like a compass needle seeking north.

I'm going to kiss him.

I want to kiss him.

I want to fall, just for a second, into the deliciousness of him.

But my rational brain slices through the haze like cold steel.

"No." The word leaves my mouth too quickly. I take a step back and grip the ropes along the bow. "We're not doing this."

"Gemma, I just—"

"I need your help," I cut in, sharper than I mean to. Work mode. War mode. Anything-but-feelings mode.

"Glad to see I've been promoted from irredeemable liar," Alderic says, that too-handsome mouth tugging into the ghost of a smirk.

My eyes narrow. "This doesn't mean we're good. We're going to work together. Professionally. Cleanly. No more secrets."

"I know."

"You lied to me."

"I know."

"I can't trust you."

Something in his expression flinches. Barely. But I see it.

"Tell me what you need." He doesn't sound hurt. But he doesn't sound not-hurt either.

Good. Let him sit with it.

His smile fades as I lay it out—every sharp-edged piece of the plan. How he, posing as Alder, who's still very much posing as him, will infiltrate Delphara's inner circle. How he'll charm her, fool the priest, and slip into places only Alder has access to. How he'll collect notes, orders, anything we can use to shatter their reign from the inside out.

And how, at the ceremony—before they can kill another girl—we'll reveal everything. In front of the nobles. The court. The people.

"You'll take Alder's place," I finish. "She trusts him.

Likes him. Thinks she can control him. Use that. Say whatever she needs to hear, get what we need. Then we burn the whole damn house down."

Alderic is quiet for a beat too long.

"You're serious," he says finally.

"I've never been more serious in my life." I cross my arms. "You said I have to help this kingdom if I want to get home. That's what I'm doing."

Silence stretches between us, taut as a bowstring.

"You're remarkable," he says quietly. "You know that?"

I roll my eyes. "And you're still not forgiven."

A flicker of a smile. "Right. Logistics, then. You need access to the queen's documents, private quarters, sacred vault of doom..."

"And you'll need time. Time to go through it all before anyone notices." I start pacing the deck, momentum pulsing through my limbs. "Which means I have to distract Alder."

He frowns. "Gemma, that could be dangerous."

"I know him. He's arrogant and smug, and I'm sure he's convinced I'm still halfway in love with him. If I pretend I want his help, if I make it look like I've come crawling back so he can play the hero, he'll bite. He won't see it coming."

Alderic's jaw ticks. "If something goes wrong—"

"He won't hurt me." I glance up. "Not physically, anyway."

The hush that follows is a little too heavy.

"Bernice told me there's a banquet tonight," I say, shifting the subject. "Delphara's making a big show of her new priest. It's perfect. Everyone who matters will be there."

"I'll need one of my outfits he's stolen," Alderic muses, "and a sword. Just in case."

"You're not stabbing anyone."

"I might stab Alder. Lightly."

I shoot him a look. "No stabbing. No improvising. No grand gestures. Get proof and bring it to me."

His grin falters. "And after?"

My throat tightens, and I turn away.

"Gemma—"

"After doesn't matter yet," I say. A lie I wish I could believe. "First, we save the kingdom."

TWENTY-SEVEN

The sun slants through the tall castle windows, gilding the dressing room. Linen shirts and embroidered jackets spill from the open wardrobe like molting feathers as I dig through them, muttering to myself.

Whatever I choose has to be perfect. It has to say, *I'm the same manipulative ass you've come to know and love, and yes, you can totally trust me even though I'm clearly awful.* Because if we're going to pull this off, Alderic has to be believable. He has to become Alder.

Which is ironic since this whole thing started with Alder pretending to be Alderic.

I hold up a double-breasted velvet coat with gold buttons, wrinkle my nose, and toss it aside. I reach for a deep burgundy jacket with gold trim and a high collar when the door creaks open behind me.

"I didn't expect to find you here."

Alder's voice curls through the room like smoke, dark, thick, and uninvited. My spine stiffens before I turn, carefully schooling my expression. The man who thought he owned me, then carved out my heart like it was payment.

He doesn't know it yet, but I'm about to rip the rug out from under him.

I lift the coat from the wardrobe like it's any other garment, not the costume for the lie I'm about to wrap around Alderic's shoulders. "I needed to grab something."

He leans against the doorframe, casual in that carefully sharpened way of his. "For me?" He's so calm. So self-assured. It makes me nauseous.

"For the banquet," I reply coolly, draping the coat over my arm.

A pause. Then a slow, amused smile curves his lips. "I assumed if I asked you to join me, you'd say no out of spite."

I bite the inside of my cheek so hard I taste blood.

Because of course he thinks that. Of course my boundaries, my grief, my gut-punched betrayal couldn't possibly be mine—they must be some petty rebellion. It must be spite. As if my existence revolves around him.

Arrogant, insufferable ass.

"Luckily, I was already informed about the banquet. I'm borrowing your coat to see if someone can fashion a dress before tonight. Something dramatic. Blood red, maybe. Or funeral black."

A flicker of emotion dances across his face—amusement, maybe, but it's chased quickly by curiosity.

He takes a step forward, and I swear the room gets smaller. "And you decided to go rifling through my clothes yourself? You could've sent someone."

They're not your clothes, I think, biting back a scoff.

You're not Lord Lockhart. You're just very good at pretending to be him.

But that's the game I'm playing too, isn't it?

"I could've," I say, lifting a brow. "But then I wouldn't get to see that look on your face when I take what I need without asking."

That gets a real smile—crooked and slow, like it's wrapping around something filthy in his mind. "Careful, sweetheart. You say things like that, and I'll start thinking you enjoy this."

I let the silence linger, feel it crawl up the back of my spine. Then I turn, slowly, and lift my gaze through my lashes like the heroine of a sad, manipulative romance.

I guess that's exactly who I am.

"I was wrong last night. About…everything."

He blinks, then pushes away from the doorframe. "You'll have to be more specific. You've been wrong about a lot of things lately."

A thousand retorts press against my teeth like the edge of a blade. I could slash him open with the truth. But I don't. I swallow the metal, wrap my lies in velvet, and keep going.

"I thought I could do this alone," I say, voice quiet, carefully frayed at the edges. "But I can't. I need you."

He crosses his arms, his expression unreadable. "That's a change in tune."

I look away, chewing the inside of my cheek like I'm trying not to cry instead of trying not to puke. "You've always been there for me. Protected me. And I—" I force a breath, blinking fast like I'm holding back tears. "I took everything for granted. I took *you* for granted."

He's silent, gaze sharp enough to cut through bone.

"Just like that?" he says finally, voice low and skeptical. "You wake up this morning and decide the world's too scary to face alone, so now I'm suddenly the answer?"

Shit.

I swallow, heart skidding in my chest.

For one awful second, I think he's not going to buy it. That he'll call my bluff and walk away, and then all of this—all the risk, all the venom I choked down to pull this off—will be for nothing.

So I do what I always do with him. I act. Only this time, I know from the start that I'm acting. I've spent so long pretending with him, twisting myself into the version he wanted, the one who adored him, needed him… The part is so easy to step into that it's hard for me to understand how I never saw it before.

The only time I've actually felt real is when I'm with the man who looks just like Alder but couldn't be more different.

I blink up at him. "You think I like this? Begging for forgiveness? You think it's easy for me to admit I was wrong?" I take a step closer, as if drawn to him. "But I was. You were right." My voice thickens with desperation. "I can't survive without you."

Alder takes a slow step toward me, eyes gleaming. "Say that again."

I grit my teeth so hard my skull aches. But I make my voice small, cracked. "You were right. I can't survive without you."

"Hmm." He circles me, a shark scenting blood, then laughs softly, but there's steel beneath the sound. "And now you're here to make it right with a few pretty words?"

I offer him a small, trembling smile. "I'm here to ask for your help. I need you to save me like you always do."

His eyes flare with something dark and he steps forward, brushing his knuckles lightly along the curve of my jaw. It's gentle, but it makes my skin crawl. "Then you'd better clean yourself up," he murmurs, thumb ghosting beneath my lower lip. "Wouldn't want the kingdom thinking you've been crying over me."

I laugh, too brightly, too breathily. "Don't flatter yourself."

He leans in, breath warm. "Oh, sweetheart. I don't need to. You're already doing it for me."

Then he turns and disappears into the main room, leaving only the specter of his grin and the wreckage of my nerves in his wake.

A shudder slips down my spine. I need a bath.

My fingers tighten around the coat until the velvet crushes in my grip. I exhale slowly, trying to purge the feeling of him from my skin, from my lungs.

He thinks he won, but he has no idea what's coming.

TWENTY-EIGHT

I slip into the hidden chamber beneath the pantry when no one's looking. My footsteps are silent as I descend the stairs, candlelight flickering across the damp walls.

Alderic is already there, leaning over the table, sleeves rolled, shirt half-unbuttoned, hair mussed from running his hands through it one too many times. A map is spread before him, corners pinned with mismatched cutlery and a chipped porcelain vase of drinking chocolate, still steaming. Beside it is a plate of ripe strawberries, thick cream, torn hunks of bread, aged cheese, and golden honey.

He doesn't look up right away. Which means I get a full, unguarded moment to look at him.

My stomach dips, low and aching, like I've stepped off the edge of something I can't quite see the bottom of. My skin prickles. My mouth dries. He looks…edible. Like every dark, aching thing I've ever wanted. And suddenly, all I can think about is how I need to feel that mouth on my throat, his hands gripping my hips, the weight of his body pressing me down as he—

"Are you mentally undressing me?" Alderic glances up, and that slow, self-satisfied grin spreads across his face like he already knows exactly what I was thinking. Which, unfortunately, he probably does.

My whole body jerks, and my face flames. "I—no," I sputter, flinging the coat out between us like a shield. "I brought your clothes."

His gaze drops lazily to the coat, then back to my flushed cheeks, and I know he's cataloging every detail of my mortification. "You only brought a coat?"

I clear my throat and straighten like I'm presenting a quarterly report instead of resisting the urge to climb him like a tree. "And a shirt," I say, flipping the velvet over my arm to reveal the rumpled linen button-down. "And pants."

His lips twitch. "Just pants? No underthings? How bold of you."

I narrow my eyes. "Do you want your clothes or not?"

He tilts his head, gaze sweeping down to the bundle of fabric, then slowly dragging back up to me with deliberate hunger. "I'd rather there was no fabric between us," he murmurs, "but I suppose this will do."

He takes the bundle, brushing his fingers against mine in the exchange. It's nothing, barely a whisper of contact, but it slides through me like silk pulled slow across bare skin.

We hover there—coat limp in his hands, a current of heat thrumming between us. His eyes drop to my mouth, linger. When they rise again, there's something molten in them, something that dares me to keep pretending I don't want this. Don't want him.

He steps closer. Just an inch. But it's enough to make the air feel thinner, tighter. The warmth of his body spills over me, skimming the exposed line of my collarbone, stealing the breath from my lungs.

I want him.

God, I want him.

Even now, with the memory of his deception still jagged in my chest, with everything he's kept from me still coiled beneath the surface—I want him.

Because there's magick. Because there's the Lovers card. Because from the moment I found him in the woods, naked and endearing and mine without even knowing it, something's been pulling me to him.

Maybe it's magick. Maybe it's destiny. Maybe it's both.

But here, in the eye of the storm, with danger pressing in on all sides and nothing certain beyond the next breath, I want something real—something I choose.

If this is the edge of a cliff, then let me jump knowing I felt something before the fall. Even if it's selfish. Even if it's reckless. Even if it's only for a moment.

He moves closer. Close enough that I feel the tremble in his exhale, the hesitation. Close enough that the world narrows to the shape of him.

His fingers rise slowly, giving me every second to pull away. I don't.

His thumb traces the edge of my cheekbone, a featherlight touch that lands like lightning. My breath stutters in my chest. My pulse kicks, too loud in the quiet.

"Gemma." My name is a raw thing in his mouth.

Not a question. Not a plea. Just a truth he can't keep inside any longer. His gaze finds my lips again, and he exhales. "I may not know how the Tower works or why its magick chose us. Maybe I'll never understand it."

He leans in, forehead brushing mine, our breaths mingling in the narrow space between us.

"But I know this." His voice drops, steadier now, full of something that makes me ache. "Whatever force pulled me to you—whatever split the sky open and set this in motion—I'd let it break me a thousand times over if it meant I'd find you again."

My throat tightens. My heart melts against my ribs.

"I've walked through kingdoms where my name meant everything. I've sat on a throne and felt nothing. I've had riches, power, adoration." His hand finds my mine, wraps gently around it. "And none of it—not a single crown, not a single victory—made me feel alive until I met you."

I'm not breathing. I don't think I can.

"I don't want this because the Tower says I should," he finishes, eyes burning into mine. "I want it because you are the only thing in this entire realm—this world—I can't live without."

I feel the crack form. A hairline fracture through everything I've tried to hold together. The part of me that's been standing guard, that's been clinging to anger and logic and reason—it falters, collapses.

I let out a shaky breath and try for levity, something flippant to counter the way he's made me feel like the center of the universe. "I thought I said no grand gestures."

His lips tip into a smile. "That wasn't a gesture. That was the truth."

And then he leans in, impossibly gentle, impossibly sure, and kisses me like it's the last thing he'll ever do.

And I let him.

Because maybe it is.

His tongue glides along the seam of my lips, teasing, coaxing. His fingers tangle in my hair, threading through the strands with just enough force to tilt my head back.

A soft gasp escapes me, and he takes his opening, his mouth slanting over mine, his tongue sweeping inside, claiming, devouring. Chocolate brushes my tastebuds as he licks into my mouth, the sweetness mixing with something deeper, darker. Something that tastes like home.

A groan rumbles in his throat, vibrating against my lips, and it sends a hot rush straight through me. My nails scrape against his chest, and he shudders, his breath coming faster, rougher.

"You taste like chocolate," I murmur without thinking.

His hands slide down my back, gripping my waist, pressing me flush against him. "Then keep tasting. Until I'm the only flavor you remember."

I don't have time to think before my fingers are fisting in his shirt, and his breath is on my neck. The space between want and ruin has never felt so thin.

He doesn't rush, doesn't demand. Alderic just watches me unravel beneath the weight of my own hunger. And then, like he can hear my every secret thought, he turns toward the platter beside us. His movements are unhurried and sinfully confident as he plucks a strawberry from the plate next to the chocolate. He dips it into the goblet, coating the fruit in thick, molten sweetness, then drags it slowly across my bottom lip.

"Open," he says, his voice rough with want.

My breath catches. Heat coils low in my belly, pulsing between my thighs. I obey, parting my lips, the molten chocolate smearing over my skin.

His gaze burns as he slips the berry into my mouth, his thumb grazing the corner as I close my lips around the fruit.

"Fuck," he breathes. "I didn't think you could look more delicious."

The taste is decadent—rich, dark, sinful. The chocolate curls over my tongue, its warmth spreading through me. I hold his gaze as I take a slow bite, the sweetness bursting between my teeth. A single drop of chocolate slips down my chin, and before I can wipe it away, Alderic leans in and catches it with his tongue.

His moan is low, wrecked.

"Chocolate and you—two of my favorite things together," he breathes, dipping his fingers into the sweet dessert and dragging them across my collarbone.

I shudder, breathless, as he follows the path with his tongue, licking the chocolate from my skin.

Alderic pulls back just enough for me to see his face—his skin flushed, his lips swollen from our kisses, his pupils so wide they swallow the blue of his eyes. He stares at me as if I'm something he was never meant to have but can't bear to let go. As if he's memorizing me, committing every inch of me to his soul, knowing that even eternity wouldn't be enough to satisfy him.

His fingers tremble where they press into my skin, the only sign that he's barely holding himself together. That if I ask for it—if I so much as whisper his name—he will fall apart for me.

His fingers drift over the curve of my hip before skimming lower, gripping me just enough to make me shiver. Then, he plucks another strawberry, dipping it deep into the chocolate, letting it coat the surface before bringing it to my mouth again.

This time, I don't just take the fruit. I lean in and catch the tip between my lips, teasing, before sinking my teeth into the juicy flesh. The noise that slips from Alderic's throat is almost feral.

Before he can say another word, I grab his collar and pull him to me, pressing my mouth to his, letting the flavor spill between us. He doesn't hesitate. His tongue sweeps inside, tasting, devouring.

His grip on me tightens as he walks me backward, his lips never leaving mine, until my back collides with the cold stone wall. The shock of it sends a gasp tumbling from my lips, and he takes advantage, his tongue licking deeper.

His hands slide down my sides, fingers pulling up my dress, spanning my hips before reaching down to grab fistfuls of my thighs. A sharp breath catches in my throat as he lifts me effortlessly, like I weigh nothing at all. My legs wrap around his waist, instinctual, desperate, anchoring myself to him, to the heat of his body against the chilled air, to the press of his hips against mine.

Alderic groans, his mouth finding the curve of my jaw. "It's sweet," he murmurs. "But not as sweet as you."

I chew slowly, chocolate and fruit juice trickling down my throat, and when I swallow, I hold his gaze. "Prove it."

Alderic groans into my mouth as his hands slide beneath me, gripping my ass in his broad palms, fingers digging into me like he never wants to let go. He grinds against my heat, his cock straining against his pants, and a deep, grateful sound rumbles in his chest.

"Gods, Gemma," he rasps, "you feel fucking perfect. All soft, all mine." His fingers knead my skin. "I love knowing there's more of you for me to hold, to worship, to feast upon."

My back arches as Alderic lifts me and carries me to the table, the strength of his arms making me feel weightless. The platter crashes to the floor, forgotten, strawberries rolling across the stone surface. The moment I settle, the fruit beneath me bursts, their juices warm and sticky against my bare thighs, staining the wood, staining me.

His fingers brush over the laces at the back of my corseted dress before he starts to tug them loose. Each pull unspools the tension holding me together, unraveling me stitch by stitch. The fabric softens against my skin as the tightness releases, the corset no longer a barrier between us. He trails his fingers along the undone laces as if savoring the moment before everything is laid bare.

"Tell me to stop," he murmurs, his breath warm against my ear.

"No, Alderic, touch me."

I lift the gown and slide it up and over my head with a slow, teasing roll of my shoulders. The fabric whispers against my skin as I peel it away and toss it onto the floor in a careless heap.

Alderic curses under his breath as his gaze rakes over me. He swallows hard, then exhales, his voice thick with hunger.

"Look at you. The perfect feast." His fingers scoop beneath my thighs, gathering the burst strawberry juice, before sliding up, smearing the sticky red stain across my skin. "And I intend to savor every bite."

I guide his hand to my mouth. My tongue flicks over the tip of his finger, tasting the tart sweetness, tasting him. Then I take him deeper, sucking the juice from his skin, slow and deliberate. My lips seal around him, my tongue swirling over the pad of his finger before releasing it with a soft, wet pop.

"Fuck," he rasps, his voice nearly breaking.

His hands flex against my thighs before gripping them harder and dragging me closer, sliding me to the very edge of the table.

And then his mouth crashes against mine.

It's wild, unrestrained, a claim as much as it is a surrender. He kisses me like he's starving, like he'll die if he doesn't taste me, devour me.

His body presses flush against mine, the thick, insistent weight of him catching perfectly against the slick heat of my bare skin. I gasp into his mouth, the friction sending a shudder rolling through me, heat pooling deep in my core.

I need more.

I tug at his shirt, pulling at the buttons, the fabric bunched in my fists as I fumble in my desperation. He helps me, impatient now, yanking the linen over his head and tossing it carelessly aside.

I drink him in, my breath catching at the sight of him—broad shoulders, sculpted chest, skin flushed with heat. My fingers trace down his abdomen, following the ridges of muscle, feeling the way they flex beneath my touch. And there, cutting across the hard planes of his stomach, is a scar. Its golden hue catches the light as I trail my fingers across the velvety softness.

Alder is attractive. But Alderic—God, Alderic is something else entirely.

"You're beautiful," I whisper, my voice barely audible, my palms flat against his chest, his heart hammering beneath my fingertips.

He cups my face, capturing my lips once more as he rolls his hips, the thick press of him straining against his breeches making me gasp, making me ache.

He reaches for the small pot of thick cream, now knocked over on its side, its contents spilling onto the table in slow, decadent ribbons. His eyes never leave mine as he dips two fingers inside, coating them in the velvety sweetness.

"Hungry?" he murmurs, voice dark, decadent.

"Starving."

His other hand flexes on my thigh as he growls.

I part my lips, and he slides his fingers inside, pressing against my tongue, coating my taste buds in the creamy mixture of milk and sugar and him. I close my lips around him, sucking slowly, my tongue swirling over his skin as I savor every drop.

"Lay back," he commands, his voice rough with desire. "I want to eat my dessert."

I do as he says, sinking back against the table, my body humming with anticipation as I watch him through heavy-lidded eyes.

Alderic scoops up more of the thick cream, dragging two fingers through the luxurious sweetness, letting it drip down his hand.

His gaze meets mine as he hooks my leg and spreads me open.

I gasp as he glides those two fingers slowly over my clit. The cool cream against the heat of my skin sends a shockwave through me. He doesn't stop, doesn't let up, doesn't rush. He moves over me slowly, again and again, spreading the sweetness until I'm writhing beneath his touch, until I'm nothing but desperation and need.

And then his fingers slide inside me. Slow at first. Deep.

A moan claws its way from my throat as he pushes farther, curling them just right, finding that place that makes my vision white out at the edges.

I arch off the table, hips chasing his hand, gasping his name like it's the only word I remember.

He bends down and his mouth is on me. His tongue licks through the mess he's made of me, slow and savoring. Every stroke of his tongue is a praise, every flick a question I answer with a cry.

His fingers press deeper, filling me with a slow, punishing, perfect rhythm, dragging me higher and higher while he continues to worship me with his mouth, his tongue, his teeth.

He devours me like he's starving. Like I'm salvation. Like this is the only thing that's ever mattered.

And when I shatter—when I come so hard I break apart in his hands—he's there to catch every trembling piece.

Alderic pulls his fingers from me slowly, dragging out the sensation, leaving me shuddering, quaking beneath him. My pulse pounds in my ears, shockwaves coursing through me, my body desperate for more even as I lay boneless against the table.

And then—his tongue sweeps over his fingers.

He groans deep in his chest, his eyes hooded as he licks me clean from his skin, savoring every last taste. "Like honey," he rasps, his voice drenched in sin. "So fucking delicious." His tongue flicks over the tip of his finger, his gaze locked onto mine. "The best dessert I've ever had."

Heat caresses my spine at his words, at the way he looks at me. Like he could feast on me forever.

I sit up, still breathless, still feeling the echoes of pleasure thrumming through my limbs. My hands find his chest, tracing down, down, lower. His muscles clench beneath my touch, but he doesn't stop me.

He watches, his pupils dark pools of hunger and need as I undo the laces of his pants, my fingers brushing over the thick length of him, straining against the fabric.

I meet his gaze, lips curving into a wicked smirk. "My turn."

I slide off the table and press my bare skin against his as I descend. My fingers forge a path down the hard planes of his chest and then the soft scar that cuts across his abdomen before my lips replace them.

Alderic groans, a deep, ragged sound as I slide his trousers down his hips. His cock is thick, flushed, a bead of precum glistening at the tip. His breath stutters, fingers flexing at his sides as if he's fighting for control.

But I don't want his control.

I want his surrender.

I press a lingering kiss to the sharp cut of his hip, my hands smoothing up his thighs, over the tension coiled beneath his skin. His muscles twitch under my touch, every part of him strung tight, barely restrained.

"Gemma," he swallows, his fingers finally giving in, tangling in my hair as he strokes his thumb along my temple in a silent plea. "Taste me."

I glance up, meeting his gaze through my lashes. "Oh, I intend to."

Before he can respond, I flick my tongue over the tip of his cock, catching that first drop of him. The taste is salt and heat, heady and rich. His whole body jerks, a sharp inhale punching from his chest. His fingers tighten in my hair, not to guide, not to control—just to hold on.

I take him deeper, hollowing my cheeks, letting the weight of him settle heavy on my tongue. His curses break against the air, desperate, ragged sounds, and God, I want to wreck him. I want to watch him come undone for me the way I came undone for him.

I move slowly, savoring every reaction, the way his abs clench, the way his thighs tense beneath my hands. I run my tongue along the thick vein on the underside of his shaft, tracing every ridge, every part of him that makes him tremble.

His breaths come faster, rougher. "Gemma—fuck—" His voice is hoarse, almost broken, and when I hum around him, taking him deeper, his hips stutter forward, chasing more.

I wrap my fingers around the base of his cock, stroking in time with my mouth, dragging him to the edge. His head tips back, throat bared, his chest heaving, his grip on me turning almost desperate.

I pull off him with a slow, deliberate drag of my tongue, my lips swollen, my breath uneven. His cock twitches, thick and aching, and the sight of him like this sends a pulse between my legs.

Still on my knees, I reach for a strawberry from the scattered pile on the counter, plucking it by the stem. I bring it to my lips, dragging it slowly across them before taking a bite, the juices bursting onto my tongue, dripping in a thin line down my chin.

I catch it with the tip of my finger, sucking it into my mouth.

With a desperate growl, he hauls me back up into his arms, his mouth crashing against mine, tasting fruit and salt on my tongue. His hands are rough, greedy, roaming over my body as he pushes me back against the table.

"I wanted this to be slow," he mutters against my mouth, his hands gripping my thighs, lifting me once more. "I wanted to—"

I drag him down to me, stealing the rest of the sentence from his lips.

There's nothing slow about this.

This is hunger. This is starvation. I am ravenous.

I arch against him, desperate, the heat between us unbearable. The tension coils tighter, every nerve in my body strung so taut I might break apart again before he even takes me. My thighs tremble around his hips, my nails digging into his broad shoulders as he strokes his fingers down my inner thigh, teasing, tracing, dragging out the moment until I'm begging for it.

His fingers glide over my slick folds, parting me, finding me already drenched, aching. He groans, a deep, guttural sound, his forehead pressing against mine as his fingers slide through my wetness. "Gods, Gemma… you're so ready for me."

"Then stop teasing."

Alderic growls low in his throat, gripping my hips, lifting me slightly, just enough to position himself at my entrance. The cool air kisses my fevered skin as he lines himself up, the head of his cock pressing against my wet heat. He holds there, lingering, his fingers flexing against my hips, savoring this moment before surrendering completely to the inevitable pull between us.

"Gemma, you do know we were always meant to find each other, don't you?"

"Were we?" But even as I say the words, I know the truth. "Yes."

I meet his gaze, and the moment I do, he thrusts forward, sinking deep, stretching me inch by inch.

It's not just a joining—it's a claiming, a tethering of something beyond flesh, beyond thought, beyond reason. He fills me completely, a slow, deliberate possession that makes my breath catch, my muscles quiver around him as if recognizing, remembering. As if my body has always known his.

"Gods," he groans, his head dropping back, his fingers tightening around my hips. "You feel—" His words break off into a shuddering breath as he pulls back, just enough to make me whimper, then pushes forward again, harder this time, setting my nerves ablaze.

My back bows, my hands fisting in his hair, dragging his mouth back to mine as he starts to move, thrusting deep, slow, letting me feel every inch of him, every stretch, every exquisite bit of friction that sends pleasure crackling through my veins. The table beneath me quakes with each delicious stroke.

He buries his face against my neck, panting, groaning,

his lips dragging over my heated skin. His voice trembles as he thrusts deeper, his hands gripping my hips like he's afraid to let go. "You feel like heaven." He lifts his head, and his blue eyes burn into me. "Like you were made for me."

At his words, I tighten around him, moaning as he thrusts deeper, stretching me. My fingers slip from his shoulders to his chest, splaying wide over the firm muscle and burning heat of his skin. His heart pounds beneath my touch, wild and unsteady, and I realize—he's just as lost in this as I am.

His lips find mine again, but this kiss is different. There's no desperation, no frantic hunger. Only something slow and deep and devastating. His tongue sweeps against mine, coaxing, teasing, until I'm arching into him, pressing closer, wanting more, more, more.

He drags his hands up my thighs, over the curve of my waist, along the soft swell of my breasts, worshipping every inch of me with his touch.

His hips roll into mine again, slow and deep, his body meeting mine like the sea drawn to shore. Pleasure builds in thick, aching waves, cresting higher, higher, dragging me to the edge without sending me over.

"Please," I beg, barely able to form the word. "Please—"

"I know," he murmurs, pressing a kiss to the corner of my mouth, then my jaw, then the sensitive spot beneath my ear. "I feel you."

He shifts slightly, angling his hips, and the next thrust hits something devastatingly perfect. My vision splinters, my breath catches, and my back arches as pleasure twists tight, winding impossibly sharp, impossibly sweet.

He continues to drive into me, each stroke landing right where I need him.

Again.

Again.

Again.

Until I can't hold on anymore.

Until I don't want to.

I shatter, my muscles rippling around him, my release cresting over me in slow, rolling waves that shake me to my core. And he doesn't rush. Doesn't chase his own pleasure. He just moves with me, drawing it out, letting me feel every lingering tremor, every pulse of pleasure still washing through my limbs.

Only when I sag beneath him, utterly wrecked, utterly his, does his rhythm finally falter. His breath stutters, his muscles tensing as he thrusts once, twice more, then finds his own release with a broken, reverent moan, spilling into me, his body pressing deeper, holding me to him like he'll never let go.

For a long moment, we don't move. Our bodies locked together, our chests rising and falling in sync. His forehead drops to mine, his lips brushing over my cheek, my jaw, my mouth.

"You were made for me," he whispers.

And it isn't a claim. It's a prayer.

And God help me, I'm praying too.

TWENTY-NINE

For a little while, the world outside this cellar, outside this moment, doesn't exist. There is only him. Only us. The heat of his skin pressed against mine, the scent of salt and chocolate in the air between us. The way his fingers still ghost over my hip as if memorizing me, as if trying to hold onto something he knows is already slipping away.

I close my eyes in an attempt to stay in this moment, tucked into this stolen sliver of time, but reality slices back into me like a blade to the gut.

Alder. The priest. The banquet. The sacrifice.

I've seen how the machine responds when Alderic and I are together. I've felt the shift. The hum beneath my skin. It doesn't want blood. It doesn't want suffering.

It wants connection. It wants the Lovers. Not just the card. But us, together.

But will that be enough?

Alderic's arm tightens around me as if sensing my thoughts.

I draw a slow breath. "We should get ready."

He sighs like he doesn't want to move, but then he pushes up from the table. Candlelight dances over the lines of his body—sun-kissed skin stretched over strong muscle, the sharp dips and angles of his abdomen, the light sheen of sweat still clinging to his chest. He is all strength, all beauty, and I take one selfish lingering look before he reaches for the clothes I brought for him.

"We have a plan. The people think Delphara is their savior, that the machines turning back on is divine will," I say, finding my dress, slipping it on, and tugging my own laces tight as I force my thoughts back to our strategy. "No one outside the castle knows the truth about what's happening here. We expose the queen. End the sacrifices. Free the kingdom."

"But that doesn't heal the Tower or the machine inside it. It doesn't fix the problem with the magick," Alderic says. "It doesn't get you home."

"No. It doesn't."

He watches me as I cross the room and take his coat from where it was haphazardly thrown over a chair. My thoughts tighten, pulling into shape, into something I've already half-mapped but haven't yet shared.

"Delphara thinks it's blood," I murmur, smoothing the velvet over my arm. "She believes that blood is the price of power. But that's not what the Tower actually wants." I glance up at him. "At least, not what I think it wants."

Alderic nods, linen shirt half-buttoned, eyes narrowing. "Go on."

"Every time I go over what's been happening, it

always comes back to us. Whenever we're together—on the island, in the kitchen, in the Tower—the machines wake up. It's not death they react to. It's us."

He gives me a slow, crooked smile. "So, what you're saying is…we were always meant to be together."

I roll my eyes. "That is not what I'm saying."

"But you're not denying it."

I scowl at him, but energy is building behind my thoughts, too strong to stop now. "The Lovers card. It symbolizes love, obviously, but it's more than that."

"It's about union. Balance. Two halves making a whole. Trust and devotion. And the reverse meaning is the opposite: detachment, disconnection, general misalignment of values." Alderic's lips twitch. "That'll teach Kane to say I never listen."

I blink. "Who's Kane?"

He waves it off. "No one important."

He pauses, brow furrowing, the playful glint in his eyes replaced with something brighter, more urgent. "It's choice," he says, the word clicking into place like a key into a lock. "That's what the card is really about. Choosing."

"Yes." My heart pounds. "The Tower doesn't need sacrifice—it needs an offering. A union born not out of duty or control but out of love. A connection so deep not even different worlds can keep it apart."

His mouth curves in that familiar, delicious grin. "It always comes back to us being fated."

I narrow my eyes. "I'm saying *the Tower* thinks we are."

He chuckles, and I'm already flying through a hundred playfully smug responses to whatever cheeky, flirtatious quip he's going to say next when his smile falters and laughter fades. He shifts, the easy confidence bleeding out of him. His shoulders drop slightly, arms loosening at his sides like he's letting go of something he usually holds close.

He steps forward, just one slow step. Close enough that I see the tension at the corners of his mouth, the flicker of hesitation behind his eyes.

"Gemma," he says softly, and the sound of my name on his tongue makes my chest ache. "Do you love me?"

The question isn't flirtation. It's not leverage. It's not a line. It's real. He's vulnerable in a way I don't know what to do with, raw and terrifyingly sincere.

"I—" My voice snags. I force a breath. "It doesn't matter."

His expression flickers. Not hurt. Not quite. But something close.

"How I feel isn't the point. Not really," I add quickly, trying to fill the silence. "The point is that the Tower thinks we feel that way. That we've chosen each other. That we're deeply connected."

His eyes search mine. "But are we?"

My throat tightens. I hate this. I hate how it doesn't feel like a trap. How there's no angle to play, no leverage to gain. Just a man offering something real, asking for nothing in return.

With Alder, everything was an exchange. Affection for admiration. Love for security. My devotion in exchange for his attention. I always knew exactly what I was supposed to give to get what I thought I needed.

But Alderic doesn't want anything from me. And I don't know what the hell to do with that.

I smile, tight, controlled. "We need the Tower to believe it. That's all that matters."

His gaze lingers on me, long and knowing, and I hate that he doesn't push. That he just nods like he gets it. And it's terrifying that he might actually understand.

"And what if we succeed? If it works?" His voice drops, rough around the edges as his fingers find mine. "What happens then?"

My chest tightens. "I go home."

The words fall like stones, solid, immovable. But they're not the whole truth. Even as I say them, something inside me buckles. Not at the thought of returning to my world, but at the thought of doing so without him.

This was always supposed to be about survival. About getting back to my life, my world, my rules. I didn't plan for Alderic. I didn't plan for the way he touches me like I matter or listens like my thoughts are sacred. I didn't plan for the warmth in his laugh or the way he watches me like I'm his favorite ending to the story he never saw coming.

And maybe I don't know what that means yet—maybe I'm too scared to admit it out loud—but I know one thing with aching clarity:

I don't want to leave him behind.

I came into this world with Alder… Does that mean I can leave it with someone else?

Could I leave with Alderic?

Would he even come?

I swallow the questions and the fear tangled up in them. I can't afford to wonder right now. So I just squeeze his hand and let my silence lie for me.

His thumb skims over my knuckles. "There's another option."

I glance up at him.

"We run. Right now. Take the boat. Sail until we're far from here. No evil queens. No machines. Just you and me and the sea." His eyes search mine, pleading. "You don't have to fight this battle, Gemma."

I close my eyes, and for a split second, I let myself imagine it. The open ocean. A life without castles, without bloodstained machines, without the weight of responsibility pressing down on me. Just the wind in my hair and Alderic's hands on my skin.

But when I open them, I shake my head. "I can't run. Not from this."

"You'd rather die to save a kingdom that isn't even yours?"

"I'd rather live with myself when it's over." I square my shoulders. "I won't be the woman who looks away when other women are suffering."

His jaw tightens, his whole body going rigid. "Gemma—"

"No." I meet his gaze, unwavering. "I choose the fight."

His breath shudders, and for a moment, I think he might argue, might try one more time to convince me. But instead, his fingers tighten around mine "And I choose you."

THIRTY

Silver banners cascade from the banquet hall's vaulted ceiling like moonlit waterfalls. They ripple with every shift of the air, shimmering above walls swathed in gauzy silks, artfully pinned to mimic waves crashing along an unseen shore. The scent of spice and roasted meat mingles with candle wax and lavender oil.

Each banquet table gleams under candelabras shaped like coral, their branches dripping with crystals. Pale blue silk covers every surface, embroidered with silver thread so fine it almost glows. Every person in the room is dressed to impress the gods themselves—or at the very least, the queen who sits like one.

At the far end of the hall, raised on a crystal dais that resembles frozen waves mid-break, sits Queen Delphara Rothmore. Her gown is the color of the Caribbean, layered in translucent fabrics that shimmer like frost. Her bodice clings to her waist, stitched with sapphires and wave-carved bone, the crest of Cups a purplish blue and painted onto the fabric like a bruise. Her crown is a twisted reef of silver and polished gems, jagged and glinting. And around her pale throat coils a chain of sapphires so dark they look black.

Her expression is serene, serpentine. A queen sculpted from the sea's coldest depths.

A few steps down, seated just beneath her on a smaller platform, is Victor. His throne is simpler, though still gilded. He sits straight, but not stiff, his expression neutral in that way only people with terrible secrets can manage. His hand rests on the arm of his chair, within easy reach of Delphara, though I get the feeling that he hasn't touched her in ages.

Laid out around them, painted in silver and positioned like art, are women. They're naked and motionless. Their bodies serve as platters—shoulders bearing fruits, bellies holding mounds of carved meat and cheeses, thighs spread for crystal dishes of figs, honey, and decanters of wine. Every inch of them arranged for display. For use. The women in this castle are always being used for something.

"Magnificent, isn't it?" Alder murmurs at my side.

I force a smile, aware of the weight of every glance in the room, every wine-glossed whisper rippling behind us.

"It's really something," I say, managing to make my voice sound awed, just a little breathless, like I've been swept off my feet by the splendor of it all.

Alder's hand settles at the small of my back, possessive, and I suppress the shudder that runs through me. Instead, I smile a little wider and tilt my head up toward him like I'm grateful for the attention.

I'm playing my part. The scared, overwhelmed woman who came crawling back. The woman who tried to run but realized she couldn't survive without her powerful, perfect man.

His hand presses a little firmer, fingers splaying across bare skin. He pushes me deeper into the banquet hall with the casual command of someone who assumes the room belongs to him. After all, these people know him as Lord Alderic Lockhart, the Queen's new plaything. And I am his chosen accessory.

I straighten, spine prickling as more faces turn toward us.

My dress clings to every curve, midnight-blue velvet catching the light in ways that make it look almost wet. The high neckline elegantly skims my throat, but the draped back falls just above my tailbone, leaving most of my back exposed to the chill and to Alder's hand.

I hadn't had time to have a dress made. Of course I hadn't. No one can handcraft an evening gown in an afternoon. Not that Alder even realizes this doesn't match the maroon coat I took from the wardrobe he's pretending is his.

One of the noblewomen who've been quietly planning a revolution beneath the kitchen offered me this dress the color of crushed sapphires. Sylvie sewed lace panels into the sides, sheer and slightly scandalous, to accommodate my figure and make it mine. Because bodies aren't mistakes to be reshaped—they're all different, all beautiful—and clothes should rise to meet them, not the other way around.

It fits like power. Like the first victory in a war I intend to win.

We move slowly past jeweled collars and polished smiles. Noblewomen drip with diamonds. Noblemen sweat in brocade. Every gaze flicks from Alder to me and back again, as if they're deciding whether I'm a trophy or a threat.

Alder leans down. "Smile, Gemma. You look like you're planning a murder."

"Maybe I am," I say, voice sugary. "Careful where you stand."

He chuckles, but his grin doesn't quite reach his eyes.

Delphara rises, and the room stills. She lifts a goblet in one hand, the wine inside glinting like fresh blood.

My stomach twists. Knowing Delphara, it might be.

"To the Kingdom of Cups," she says, her voice low and mellifluous, woven through with something sharp. "To the return of glory. To the machines that sleep no longer. To the gods who demand our devotion. And to the offering that will awaken the land once and for all."

Applause erupts like thunder cracking through the room. Silver goblets clink, laughter bubbles, and the Queen's smile turns wicked as she basks in it.

Victor rises slowly beside her, goblet in hand. His expression is all polished civility, but there's a slight tremor in his arm, a tightness in his jaw. "To the cost of progress." He lifts his glass. "And how steep a cost it is."

The applause that follows is more hesitant, less certain. But Delphara's smile doesn't waver. Instead, she turns toward Victor and rests her fingers against his wrist.

And just like Clara's sacrifice, it begins.

A glow unfurls beneath her touch, and if I hadn't seen it before, I would assume it was a flash of light off gemstones. Sea-blue dances across Victor's skin, pulses once, twice, then melts into silver. It flashes like a blade before sinking into him and disappearing.

He stiffens, blinks, then he smiles like nothing happened.

But I know better now. I know that smile. I've worn it myself. Obedience disguised as devotion.

Delphara leans forward and murmurs something only he can hear. He nods.

My stomach sours again.

Movement catches the corner of my eye. One of the masked guards has approached Alder. I watch, careful not to shift too suddenly, as the guard passes him a folded piece of parchment.

Alder opens it. Reads it. His expression doesn't change, but his focus moves from the note to Delphara.

"Gemma, sweetheart, I have to go attend to—" Alder begins to tuck the note into his pocket and walk away when a man in a seafoam green brocade sidles up beside him.

"Lord Lockhart," the man says. "I was hoping to speak with you about the new terms from Pentacles. I have been told you've brought a rather compelling counterproposal."

Alder slips seamlessly into his role, that easy smile lighting his face as he extends his hand. "Of course," he says. "Always happy to discuss business. Especially when it's profitable."

Whatever was in that note, wherever Alder was going to disappear to, it has to wait. Because now, it's time.

Alder is laughing at something the man beside him said, charming and effortless in his golden silk jacket.

He's glowing under the chandeliers, every inch the lord of the realm.

I smooth my hands down my gown, letting the confidence I don't completely feel straighten my spine and lift my chin as my stomach does cartwheels.

I excuse myself from Alder's side with a smile that feels almost real and speed walk toward the refreshments table. One of the naked women lies artfully across the tablecloth, grapes cascading over her hips, a platter of cheeses perched delicately on her thighs. Beside her, mercifully clothed, stands an attendant in a crisp, pale-blue dress, looking far too composed for someone literally working a buffet made of bodies.

She perks up the moment she sees me. "Wine, my lady?"

I offer her my goblet and channel every unhinged rom-com heroine who's ever done something insane in the name of a plan. "To the top, please."

She pours carefully and stops when the glass is halfway full.

"More."

She blinks. "Of course." Another inch. She tips the carafe again. The wine rises, dark, almost black beneath the lights.

"Keep going."

Her brows lift slightly, but she obliges.

"More."

Now the wine's right at the rim, threatening to slosh with the slightest breath. Perfect.

I take the goblet with both hands, careful as a bomb technician. "Thank you."

She stares at me like I'm already halfway to unhinged. I smile. It sure is starting to feel that way.

Alder's deep in conversation with Lord Seafoam from Trade and Brocade, flashing that practiced grin like it's currency.

I hover a beat. One breath. Two. Then I move.

It's time to make a mess.

I aim for maximum damage, lift my skirt dramatically, and trip.

My slipper happens to catch on the smooth, polished floor. My arm happens to flail with theatrical flair. My goblet happens to launch forward like a missile. And wine happens to sail through the air in a slow, glorious arc.

Gasps erupt across the room like fireworks.

Alder jerks back with a curse as the scarlet wine splashes across his gold silk, blooming like a fresh wound across his chest.

I suck in a breath, hands fluttering like I might actually want to fix the problem I one hundred percent created on purpose. "Oh my God. I'm so sorry! I am so clumsy!"

A nearby noblewoman titters behind her fan. Someone snorts into their wine. Delphara, from her throne of crystalline judgment, lifts one perfectly arched brow.

Alder stands there, dripping and furious, arms out like he doesn't know what to do with himself. "It's fine," he says, teeth clenched. "I'll change."

I clutch his arm, dabbing uselessly at the stain with a napkin I collected from a passing attendant. "It's my fault. I feel awful."

"You should," he mutters.

"Come," I say brightly. "Let me help you out of that ruined suit."

And with every eye watching, I guide him from the room, my heart racing.

The din of the banquet hall fades as we round the stone corner, footsteps echoing down the long corridor like a ticking clock.

Alder walks beside me rigidly, his silk jacket and shirt clinging to him in damp, crimson-splotches.

"I'm so sorry again," I say sweetly, clutching his sleeve and forcing him to look at me. "It's just…those goblets are so slippery, aren't they?"

He huffs a breath and dabs at his chest with a silk handkerchief like it's the greatest tragedy ever to befall him.

And there, tucked into the shadows exactly where he's supposed to be, Alderic waits. Perfectly poised to step in as the man walking beside me the moment we get far enough away.

Our eyes meet for the briefest second. I offer him a subtle nod, then keep walking. Keep pretending.

There's a flash at the far end of the corridor. A blur of hair and wide, familiar eyes.

Sylvie?

We really have to stop meeting like this.

I wish she'd trust me. But I don't blame her for keeping her distance. Not when trust is a luxury most women here have never been afforded.

"Are you even paying attention?" Alder says, voice edged with irritation. "Or are you planning to spill something else on me?"

My pulse lurches. I glance again, but the hallway is empty. Just a shimmer of torchlight, a whisper of movement that might've been real or might've been my nerves tangling with the shadows.

"Of course," I lie. I have so many more important things to worry about than Alder's most recent snarky complaints.

Even if Sylvie doesn't feel confident with the full scope of the plan, she knows the stakes. She knows what we're up against. What we're fighting for. What we're trying to stop.

I square my shoulders, bury the tremble in my spine, and lead Alder toward the trap he doesn't know he's walking into.

Everything's in motion now, and there's no turning back.

I step onto the staircase that leads to our shared chambers, nerves tight, breath shallow, my mind already racing through the next steps of the plan.

I just need to get him to the room. That's it. One last performance. A little flirtation. Some false vulnerability. Keep him distracted long enough for Alderic to slip into the banquet and take his place.

I'll keep Alder talking. Maybe I'll pretend I want to help him change, maybe I'll start undressing him myself. The thought makes bile rise in my throat. I've never been good at being a tease, but I'm going to have to become an expert now.

I'm halfway up the steps before I realize he isn't following.

Alder keeps walking, unhurried as he moves past the staircase and deeper into the corridor, the soft scrape of his boots echoing off the stone.

I pause on the third step. My pulse flutters. A strange chill slips down my back. "Where are you going?" I ask, voice pitched too high. "You need to change."

A small, amused breath escapes him. "Do I?"

"The wine…" I swallow hard. "Your outfit is ruined. I thought—"

He smiles. It's not a smile meant for ballrooms or banquets or seduction. It's razor-sharp and venomous. "Sweetheart," he says, each syllable so quiet, so careful, it feels like it's been dipped in poison. "Did you really think I didn't know what you were doing?"

My stomach lurches, dread hitting in one nauseating wave.

From the shadows, they emerge. One masked figure. Then another. Then more—slipping from alcoves and side corridors like they've been waiting all along. Like they were always going to be here, just out of sight.

Like the plan was never mine to begin with.

Silver masks gleam beneath the flickering torchlight, blank and inhuman, their expressionless eyes locking on me. Their armor catches the light in jagged flashes, bodies silent, hands already reaching.

No.

No no no no no.

My breath stutters. I take one step back. Then another. My slipper catches on the edge of my gown. I stumble, one arm flying out, the other groping for the stair rail. The wrought iron bites into my palm as I steady myself, heart crashing against my ribs.

"You've been busy," Alder continues. His voice is low, lilting, almost amused. "Scheming with the kitchen girls. Whispering in dark corners. Plotting to take down a queen."

He walks toward me, casually, and the floor feels like it tilts beneath my feet. "You almost got away with it too." His smile sharpens, slicing straight through me.

My heel slips. I jolt, nearly falling backwards up the stairs, clutching at the banister like it might save me. The gown tangles around my legs, and my pulse screams in my ears.

"Guards," he shouts. "Take her."

Panic claws at my throat. I whirl and run. The hem of my gown snags on the stone, tears at the seam. I don't care. I don't look back.

I have to move. I have to get away. I've walked right into a trap I thought I'd set. And now it's closing. Fast.

Hands seize me from behind. A sharp yank, a rough, crushing grip.

Gloved fingers clamp over my mouth, my shoulders, pinning me before I can scramble away. My pulse spikes like a struck bell.

I twist, my teeth snapping at the hand stifling my mouth, but thick leather blocks the bite. A cry builds in my throat, but it dies beneath the pressure of the palm crushing my jaw. I can't make a sound. I can't breathe. No one can hear me.

No one is coming.

I thrash—wild, desperate, feral. I buck and twist, fighting against their arms, refusing to make this easy. My legs kick. My nails scrape skin and armor and anything I can reach. But it's like fighting stone. Their grip doesn't loosen. My lungs scream for air. My limbs burn. Each heartbeat crashes like symbols in my ears.

I'm being taken. Like Clara. Like all the girls before her. A sacrifice ripped from the world and cast into darkness. A warm body to feed the cold machine while the rest of the kingdom raises their glasses and toasts to power, blissfully unaware their comfort is built on slaughter.

I made the same mistake every heroine makes: I thought I was different. I thought I was special. I thought that, against all odds, I would be the one to stop it. That I'd change the story.

But Alder has always been a step ahead. Watching. Calculating. Pressing until I cracked just enough to let him slip back in. He's always known how to twist things—how to make me second-guess my instincts, question my truths. How to rebuild my thoughts until I couldn't tell where he ended and I began.

It makes me sick to think I ever believed I loved him. Like his PR team, I thought I'd be the one who fixed him, who transformed him into the man I believed he could be.

But no woman can change a man. She can only change herself.

And I was never fighting to change him. Not really. I was fighting the version of myself who knew not to let him win.

And I am done losing.

I am not the same woman I was six months ago. I am not fragile. I am not breakable. And I am not going down without a fight.

THIRTY-ONE

Rage ignites, fast and consuming, burning through the helplessness that had begun to frost my veins. It melts into something fierce, something violent. A scream rips from my throat, raw, unhinged, as I drive my elbow back.

Bone hits bone.

One of the guards grunts, the air punched from his lungs, and his grip falters just enough. I twist, teeth bared, legs kicking. My foot connects with a shin, a knee, and I slip free for one breathless second. I sprint, vision blurry with adrenaline, pulse vibrating like a gong in my chest.

Up. Oh, God, I'm going up.

The realization hits midstep, but I keep moving. I'm doing exactly what every doomed heroine in every slasher movie I've ever screamed at does—racing up the stairs, away from escape, toward a room with one exit and no good outcomes.

"Not the stairs, you idiot," I whisper to myself, breath ragged, "not the stairs—" But I'm already there, crashing against doors one after another. Locked. Locked. Locked.

The third one gives. I shove it open and lurch inside—

A thick-gloved hand slams over my mouth, wrenching me back before I can even inhale to scream.

Another hand clamps around my arm, bruising and brutal, and I'm dragged into the hall as the door bangs shut behind me.

Back down the stairs we go. Back through the castle's throat, into a hidden passageway, into the dark.

My stomach lurches as stone grinds against stone and the last sliver of light disappears and I'm sealed in the dark.

It takes a minute for my eyes to adjust to the torchlight lining the walls. The passage is narrow, carved from rough, unpolished stone, and it stinks of damp earth and something older—something rotten beneath the surface. My heels scrape uselessly against the uneven floor as I'm hauled deeper into the belly of the castle, into some secret artery no sunlight has ever touched.

The walls press closer with every step. The ceiling lowers. The floor tilts. I can't tell how far we've gone, how long we've been moving. My body aches. My lungs burn. My voice is swallowed by gloved hands.

And then cold air slaps my skin. The stone gives way to sky as we step out of a doorway carved into the castle's exterior.

The hidden door grinds shut, vanishing into the castle's stone skin. Above, gray clouds sag over the sea, the sun nothing more than a smear of light behind them.

The Tower's isle rises from the churning sea like a

broken tooth, jagged cliffs, pointed trees. Within those trees, the Tower watches, ancient stone and whispered ruin, waiting for me.

The hand over my mouth loosens, and I suck in a crisp, briny breath. A rough yank on my arms wrenches me forward, dragging me to the stone bridge that stretches from one island to the other.

They're taking me to the Tower.

They're taking me to die.

The wind shrieks around us. Waves slam into the rocks below, white spray leaping over the sides of the bridge like grasping hands. Salt lashes my skin, stings my eyes. My hair whips across my face as I stumble, half-dragged, half-carried across the stone.

And still—beneath the roar of the sea, beneath the thunder of my heartbeat—I feel it.

That pull in my chest, like a thread cinching tighter with every step I take toward the Tower.

No.

I dig my heels in, panting. I don't want to feel it. I don't want to be drawn to it. I don't want to be another offering to something that's already devoured too many women and left nothing behind but the husk of hope, spoiled and crawling with rot.

"I'm not the answer," I rasp, twisting in the guards' grip. "You've got it all wrong. Just stop."

They don't. Their hands clamp tighter around my arms as we cross the bridge.

"Wait, please," I beg, the words tumbling from my mouth in broken pieces. "If you'd stop—if you'd just listen—I can help you. I can fix this. I can—"

At the far end of the path, where the bridge bleeds

into sand and the sand gives way to shadow, Alder waits. He's motionless as a statue and immaculate except for the bloodred wine staining his chest. The dingy light of the storm-draped sky turns his golden hair to ash as he stands at the forest's edge.

Alder ruined my life once. And now he's going to be the one to end it.

"That's not the real Lord Lockhart! That man is an imposter. He is lying to you!" I shout, straining against the guards' hold. "*The queen* is lying to you!"

No response. Just heavy boots crunching sand.

"These sacrifices—" My voice cracks. "They won't save your kingdom. But I can. I know how to fix the machines. I know how to bring it all back."

Still, they don't stop.

The trees loom taller now, their branches curling above the path like claws. Alder doesn't flinch as we approach. Just stands there with his hands behind his back, a general surveying the battlefield.

The guards shove me forward, and I fall hard, knees hitting the ground before my palms slap cold sand.

"Sweetheart, you've always been easy, but getting you here was embarrassingly simple."

My stomach twists, bile rising in my throat.

I push myself upright, breath ragged, throat raw. Sand clings to my skin, to the velvet folds of my torn gown. Fear coils in my stomach but so does rage. A low, simmering fury that steadies my hands even as the rest of me shakes.

Alder cocks his head, the faintest smirk tugging at the corner of his mouth. His gaze rakes over me like I'm a riddle he's already solved. Like I'm right where I've always belonged: at his mercy.

I grit my teeth, forcing the tremble from my limbs as I inhale sharply through my nose. My body's screaming with panic, slick with sweat, but I lift my chin.

"And you've always loved underestimating me," I say, voice shaking with fury. "Let's see how that works out for you."

My gaze flicks past his shoulder.

There—a narrow break in the tree line where the pines thin and the path dips, half-hidden by rock and brush. Not much, but enough.

Adrenaline explodes through my veins. A sharp, dizzying burst of survival that propels me forward in one violent surge.

The world is a blur of gray and green as I tear across the sand and into the cover of the pines.

My pulse roars in my ears, drowning out the crash of the waves. The taste of salt fills my mouth, chased by the bitter tang of fear. I push harder, faster. My chest burns, my legs scream, but I keep running.

The world narrows to the rhythm of my breath, the pounding of my feet, the sting of bramble against my legs. I dart between twisted trunks and gnarled roots, ducking under branches, searching for a path to safety.

And just when I think I might make it back to the bridge, to the castle, to Alderic and the women, just when hope flares, foolish and fragile in my chest, I look back. One single, stupid heartbeat of a glance.

And I slam into something solid.

The impact knocks the air from my lungs, the world pitching as I stumble back. I flail for balance, but before I can catch myself, a hand shoots out and clamps around my wrist.

I don't need to look.

I already know.

But some part of me still can't understand how he got in front of me so fast. *How did I get so turned around?*

Alder stands before me like he was conjured from the deepest, coldest depths of the sea. His fingers tighten, and his eyes gleam with something close to victory.

"It's cute and so like you to think that Delphara and I were in the dark," Alder says softly, mockingly. "We've known from the beginning who he really is. What the two of you do to the machines when you're together."

My stomach drops.

Alder smiles wider, and it's all teeth. "You used to dream of being someone, didn't you, Gemma? Someone important. Chosen. Special." He leans in, his voice a poisonous whisper. "Well, you were right. You are going to be someone. You're going to be the key. *My key*. To power. To everything I've ever wanted." He tilts his head, voice velvet-smooth and venom-laced. "It's about time you finally proved your worth."

A flush of rage burns through me, snapping the fear clean in two. My hand slices through the air and lands with a crack, my nails raking down his cheek, carving deep, angry red lines into his perfect skin.

Alder stumbles back, stunned, a sharp curse hissing from between his teeth as his fingertips brush the blood beading along the jagged lines my nails left behind.

I don't waste a second—I bolt.

The castle rises ahead, dark and distant. I have to get there, to Alderic. If Delphara knows the truth—if she's figured out who he really is—then there's a chance he's already been taken. And they know about the women…

I have to save them.

All of them.

The wind claws at my hair, my skirts twisting around my legs as I push harder. My breath tears from my throat in ragged gasps. The bridge stretches before me, the only path back to the castle. I'm almost there. Almost—

The scent of the ocean and something ancient fills my lungs.

No.

I skid to a stop, my chest heaving.

I'm not on the bridge. I'm standing at the mouth of the Tower.

The withered apple blossoms curl against the stone like burned parchment, brittle and blackened. The sea roars below thc cliffs, spray shooting in foamy white arcs, but I barely hear it over the hammer of my own pulse.

Panic surges as I spin around and sprint back the way I came, chest burning, limbs screaming in protest, feet pounding the earth.

But the moment the bridge comes into view, I'm back. Back at the Tower.

The world has twisted in on itself.

The air thickens, heavy with the stench of old blood and older magick. It wraps around my throat, seeps into my lungs, presses down until I can barely breathe.

The bridge is gone.

The castle is gone.

There is only the Tower.

The great doors groan open. The sound rumbles through the earth, through my bones, shaking loose whatever part of me still believed I could outrun this.

A figure stands at the threshold.

His fanged, silver mask gleams in the dim, watery light—expressionless, endless.

White robes spill around his feet, across the stone, untouched by the wind that whips through my hair, the salt-laden air that burns my skin and fills my mouth with the taste of sea and ruin.

I take a step back.

The Tower pulls me forward.

No matter how far I run, I will always end up here.

THIRTY-TWO

The Masked guards close in around me. A wall of steel and flesh, faceless and merciless, pushing me toward the Tower. My gaze skims frantically over their shoulders, searching for Alder. But he's gone.

A shuddering breath catches in my throat as I'm shoved forward, my feet stumbling, my heart thundering behind my ribs like it's trying to escape. My body shouts at me to fight, to run, to do something, but I'm out of options.

The priest's voice rises over the howling wind.

"Tonight, we are delivered," he proclaims, lifting his hands. "And tomorrow, we shall rejoice!"

He walks slowly, the fabric of his white robes whispering over the stone. His silver mask catches the torchlight, glinting like a blade.

I try to dig in my heels, but the guards drag me into the Tower like a doll.

The machine rises before me—an ancient, monstrous

thing of silver and stone, its gears and levers frozen with time, with starvation. The skeletal remains of withered apple blossoms cling to its base, their brittle petals tangled in the rusted framework.

Hands clamp down on my shoulders and shove me against the machine. I thrash, kicking wildly, twisting against the hands that hold me. A scream tears free, guttural and desperate, but no one flinches. No one stops. Cold, rusted metal scrapes my back, pain biting into me like hungry teeth.

A sharp, metallic clank—one shackle. Then another.

Iron snaps around my wrists. My arms are yanked upward until my shoulders shriek with pain, my back arching from the unnatural angle. The guards loop my shackles over a rusted iron hook. It catches on my forearm and tears into flesh as my shoulders strain against the weight of my own body.

A warm line of blood snakes down my arm in a crimson ribbon that slides slowly and steadily toward the crook of my elbow.

The first drop falls and splatters against the machine. The steel beast exhales, a sound like the rusted rattle of something long dead.

Another drip of scarlet rolls down my arm, hitting the metal with a soft, sickening pat.

A shiver racks through me, every muscle locking tight as the machine against my back begins to hum with anticipation, with hunger.

It's been waiting—for me. For this. For blood.

I was so sure it wasn't sacrifice that the machine needed. It thought it was balance, choice, connection, love.

But maybe I just needed something to believe in, something to make this whole world make sense. Maybe I couldn't see past my own desperate hope. I wanted so badly to rewrite my story.

But I was wrong. The machine isn't stirring for love or devotion or any of the sacred things the Lovers card is supposed to mean.

It's responding to blood.

A wave of nausea crests in my throat.

But…*why*?

Before the thought can settle, the Tower pulses. A slow, guttural thrum that reverberates through the stone.

The priest steps forward, his white robes nearly brushing my legs, his mask tilted ever so slightly as if admiring his handiwork.

"The gods are generous," the priest says, his voice distorted by the mask, warped and watery. "Plucking you from your small, simple life and bringing you to the place that could use you the most."

He lifts a hand and presses two fingers to my forehead in a mockery of a blessing.

I lurch at him, baring my teeth. "Go to hell." My bound wrists yank me back, pain snapping like lightning under my skin. "You think sacrificing me will make your gods happy? You think this will save your kingdom?"

A monster in priest's robes.

A butcher in his white apron.

"Tell me," he says. "Has the blood we've spilled failed to work?"

I freeze.

Because he's right—the machines have stirred. The

kingdom has flickered with signs of life. And that's the part I overlooked. That we all overlooked.

I've been so focused on stopping the sacrifices, on putting an end to the slaughter, that I never paused to ask why they worked in the first place.

And now, with my life mere moments from ending, the answer crashes into me like a wave.

The blood Delphara spilled, the women she and her priests slaughtered…it worked. For a while. But only because it brushed up against the true magick. The shadow of it, the twisted reflection. Not union but division. Not devotion but betrayal. Not love freely given but trust violently broken.

The reverse meaning of the Lovers.

It was close enough to the source to flicker the machines awake. To mimic power. But it was never going to heal the kingdom. Never going to restore what was lost.

Because this kingdom needs connection—love, freewill.

And what Delphara offers is not love. It's control. It's the illusion of unity built on blood and fear.

The priest lifts his hands, palms upward, as if welcoming a divine truth. As if calling the Tower itself to bear witness. "The time has come to restore what was broken. To resurrect the order that once gave this kingdom power. Tonight, the cycle begins anew. The Tower will rise. Cups will flourish. And prosperity will once again flow through this kingdom like water…like blood."

The words don't echo—they root. They claim. They sink into the walls, the floor, the bones of the

Tower itself. The machine's hum deepens, vibrating under my skin.

"We thank the gods with this offering. With this sacrifice." The priest tilts his head back, bathed in flickering torchlight, pristine mask gleaming.

Except it isn't flawless—a single line of blood slips from beneath the silver edge. A vivid crimson stream against pale skin.

Everything stills. The machine. The Tower. The shackles. My thoughts.

The world is suddenly silent. Heavy. Wrong.

He raises a hand and smears the blood at his throat with his fingers. The pristine white robe stains beneath his touch, blooming like dye in snow.

And then he laughs.

The sound is low and warped, twisted at the edges, like a memory gone sour. It scrapes against the walls of the Tower, against the inside of my ribs.

His fingers find the edge of the mask. They linger there, as if savoring the power in the reveal. Then, with a quiet scrape of metal against skin, he begins to lift.

Blood snakes down his cheek in a scarlet thread, catching the flicker of the torches as it carves its way along the sharp line of his jaw.

And then I see it.

That smirk.

That same condescending twist of his mouth that once told me I was overreacting, spiraling. That I was hysterical. That I was worthless.

It's not just a smile—it's a weapon. One I've seen before. One I'll never forget.

Alder's blue eyes drag over me—my bound hands,

my trembling body, my unraveling mind—and linger. They drink me in like victory champagne.

And I break.

Not with a scream. Not with a sob. But with a realization. This is the end of a cycle twisted by this man who mistook obsession for fate—and power for love.

Alder is the Queen's new priest. That's what he's been doing here this whole time.

"I told you, sweetheart," he says. "You won't run from me again."

THIRTY-THREE

The Tower shudders as if flicking off flies. The iron shack- les bite deeper into my wrists, and my pulse thrums in sync with the Tower's ancient magick. The doors groan open, loud and slow, the sound echoing through the chamber like a death knell.

I wrench my head toward the sound, heart stuttering as storm-gray light spills into the chamber, casting long shadows against the damp stone. Silhouettes emerge, and the sharp staccato of the Masked guard's march echoes throughout the chamber, their silver masks catching the light. At their center, flanked on all sides and barely upright, is Alderic.

My breath lodges in my throat.

He's not supposed to be here. He was supposed to be safe. He was supposed to blend in and stay alive, and now he's bleeding because of me.

His wrists are bound. His shirt clings to him, blood-soaked and torn. There's a gash on his forehead, stark against his white skin, and crimson runs down the side of his face. His steps drag, his legs barely cooperating.

"Alderic!" My voice cracks as I strain against my restraints, fury and fear roaring in my chest.

His head jerks up. Wild eyes search the room and then lock on mine.

"Gemma!" The breath leaves his lungs like a gut punch. His shoulders collapse with it as he exhales my name like it's the only thing that's kept him alive. His face crumples with too many emotions at once—devastation, disbelief, desperation, relief.

And God, it nearly undoes me. But I don't get to falter right now. I don't get to feel anything. I need to be steel. For him. For me. For whatever's coming.

"She told me..." His voice is hoarse. "Sylvie. She found me. Said you were taken. I came as fast as I could but... I thought I was too late. I thought they'd already—" He doesn't finish. His knees buckle, and a guard yanks him upright before he can fall.

"You're not," I whisper, tears threatening to spill. "You're not too late."

Our reunion is short-lived as another figure glides forward, sweeping in from the shadows behind him like mist from the sea.

Queen Delphara Rothmore—of course she's here.

Her smile, when it finds me, is slow and serene like the sea moments before its pull turns deadly.

She turns to Alder, voice sweet as pie. "It's time."

Alderic's gaze cuts across the chamber. His breath catches. His body goes rigid. And for one suspended second, he doesn't move. Doesn't breathe.

White robes swirl around Alder's ankles like steam, the silver priest's mask dangling from his fingertips.

Alderic shakes his head once. Twice. Like he can undo what he's seeing. "No, it's not—you're not—" Fury replaces disbelief as the realization sets in. "You," he spits, eyes blazing. "*You're* the priest?"

"I knew you were a little slow, but I thought you'd catch on faster than this." Alder's smirk curves like a scythe. He spreads his arms and lets the mask fall from his hand. The sound it makes when it hits the floor echoes louder than it should, like a gavel, like a death sentence. Like the sound of my last stupid hope cracking in half.

Alderic stares at it. At him. At me.

"Gemma, I'm sorry," he says, voice raw. "I'm so—" His words dissolve into a choked breath, rage and heartbreak etched into every line of his face.

Alder strolls forward, hands clasped behind his back. "So desperate to be the hero. So willing to play protector." He stops inches from Alderic and tilts his head. "How does it feel to know that the woman you tried so hard to save played right into my hands?"

"You don't speak about her," Alderic growls, bound fists clenched.

"Oh, come on. You really think she wanted *you*?" Alder crouches in front of him. "She spread her legs because your face looks like mine. That's all this ever was." He flashes a wicked smile. "You were a safer version of the person she can't resist."

Alderic explodes forward, a snarl ripping from his throat, but the guards crash over him like a wave. Blades flash, steel sings, fists slam into his ribs as they wrench his bound arms. He fights like a man possessed—like a man who has nothing left to lose.

One guard stumbles under the weight of Alderic's fury. Another loses hold of his dagger entirely as Alderic jerks free, only for more hands to seize him again, dragging him backward. His roar echoes through the chamber as metal scrapes stone and blood spatters the floor.

I want to move, to tear this place apart, but all I can do is watch as they beat him.

He clenches his jaw, breath coming hard and ragged, but he doesn't fall. Doesn't give Alder the satisfaction of seeing him break.

"Alderic!" My wrists pull against the restraints, my whole body screaming for movement, for a fight, for him.

The guards drag him to my feet, force him to his knees. Blood streaks down his forehead, his arms, dripping into the cracks of the stone. He meets my gaze, blue eyes burning with pain and fury, and I don't know if I want to cry or scream or tear open the sky with my bare hands.

Alder turns slowly and tilts his head toward Delphara. "Told you she'd keep him busy."

My rage detonates. If I could get free, I would end this whole kingdom. "*Fuck. You.*"

"You'd like to, wouldn't you?" Alder's grin sharpens. "If only there were time."

"Enough." Delphara's voice cuts clean through the chamber. "I admit, I had my doubts. However, you were right to let him move about the islands. A clever trap, indeed."

Alderic thrashes again, twisting against the hands pinning him down and the twin blades now pressed to his ribs. "Cowards," he spits. "You hide behind your masks and your magick and call it power."

Delphara doesn't flinch. She steps forward, her voice calm, almost kind. "That one dies first."

Alder doesn't even look at Alderic. He simply nods.

My lungs seize. My vision narrows. The air feels too thin, the walls too close. My pulse beats in my ears, frantic and stuttering.

This can't be happening.

"Alder…" It slips out—a plea wrapped in panic.

He looks at me, and the cruel curve of his mouth deepens like a crack in ice. "Oh, sweetheart," he purrs. "Now you want to beg?"

Delphara begins to chant. The low, lilting hum slips from her lips and winds through the air as the Masked guard joins in. Their voices rise together, a replay of the bathing chamber. Of Clara. Of death.

"Too little," Alder murmurs, stepping toward me. "Too late."

Delphara lifts her arms, eyes closing as her fingers begin to move, tracing invisible shapes in the air. Sparks of blue magick flicker at her fingertips—cool, crystalline drops that shimmer like rain suspended mid-fall.

The Tower groans in response. Water weeps from its ancient stone, slipping down the walls in rivulets that pulse with silvery light. The stones beneath us dampen with seawater, pooling in patterns that spiral beneath my feet.

"Now," Alder says as he steps forward, his smile cold and final. "Shall we begin?"

THIRTY-FOUR

The walls of the Tower loom around me, pressing in, heavy with centuries of sacrifice, of death, of blood offered in devotion, of magick twisted into fate. The machine hums behind me, patient, waiting, its ancient gears groaning, its rusted lungs sighing.

"You said Sylvie saw them take me?" I ask Alderic, my voice a whisper beneath the melodic chant.

He nods once, a flicker of something fierce sparking in his eyes.

We don't have to say the rest aloud. We both understand what it means.

I lift my chin. My pulse steadies. My breathing smooths. The fire rising inside me is no longer fear—it's fury. It's power. This fight isn't over. It's only just beginning.

Alder tilts his head, studying me as if sensing the shift, as if seeing my strength rekindle, the moment everything changes.

“Sweetheart,” he drawls, “are you about to do something reckless?”

I meet his gaze, smile, and the Tower answers.

A crack splits the air. A sound older than time itself. A sound like stone breaking, like history unraveling, like a god exhaling after centuries of holding its breath.

The Tower doors—doors that had vanished from maps, from the island, from the Kingdom of Cups itself—open.

This ancient chamber appears only for three people: me, Alderic, and Alder. But we’re already inside. And now, it’s appeared to and is opening for someone else, not with force but with invitation.

A breath of air rushes into the chamber, swirling around me, rustling the hem of my gown, curling through my bloodstained fingers. The iron shackles rub my wrists raw and hold me in place, but I don’t feel trapped anymore. Because I know, in the marrow of my bones, in the deepest part of my soul, the truth Alder and Delphara never saw coming.

The Tower, this machine, was never meant to serve them.

Alder turns. His smirk falters, and his fingers twitch at his sides, but there’s no escaping what’s coming.

Footsteps echo beyond the entrance. A whisper of sound slithers through the chamber—the soft shuffle of leather on stone, the shifting of bodies in the growing gloom. Shadows stretch across the floor. The flicker of torchlight catches on steel. Then, a flood of movement, and they’re here. A surge of bodies storming the Tower.

A sea of women spills through the entrance of the ancient chamber that should not exist, that they should not have been able to find. Their fury is a tempest, a hurricane. They are a force of nature, their battle cries filling the air.

The guards barely have time to react before the first strike lands and chaos erupts.

A blur of action—steel flashing, skirts whipping as women who have been overlooked, dismissed, silenced for too long fight back.

Bernice, her skirts hitched up, brandishes a kitchen knife like she's been waiting her whole life for this moment.

Sylvie, her face grim, eyes blazing like embers in the dark, swings a stolen sword, cutting through the ranks of guards.

The noblewomen—the same women in the hidden cellar beneath the kitchens—fight alongside them, wielding daggers, broken chair legs, whatever they could find. One swings a dented candelabra straight into the temple of a guard, another ducks low, slicing at the back of a knee with a piece of metal, sending her opponent sprawling.

Steel clashes. Boots scrape against stone. Women emit war cries. And the Tower trembles beneath the force of a battle decades in the making.

Alder's smirk shatters, jagged and frantic. He reaches out, fingers grasping the air like he can regain control, twist this moment into something that still belongs to him.

Delphara's lips peel back in a snarl, her regal composure cracking at the edges. She clutches her heavy skirts as she scrambles back, a cornered animal seeking an exit that no longer exists.

Alder doesn't run—not at first. No, that would mean admitting defeat, admitting failure. And Alder doesn't lose. Not him. Not ever.

A guard collapses at his feet, blood staining his blue robes, a dagger buried in his ribs. And suddenly, there is no denying it. If this ever was Alder's kingdom, it's not anymore.

His chest heaves as he turns on his heel, his white robes lashing the air as he searches for an escape. But there's nowhere to go but through.

Bernice slashes at a guard, her knife flashing. Sylvie advances, blade slick with blood. Noblewomen and maids stand shoulder to shoulder at the entrance, driving back the last of the Masked guard.

Delphara's breath comes too fast, her hands shaking as she grips her skirts and shoves past a wounded guard, her pinched face twisting with disdain, with desperation.

Through the fight, Bernice's voice rings out. "Gemma!"

Sylvie stands beside her, panting, her sword slick with blood. Her red hair is half torn from its braid, wild around her face, and her gaze burns with something between fury and triumph.

A cry bursts from my lips—relief and disbelief in one breath. They came. They came for me. They came for themselves.

"They were counting on us not to fight," Sylvie shouts, whirling as a guard lunges toward her. She pivots, drives her sword deep into his gut. He lets out a strangled gasp, his body crumpling to the floor. She doesn't flinch. She yanks the blade free and calls out, "The Tower appeared out of nowhere as if from—"

"Magick!" Bernice bellows, hacking at a soldier's arm with the same kitchen knife she's wielded like a warrior's blade. The guard stumbles back, clutching the wound, but Bernice is already closing in.

I press my lips together, swallowing against the burn in my throat as hope ignites in my chest, bright and impossible to contain.

This is what Alder and Delphara never anticipated. The ones they ignored, the ones they crushed beneath their heels, the ones they never saw coming. The women of the Kingdom of Cups, rising together.

And winning.

Behind them, the chaos swells, a chorus of steel against steel, of battle cries and bodies hitting stone. The torchlight catches his face as he advances with the women, bloodied, pale, but unmistakable—King Victor Rothmore.

He's slower than the others but no less determined, his face set with grim resolve. His ornate doublet is torn, the intricate silver embroidery stained with crimson splotches. One hand clutches a blade, the other pressed to his ribs like something inside him is already breaking.

"Delphara!" he roars and pushes through the clashing bodies.

The machine groans. Its gears shift, grinding against decades of rust and ruin, hungry for more. The sound vibrates through me, through the Tower itself.

With the guards distracted, Alderic moves.

A sound tears from his throat—half-roar, half-battle cry—as he wrenches against the chains binding his wrists. For a heartbeat, nothing gives. Then, with a guttural snarl, he hooks the shackles around the edge of the machine and twists hard. Metal scrapes against metal, and one shackle snaps open with a sharp clang. The second follows a beat later, forced open with another burst of strength.

He surges forward, snatching a sword from the blood-slick grip of a fallen guard.

Before I can process the motion, he's in front of me—fire in his eyes, fury in every breath. The sword flashes in the low light, and with one clean, brutal arc, he drives it down on the chain binding my cuffs to the hook suspending me off the ground.

The metal shatters with a shriek. The broken chain hits the stone floor with a clatter I barely register, lost beneath the roar of battle, and the relentless pounding in my skull.

Before I can fall, Alderic catches me. His arms slide beneath me, sure and steady, pulling me tight against him, as if letting go isn't even an option.

My feet brush the floor, but they're useless. My knees give out instantly. Pain screams down my arm. The place where the hook tore through my forearm is bleeding again, crimson streaking down my skin, dripping onto the stains of sacrifice and battle painting the stones. I try to straighten, try to plant my feet, but my legs won't cooperate.

Alderic's golden hair is dark with sweat and blood. A bruise blooms beneath his eye, and cuts slice across his chest and arms, but none of it dims the brilliance of him, the fire in his blue eyes, the reckless devotion in his gaze as he looks at me.

His tunic is torn, fabric sticking to the hard planes of his chest, the muscles beneath tense and taut, ready for battle. One hand holds the sword, still poised for violence. The other steadies me with trembling fingers, slick with blood but achingly gentle, cradling me like I'm the only thing in this cursed kingdom worth saving.

He is fury and tenderness. Ruin and refuge. He is mine.

And in the center of the battle—the war we were fated to start, fated to *win*—he leans close and whispers, "Forgive me. I wanted my dream to be yours. I never stopped to see that you had your own."

The words hit like a blade and a balm. Relief and rage. Gratitude and grief. Love so vast it hurts. My chest tightens, a storm surging inside me—everything we almost lost crashing into everything we still could be.

My throat tightens. My breath catches. My fingers splay against his chest, desperate for proof that he's real. That I am. That we're still here. His heartbeat thrums beneath my palm. A pulse of life, of hope, of survival.

A guard slams into us, the jolt tearing me away from Alderic.

My slippers skid across blood-slick stone. I stumble and catch myself on the machine. The world tilts. A snarl grazes my ear as the guard staggers upright and vanishes back into the chaos.

A jolt of electricity tears through my arm as I grip the corroded metal. The gears grind, shifting, sluggish but building speed. The air changes. Magick crackles, snapping against my skin.

Power hums in the walls, vibrating through the stone, echoing the frantic rhythm of my heart. Everything is moving—gears, wind, fate. And beneath it all, *him*. The one thing that's been constant in the chaos.

"You asked me if I love you..." The words spill from my lips, unplanned and unstoppable, like I've been holding them for lifetimes.

Alderic's eyes find mine, and the love I see there makes everything else fade.

"I didn't want to let myself. I didn't think it mattered."

He closes the distance. His hand finds mine on the machine. Our fingers lace together, and the pulse intensifies—a golden spark pouring from our skin onto the gears beneath.

"But it does. God, it does. Because I do." My voice shakes, but I don't care. "Alderic, I love you."

His mouth claims mine like a vow. Like a promise. Like the beginning of something neither of us ever expected but both of us chose. It's a collision of souls that were always meant to find their way to each other.

A violent shudder rips through the Tower. The machine's gears grind against one another, screeching as they pick up speed. Metal shrieks, stone splits, the earth trembles under our feet.

Heat surges up my arm, searing, consuming, boiling water racing through my veins, something ancient and insatiable awakening in my blood. The hair on my arms rises, my pulse hammering as if it's trying to match the machine's frantic, climbing rhythm.

A force slams into my chest—a heartbeat, but not mine. It pushes, pulls, demands. My knees weaken beneath the weight of it, as if the machine itself is reaching inside me, recognizing me, tethering me to its power.

And then, I hear it. Not the grinding of metal, not the crumbling of stone—but something deeper. A whisper, a crash of waves, the exhale of the ocean against the shore.

The Tower is speaking.

The machine is fully awake.

Alder emerges from the fray and barrels toward us. Guards and rebel women fall like dominoes as he tears through them, wild, unhinged. His face is twisted with fury, lips curled back, nostrils flaring, teeth bared.

"You're not the one!" he roars, voice cracking at the edges, ragged with disbelief. "It was never supposed to be you!"

He grabs a noblewoman by the front of her gown, rips a dagger from her belt, and tosses her aside like she weighs nothing. The blade gleams in his hand as he advances, steps erratic, like gravity can no longer keep him bound to the earth.

"It can't be you!" he spits, each word laced with venom. "It won't be!"

His entire body trembles as he glares at me like I've broken the universe in half. Like I've stolen his destiny. Like I was never meant to matter—and now, suddenly, I do. And he can't bear it.

He curses, his fury unraveling, his composure gone. "It's me! *I* was chosen! You're nothing—a body meant for sacrifice, to do with as I wish—"

A growl rips from his throat as he lunges. The point of the dagger flashes. His grip on the hilt is white-knuckled, his movements frenzied, driven by something beyond rage, beyond desperation. His entire world is collapsing around him, and if he cannot control the machine or the Tower, if he cannot control this fight and these people, then he will control the one thing he's always thought was his.

Me.

Alder swings the blade.

I don't think. I don't hesitate. I step forward. Use his own fury, his own arrogance, his own unstoppable momentum against him. I plant my feet—and shove.

His body lurches backward, eyes wide as he realizes he's lost, arms flailing as he stumbles into the machine. The instant his back hits the cold steel, the gears snatch him. They come alive and bite into his limbs like mechanical teeth. The metal jaws clamp onto his shoulders, his legs, his chest.

Alder's scream is bloodcurdling and broken and echoes off the Tower. He thrashes, jerking, twisting, fighting, but the machine tightens its hold.

The cogs spin, grinding into his flesh and splintering bone. Blood gushes in thick, pulsing rivers, drenching the ancient steel. It seeps into the hollow grooves, into the carved, wave-like veins of the machine.

Alder howls. He scrambles for purchase, fingers breaking against metal as he claws for escape.

But there is none.

The machine grinds, groans, devours. It drinks deep of his blood, what's left of his body twitching as the last of him is swallowed by the churning core.

And then, he's gone.

The Tower trembles.

The machine hums, then roars—a thunderous sound that splits through the stone, through the walls, through my bones. The ground lurches, a deep, shuddering quake that sends dust raining from the high ceiling.

A low, keening whine builds in the air, rising higher, sharper, until it claws at my eardrums and shakes my lungs.

The roots of the machine—twisted, rusted tendrils of metal that have slumbered beneath the earth for decades—begin to move.

A shudder. A shift. Then, the ancient steel roots tear from the stone, lifting from the ground in jagged, groaning movements, shaking loose debris, snapping through the foundation, a giant uprooting itself.

A crack splits the floor, then another, and another. Stone buckles. The entire Tower moans as if alive, as if breathing.

The machine has power, and the Tower is coming apart.

THIRTY-FIVE

A primal roar splits the air. It's the sound of stone crack-ing, of metal shrieking, of a beast waking only to realize it's dying, changing.

The floor trembles. Walls groan. Above us, cracks spiderweb through the ceiling as loose debris rains down in sharp, splintering bursts.

Screams erupt. Bodies slam into one another in a desperate scramble for the exit.

"The Tower is collapsing!" My voice tears out of me, nearly lost beneath the cacophony, but it's the only thing I have left to offer—a warning, a scream, a plea. My legs won't stop shaking. My ribs feel too tight to contain my lungs. "Get out now!"

Alderic is already moving, a blur of motion through the chaos. He reaches for one of the maids who followed Bernice and Sylvie into rebellion and hauls her to her feet, shoving her toward the open door.

"Go!" he instructs. "Keep moving! Don't look back!"

Even in the chaos, even with blood glossing the floor and stone falling through the air, Alderic looks like the version of the man I always hoped existed—one who fights for something beyond himself.

Another woman stumbles, knees bloodied from the stone. Alderic catches her arm, steadies her, and presses a dagger into her shaking hands.

"Run," he says. "And if any guards try to stop you—fight."

The women surge forward in a rush of skirts and slippers, sliding on blood-slicked stone, climbing over the fallen bodies of the Masked guard. Some are weeping. Others are silent. All of them are running.

The air is thick with smoke and dust. The scent of iron and ash.

The machine wails again, a mechanical scream that rattles through the skin of the Tower, through the spine of the kingdom.

The walls begin to warp, buckling like ribs under pressure. Somewhere behind us, a support beam gives way with a groan, collapsing in a shower of sparks.

Screams ring off stone. Chaos churns. And through it, a shadow staggers into the light. King Rothmore emerges from the fray. His face is pale, his steps uneven, but his grip is iron. Because in his arms, he drags Delphara.

Her once-glorious gown is soaked in red—his blood, her blood, the kingdom's. Her crown is tangled in her hair, tilting like a toppled monument. The Queen of Cups, stripped of grace. For the first time, there's fear in her eyes.

It should feel satisfying, watching her

crumble—watching the woman who played goddess choke on her own undoing. But it doesn't. It just feels… sad. But necessary.

"You will not hold power over me or my people another day," Victor rasps.

Delphara thrashes. "You ungrateful…" she hisses, her nails raking down his forearm. "You think you have a plan to end my rule?"

"There was no rule," he says hoarsely. "Only fear. Only the illusion of choice."

"You swore yourself to me," she spits. "You made the pact in exchange for a return to glory. *You are mine*."

Victor tightens his grip, blood dripping from his fingertips. "I made a mistake, and I've paid for it every day since. But this…" He exhales raggedly. "This is where it ends."

Delphara screams, twisting, trying to break free. But the king does not let go.

"Even if you end me," she whispers, "you will still be mine. My magick lasts beyond the grave. You will never be free of me."

Victor's jaw tightens. "Then I die gladly," he says, voice rough with resolve. "If it means saving the kingdom I betrayed, then let my blood be the price. Let the rot end with me."

For the first time, I see him—not the king, not the pawn but the man. The man who couldn't undo the past but still tried to stop the future from bleeding.

With the last of his strength, King Victor Rothmore seizes Delphara's wrist and yanks her close. She shrieks in protest, hands clawing at him, but it's too late. With one final, defiant breath, he throws himself—and the queen—into the gaping mouth of the collapsing machine.

Delphara's scream cuts through the Tower like a blade. For a moment, time stills. Her magick erupts from her in a final shower of blue and silver light that spirals upward like mist rising off a violent sea. The spell tethering her to the King and the kingdom itself shatters.

A boom pulses outward.

Magick explodes from the Tower's heart, and the force of it throws Alderic and me backward. I scream as we're hurled through the air, through the crumbling doors, past the threshold, and into the open world beyond.

The machine howls as it consumes itself, its core shrieking with the power of those who tried to control it. It consumes their ambition, their cruelty, their greed, and it erupts.

A burst of light, silver and scorching, pours from every crack in the stone. It races along the seams of the Tower, eating through rot, devouring decay. It glows brighter and brighter until it is everywhere.

I can't look away. The Tower isn't dying—it's being reborn. And with it, maybe, so am I.

The Tower exhales everything it's held, every scream it silenced, every injustice it endured—it releases all of it. A final, magnificent breath that floods the kingdom in a radiant wave. Magick surges across the bridge, over the castle island, through the valleys, and down into the quiet villages beyond. Machines stir in distant cities. Wheels spin. Lights flare. The sound like a thousand beasts waking at once, stretching after centuries of restless sleep.

The light rushes back to the Tower in one last sweep. It burns away the withered apple trees. Bark turns to ash and roots crumble, their papery remains swept away by the wind. For a moment the earth around the Tower is bare.

Then something new takes hold.

Vines twist through the soil, thick and green, bursting with ruby-red fruit. The scent of strawberries lifts on the wind—wild, sun-warmed, impossibly sweet—and wraps around the stone like a promise.

The Tower no longer groans under the weight of its own ruin. It's no longer a tomb but a beacon. It gleams, transformed. The ancient stone shimmers, smooth and silver, reflecting the waning light of the setting sun that's broken through the clouds.

The women gather at the foot of the Tower, breathless with wonder, eyes fixed on what remains—not ruins, not wreckage, but change. The magick that once fed on blood now hums with something gentler. Something new. It nourishes. It restores.

This is not the end. It's the beginning. A kingdom reborn. A kingdom freed.

But freedom is never tidy. It's not neat or ceremonial. It's uncertain, unruly, uncharted.

The aftermath hangs heavy in the air, thick with dust and salt and silence. Not the silence of peace, but the silence that follows a scream—a breathless, suspended hush where the world waits to see what comes next.

Some women clutch bloodied blades. Some hold onto each other, their arms looped tight, their bodies trembling with exhaustion. Some bear wounds that will scar, jagged reminders of the battle fought and the lives lost.

But they all stand. Fierce. Unbroken. Free.

Sylvie steps forward, her hands stained with blood, her sword hanging at her side. "The king and queen of Cups are no more," she says, hoarse but steady. "We will need a new ruler." Her gaze finds Alderic. "You led Pentacles once. You could lead here."

A murmur ripples through the gathered women. Some nod. Some shift uneasily. Others look to Alderic, to me, to the Tower that now watches in silence.

Alderic steps forward. For a moment, the wind dies. The sea stills. The magick holds its breath, and so do I.

Maybe he'll step into power and become what everyone needs. But that's the old way, isn't it? One throne for another. One ruler for the next.

And then, softly but clearly, he says, "The rule of kings is over."

I turn, my gaze sweeping over the women before me—Bernice, Sylvie, the noblewomen, the attendants, the ones who fought in shadows and stitched the wounds of this kingdom long before anyone called them warriors.

I never thought I'd speak for a kingdom. But the Tower's magick brought me to Towerfall for a reason, and it feels an awful lot like I've been speaking for it all along.

"You have always ruled Cups," I say, voice shaking with the truth. "You've kept it alive. You've bled for it while the world looked away. You stayed and you fought."

Bernice steps forward. Her apron is torn, her dress streaked with blood, but there is nothing fragile about her. She is solid, steady, unshaken.

"No more hiding. No more kneeling. No more serving men who never saw our worth." She looks at every woman gathered, her voice rising. "Gemma speaks the truth. This kingdom is ours. And now, we take it back."

There's a beat of silence, and then a single voice rises.

"No more crowns."

Another, louder. "No more thrones."

A third, fierce, unyielding. "No more rule without us!"

The dam breaks. Voices rise like thunder. A roar of women, of power unchained. It drowns out centuries of silence, of being used, of being told to wait their turn.

No more monarchs.

No longer controlled.

Never powerless.

They do not hesitate. They do not waver. They do not ask permission.

They claim what has always been theirs.

THIRTY-SIX

Magick hums against the breeze, an ancient, living vibra-tion I feel in my bones, in my blood. The Tower's isle glows beneath the fading light, its silver walls no longer hidden, no longer forgotten. It stands tall against the horizon, gleaming—a beacon of what is possible, of what will be. It looks almost beautiful now. Strange how something that nearly killed me can also feel like the beginning of something new.

Ahead of us, the women's footsteps echo across the stone bridge, steady and sure, as they return to the castle where other women gather. Those who watched and waited, who feared and hoped and dared to believe, they surge forward, a tide of voices and open arms and wide eyes, meeting in the middle like waves crashing together.

They call to one another, voices bright with victory and laughter. Fierce cries of triumph ring out into the twilight-tinged air. The sounds spill across the water, unrelenting, unstoppable. Like them.

I should be crying or collapsing or doing something equally dramatic to mark the moment. But all I can do is watch them, hollowed out and overflowing all at once. This isn't just a win. It's a reclamation.

I press a hand to my chest and exhale. The fight is over, but my heart still races.

Alderic stands beside me, bruised and bloodied and breathless, his tunic torn, his knuckles scraped raw. He looks like hell. And yet, he's gorgeous. A little more golden in the silver dusk. A little more real in the stillness.

And there's something in his expression now that wasn't there before. Lightness.

I feel it too.

The weight I've been carrying for so long—fear, doubt, the crushing belief that survival meant selling pieces of myself—has finally slipped from my shoulders.

He wraps an arm around me, pulling me close. His lips press against the top of my head, a breath of warmth brushing my sweat-damp skin. A promise. A quiet vow in a world that no longer demands sacrifice.

I slide my fingers between his, threading them together as I tilt my face up to his.

His gaze is steady, searching. Lit with something too vast to name and too fragile to look away from.

Without a word, he reaches into his pocket and pulls out the Lovers card. "I think you dropped this."

My breath catches. "I wasn't sure I'd get it back."

He tilts his head, eyes glittering. "It's always been yours, Gemma. I was just holding onto it until you were ready to take it."

Something warm twists in my chest. "That's oddly romantic for a man covered in blood and dirt."

"What can I say?" He brushes a grimy strand of hair from my face and softer, teasing, says, "You bring out my poetic side."

"So," he murmurs, a weak smile tipping the corner of his mouth, "what now?"

I take the card from him and hold it between us like a question, like an answer.

The card that brought me here. The card that cracked open my world.

This card tore everything apart. It also stitched it back together. I don't know if I believe in destiny—but I believe in this. In him. In us.

Beneath my fingers, the ink shivers. The figures shift, tangling into each other just like they did the night the Tower called me here. Magick stirs. Not loud. Not grand. But steady. Familiar.

Alive.

"It can take you home."

I study Alderic—the man who never asked me to be small, who never demanded I fold myself into something more palatable or give myself away just to be accepted. The man who fought beside me, fought for me. The man who lets me be me. Who chose me, not in spite of that, but because of it.

I glance down at the card. The ink continues to swirl, its edges warm beneath my touch. A tether. A choice.

I trace my fingers along its soft corners as I lift my gaze back to Alderic. His golden hair is tousled, and his eyes are so blue it's like staring into the horizon. But better. Because the horizon is distant, always just out of reach. But this? This is here. This is mine.

"Would you come with me?" I ask. My chest tightens

around the question, my voice hushed and uncertain despite everything we've been through.

He draws in a slow breath, his fingers closing around mine.

"Gemma." It's just my name. But it lands like something sacred, something sure. "I would follow you to the ends of the earth."

The breath leaves me in a stuttering exhale.

"This was never my world," he murmurs, his voice thick with emotion. "You are."

A slow, aching warmth unfurls in my chest, expanding, blossoming. The fear, the belief that I would always have to choose between freedom and love, between myself and someone else—it vanishes.

I reach up, curling my fingers into the front of his torn tunic, and tug him down. His breath mingles with mine as our lips meet.

Soft at first—a kiss of relief, of gratitude, of *I'm still here and so are you.*

Then deeper. Fiercer. Like he's saying a prayer, making an offering at my altar.

When we finally part, I press the card between our joined hands.

The magick pulses, warm and bright. The ink shifts again. The two figures entwine, melting into each other, moving as if they already know what comes next.

I look up at Alderic, my heart so full it feels like it might burst. "Let's go home."

Magick answers in a swell of silver light.

And together, hand in hand, we step into forever.

EPILOGUE

SIX MONTHS LATER

The bell above the door chimes softly as Alderic and I step inside, the delicate sound ringing through the boutique. It's warm here, cozy in that intoxicating way only small shops and bakeries manage to pull off.

Outside, the South Carolina winter is colder than usual, the kind of biting chill that lingers no matter how many layers I put on or how sweaty I get inside my coat. But here in Wilder Ever After, it's summer again, the air rich with lavender and the faintest hint of something sweet.

The wedding boutique looks exactly as I remember. Faceted crystals dangle from the ceiling like suspended starlight and scatter tiny rainbows across the glossy hardwood floor. Floor-length gowns shimmer along their racks, pools of ivory and champagne, intricate beading catching the golden glow of the pendant lights.

Bundles of herbs tied with twine rest beside a collection of candles shaped like goddesses. Veils float from silver hooks like ghosts caught mid-spin. And nestled among a delicate cloud of lace and silk, a small vase of fresh strawberries sits on the counter—ripe, red, and waiting.

"It's like they knew we were coming." Alderic pops a berry into his mouth and reaches for another. "You know, I've been thinking…we should make chocolate covered strawberries our signature dessert. Every Fated Feasts catering package comes with a platter of indulgence."

I smile, my heart swelling in that way it always does when he talks about our business. "You just want an excuse to play with sweets."

"And what if I do?" He chews thoughtfully, his voice rich with mock offense. "I'd argue my cake decorating skills are a public service. Honestly, I should be knighted."

I laugh, bumping his thigh with my hip. It's true, though. As it turns out, he's ridiculously talented with a piping bag…among other things. He once turned a dozen cupcakes into a Baroque-style fresco. I handle the customers, the spreadsheets, the bank accounts. He handles the sugar and spice and everything delicious.

We built this together—a thriving catering company. A life. A future I can't imagine without him. Not because I *need* him. But because I *chose* him. Because I finally chose myself, and that choice led me here.

I lace my fingers through his, squeezing gently. "Come on, sugar daddy," I whisper. "Let's go see my dress."

Alderic grins, sliding his arm around my waist as we move deeper into the shop. His golden hair tousled from the brisk winter wind, his ocean-blue gaze glitters as he takes in the boutique's eclectic charms—the velvet-draped windows, the wax dongs, the strands of talismans that dangle from the ceiling like captured constellations.

"Remind me why I don't get to try on anything?" he asks, his voice low against my ear.

"Because if I let you loose in the crystal vaginas, I'll never get you out again."

"It's you two!" Elsie emerges from behind a display with a grin so wide and unapologetic, it could melt the frost off a January windshield, her gaze bouncing between Alderic and me. So much like Sylvie and yet so different.

The boutique manager waves from the shadowed corner of the shop where she adjusts a display of dried lavender bundles and moonstone charms. Her long, flowing skirt brushes against the polished wood floor as she approaches. The silver pendant at her neck glints like an open eye. Her salt-and-pepper hair is twisted into a perfect coil on the top of her head, and her lips are painted the same shade of deep wine-red as the last time I saw her. From beneath thick, black lashes, her dark gaze locks onto mine, seeing, knowing.

But this time, the weight of her focus doesn't make me nervous. It doesn't make me want to turn away. This time, it feels like recognition. Like understanding whispered across realms.

"I'm here to try on my wedding dress," I say, standing a little taller.

The manager hums, and her fingers drift through the air in an absent-minded pattern—one I half expect to shimmer with magick.

"Ah," she murmurs, nails trailing along the silver pendant at her throat, clicking against the metal. "And to think, last time we met, you stood at a crossroads." She smiles. "I am happy to see the path you chose."

It feels like she knows every road I've walked. Every turn I took. Like she knew, even then, that I would find my way back here. That I would find my way to him.

Alderic lifts a brow. "Are the beginnings of all wedding gown fittings this dramatic?"

Elsie giggles, swatting at his arm. "Only the *really good* ones."

"I'm sorry," I say, looking him up and down. "Are you calling my wedding gown fitting dramatic?"

He shrugs, completely unrepentant. "At any moment, doves might spontaneously appear."

I shake my head. "You're the one who asked to come along."

"Oh, I'd sit through a hundred fittings if it meant I got to watch you undress and call me your husband."

My cheeks flush. "You like being called that?"

He arches a single brow. "Say it again and find out."

I roll my eyes, but it's useless. I'm already leaning into him, into the warmth of his hands as his fingers brush my skin. He's looking at me like I'm some kind of miracle, like I hung the stars just to lead him home.

"I know that look," I murmur, my voice catching on the swell of emotion in my throat.

His thumb traces lazy circles along my wrist. "Just thinking about fate," he says. "And how if I'd known it would end like this—that you were waiting for me on the other side of everything—I would have run faster. I would have torn the world apart to get here sooner."

"You're here now," I whisper. "You don't have to run anymore."

His lips slant over mine, warm, certain, tasting of strawberries. And in that kiss, I feel it: the shift of something cosmic, the quiet click of destiny falling into place. Not a surrender, but a return.

Not to the version of me who played it safe, or the woman who made herself smaller to survive.

But to the one who chose herself.

Finally—*finally*—I'm home.

Reading Group Guide

1. Gemma's voice is sharply contemporary, even as she's pulled into a fantastical world. What were your first impressions of her as a protagonist? Did you find her relatable or surprising?

2. Much of Gemma's journey is about reclaiming her own narrative. Where in the novel do you see her making pivotal choices? How does her sense of agency change by the end of the story?

3. How does the relationship between Gemma and Alder (and later, Alderic) play with or subvert classic "enemies-to-lovers" or "second chance" romance tropes? Did their dynamic keep you invested?

4. How does Gemma's journey into the Kingdom of Cups compare to other portal fantasies you've read or watched? What was your reaction to the

genre-blending of contemporary romance and magical fantasy?

5. How does the book explore the difference between love as rescue and love as revolution? Who, in your opinion, holds true power in the story, and why?

6. Discuss the roles of secondary female characters (Sylvie, Bernice, Elsie, and others). How do these characters contribute to the novel's themes of solidarity, survival, or resistance?

7. How did you experience the setting of Cups? What worldbuilding details—rituals, magic, machines, the castle, etc.—were most memorable or evocative for you?

8. What did you think of the narrative device of splitting Alder into two characters? Did it deepen your understanding of Gemma's internal conflict, or did it complicate your reading experience?

9. How does Gemma's journey in Cups parallel (or diverge from) her journey in the real world? What does the story suggest about healing from the past and starting anew?

10. How does the novel comment on, play with, or subvert traditional romance or fantasy tropes? Were there moments where you felt the author was winking at genre conventions?

11. After finishing the novel, what does "The Lovers" mean to you? Is it about romance, self-love, partnership, rebellion—or something else entirely?

Acknowledgments

Every book is a miracle. A ridiculous, messy, joyful, teeth-gnashing miracle. And this one wouldn't exist without the people who held me up, kept me from melting down, and let me spin wild stories while whispering "you've got this" on repeat.

To Christa Désir, my fierce and brilliant editor. Thank you for believing in this book when it was a complete mess. Your insight and heart made it better in every possible way.

To Letty Mundt, the ultimate project manager. There is no mountain too high, no chaos too chaotic. You keep everything moving with grace, power, and spreadsheets that might actually be made of magick.

To Brittany, Madison, Alex, Kavita, and Jolene, my dream team. This book wouldn't reach the women who need it if it weren't for each of you. Thank you for championing it, lifting it, and giving it a fighting chance in the world.

Falyn, you reminded me that softness isn't weakness. That stillness is strength. Thank you for showing me what it means to breathe.

Melissa/Megan/Mellie, you see me and love me anyway. Thank you for understanding me like no one else can.

Alisha, I am honored to call you my friend. I hope one day my butt looks as amazing as yours.

Brooke—my motivator and my Tuesday coffeehouse co-conspirator. Thank you for always letting me be fully, wildly myself.

Gina, your friendship brings me joy, laughter, and just the right amount of "get your shit together" energy. I'd be a puddle without you.

Emily, my genius writing coach. Thank you for making my books sharper, better, and smarter, and for answering every "wait, what if…" text I send in full panic mode.

Dr. Amanda, thank you for helping me rebuild my relationship with my body and brain. Your patience, wisdom, and quiet support have been life changing. I wouldn't be standing—let alone writing—without you.

Steven, my badass agent, thank you for always having my back, fighting the good fight, and making this dream feel possible (even when I'm crying in my car).

Mam, you annoy the bejesus out of me, and I love you. When are we going to luncheon?

Douglas, you're the reason I get out of bed each day. (And not just because you open the blinds.)

And to you, my wonderful reader. Thank you for showing up. For feeling with me, crying with me, laughing, screaming, rereading, and telling your friends. You're fucking great. No notes.

About the Author

Kristin Cast is a #1 *New York Times* and #1 *USA Today* bestselling author with over 30 million books in print.

She is proudly neurodivergent (ASD + OCD) and deeply consumed by character-driven chaos, emotionally vulnerable heroes, and smart, sexy heroines who always get the last word and the hot guy. When she's not writing, you'll find her devouring thriller, horror, and romance novels, practicing witchcraft, and being the exact kind of unhinged that makes group chats worth opening.